Praise for T.J. MacGregor and her previous thrillers

DEATH FLATS

"If you love great suspense, DEATH FLATS will make you feel you've *nearly* died and gone to heaven."

NANCY PICKARD

DARK FIELDS

"A top-notch suspense novel . . . The true magic of this book is that the reader can become so wrapped up in the plot that he can't figure out who really committed the murder. . . . MacGregor's writing style is unique."

Mystery Scene

DEATH SWEET

"The weaving of the two plots is skillfully done, and the resolution well-executed."

The Drood Review of Mystery

ON ICE

"Chilling."

The New York Times Book Review

Also by T.J. MacGregor
Published by Ballantine Books:

DARK FIELDS
KILL FLASH
DEATH SWEET
ON ICE
KIN DREAD
DEATH FLATS

As Alison Drake:

TANGO KEY
FEVERED
BLACK MOON
LAGOON

SPREE

T.J. MacGregor

BALLANTINE BOOKS • NEW YORK

Copyright © 1992 by T.J. MacGregor

All rights reserved under International and Pan-American Copyright Conventions. Published in the United States of America by Ballantine Books, a division of Random House, Inc., New York, and simultaneously in Canada by Random House of Canada Limited, Toronto.

Library of Congress Catalog Card Number: 92-90141

ISBN 0-345-37346-4

Manufactured in the United States of America

First Edition: August 1992

For my parents,
Rose Marie & Tony Janeshutz,
with love & thanks
for all those Saturdays,
my sister, Mary Anderson;
and for the Megger.

Society wants to believe it can identify
evil people or bad or harmful people
but it's not practical.
There are no stereotypes.

—TED BUNDY

Special thanks to the Haldemans—
Jay, Vol, Heidi, and Flats—
for all their hospitality, &
to my husband, Rob,
who keeps it all in perspective

Monday, November 4
Gainesville, Florida

2:15 A.M.

These moments at the beginning set his nerves on edge and filled his mouth with the taste of metal, as though he'd bitten into a strip of aluminum foil.

Everything, in fact, seemed excessive: the cries of the crickets outside, the softness of the light, the wheeze of the woman's breathing. The screech of the chalk as he pressed it against the wooden floor was high and sharp, the noise of an owl in a predatory swoop. It irritated him nearly as much as the stink of the alcohol that his teacher was swabbing across the back of the woman's hand.

Rick slipped off his shoes, stepped inside the circle. His movement stirred its boundary of white dust, dust that would be gone by the time they left, its grains ground into the old wood, stuck between the planks, as impermanent as the shirt he wore. But for now, he felt protected inside it and believed it to be as magical and powerful as his teacher said it was. For now, he could believe almost anything: that he could breathe fire, speak in tongues; that he could walk outside and rise through the blanket of fog like a balloon, a bird, a witch on a broom. Such was his teacher's hold over him.

His teacher's voice was music. It disturbed the quiet in the farmhouse, filling the strange air with the ease of light or water, shaping it, changing it, transforming it. But even the voice couldn't mitigate the stink of the alcohol, a stink that reminded Rick of hospitals and sickness, of the loose, wrinkled flesh at Mother's throat that vibrated when she talked.

When they finished here, he would wash everything down with Clorox or Pine Sol. He hadn't decided which

1

yet. Either one would swallow the odor of alcohol. Either one would disinfect, kill germs, bring order to disorder. Christ knew, this place could use a good cleaning. Mold grew under spigots, dead insects littered windowsills, and there was no telling how many cats and dogs had pissed on these floors. But the circle neutralized bacteria, rendered them as harmless as grass.

He became conscious of a sound and realized it was coming from the woman. She was shrieking into her gag as his teacher approached her with a syringe and quietly explained its purpose. Rick wished she wouldn't scream. He hated it when they screamed.

A few years ago, in Texas or Alabama or maybe it was Georgia—he couldn't quite remember anymore—they'd done someone who hadn't screamed. Who hadn't even whimpered. That was the way it was supposed to be, quiet but fearful, as though God had extended a giant hand and stitched the person's mouth shut.

"It's novocaine," his teacher said. "Just novocaine. So you don't feel anything. I already explained it to you. Now please open your hand, palm up. Otherwise you're going to be in a lot of pain."

His teacher tried to be kind. He appreciated that. There were already too many people in the world who didn't give a damn about the basic courtesies, much less about kindness. The jerk on the interstate who swerves his El Dorado in front of you, the fat broad who sneezes on the back of your neck in the grocery checkout line. But the woman didn't appreciate the gesture. She kept screaming into the gag and strained against the ropes that secured her to the chair. Her eyes were wide, utterly terrified. She didn't unclench her hands.

"Open her hand, Rick," his teacher said. "I don't like it when they're in pain."

He took hold of the woman's wrist and worked her fingers open. In the spill of light, her palm glistened with sweat. He was grateful for the rubber gloves that separated his skin from hers; it nauseated him to think of her body fluids touching him. Sweat, blood, semen, tears, urine: they were all the same to him, alive with germs, as personal as a fingerprint.

2

"You'll just feel a sharp sting, that's all," his teacher told the woman, and slid the needle under the skin at her wrist.

She moaned and squeezed her eyes shut. He looked away. A needle was the ultimate invasion. He submitted when he had to, when the law required it, but given the choice he did without. Like at the dentist's. No novocaine for fillings. No novocaine for root canals. No novocaine, period. In a dentist's chair he stared into the light and cut off all sensation between his mouth and his brain. It wasn't that difficult to do when you were desperate.

He hoped the woman was desperate.

His teacher handed him the spent syringe. He stepped to the boundary of the circle and placed it next to the empty vial on the counter. Then he picked up the scissors and a saucer and moved back into the circle. The woman's eyes were open again and frozen on the scissors. Her cheeks were wet with tears; her nose was running. He wiped it with a paper towel, wiped it gently, as though she were a child, and dropped the wad outside of the circle.

"I'm just going to cut a little of your hair," he said.

But she didn't believe him; she craned her neck, trying to keep him in sight as he moved behind her. "Hey, c'mon, turn your head around. All I'm going to do is snip a couple of locks, I promise. No tricks. You have my word, Catherine."

He touched just her hair, that was all, a soft, gentle touch at the crown to show her he meant what he said. He felt her relax a little. He ran his fingers up under her hair, then let it fall. She might not be much of a housekeeper, but Jesus, she had gorgeous hair, black and thick, shiny and clean. It smelled like pears. He bet she didn't have to do anything special with it, either. No hot-oil treatments, no expensive cream rinses, nothing like what his wife or his mother used to go through with their hair. Good genes, pure and simple.

He snipped locks from underneath, where it wouldn't show, and his teacher looked on, smiling, pleased. He placed the strands on the saucer, then stepped out of the circle again. He set the scissors and the saucer on the counter and took a Baggie from his pocket. Inside was a

3

white, sterile handkerchief. He removed it, smoothed the edges flat, and placed the strands in the center of it. He folded the hanky with the utmost reverence, three even folds lengthwise, the ends tucked under and sealed with wax the color of rich chocolate.

From another white handkerchief to his left, he picked up a pocketknife and a white plastic cup. The cup, also sterile, was still in its cellophane wrapping. He opened the knife as he stepped back into the circle and handed it to his teacher without touching the blade.

"Let's make sure that novocaine's taken," his teacher said. The woman screamed and threw herself around as much as the ropes would allow. He and his teacher stood there watching, saying nothing, and pretty soon she exhausted herself and started to cough. "I told you it's easier not to fight things. If you keep this up, the novocaine's going to wear off and I don't have any more and then you're going to be very unhappy. Would you please open your hand?"

Her fingers unfurled. In his mind, they became the petals of a golden flower, conduits of knowledge. She turned her head to the side, sobbing softly, as the teacher touched the blade to the center of her palm and pricked the skin. A single bud of blood appeared, a ruby against her pale skin.

"Did you feel anything?" his teacher asked.

The woman shook her head violently and kept her eyes averted. Her shoulders continued to tremble. He tore open the cellophane on the cup and watched as his teacher drew the blade down the middle of the woman's palm, through the heart line, the life and head lines, and then again across the top, in the shape of a cross. Rick took over, milking the wound, catching the blood in the cup. He made sure none of it got on his gloves.

But through his gloves he felt the blood's warmth at the bottom of the cup: August sidewalks against bare feet, warm Gulf breezes, morning toast. This was the simplest and most complex of fluids, the alchemist's *prima materia*, the current of life.

When the cup was half full, he turned the woman's

hand so the palm was facing up and gently closed her fingers. "Keep pressure on it to stem the flow."

He capped the cup, went to the counter again, set it inside the waiting Igloo cooler on a bed of ice, like shrimp. He washed off the pocketknife, dried it with a paper towel, and placed it next to the empty vial and syringe. When they were finished here, he would sweep all their trash into a white garbage bag that they would take with them. By cleaning up all at once, they were less likely to overlook anything.

He studied the five knives his teacher had arranged on a white towel directly behind the woman and chose the one with the ivory handle. It had a history. He'd found it some years ago in a house that was reputedly haunted. Its handle, from the days before anyone cared how many elephants were killed in Africa, was beautifully carved. It depicted Kali, the four-armed Hindu goddess, naked and full-breasted, standing watch over the entwined bodies of a pair of lovers. A serpent coiled around one of her arms like a bracelet; in another was cradled a child. One hand held a knife with a curved blade; in the palm of another were the petals of a lotus flower. Life and death, violence and peace and resurrection: Those were the things he saw in the handle.

He took up his position next to his teacher and held the knife in front of him, blade pointed toward the ceiling. The woman shrieked. Abject terror flooded her eyes.

Death is just a breath that isn't taken, he thought, then grinned and stepped forward, the taste of metal thick against his tongue and the roof of his mouth.

5:18 A.M.

Andrea Tull clutched the blanket to her throat, her eyes skipping through the darkness as she strained to hear whatever had awakened her. She hoped for the usual culprits: drunken students stumbling back to campus after a party, cats fighting in the street, pipes clanking in the walls. But she heard only the thick silence of a world at the edge of sleep.

She threw off the covers, turned on the lamp, swung

her legs over the side of the bed. Her toes curled and uncurled against the pine floor like pale white worms that wanted desperately to burrow, to hide. She reached for the blanket at the foot of the bed, drew it around her shoulders, and walked across the room to shut the window.

The temperature had dropped during the night, and this old place harbored a chill the way a dog did fleas. She hated it, hated the cool seepage of air through the glass, the floorboards, under the doors: invisible, odorless, relentless. She longed for the sunbaked air of Key West, for the odor of salt and sea, for the small, familiar rooms of her own home.

Small, yes, she liked her rooms small. In a small room the space was charted, seen, nothing was hidden. But this loft, owned by a sociology professor at the university who was on sabbatical, was cavernous, vast. High ceilings, few walls, too much openness. Here, she felt exposed.

Her gaze fixed on the front door at the end of the long hall. Walk out there, she thought. Put your ear to the wood, be sure no one is on the other side. But as she stood, the phone rang. The sound stabbed at her. Her legs froze. She knew who it was, who it had to be.

She glared at the phone, willing it to stop pealing. Her heart hammered. Cold and heat flashed across her skin in alternating waves. She was grateful the light was on. She wouldn't be able to listen to him in the dark, to his soft, lubricious voice, a mask that hid more than his identity.

She didn't have to pick up the receiver. But she knew she would. She wanted to know. Needed to know.

Deep breaths. Her knees creaked as she sat on the edge of the mattress. Maybe he was close enough to throw pebbles at her window and that was what had awakened her. She reached for the pen and notebook on the floor, turned on the recorder that was connected to the phone, and picked up on the fourth ring.

"Hello?" Her voice was hoarse with sleep, much too soft. A fearful soft. She hoped he didn't hear it.

Breathing, then: "I woke you."

That voice, the color of burgundy, was an asexual

whisper, and yet she thought of it as male. Her hand was so damp, the receiver nearly slipped from her grasp. She mustered what she could of her usual irreverence. "I don't know why that should come as any big surprise. It's the middle of the night."

His laughter was a cool, clear sound, the sound of stars whirling in their solitary journeys through the blackness of space. "It's morning, Andrea. Not light yet, but morning. That's important."

She glanced at the clock, scribbled down the time. When she spoke, the words stuck to her tongue, insects to flypaper. "What's important is that I've only had about three hours' sleep. So if you don't mind, get to the point."

Another laugh, softer this time, almost feminine, coy, but no longer melodic. It was like the silence, ubiquitous and furtive, and it chilled her. "The point. Okay. The point is the fog, Andrea. There's ground fog this morning. Can you see the fog where you are?"

Near water? She scribbled the words, her mind fluttering like a flag in a high wind. "Sure." She hadn't moved from the bed and, in fact, could not see out the window from where she sat.

"Tell me what you see."

He was testing her. Hang up, she thought, but didn't. She walked over to the window, the phone's long cord scraping against the floor. Her feet felt abnormally heavy and thick, as though she'd grown extra toes and heels during the night. She yanked the curtains to one side, saw wisps of fog curling like commas against the ground and sidewalk. Fog that would burn off as soon as the sun rose, fog that was porous, like gauze or ectoplasm.

"I see a streetlight and ground fog. That's it." She pulled the curtain into place again, covering the glass, and backed toward the bed, suddenly certain he could see her from wherever he was calling. A phone booth in the parking lot?

She listened to the silence that connected them, hoping to hear something in the background that would identify where he was. "What do you hear?" he asked, as if he'd read her mind.

7

"My eyes shutting. Talk to you later."

"She's dead." The words rushed out in an urgent whisper. "It was easy."

The back of her neck prickled. Andrea gripped the receiver and squeezed her eyes shut. *Hang up. Call the cops.* But the receiver remained glued to her ear and she opened her eyes, staring at the notebook in her lap, at the pen poised between her fingers. Her heart slammed against her ribs, a caged, panicked bird.

"You still there?"

Softly: "Yes. Who's dead?" *Give me a name.*

"No names. That's not how we do things, Andy. You know that. We follow the rules."

Andy. Her nickname drifted through the spaces between his teeth. The inside of her mouth flashed dry and she sipped from the glass of water on the nightstand, waiting, wondering if he could hear her swallow. "You withheld information the first time. That's hardly fair."

"There have to be *some* things for you to figure out. Otherwise you'd get bored, Andrea. Admit it."

Not to you. "Maybe I don't want to figure anything out. Maybe I don't even want to write this story."

Laughter again, low and soft, a hiss of poisoned air. "It was on a farm and there was a lot of fog. . . ."

His voice seized her and her pen raced across the page, betraying her.

1

Swollen, leaden clouds hung low over Gainesville's shallow hills. To Mike McCleary, they looked like sponges that invisible hands wrung ineptly, squeezing out a chilly drizzle. The dim afternoon light completed his gloom.

He had turned west off I-75 ten minutes ago and was now on Route 24, a two-lane country road. The pines on either side glistened in the dampness like Christmas trees and the asphalt unrolled in twists and loops, a dark, wet ribbon. The Miata's windshield wipers kept up a steady, monotonous rhythm and had smeared dirt in inverted half-moons across the glass. The car's heater, which had never been used, pumped out enough air to keep his feet warm but little else. He simply wasn't dressed for this weather.

His light leather jacket wasn't intended for anything cooler than sixty, and the dampness had already penetrated his running shoes. But he hadn't been thinking straight when he'd packed last night. He hadn't been thinking at all. He'd been reacting to a phone call from his father.

He stepped on the accelerator, as if to outdistance the memory of his father's voice. But the words—*your sister*—were shouts in a canyon, echoing forever. Catherine, the baby of the family, the youngest of five, thirty years old, had been murdered sometime before dawn yesterday out at the farm where she'd been living. A fact. One of several. And no matter how he looked at it, that fact remained as immutable as granite.

He thought of the way the control in his father's voice had slipped several times, telling him everything he needed to know about what it was like to be seventy-six years old and to discover you had outlived one of your children. The baby of the family, no less, the child that was unplanned, born to your middle age.

Like McCleary's own daughter.

As soon as he'd hung up with his father, McCleary had called Steve Bristol, the homicide detective at the Alachua County Sheriff's Department who had broken the news to his parents. He needed to hear it from a cop. The details, the facts, what was known and unknown. He and Bristol had agreed to meet at Cat's farm this afternoon, a meeting he dreaded.

For most of the trip, the farm had been blurred and indistinct in his mind, like a town he had driven through en route to somewhere else. But now bits and pieces of it were fitting together, becoming clearer as he neared the turnoff: forty acres of rolling countryside rich with orchards, vines, a pond as round as a pancake, the rambling old house of cedar and glass.

He didn't allow himself to remember the rooms, those intimate spaces where she had lived and breathed. It would be too easy to imagine her there, to stumble upon some recollection of Cat laughing, Cat clowning, Cat moving in that quick, impatient way she had. In the aftermath of violence, memory could be as lethal as the act itself.

He pulled into the first gas station he saw, filled the tank, went into the men's room. Ice-cold water sputtered from the rusted faucet. When he splashed it on his face, it shocked the lethargy from his system. But his grief remained, coiled under his heart like a recently detected tumor. And it was grief that had aged the man who looked back at him in the mirror. The creases at the corners of his smoke blue eyes were deeper, the streaks of white in his dark hair and beard were more profuse, his shoulders were stooped. He stood six feet, but seemed to be shrinking, aging even as he stood here, muscles turning flaccid, cells dying, layers of skin sloughing off.

He rubbed his face dry with a paper towel and thought of stage makeup, of Cat removing it from her cheeks, of Cat in dressing rooms backstage in theatres, in TV studios, in her one starring movie role, a grade-B horror film called *Magenta Nights*. The movie, in which she'd played a woman named Claire who had second sight, had become a cult classic. It had landed her in Hollywood for a while, doing bit parts and some commercials. She'd hated it—the work, the city, the state, the life-style. When *Nights* eventually started bringing in money, a lot of money, she'd headed East to live theatre again, her first passion.

After several years in Miami at the Coconut Grove Playhouse, she'd ended up at the Sunshine Repertory here in Gainesville and had bought the farm. It included eight cows, a dozen sheep, six chickens, orchards of apples and muscadine grapes, blueberries, and Christmas trees. Cat had bought some secondhand equipment, hired a caretaker, who lived in a separate house on the land with his wife and two sons, and rescued a sheepdog from the pound to keep her company.

McCleary wondered where the caretaker and the sheepdog had been the night she was killed.

Get moving, old man. He wadded up the towels and tossed them in the basket on his way out.

South on Route 24 to the town of Archer, south on Route 41 to Southwest Ninety-fifth Avenue, turn onto the limestone road, cross the railroad track, take the right fork, and keep going until you can't go any farther.

He heard her voice repeating the directions. He'd been here only twice, when he helped Cat move and shortly after his daughter was born. But the way to the farm returned to him like a lost pet.

The landmarks hadn't changed. Archer was still a nothing town—a gas station, a few fruit stands, a veterinarian's office, and Hitchcock's, a grocery where the hicks and the motorcycle gangs hung out. It was the last outpost before the countryside opened up to pastures burned brown by the dry summer, to wooden fences, barbed wire, horses, cows, sheep. In South Florida you had to drive for hours to see this much empty land.

He crossed the railroad track, long since rusted. It dated back to the 1850s when the old Florida Railroad

11

had been built, connecting the state with the rest of the world. The railroad ultimately had proven vital in the founding and development of Gainesville. But these days the main draw in town was the university, one of the twenty largest in the country. It accounted for nearly half of the city's eighty thousand inhabitants and covered two thousand acres downtown.

Quin's alma mater.

The road forked; he kept right. Sheep grazed in the brown fields, cows stood motionless in the drizzle, the barbed wire that crowned the fences gleamed in the wet light. Pastures gave way to pines, to live oaks garnished like a giant salad in Spanish moss, to palmetto shrubs and hickories and, finally, to the Christmas trees that lined the road to Tree Frog Farm.

He spotted the house through the trees. It was longer than it was wide. The end closest to him was a storage room attached to the rest of the house by a porch that was a hundred and fifty feet long. The junk in the front yard appeared: a rusting tractor, a broken-down pickup, a refrigerator that lay on its back, its front door gone, its interior a bed of weeds.

A cream-colored Pontiac was parked parallel to the porch. Detective Bristol's car, he guessed. McCleary pulled up next to it and got out, raising his collar against the drizzle. It still managed to seep down inside his jacket and shirt, chilling him.

A breeze blew up the path that led to the pasture where the cows stood at the fence, mooing. It stirred the tinsel that clung to the branches of last year's Christmas tree, which was stuck in the ground to his right like a scarecrow. Next to it was a birdfeeder, but there was no seed in it. An inch of water had accumulated between its plastic walls. The sight of the tree, forlorn and solitary and brown—*so past tense*—made his throat go tight and hot. For a second, he thought he was going to puke.

When the feeling passed, he moved woodenly toward the screened porch where he and Cat had sat several nights in a row, buzzed on beer, talking, their voices drifting out into the pine and loquat trees. These memories were bright and beautifully textured, like oil paintings that possess mystical dimensions of time and space.

There was a ramp rather than stairs; the former owner had had an invalid sister. The door still creaked and its screen was still ripped. Everything, in fact, was exactly as it had been the last time he was here, cluttered but with a peculiar order that had made sense only to his sister. To his right were tremendous cans of feed for the chickens, the sheep, the visiting ducks; a piano so dusty he could have written his name on the top; a pool table covered with Christmas paraphernalia; a table strewn with ashtrays and books and magazines; a refrigerator; and a 1957 Wurlitzer jukebox complete with 45s, its front smashed in.

To his left were a kiln; assorted clay pots and glass jars that held hardware supplies; dozens upon dozens of square plastic pots with seedlings in them; more feed; more storage cabinets; more magazines. His sister, the packrat.

He walked past the feed cans, the piano, and the pool table and opened the doors to where Cat had lived. A stone fireplace, vaulted ceilings, wicker furniture with tropical-patterned pillows, a pine floor broken up by throw rugs. The mantel over the fireplace was littered with photos, pinecones, clay vases that held wildflowers, hairclips, paperbacks—anything that wouldn't fit anywhere else.

To his left was a dining room separated from the living area by a pair of wooden posts. Behind it, the wall was papered in snapshots that were a Catherine McCleary history dating back almost to her birth. Family and theatre, men and theatre, friends and theatre.

His sister's face took shape in his mind: those large eyes the same shade of blue as his own, her shoulder-length black hair, her pretty mouth, those high cheekbones. Twelve years and three other sisters had separated them, but he'd been closest to her.

Cat was the iconoclast of the family, the one who had fixed on a dream that nothing had shaken. At eighteen she'd struck out for New York armed with nothing more than an immense talent and an indomitable optimism.

13

Within three years she was regularly employed in Off Broadway plays, doing what she loved best, and nearly starving. She began to supplement her income with TV commercials, and one of these, a clever panty-hose number, had inadvertently landed her an audition for *Magenta Nights*. If he had to choose a point where her life had changed, that was it. Nylon stockings. Nylons had brought her here, where she had died. Nylons, Jesus.

He heard Flats's bark; Bristol was returning to the house. A part of McCleary wished to postpone their meeting. He didn't want all the facts just yet. But then the barking stopped and the silence enclosed him and within it echoed the voice of his sister's ghost: that exuberance, that passion, that irresistible optimism. He could almost hear her laughing.

He hesitated in front of the bedroom door, then opened it. A clutter of books and laundry, notepads and clothes leaped out at him. The walls were papered in memorabilia: a framed poster from one of the plays she'd done in New York; a Halloween mask; a framed review from the *Village Voice* with her name highlighted in yellow; a five-by-seven photo of the entire family—Mom and Dad, sisters, himself, in-laws, nieces, and nephews. The king-size bed was bare and a white stain shaped like Texas stood out in the middle of the mattress. It smelled of bleach.

To the left of the bed was a masking-tape outline of her body. McCleary had seen dozens in his life, made of chalk and electrical tape, fat and thin, large and small, but this was the only one that nearly broke his heart.

He forced himself to focus on details, like the absence of blood in the room. She hadn't been killed in here. Why not?

He heard the creak of floorboards and walked out onto the porch, where a man he presumed was Bristol was unbuttoning his raincoat. He was about six feet, wide and brawny through the shoulders. His khaki hair, neither graying nor thinning, fell across his forehead. His eyes, set deeply in his face, were a strange, flat blue, a lake on a windless day. His jeans and long-sleeved cotton shirt were rumpled. He leaned heavily on a mahogany

14

cane, stuck out his hand, introduced himself. Then he said: "The cows and sheep are hungry."

"Is there any hay in the barn?"

"I don't know. I didn't get that far. There's one sheep that looks like she may go into labor at any time."

"Is she separated from the others?"

"No, but there's a couple of sheep in a separate pen. The males, I think."

They spoke with the casual familiarity of old friends who had nothing more important to discuss than sheep and cows, which was fine with McCleary. It allowed him to prolong the illusion that he was twenty years old, visiting his parents' farm in upstate New York. Any second now an eight-year-old Cat was going to come tearing through the French doors, shouting, "Mikey, Mikey's here," with an uncontained glee he'd never heard since. A lump swelled in his throat; he had difficulty swallowing it.

"I guess we'd better look for some hay to feed them. That was Flats I heard barking, wasn't it?" he asked.

Bristol nodded. "Yeah, she's been staying with me since yesterday. She's checking out your car." Bristol lifted his cane, pointed at a feed can. "How about if we start there?"

"Good idea."

Once they had a bucket of feed, they exited through the back-porch door and started down a path to the sheep's shelter. They passed a wire chicken coop with a flimsy roof that had caved in and the new coop, built of sturdier stuff. They passed a rusted boat motor, a soiled gray tarp, a bale of hay. McCleary tucked one of the bales under his arm and carried it into the shelter where the sheep were.

There were five sheep under the roof, three females, including the pregnant black sheep, and two babies about eight weeks old. Another six sheep were sequestered in open pens that were separated from the shelter by a rickety wooden fence. They scampered over to the feed trough, bleating, crowding one another. As McCleary dropped the bale into the trough and divided it with his fingers, Bristol poured feed into the other end of the trough. Then he turned on the hose and filled the water buckets, which were bone dry. "I should've checked here yesterday."

Yesterday, November 4, when Cat was found.

"Where's Eddie, the caretaker?"

"Your sister's neighbor told me he and his family left four days ago for Tallahassee. Family illness. I found his number on the refrigerator door and called. His alibi checks out."

"Eddie didn't kill her," McCleary said. "He has trouble killing an ant. Where was Flats when it happened?"

"Roaming, probably. Let's head down to the barn to see if there's any more hay so we can feed those cows." They started out of the shelter, into the drizzle, Bristol limping along with his cane. "She was found by an actress in the company. Tess Schulman. You ever meet her?"

"Sure. She and Cat worked together at the Coconut Grove Playhouse three or four years ago. She moved up here first to take some drama courses. Then she hooked up with Sunshine."

"Well, she was worried because Catherine had missed rehearsal that morning and didn't answer the phone. She'd been dead at least twelve hours when Tess found her. We believe she died sometime very early on the fourth."

"How was she—"

"I'm getting to that, Mr. McCleary." Bristol whacked his cane at the weeds that grew in thė path. "There's a lot more here than a murder."

McCleary didn't like the sound of that. "Look, I didn't come here just to tidy up Catherine's affairs. I intend to stay until I know who killed her and why. So just spit it out, okay?"

Another whack at some weeds, then: "Her throat was cut. One of her hands was amputated. We believe she was killed in the kitchen—that's where we found residue of blood—and we found her in the bedroom." He spoke slowly, carefully, in a monotone, a reporter providing the facts; McCleary's gut slid out from under him. "There was a white powder on the floor, which Forensics said was chalk. Her hand wasn't found.

16

"The knife that was used on her was in the brush at the front of the house. No prints on it, her blood all over it. The Hindu goddess, Kali, is carved into the handle. There's a stain on the bed—"

"I saw it. Bleach."

Bristol nodded and continued in the same soft, even voice. "She'd been rubbed down with it. It had been poured between her . . . her legs." He paused, ran his fingers through his hair. It was the first time he'd shown any emotion at all. "I'm really sorry you have to hear this, Mr. McCleary, and I'm sorry I'm the one who's telling you." Another pause, briefer this time, then he continued in the same quiet voice. "The bleach screwed any chance of determining if she was raped."

"And the hand?" What the hell was that supposed to mean?

"We don't know. Maybe for effect. Catherine's was the second murder in this area in ten days. The MOs aren't identical, but they're close enough. The first woman was an attractive brunette, like your sister, killed with a knife. Her left hand was missing. No bleach this time, but she'd been washed down with Pine Sol. Her body was also found in a different location from where she was killed and the knife was in a flowerbed outside. We didn't lift any unknown prints. There was a residue of chalk on her kitchen floor as well."

Bleach and Pine Sol: a preoccupation with germs? "Was she a student?"

"No. An English professor. Lucy Davenport. Divorced, lived alone. We kept some details out of the press, and your sister's name hasn't been released yet. The media just knows a second body was found."

"That won't last long."

"No, it won't. Her name and a few details will be released tomorrow. We're going to say we believe the murders are linked, but otherwise the lid on this one is real tight. By the way, if you hear from a woman named Andrea Tull, it'd be in your best interest not to talk to her."

The name seemed familiar, although he didn't know why. "She a reporter?"

Bristol snorted. "She's a goddamn pariah who calls herself a true-crime writer. Her last bestseller was about a murder in your neck of the woods: *Home Before Dark*."

No wonder her name had rung a bell. "The Mendez family murders."

"Right. She's teaching a writing course on campus this semester. I understand her last book wasn't a blockbuster, so she's really looking for a hot ticket this time."

They reached the barn. Its doors were thrown open and Cat's blue Wagoneer was parked in front. The key was in the ignition, which didn't surprise him. Cat had felt safe out here. Too safe. "Was the Wagoneer here when you arrived?"

"Sure was. And it was dusted for prints. Nothing turned up."

They fell silent as they entered the barn. McCleary was grateful for the reprieve, for the reality of hay and old wooden beams, for the sound of rain on the roof. There wasn't a lot of hay, but they loaded it into the back of the Wagoneer and drove down toward the pasture. The cows saw them and loped through the wet gloom, mooing. As they tossed the bales over the fence, McCleary heard Flats's excited barks and glanced around.

The black-and-white sheepdog tore down the road toward them, a hundred and fifty pounds of muscle and fur. She leaped and her front paws slammed into McCleary's chest, nearly knocking him over. She slathered his face with kisses, whimpered, and trembled, and he laughed, hugging her, inhaling the scent of rain in her fur.

She jumped into the front seat of the Wagoneer and rode back to the house with them. Then she tagged McCleary's heels when they went inside, as though she were afraid that someone else whom she loved might abandon her. He knew the feeling.

He and Bristol settled at the dusty round table on the porch. The detective rubbed his bum leg, shrugged off his wet raincoat, hooked his cane over the armrest of the chair, and picked up the conversation as though there had been no lapse.

"So far, the prints we've lifted are a dead end. Have you been into her den?"

"No. I only got as far as the bedroom."

"You'll find six *X*s on the floor that mark the placement of personal objects or clothing. They're listed in the file. They appear to form some kind of pattern, but no one's got a clue as to what it means. There was a pattern at the first homicide, too."

"I'd like to see the photos from both scenes."

"No problem. You'll have access to whatever you need."

Just like that. "You ran a check on me." It wasn't a question.

Bristol nodded. "I didn't know if you'd want to get involved in the investigation, but frankly I'm relieved that you do. We need all the help we can get."

"Is there anyone working on a psychological profile?"

"Yeah, a guy who teaches at the university. He's considered an expert on criminal and aberrant psychology. You'll have a chance to talk to him. In fact, one of my people is going to bring the photos and the profile and everything else by. I left the station in such a hurry this afternoon, I forgot my briefcase."

A cruiser turned into the driveway a few minutes later. Flats raced down the porch, barking, and McCleary hurried after her to restrain her. The woman who came up the ramp had a face that had been pieced together carefully, like a quilt. Her brows were plucked into smooth arches over hazel eyes that boasted just the right touch of mascara and shadow. Her prominent cheekbones were accentuated with a hint of color. The precise cut of her walnut hair drew the eye to her jaw, where her hair ended, and focused attention on her mouth, which was a glossy peach. Even her clothes were careful: tailored khaki slacks, a cotton shirt with fancy pearl buttons, a red pullover worn the preppy way, tied loosely at her shoulders. The dusting of freckles on her cheeks endowed her with a kind of youthful innocence you might find in a freshman. Except that she was closer to thirty-five, McCleary guessed, than eighteen.

She stopped at the screen door, where Flats was snarling, and shut her umbrella. "I don't think this pooch likes my perfume," she said.

"It's the red sweater, Angie," said Bristol, pushing the door open with the tip of his cane as McCleary held on to Flats's collar. "Like a matador's cape, you know?"

"So much for the theory that dogs are color blind, huh."

"Detective Wilkin, Mike McCleary," said Bristol.

"Angie," she said with a smile, then stepped uneasily through the door holding her briefcase against her and clutching the umbrella like a sword. "I'm really okay, dog."

"Let her sniff your hand," Bristol suggested as Flats continued to snarl.

"You must be kidding."

"I'll put her inside," McCleary said, and led the dog into the house.

When he returned, Bristol and Wilkin were at the table, the open briefcase between them. Bristol was removing files, stacking them neatly to one side. "Everything you need is here."

"So's the profile," Wilkin said, lighting a Marlboro with a dramatic flourish, as though she were on camera. "I swung by the campus on my way over here and picked it up. Dr. Farmer thinks we're dealing with a serial killer." She glanced at McCleary. "He's the shrink we're using. Anyway, his conclusion sounds reasonable to me."

Bristol rubbed his jaw and shook his head. "I disagree."

She turned those hazel eyes on McCleary again, commiserating. "We disagree on just about everything. I think he does it just to be contrary."

"That's what my wife says all the time," Bristol remarked.

"If not a serial killer, then what?" McCleary asked.

"This guy's on a spree, Mike. A goddamn spree."

Which would make him easier to find.

The archetypal serial killer was methodical, fastidious, calculating, and coldly patient. Ted Bundy, for example, had chosen his victims carefully, spaced the murders over many months and miles, and crisscrossed state lines and police jurisdictions to confuse investigators. Some of his victims had been disposed of so shrewdly, their bones had never been found.

In contrast, the spree killer had a pattern of lashing out. The bloodiness, and aggression were signs of a contained rage that suddenly exploded, and were often associated with psychotic disturbance. Richard Speck, who had attacked nine nurses in a spree in Chicago, killing eight of them, was the name that immediately came to mind. A killer in a frenzy was more likely to leave clues behind. He tended to be reckless and imprecise and was also more likely to have a connection, however slight, to his victims that could link him to the crime.

In theory.

And that was the problem. It was all theory. Sometimes the theories proved out, sometimes they didn't. But one way or another, he was going to find the sick fuck who'd done this.

2

IT SEEMED TO Quin that the Mickey Mouse clock in her daughter's room didn't tick as quickly as the others in the house. Maybe the passage of time was actually slower in here, the way it was the farther from Earth you got. Or perhaps, in some mysterious way, it reflected Michelle's perception of time. In a baby's world, where your past could still be counted in months and your future was practically infinite, anything was possible.

She lifted herself up from the blankets and quilts on the floor of the nursery where her daughter, nearly nine months old, had fallen asleep. Since she'd started cutting teeth four months ago, this was where she nodded off nearly every night. Her head was against a small down pillow and her favorite quilt was pulled up around her. The quilt was a gift from Cat, a patchwork of brightly colored squares, each with a different animal on it. Michelle's nickname, Ellie, was stitched across the middle of it in red. Cat had given it to her when she was barely an hour old. Quin could still see Cat standing in front of the nursery window on the maternity floor, beaming as a nurse fitted the quilt into Ellie's bassinet.

Cat was wearing one of her weird outfits that day, Quin remembered. It was a flowered skirt with a checkered blouse and a vest the same deep red as her hat. Any other woman would have looked demented in the combination, but Cat had carried it off with that dramatic flair that had underscored everything about her.

Cat had spelled McCleary during Quin's thirty-hour labor, gripping her hand with each contraction, urging her to breathe as she'd been taught, breathing with her, hurting with her, riding out each wave of pain until it subsided and another began. In between contractions Cat had massaged Quin's lower back, given her 7UP, convinced the nurse to delay hooking up an IV, and reported on all the other women in labor and delivery.

The woman next door's stuck at two centimeters, Quin. You're way ahead of her at five. . . . Hear those screams? One-ten's on her way for an emergency C-section because her OB is jumpy. Yours isn't. Keep up that breathing. And when the pain grew so extreme that Quin no longer cared how to breathe or even if she did, Cat cheered her on. *You're at eight, Quin, eight centimeters, not much farther, c'mon, c'mon, scream fuck, scream anything, just scream.*

When Cat had left, her presence in the room had been so strong, Quin had still felt her around. Just as she did now. Cat lingered everywhere in here—in the quilt, in the toy chest against the wall, in the stack of children's books on the shelf. Her gifts had always arrived in time for Ellie's birth date on the seventeenth of each month, or for no reason at all.

The last one had been delivered yesterday, four little books called *New Age Tales for Tots*, bundled together in red ribbon, a random gift. Included with them was a computerized horoscope for Ellie—a natal chart—and five pages of interpretation. Cat had highlighted parts of it in yellow and added notations of her own about Ellie's innate talent for drama, her predisposition for stomach ailments, problems to watch for as she grew older. Cat, a fellow Aquarian, felt she had the inside scoop on what her niece was about.

Ellie rolled onto her back with a soft, contented sigh and Quin sat there a moment, watching her sleep, aggrieved that she would grow up without knowing Cat. The terrible vacancy she'd felt since last night's phone call filled suddenly with a rush of love for her daughter that nearly overwhelmed her. She'd never expected the love to be like this, fathomless, without parameters or boundaries or conditions, a love that seemed to be an entity unto itself.

Ellie's hand was curled up under her chin, a thinker's pose, and her perfect little mouth was slightly parted, as though she was going to laugh. Even in repose, her strong resemblance to the McCleary side of the family was evident. Here was the fine bone structure that had made Cat such a mercurial beauty, the sweeping forehead, the high cheekbones, the bow mouth. But her curly blonde hair came from Quin, who'd been a towhead until she was three, and her eyes were Quin's, pale blue ringed in a darker blue. Ghost eyes, McCleary called them.

Quin tucked the quilt around Ellie and tiptoed out of the room, closing the doors as she left. The three cats, Merlin, Tracy, and Hepburn, were sprawled on the tile floor, relieved that the baby intruder was finally in bed. Since her arrival, and particularly since she'd started walking a month ago, Tracy and Hepburn were rarely seen during the day. They burrowed into closets, hid under beds, catnapped in the atrium. Only Merlin, the black cat and the eldest, took any interest in her at all.

Merlin seemed to regard Ellie as a kitten without fur, to be protected when she slept, to be preened when she was awake, to be swatted when she got too frisky. A lick from Merlin was enough to send Ellie into paroxysms of delight, and when he spurned her, she was crushed.

Quin ran the water for a bath, stripped off her shorts and T-shirt, left them where they fell. Her plane for Gainesville didn't leave until eight-thirty, but she was already packed, had arranged for someone to come in to feed the cats, had notified the baby-sitter. She'd called McCleary to let him know she was coming but had ended up leaving a message on the machine. Better that way. He would try to talk her out of it or would suggest she catch a plane tomorrow morning. But this way Ellie would, she hoped, sleep through the trip.

She looked at herself in the mirror, five feet and ten inches of long bones and skin that were almost back to normal. Before she'd left the hospital, she'd lost twenty of the forty pounds she'd gained while pregnant, and she had shed the rest in the last few months. She was now back to her usual 109. She had hipbones again, her bra size had shrunk to a depressing thirty-four A, her old clothes fit. Her umber hair wasn't quite as shiny or thick as it had been when she was pregnant and her complexion had lost its salubrious glow, but her body was her own again.

And my life, she thought, slipping into the warm water, is irrevocably changed.

She and McCleary now ran in shifts every morning, pounding out their solitary three miles while the other attended to Ellie. She missed the shared ritual. Breakfast was no longer a peaceful affair with small talk over the morning paper. It was a contest of wills with Ellie about food and staying in her high chair. It was high-wire tension between her and McCleary over who would do what and when. Although they still worked together, Quin didn't go into the office until noon, when the baby-sitter arrived, and was usually the first one home at six.

There were several problems with the arrangement, but primarily it came down to an inequitable division of labor. *She* was the one who usually had to drop whatever she was doing and head home. *She* was the one who usually fed Ellie, bathed her, got her to bed. Never mind that she and McCleary were professional equals; on the home front, the feminist movement had never happened. Ellie had changed the dynamics of the marriage, the balance of power, by conjuring the traditions in which Quin and McCleary had been raised. Dad's business was bringing home the bacon; Mom's was raising the family.

On a more depressing note, sex had taken a backseat to everything else. Their moments of intimacy were stolen in the evenings after Ellie had gone to bed and only when they weren't exhausted from her erratic sleep patterns. She was afflicted with what her pediatrician had dubbed *the REM sorrow*. After the second dream period in every three- to four-hour block of time throughout a given night, she awakened and couldn't put herself back to sleep. So she cried for a bottle. She cried to be held. She cried for the coveted spot between Mommy and Daddy where she could sprawl, coo, and knead her feet against the nearest back or leg, thus ensuring that she would be an only child forever, amen.

These days, it seemed there was a great mystique about babies and families; mothers forty and older were particularly fashionable. But the truth, Quin thought, was that no one and nothing prepared you for the reality. Not at twenty, not at forty, not ever. A baby dominated your life, claimed it, possessed it entirely.

Nature, in her infinite wisdom, had encoded numerous complex emotions into your genes to make your heart melt every time you looked at what you had created. But even so, these last months had not been easy. She supposed the formality of marriage was the cement that kept the relationship intact during times like these.

As she pulled the plug a few minutes later, she caught a faint whiff of something, perfume, yes, it was definitely perfume, and not anything she owned. This was a light scent, one of those she sometimes sampled as she cruised through the department stores in the mall. White Linen, she thought, that was it.

Cat's favorite.

Goose bumps instantly erupted on her arms. She didn't move. Water swirled noisily down the drain. She had read about these things, small-time hauntings by someone you loved, a violent death, unfinished business, the soul in torment. And she suddenly hoped something else would happen—that her towel would slip off the shower rack above her, that a whisper of air would graze her cheek, that the lights would flicker (but not go off, thank you very much). The scent, though, gradually thinned until it was gone.

Quin realized she was sitting in an empty tub, shivering, tears coursing down her cheeks.

On the plane, jammed in a seat meant for a midget, with Ellie asleep in her lap, she nodded off and dreamed that she was in a cavernous house. There were no windows, but dozens of hallways twisted this way and that, some leading up or down to other floors or into other rooms connected by more corridors, some leading nowhere. She could hear Cat calling her but couldn't tell where her voice was coming from. It grew more and more faint and then finally vanished, like the scent of the perfume.

She came to abruptly, her right arm numb, a crick in her neck, her own face staring back at her in the dark-

26

ened window. The act of murder, she thought, was like that cavernous house. A foundation, different levels, labyrinthian leads, and the soft, small voice of the victim, calling for friendship or justice or, at the very least, retribution.

She closed her eyes again, but sleep eluded her for the rest of the flight.

3

(1)

IT WAS IMPORTANT to know the name of the person you intended to kill, Rick thought. Ted Bundy would disagree with him on that point, but he had gotten caught and fried, so what did he know?

The woman seated next to him was Susan-but-my-friends-call-me-Suzy. She was a redneck hick in jeans, boots, and a sleeveless tank top that her nipples strained against. She claimed she trained horses here in Ocala, but he suspected she had stretched the truth a bit and probably worked at menial labor on one of the horse farms. The sun had weathered her skin and left her dark hair brittle, dry, with broken ends. She was a nobody who wouldn't be missed when she was gone.

"Wanna b'me 'nother beer, hon?" She leaned toward him, her speech slurred from too many beers, and the long ash on her cigarette dropped into his lap. Rick brushed it off and she giggled. "Oopsy-doopsy, sorry." She touched his arm and he flinched. "L'split, g'somewheres else, wh'd'ya say?"

"I thought you wanted another beer."

"N'here. Be right back. Gotta hit t'john."

"I'll meet you outside." He didn't want to be seen leaving the bar with her.

As soon as he was in the parking lot, he removed an alcohol wipe from his pocket, tore it open, and rubbed the place on his arm she had touched. No telling what kind of germs she carried. He withdrew a pair of scissors from under the driver's seat of his car. Brand new, shiny, purchased this evening at K Mart in downtown Ocala. He'd also made other purchases so the scissors wouldn't stand out in the clerk's mind. Rick pocketed them and

28

stood against his car, waiting for my-friends-call-me-Suzy, not allowing himself to think beyond this minute.

It had to be spontaneous, as much of a surprise for him as it would be for her. He hadn't even planned which city. He'd simply left Gainesville late this afternoon and driven south. By the time he reached Ocala's rolling countryside of emerald hills, he'd decided that if he saw a Wal-Mart first, he would go inside and buy a hunting knife. If K Mart was first, it would be scissors. He'd been thirsty when he'd exited K Mart and wanted a beer. This redneck joint was the first place he stopped, country music pumping from the jukebox, some good ole boys playing darts, and Suzy straddling the bar stool next to his. Serendipity, that hidden and mysterious pattern of things, always seemed brightest when he planned nothing. Like the old days, he thought, except that his teacher wasn't with him tonight. He needed this solitary excursion into darkness.

"There y'are, hon." She weaved over to him, a cigarette hanging from a corner of her mouth like some grotesque appendage. "Where we goin'?"

"You tell me."

"Got jus' the place. Y'gotta drive, though."

She swung into the Firebird's passenger seat, turned on the radio, tuned in a country station. The air stank of smoke. He never smoked in his car. He reached over, took her cigarette, tossed it out the window. "No smoking in here. I'm allergic to it.'

"Y'allergic to grass, too, hon?"

He laughed. "Nope."

"Oh, good." She slipped a joint from a pocket. He thought of her mouth on it first, the germs that would be crawling on the damp paper, and said he'd light it. "A gentleman to boot. Goddamn." She laughed and held it out.

He smoked it halfway down, passed it to her, and she smoked the rest of it, her fingers tapping her thighs in time to the music. Now and then she told him to turn here or there, but she was so loaded she didn't notice that he didn't follow her directions.

"What'd y'say y'do, Rick?"

"Oh, this and that."

"Shee-it, tha' sounds like this guy I knew," she said, and told him about the guy.

They passed horse farms, huge spreads of land set back from the road, all with fences so white, they shone like luminous teeth in the dark. Then they were deep in the country, a wall of pines on either side of them, the sweet November air sweeping through the car. He pulled onto a dirt road and followed it far enough to make sure it wasn't someone's driveway, then stopped.

Suzy sat up straight and looked around, blinking, then turned down the radio. "Wha' we doin'? Where're we, anyhow?"

"Got another joint?"

"Sure thing. Somewhere in here." She dug into her pocket, pulled it out, wagged it in the air.

"Let's smoke it in the trees."

"Ground's wet, hon. G'something to sit on?"

He had a paint-stained sheet in the trunk and carried it into the trees with them. They spread it on the pine needles and Suzy leaned back on her elbows and chattered about horses, her friends, her small-town life. He lit the joint and took a couple of hits. The sweet scent floated into the sweeter aroma of pines and damp earth and reminded him of a man he and his teacher had taken down one afternoon in Tacoma. An aging hippie who'd thumbed a ride. Hines, his name was, like the ketchup. Funny how sometimes their names stuck with him and sometimes he forgot their names as soon as they were dead. He wondered if, next week or next month or a year from now, he would remember my-friends-call-me-Suzy.

He passed her the joint and his hand slipped into his pocket for the scissors. When she stretched back onto her elbows again, the joint in her mouth, he moved toward her as if to kiss her. He sank the scissors into the side of her neck, jerked them out again. She hardly made a sound, just a single sharp gasp of surprise, of pain, a sound as clean and unencumbered as the air. He was already standing as she struggled to sit up and pressed a foot against her chest to hold her down. Her blood

30

spurted, of course, he had punctured the carotid, but it didn't touch him.

She was still alive when he rolled her up in the sheet; he could hear the strangled wheezes of her last breaths. But she wouldn't last long and the sheet was necessary. It was all that stood between him and her blood. He left her in the trees, wrapped up in the sheet like a sausage, cleaned the scissors on the ground, and started back toward his car. Halfway there he realized he'd forgotten something and hurried back to where she was.

She was no longer breathing, and Rick actually felt a little sorry for her. If she'd stayed home tonight, if she'd gone to another bar, if she'd been sitting at another stool, she would still be alive. The luck of the draw was often cruel.

He worked the sheet loose at the top of her head and snipped off several strands of hair. Such ugly hair, really, but he would add it to his collection. In her honor. He folded the hair inside a handkerchief, tightened the sheet again, and strode back to his car, whistling softly, pleased with how easy it had been and that he had done it alone.

As soon as he was on the road again, he had forgotten her.

(2)

Andy was sure she had a gene missing. The direction gene. The gene that got you from point A to point B even when you couldn't see water. She was used to Key West, where you could watch the sun push up from the Atlantic in the morning and watch it sink into the Gulf at night. Key West was simple. Gainesville in the boonies was not.

She was on a dirt road in east fucking nowhere, freezing her ass off and poring over a county map that made her dyslexic. The heater in her BMW didn't work, there wasn't a house within sight, and she couldn't tell from the map whether she'd taken a wrong turn or just hadn't gone far enough.

She threw the map into the passenger seat, flicked off the overhead light, sat there fuming. She decided to backtrack to the paved road, which was supposed to be Routes 27 and 41, and start over again. She made a sharp U-turn, the Beamer's tires splashing through puddles. The sky had cleared and was studded with stars. Had stars been visible through the fog the night Catherine McCleary was killed? Was this incredible sky what she'd seen when she'd driven in from town that night? Had he followed her out here from Gainesville or had he already been at the farm, waiting for her?

She reached for the cassette recorder on the dash. Her tapes were her primary records during her research for a book. Though she occasionally took notes, the recorder was faster and the tapes provided a sense of immediacy when she began to write weeks or sometimes months later.

"November fifth, nine-forty-five P.M., en route to Tree Frog Farm. It's a long, lonely drive after the turnoff from the highway. Nothing out here but fields of darkness and the suggestion of shapes that are trees, brush, fences. The headlights seem weak in all this space, this blackness, no brighter than a couple of matches. And, frankly, I don't like being here. I don't like the vastness.

"Gravel pings against the side of the car. It's a sharp, distinctive sound that lifts from the hum of the engine with a kind of erratic rhythm. It's too cold and too spooky to drive with the windows down, so they're sealed tight even though the heater doesn't work well. My feet are blocks of ice.

"It was warmer the night Catherine was killed. The ground fog out here must have been like soup, swirling across the empty road, climbing fence posts and tree trunks. Even if she wasn't able to see the stars, their light probably spilled into the fog, making it look as if it was lit from within, like a lantern. The moon didn't rise that night until ten and it was just a thin sliver, not enough to make a difference out here.

"According to my source at the sheriff's department, Catherine left the theatre around eight that night and had been dead at least twelve hours when she was found about four yesterday afternoon. When the Rasper called me, I think he'd just come from

32

the farm. He frightens me. His voice frightens me. I frighten myself. I should have talked to the cops. But Bristol would take this away from me. He would claim it. Use it. Twist it to suit himself.

"The first call was on October twenty-fourth, the same night he killed Lucy Davenport. It had been a long day in classes and I was beat that night. So when the phone rang and I heard him whispering, I thought it was a perv call and hung up. He called right back and in that terrible raspy voice said, 'Don't hang up. I have a story that's going to make you rich.' What goddamn arrogance. But I stayed on the line, didn't I? I listened to the whole thing, didn't I? How he killed her. How she screamed. How all I had to do was listen to him and write it down. He didn't tell me her name or where she lived. But, lucky for me, the secretary at the sheriff's department likes to gossip and thinks I'm next to God, so I just gave her a call when it was on the news the next day and got some details. Then I phoned my editor; she said go ahead. Then Ms. Gossip supplied Catherine's name yesterday, gave me bad directions to the farm, and now here I am. Spooking myself.

"I can't say I'm particularly proud of the way I'm handling things. But a bomb after a bestseller makes you feel like the only fatso in a room filled with Cher clones, desperate enough to risk almost anything. And maybe, just maybe, it'll put me on The List again."

The List was the *New York Times* bestseller list, the only list that counted. The mass-market edition of *Home Before Dark* had spent fifty-seven weeks on The List, fluctuating between the fifth and the eighth spots, and had earned her half a million dollars. There had been three books since. Two had sold very well but hadn't hit The List. The last one had fallen *well below expectations*, publishing jargon that meant it hadn't earned out its advance and that sales had, in fact, been bad enough so that now she felt like a student on probation.

True crime, her agent had said, was maxing out. The next story would have to be *very* good, *very* different. And this one was. Right place, right time, and she had the jump on every other crime writer in the country. She wasn't sure yet if she would include the Rasper's calls in the book. It depended on how things developed; everything depended on that.

She set the recorder in the passenger seat, switched on the light, consulted the map again. She realized she'd gotten lost because she'd taken a right instead of a left on Southwest Ninety-fifth Avenue. "Heeeyy, ye moron," she muttered. "Read the map and ye shall find. Got it? Are we going to get there now?"

More pasture, more stars, more wooden fences. But this time she crossed over the railroad tracks and knew she was headed where she should be. The road forked; she hung a right. Half a mile later the Beamer's headlights struck a No Trespassing sign. To the left of it was a second sign that read:

TREE FROG FARM
ENTER AT YOUR OWN RISK

"Cute, very cute. Your own risk." The gate was shut. She pulled right up to it, removed a flashlight from under the seat, and opened the glove compartment. The .38 inside was loaded, the safety was off. No sense carrying a weapon if you had to fuss with it before you could use it.

She'd bought the gun after her tour for *Home*, when she'd become fair game for every fruitcake who thought he had a story she'd be interested in. She'd been living in Miami then and the weird calls and letters had poured in, along with one very persistent nut who'd parked himself across the street from her house until she'd filed a restraining order against him. When he'd violated it, she'd met him at the door with the gun in hand and threatened to blow off his balls if he ever set foot on her property again. Two weeks later she'd moved to Key West. Although the town had its share of fruitcakes, they were the harmless variety, their brains fried to a golden brown by the sun and endless margaritas.

Outside the car, the cold grabbed her by the ankles and chewed its way up her legs. Jesus, if she'd wanted cold, she would have gone to Minneapolis in January. Her body freaked when the temperature fell below fifty.

Jeans and high-tops and a cotton jacket just didn't cut it. She needed long johns, an electric blanket, hot coffee spiked with rum.

She flicked up the latch on the gate, pushed it open, and hurried through. Since this was where Catherine McCleary had died, she wanted to poke around, get a feel for the place, see what Forensics had left behind. But just in case someone was staying here—family, a caretaker with dogs—she opted to go in on foot, upwind from the house.

Andy felt a twist of conscience as she negotiated the muddy road. But it wasn't *her* fault that she was now acting like the criminals she wrote about. If that bastard Bristol had cooperated in the Davenport homicide, given her access to photos, to autopsy and investigative reports, she would have reciprocated with the tapes of the killer's calls and this sneaking around wouldn't be necessary. Now they were adversaries. Now she was in the rather unpleasant position of having to dig up some dirt on Bristol that she would use if he tried to make things difficult for her.

She imagined herself and Bristol on *Oprah*, he with his mahogany cane, his quiet, even voice, his odd charm, and herself twenty pounds slimmer, her new body fitted into a sleek little number. Something blue that would set off the slate of her eyes and the dark luster of her long hair. Her manner would be more abrasive than Bristol's, but it wouldn't matter. She would win over the audience. She knew the ropes on talk shows. She would look TV-right.

Despite her excess pounds and the dimple in her chin, Andy was, by her own dispassionate assessment, quite pretty. Her oval face was photogenic, framed by straight black hair that fell past her shoulders. She usually wore it in a single thick braid, a deliberate slight to her ex-husband who had liked it loose. Her eyes, slanted like a cat's, gave her a somewhat exotic look that she heightened with makeup, clothes, accessories. And one way or another, she would shed the twenty pounds she'd gained when her marriage had fallen apart. She would do it even if she had to have her stomach stapled.

The road to the house was lined with Christmas trees. Their sweet scent clung to the chilly air and mixed with the odor of smoke. The only place the smoke could be coming from was the farmhouse, and sure enough, a few moments later, she spotted a sports car in the front yard.

Family. It had to be.

She lingered at the edge of the trees, listening to the dark, imagining the Rasper here that night, tendrils of fog cutting him off at the ankles, his body taut. She squinted her eyes and he seemed to take shape in the dark, as if through some strange portal in time:

He approaches the house, silent as a ghost, a pouch of tools hanging from his belt. A syringe, novocaine, knives. His hands are sheathed in rubber gloves. His shoes have smooth soles; he wears jeans and a dark shirt, clothes that blend with the absence of light. Crickets cry out, dry twigs snap underfoot, and inside, Catherine sleeps like a princess. . . .

No, there was something wrong with that picture. She felt it, this wrongness, as a sharp insistent nudge against her ribs. But she couldn't identify it. Couldn't fine-tune it. Not yet.

Fierce barking broke into Andy's reverie, barking that was close, coming from the house. She tore back down the road, past the Christmas trees, damning her excess weight, cursing her ex-husband for the divorce that had driven her to seek solace in food, swearing off M&M's, rich foods, three sugars in her coffee. She gasped for breath, the cold chilled her lungs, her hands balled into tight fists.

The barking was closer.

A light winked on.

She saw her Beamer just ahead, a marvelous dark shape against the greater blackness, her refuge, her goddamn salvation. Then she tripped and her arms flew out to break her fall and the gun slipped from her hand. She caught herself before she hit the ground, but the gun was gone and the dog was right behind her, tearing through the trees.

Andy raced on, reached her car, hurled herself inside. Her hands shook, her teeth chattered, but the car cranked

36

up immediately and she ripped through the gate in reverse. As she swung around, the dog raced into the glare of her headlights. Andy gunned the accelerator, tempted to run the fucker down. But Christ, she *liked* dogs, how could she run over a dog? Especially a dead woman's dog?

So she swerved away from it and hauled ass down the road, tires spitting mud and gravel.

4

(1)

TAILLIGHTS. THAT WAS all McCleary saw when he reached the gate, taillights shrinking in the distance, red dots floating in the cool dark like an animal's eyes. He stared after them until the car turned and they vanished.

It could have been anyone—students who took a wrong turn, lovers looking for a place to park, a real estate agent, a visiting alien. But he knew better. Flats trotted up to him, delighted with herself for chasing off the intruder. He congratulated her. She barked, then put her nose to the ground, pursuing a scent.

He followed her with the flashlight and when she stopped, the beam found a footprint. Then another and another. They ended with the trees, where his Miata was clearly visible. Most of the prints weren't very good. The ground was too wet. But he found one that was perfect. It measured a hand length and the impression was deep. Next to it he left his own footprint and compared the two. He stood six feet tall, weighed 180 pounds, and wore a size ten medium-width shoe. This guy was shorter and fifty or sixty pounds lighter.

Flats pranced over and dropped a gun at his feet. A .38. McCleary laughed out loud. "Good work, girl. I think you have a future in this field. Guess our guy got a little spooked, huh?"

He used a handkerchief to pick up the gun. If it had a serial number and had been a legitimate purchase, then Tim Benson, his old partner at Metro-Dade, would be able to track down who owned it. It was a start.

McCleary reached the answering machine at Benson's place. He left a message, included the serial number on the gun, and asked him to call when he had something.

Then he put another log on the fire and crouched in front of it, hands held up to the warmth.

The rhythms of the house rose around him—hums and clicks, creaks and sighs, gurgles from the pipes. He never thought he would miss the noise his daughter made: the sharp, bitter cries, the quick peals of laughter, the whines of frustration, the inviolate proof of her presence. Life had been simpler before she'd come along, but not as rich, as wondrous.

Sometimes at night when he couldn't sleep, he lay in the silent dark, listening for sounds from her room. A sigh, a small cry, the squeak of her mattress, anything. It alarmed him when minutes ticked by and he heard nothing but the stillness stretching from one end of the house to the other like an oil slick. He would imagine the road not taken, Ellie unborn, her bedroom as a den, the floors clean of her toys and her plump little books, the cats still ruling the roost. And he would feel as he did now, fear rushing up behind him like a mugger, a thief, a maniac who intended to snatch her, harm her, do her in.

The threat of losing her, of something happening to her, had never loomed as hugely as it did right now. But he wanted her with him, with him and Quin, where he could see her, talk to her, hold her. Benson, father to a son now midway through adolescence, had once remarked that you were better off in this business if you were single, childless, and had no personal life whatsoever. The man who was emotionally unattached had nothing to fear except solitude. Undoubtedly true, but McCleary was glad it wasn't true for him.

He went into Cat's den. He had already searched the room, a task that had been complicated by his sister's random disorder. Her desk drawers were stuffed with papers and notes and cards, makeup and brushes and pens; nothing in her filing cabinet was labeled; books were jammed every which way on the floor-to-ceiling shelves. The computer was the only thing he hadn't had a chance to explore.

It was an IBM clone that Cat had bought to keep track of the farm's business. Spots of coffee and ashes and ink

39

stained the keyboard, the screen was dusty, and bits of Flats's fur seemed to be growing from the edges of the disk drive. But the machine was a beauty. According to the setup, the computer had sixty megs of memory on a hard drive, eight megs of RAM memory, an internal modem and fax. Cat had equipped it to the hilt with software that included programs for astrology and numerology, part of what the family called her *weirdo interests*.

He accessed the communication program. The menu indicated that she subscribed to an electronic network called Kazaam. This was the facet of computers that made the world seem incredibly small, linking people all over the country through bulletin boards on a variety of subjects. Post your message without ever leaving home and tune in tomorrow for the responses, he thought. The only reason Cat would subscribe to a network was if it had something to do with theatre or acting.

The program was set up to automatically dial the local access number, and when he was connected, it also supplied Cat's personal code. A moment later, he was in.

Hello, Catherine McCleary. Logon time 911103, 22:05 P.M. EST. Last logon 911101. 5 letters waiting.

The screen automatically scrolled to the communications menu. McCleary selected the entry for Cat's electronic mailbox:

11/02/91, 21:05 p.m., Phaedra Books
Mi amor, no answering machine on! I've got that poster you people need for scene 2. You want to pick it up or should I drop it off?
Emilio

11/03/91, 23:31 p.m., Hippodrome Theatre
I guess you're still having trouble with your answering machine. I hope you see this tomorrow morning before you drive into town. Melody changed rehearsal time on us again. She wants us there by ten. She said she'd post it in your E-mail, but she forgot, so I'll post

it before I split. Could you swing by the bookstore on your way in? Emilio has the poster for scene 2. And hey, you were terrific today!

Tess

11/04/91, 00:01 a.m., Hippodrome Theatre
Hello, sweet thing. The fog's rolling in and I'm on my way.

11/04/91, 11:17 a.m., Hippodrome Theatre
Still no machine? Did you oversleep or what? Rehearsal started at ten!
Call me!

Tess

11/4/91, 14:25 p.m., Hippodrome Theatre
Okay, Cat. What's going on? You in bed with that mysterious man in your life? Is that why you missed rehearsal? Call or I'm coming out there and then everyone, including me, is going to be red in the face.

Tess

Sweet thing . . . fog's rolling in: an unsigned note from her lover? What lover? Although Cat had rarely been between men very long, she would have mentioned it if she were seeing someone special.

But on the other hand, what he knew about her life here would fit into a thimble. It wasn't due to any breech in closeness, just to circumstances. He did know, however, that the Sunshine Repertory was a small group that received funding from the university and private grants. It was part of the theatre department, yet also separate from it. The theatre they used, the Hippodrome, was owned by the city. But that was all he knew. He wasn't even sure what play she'd been rehearsing for.

He pushed back from the computer, thinking about the objects the killer had left on the floor in here. Six personal items arranged one above the other from the door to the window. He opened the file Bristol had given him and found the list: a pair of red and pink panties; a

41

beige garter belt with tiny orange flowers on it; a pale yellow leather belt; a light green bra, thirty-six B; a necklace with a blue stone in it; a purple sweatband. Some of the colors were odd, but not for Cat; her wardrobe had never been the least bit conventional.

The photos taken in this room hadn't been developed yet. But he needed visual input, so he went into Cat's bedroom to look for the items. Although he found everything except a garter belt and a sweatband, the items weren't identical to the ones the killer had left; those were now part of the evidence package. But it helped to see the things laid out, arranged as the killer had arranged them.

Helped, yes, but it didn't tell him anything, and maybe that was the point. It was possible the killer had left them just to throw the cops off. *What're you saying here, guy? C'mon, talk to me.*

The items were things Cat had worn.

They were evenly spaced.

They corresponded to ascending parts of the body, groin to head.

He connected them point to point with a mental line, seeking a discernible pattern in the layout, then duplicated it on a piece of paper. He turned the paper around, viewing what he'd drawn from different angles. It looked like a house and not a very well-constructed house at that.

McCleary spread a map of Gainesville on the floor, located the farm and the street where the English professor had been killed, then measured the distance between them. Thirty miles, give or take. He drew the house to the same scale as the map and placed it over the map, the longest edge of it against the farm. Davenport's home didn't fall within the area no matter how he moved the paper around.

He studied the objects again, rearranged them, lined them up side by side, named them out loud. He waited for the nudge of a hunch, the glimmer of an idea; waited for something in his perception to shift. But after ten minutes he was still looking at four objects on the floor, with gaps where a sweatband and a garter should have been. Undaunted, he put everything in a paper bag and stashed it in a corner. Sooner or later something would click, and when it did, when he saw the pattern, it would be so blatantly obvious, he would be appalled that he could have missed it at all.

(2)

Cat's Wagoneer had a dozen personal touches, Quin thought, that were as idiosyncratic as she had been. An air freshener shaped like a toucan hung from a knob on the radio. A huge pair of dice like you'd find in a Mexican taxicab dangled from the mirror. Animal-shaped magnets clung to the door of the glove compartment. And the car was imbued with the smell of hay and grass, water, earth, space. The windshield, in fact, was nothing but space, a panorama of black sky and stars that winked like sequins.

Quin kept glancing around to check on Ellie, who had slept during the entire flight and awakened only briefly to grin at McCleary when he'd buckled her into the car seat. It was an old rusted thing he'd found in Cat's storage room, some object from her past she couldn't bear to part with. Quin, a fellow pack rat, understood the sentiment completely.

To McCleary, though, the car seat symbolized the disorder that had afflicted his sister's life. That was just the word he'd used, too, *afflicted*, as if with disease. He contended that it was going to make their investigation that much tougher; she didn't think it would affect things one way or another. The answers to Cat's murder weren't going to be found in a filing cabinet.

He talked steadily as he drove, bringing her up to date on everything. One of the advantages of working together was that they spoke in a kind of shorthand when it came to imparting information. He described Bristol, for instance, as anal retentive, and she had an immediate impression of a smooth, polished cop who was into control. Detective Angie Wilkin? Liz Claiborne perfect, tough lady clotheshorse. But when he got to the part about the electronic computer network, he lost her. Her knowledge

43

of computers didn't extend beyond the word-processing program. So she interrupted and he explained and she asked more questions and pretty soon they were bogged down in detail and arguing about things that had nothing to do with his sister or her murder.

Like what Ellie was wearing. "She's not dressed warmly enough for this weather, Quin. You should've brought her jacket."

"I did bring her jacket. She was sweating in it, so I took it off."

"Maybe you should've kept her awake."

She rolled her eyes and stared out the window, wondering why he was so intent on starting an argument. "If I'd kept her awake, Mac, she would've been hell on the plane."

"Well, now she'll be up by four and ready to rock and roll."

"Look, if you think you can do it any better, *you* fly home with her and I'll drive."

She immediately regretted her tone of voice, what she'd said, that she'd gotten defensive so quickly. These old patterns in the marriage were like clichés, easy to lock on to, to repeat, particularly now, with Cat dead and both of them trying to sort out what they felt. She apologized. He merely nodded and they fell into an uncomfortable silence.

Quin watched the stars and wished for food, for sleep, for a night of hot sex. Of the three, she figured that only the first was most likely to materialize. It astonished her sometimes that after eight years of marriage, McCleary's bout with amnesia that had led to their seven-month separation, his affair with Sylvia Callahan, and the birth of a daughter, they could still end up like this, as silent and distant from each other as strangers sharing a compartment on a train.

When the Wagoneer came to a stop alongside McCleary's Miata, she turned to open her door and he touched her shoulder. "Let's start over, okay? I'm glad you came up here, Quin."

His hand was still against her shoulder and she turned to look at him. "I know you are. But maybe you'd rather do this on your own. It might be easier without Ellie and me.''

''No.'' He wound a strand of her hair around his finger. ''It's easier with you here.''

There was no self-pity in his voice, just the soft, wrenching undercurrent of emotion that violent death always bestowed on the survivors. Quin hugged him and he kissed her, his hands roaming through her hair, across her back, sliding up under her skirt, asking. His need, sudden and desperate, had little to do with passion. It was McCleary reaching out to connect with life, to affirm it, to draw it around him like a kind of shield against his sister's death.

They made love in the Wagoneer's front seat with the awkwardness of teenagers at the drive-in whose hands smelled of buttered popcorn. They shifted this way, that, sometimes swaying like branches in a summer wind, sometimes faltering, seeking the rhythm that was the sum of the marriage's intimacy. There was, for her, a peculiar quality about it—her panties tossed on the dashboard like an empty pack of cigarettes, McCleary sitting up straight in the passenger seat as she straddled him on her knees, her skirt settling around them like the soft folds of an exotic flower, her hands on his shoulders, pressing, releasing, one of his hands at her hip, the other lost under her skirt, hidden, furtive, and Ellie asleep in the backseat.

She became aware of some small sound in the darkness beyond the car, probably a bird or a rodent scampering through brush. But in her mind it became the lingering presence of whomever had killed Cat, a kind of psychic residue that, if she looked for it, would glow like radioactive dust.

The weight of the night pressed against her spine and she wanted to look around but didn't. The feel of him inside her became a distraction, an intrusion, an annoyance. She hated herself for it, hated that she couldn't offer what he needed, that she couldn't accept what he offered, but she couldn't help it. Her body followed the track of her mind, leaving her tense and dry. It was uncomfortable when he began to thrust toward his own completion, leaving her so far behind that she might as well have been absent altogether. He came and she didn't, and irritation filled her.

This irritation followed her into the house, into the guestroom where McCleary had made a bed for Ellie in a playpen he'd found in Cat's storage room. She set out diapers and a few other essentials on the low bureau, working in the dark so she wouldn't wake Ellie, and the irritation nipped at her heels like a dog demanding attention. She shouldn't have come here. She didn't belong. There would be no baby-sitter to free her time for the kind of investigation Cat deserved. She was unequipped to balance everything, and it terrified her to think of their marriage sliding off into darkness again. This time there would be no way to pull it out and patch it together once more.

McCleary brought the rest of the things in from the car, set them down. He came up behind her as she stood at the bureau, arranging and rearranging her and Ellie's things, and nuzzled her neck. When she didn't react, he ran his hands up under her skirt, over her buttocks, as if sculpting them.

"Don't, Mac," she whispered.

But he pressed up against her, his mouth warm against the back of her neck, his fingers seeking her. Her hands found the edge of the bureau as she gradually bent at the waist, her body like a strip of rubber curving from an intense heat. "Let me," he whispered, and she turned in his arms and he unfastened her skirt and worked it down over her hips.

She leaned back into the bureau, its edge cutting her off just above the knees, one hand against it, the other gripping his shoulder. He played her like a piano, his hands here, there, his mouth now falling in a hot glide down the center of her. Her consciousness splintered. She was aware of Ellie in the playpen, of shadows eddying across the ceiling, of the soft, choked sounds she made. A dark, hot pulse beat behind her eyes. She heard herself say No wait oh God, but he didn't wait, didn't stop, he just kept on and on until her pleasure found the edge of her grief and she collapsed with a sob against him.

She stood under the spray of hot water, thinking of McCleary's death last fall, a flatline for twelve seconds on the operating table in the ER, the result of a gunshot wound. It was Cat whom Quin had thought of first when it had happened, Cat who she believed would explain it to her, to him, to both of them.

But Cat, in fact, had merely listened as he'd told her how he'd lifted out of his body and watched the doctors work on the man below him. He'd claimed to have traveled to some other place where he'd talked with Sylvia Callahan, who had been killed during the investigation of the case that had brought her back into McCleary's life. Callahan, he'd said, had guided him, explained his choices, offered glimpses of his future if he chose to return. When he'd finished, Cat had smiled and said, "Welcome to the weirdo club, bro."

Cat, with her endless cosmic musings, had talked about his experience at length when Quin had visited her a year ago, noting changes in his behavior, in his approach to people, to life. It struck her as ironic that an expansion of awareness could result from what appeared to be an annihilation of consciousness. But the experience had most certainly changed McCleary and in ways she was still discovering.

Only one incident in her own life was remotely similar. It had happened the night after Ellie was born. The nurses had just taken her back to the nursery after a feeding and Quin was falling asleep when someone had called her name. She'd lifted up and glanced around, thinking one of the other three women in the room had spoken, but they had all been asleep. The door to the hallway had been shut, so the sound hadn't come from out there. She'd decided she'd imagined it and had closed her eyes once more.

When it had happened again, she'd seen the person in her mind's eye, a lovely young woman of perhaps thirty. She'd said her name was Michelle Maya McCleary, Ellie for short. She was trying to verify where and when she'd been born and the address where her parents had lived at the time. Quin had sensed that the world in which she lived was vastly changed from the world into which she'd been born. These differences weren't only societal but geological, that the Earth itself had undergone some violent transformation.

Quin had given her the information, the woman had thanked her, and that had been that. It was hardly the brush with the cosmos that McCleary's near-death experience had been. But it had altered something vital in the way she perceived the world. And maybe, just maybe, that change had made it possible for her to smell a fragrance that couldn't have been there.

(4)

The French doors were thrown open to the cool night air and the cry of cicadas. Logs crackled in the fireplace and emitted tiny puffs of smoke that smelled of pine and autumn. Flats, curled up on the floor between Quin and McCleary, raised her head now and then, listening to something outside that they couldn't hear. Quin wondered if she was waiting for Cat to come home.

"You think she knows Cat is dead, Mac?"

"I don't know."

Quin unwound the towel from her wet hair and began to comb it. "I had a cat once who saw ghosts."

He glanced up from the case board he was working on. "What cat?"

"A tabby when I first moved off campus. It was a really nothing apartment that was supposed to be haunted by the woman who'd lived there before me. She'd hanged herself in the living room. Some of her furniture was still in the place, including her favorite stuffed velvet chair, right? One night I saw that cat literally stop in midair as she was leaping for the chair. She hit the floor and took off, all her fur standing straight up."

"Indigestion."

"The woman's begonias were in the sill and they bloomed that night. They hadn't bloomed since she'd died."

"Are we debating this?"

Quin, thinking about the scent of White Linen, said, "Hey, you're the guy who died. You're supposed to have the answers."

"I don't believe in spooks." He nodded toward the case board in front of her. "You finished?"

"I guess so. There isn't much since I'm just working from secondary information."

"Doesn't matter. Let's compare and see what we've got."

A case board was a visual way to organize data relating to a crime and something McCleary rarely used anymore. He was one of those fortunate people who was able to keep a great deal of information in his head and shuffle it around, like furniture, without losing track of where everything was. There were already so many variables in Cat's murder that he'd suggested they each put together a board and then compare them.

Their techniques differed vastly. His board was detailed and neat, with photos of the crime scenes pinned across the top, two lists of personal objects pinned below them, lists divided according to facts, speculations, leads, people and locations that had to be checked out. There was also a miscellaneous catchall. It was a left-brain diagram that would require right-brain leaps of faith.

Quin tended to use a board for brainstorming, a kind of right-brain purging that then required filling in the blanks with good old left-brain detection and synthesis. It was arranged in a circle, with the outer comments and observations connected like spokes of a wheel to a single phrase in the center that said *Occult/Theatre*.

McCleary pointed to the central phrase. "You think those are the most important factors?"

"Don't you?"

"They're important, but I don't know if they belong in the center."

"I think they do. Metaphysics and theatre were Cat's two lifelong passions."

"But there's no connection to Davenport. She was an English professor with an interest in erotic art, Quin."

"Who says there has to be a connection?"

"If these were spree killings, then there's probably some link between them, even if it's small."

"Says who?"

"All the data on this kind of—"

"Screw the data, Mac. I think we should look at them separately and see where they lead."

From their room came a soft, sleepy cry, a reminder that it was no longer just the two of them. "How're we going to do this with Ellie?" he asked.

She started to say they could take turns, like they did on weekends at home when they were working on separate cases. But that was hardly fair to McCleary. No matter how much she had loved Cat or how desperately she wanted to be involved in the investigation, Cat was *his* sister and he needed the space to pursue this. Taking turns was not even an option; she would just have to figure out what to do about child care. "I'll take care of it."

The astonishment on his face spoke volumes about what he had expected her to say. He blurted, "How?"

"I don't know." She shrugged and got up to tend to Ellie. "I'll figure something out."

Ellie was standing up in a nest of blankets in the playpen, crying for a bottle, a change of diapers, a hug, all of the above. When she saw Quin, she jabbed her finger toward the far wall. "Dadda, uh uh uh, Dadda."

"No, I'm Mama."

Quin picked up Ellie and put her on the bed to change her. Her head sank into the feather pillow and her blue eyes fastened on Quin's. She reached out and touched Quin's cheek. "Mama," she said.

"Yay, Ellie."

She grinned and clapped her little hands. "Mama, Mama."

Quin felt absurdly pleased. Ever since Ellie had begun trying to speak, she'd mastered only a few words, and *mama* wasn't among them. *Dadda*, which McCleary had been repeating to her since she was about five minutes old, was her favorite, with *kitty* a close second.

"Mama."

"You'll see, El. We'll do okay, you and me. We'll

spend more time together while we're here. And maybe we can find a good day-care center where you'll have other kids to play with for part of the day. How would that be?''

Ellie struggled to a sitting position and stabbed her finger at the wall. Quin glanced around. The bureau was nearly lost in shadow. ''Nothing there, cutie. Now let's get you into something a little warmer. Your legs are cold.''

As she dug into the duffel bag, looking for a pair of long pants, the air seemed to turn cooler, as though a door or window had just opened, admitting a draft. The phone rang in the front room. McCleary answered it, his voice a dull buzz, a static punctuated by Ellie's insistent *uh uh uh*. The back of her neck tightened. She was suddenly certain that if she looked around, she would see someone stepping out of the closet or taking shape from the shadows that had hidden him. Her breath stalled in her throat and her body creaked like an old floor as she shifted on the bed, turning. Ellie had fallen silent. The inside of Quin's mouth flashed dry.

She saw the far wall, the bureau, Ellie's little bag on top of it, everything folded up inside shadows. And for an instant she thought she saw something else in the mirror, a flutter of movement, a shape, fleeing. Then it was gone.

''Quin?''

McCleary in the doorway. Ellie saying ''Dadda,'' inviting him in. The world clicked into its normal speed again. ''Who was that on the phone?''

''Benson. You won't believe who that thirty-eight belongs to.''

Right now, she'd believe anything. ''Who?''

''Andrea Tull.''

5

A FEW HOURS of sleep after Ocala, he thought, and he was as good as new.

Rick pedaled his ten-speed through the chill of the city's four A.M. streets. Islands of light the color of Popsicles broke up the crisp, black shadows. The air was very still, as though waiting for something.

He could have been anyone, a man biking home after a late night with friends, a student suffering from insomnia, someone's husband. He liked the idea of himself disguised by the ordinary trappings of life—husband, father, family man—when, in fact, he was none of these things.

He crossed Southwest Twelfth Street and biked parallel to the campus, where the live oaks were larger, the Spanish moss was thicker, the shadows deeper. The past still breathed here. He knew if he squinted his eyes and gazed obliquely to the right or left, the curtain of time would lift on 1539, when Gainesville was known as the Potano Province and Hernando de Soto marched through, dogging the heels of his buddy Pizarro. Or it would lift on 1763, when the Creek Indians took possession of the area and renamed it Alachua.

In 1830, a trade post was established and a white settlement called Hog Town grew up around it. Twenty-three years later Hog Town became Gainesville, named in honor of General Edmund P. Gaines, a Seminole War leader. It drew families from Georgia, Alabama, and the Carolinas, hardy cotton growers who laid out large plantations and lived scenes from *Gone With the Wind*.

Rick wasn't sure when the cotton industry died out. Maybe when the South lost the Civil War, maybe with the coming of the railroad in the early 1860s. But as transportation improved, citrus became more important and today it was right up there with tourism and Disney World.

The university itself preceded Florida's admission to the Union, but the first college—of arts and sciences—didn't open until 1853. The state-owned colleges were consolidated into three in 1905, and a year later a hundred and thirty-six students arrived for the first college session at the University of Florida. Rick's great-grandfather had been among them. That made him a fourth-generation Floridian, a rare bird in a state where most people hailed from somewhere else.

Until the outbreak of the first world war, only a single crushed-rock road connected the university to the town. Its location was so rural, the east gate had to be locked to prevent cows from roaming onto the grounds and consuming the shrubbery. Until the war, in fact, the school's annual enrollment didn't exceed five hundred students.

Now there were nearly forty thousand students and eight hundred buildings on campus, most of them red brick and covered in vines. Twenty-one of them were recognized in the National Register of Historic Places, and had hosted such visitors as Robert Frost and William Jennings Bryan. The campus was impressive, all right, and much of Rick's own past was connected to it. The student center, the library, and McCarty Hall were all familiar landmarks from his undergraduate days. Farther back, into his childhood, Stadium Road was connected to memories of his father, the two of them en route to football games or on their way out of town to one of the sinkholes.

His old man had died suddenly of a heart attack seven years ago. He was seventy-five at the time, still robust and quick, but one morning he just didn't wake up. A month later Mother had suffered a massive stroke and had been in a nursing home ever since.

Fortunately, his parents had made a great deal of money when they'd sold Farmer Books a year or so before his old man's death. There was more than enough to ensure the best care for Mother, care that had restored most of the stroke's physical damage but that couldn't repair a mind that was failing. Now, bit by bit, her heart was following the route his old man's had taken.

For the last two weeks, she'd been in Shands Medical Center with a cardiac arrhythmia that wasn't responding to treatment. There had been some talk about putting in a pacemaker. Low risk and high yield, the doctor had said, as though talking about an investment. But the doctor wasn't pushing eighty. It wasn't his heart.

Rick turned on Newell Drive, which led into the medical complex. Shands was one of the top hospitals in the state, a teaching facility where the latest advances and therapies were the norm. ICU didn't have set visiting hours, and since Mother had a room to herself, he could come and go pretty much as he pleased. The nurses all knew him and did whatever they could to accommodate him. When his schedule permitted, he caught a couple of hours of sleep on the empty bed in her room so he could have breakfast with her in the morning.

She seemed to enjoy the company, babbling like an infant, pausing now and then to touch his arm and laugh. It made him nervous when she touched him. Sometimes he could feel the germs milling around on his skin like a gang of hoodlums and it took everything he could muster not to flee for the nearest bathroom to wash up. It wasn't her, but the hospital. All hospitals, even Shands, were filthy places, breeding grounds for bacteria and viruses. He knew. He'd spent two years in med school before he'd found his calling.

It would be a relief when she was back at the nursing home, which was cleaner, and where she had her routine, her friends, her world, such as it was.

He waited for the light at the intersection to change. A police car cruised past on Museum Road, the fourth he'd seen since he'd left his house. Security on campus had been beefed up since news of the second murder had been released. But only a fool would believe that a few more cruisers and undercover cops on foot patrol would protect nearly forty thousand students and faculty.

The light flashed green and he sped out from under the protection of the trees, away from the shadows, across the street. The green from the streetlight washed over him; he burned like an image on an X-ray, bones exposed, muscles bared, nothing sacred. The chilly wind slammed into him. The cold bit at his cheeks. Then he was under the trees again, the shadows hiding him, embracing him, holding him in an envelope of safety until he reached the hospital.

Breathless, he hopped off his bike, glanced around nervously. No one in sight. Not at this hour. But his body had already reacted, sweat spilling out of him like water from a hose. When he unzipped his jacket, he could smell himself, the faintly sour stink of his paranoia, and wished he could shower before seeing Mother.

He slipped his bike into a slot in the empty bike rack and padlocked it to the metal bar. Inside the lobby, the air steamed like the tropics. He shrugged off his jacket and caught sight of himself in the mirror. As Mother used to say, God had blessed him with a face that could start a religion. Its topography of sharp, bold lines created an image of strength, solidity, firm opinions. His eyes, large and deeply set, were a warm, caramel brown flecked with gold. Eyes you wanted to trust. His curly hair was a shade darker than his eyes and was still thick, even at the front.

For most of his life, his face had endeared him to women but not to men, which was just as well. He'd never understood the kick of bachelor parties and beers with the guys. Women were so much more interesting. He liked the way they looked and smelled, liked their curves, the smoothness of their skin, the silks they wore, their often strange and subtle differences from one another. He liked conversing with them, discovering them, unearthing their secrets. Women trusted him.

With the exception of his father and Ted Bundy, his significant relationships had all been with women.

He walked up to the visitors' desk. It was manned by volunteers who were, naturally, all women, most of them elderly widows with time on their hands. He loved them all, loved the soft blue of the veins that stood out in their ankles, loved their wrinkles and their false teeth and their bouffant gray hair.

Mabel, who manned the graveyard shift, smiled when she saw him and pushed a pass across the desk. "Morning, Ricky. You having breakfast with your ma?"

"If she'll have me."

"Well, be forewarned. I hear the breakfasts this morning are real bad. Scrambled eggs like goo, barely cooked bacon. My advice to you is to send it back if you don't like it. Let those kitchen people know exactly where you stand."

He laughed. "You leading this revolt, Mabel?"

"Somebody has to."

"You've got my vote." He touched the back of her hand because he knew that she liked it. "See you later, hon."

As soon as he was in the elevator, he pulled a square packet from his pocket, tore it open neatly at the top, and removed an alcohol wipe to disinfect his hand. He remembered reading, years ago, about Howard Hughes's fear of germs. Obsessive, the press had called it. Compulsive. Granted, Hughes had allowed it to go to extremes, but the basis of the fear was something Rick understood very well. It wasn't just a terror of death; it was more specific than that, the horror of dying of disease, of being eaten alive from the inside out.

Hughes wouldn't have done very well in this era of AIDS.

The difference between himself and Hughes was that Rick didn't allow his fear to control him. He took steps to minimize infection and was diligent about vitamins and the right foods and exercise. But emotions could kill you as surely as a virus, so he also worked to break through the conditioning of his upbringing, to rid himself of guilt. The concept of sin barely existed for him anymore.

ICU was on the second floor. It reminded him of the bridge of the Starship *Enterprise*, where everything took place against a backdrop of beeps and hums and clicks from a dizzying array of machines. Some of the patients were as good as dead. For them, the death of the body would be a mere formality. Others hovered in a kind of twilight, neither Here nor There. Then there were patients like Mother, stuck in the between, one foot Here and one foot There, minds scattered like seeds in some hot, unforgiving wind. He intended to go fast when he went. No lingering disease like cancer, no stroke, just a heart attack while he slept. Like his old man.

The nurse, Sally, informed him that Mother had had a bad night. "She had a tantrum because the orderly wouldn't kill the giant moth on the TV screen."

Giant moth. Yeah, Mother was having a fine night. "How's the new medication working?"

"Too soon to tell." She smiled sweetly and touched his shoulder. "We're all hopeful. Are you going to be here for breakfast?"

"Yes."

"I'll notify the kitchen to bring up an extra tray." A light blinked on her computer screen. "Oops, got to run."

Her uniform rustled against her white stockings as she hurried down the hall. She had wonderful hips and beautiful skin. Mother thought she resembled his sister, Josie, but Rick disagreed. Sally was merely cute; Josie would have been a beauty if she had lived.

The soft, uneven beep from the cardiac monitor suffused the silence in Mother's room. He longed for the deep, even rhythms of the heart he remembered as a child, the rhythms that had comforted him when he awakened from a nightmare, when he was sick, when she had rocked him, his head resting against the cushion of her breasts. The air smelled of sickness.

He didn't like the story the monitors had to tell. Her heartbeat for the last four hours was like a Morse code telegraphed by someone zapped on speed. Brain waves: drug-induced delta, with bursts of REM only in the last thirty minutes since the drug had begun to wear off.

She was sprawled on her back, arms thrown out at her sides, the sheets kicked off, her hospital gown hiked to the thighs, her legs all bone. Her head was turned toward him, her lips parted, her breath a noisy rasp. Her skin was pale, translucent. But it was her hair that hurt him most, a tangled fishnet against the pillow, strands plastered to her cheeks. Her hair had always been her greatest

57

vanity, and as she'd gotten older she worked hard to maintain its luster. The beauty shop, hot-oil treatments, softeners, expensive shampoos, vitamins. He remembered it as a dark fortress, a veil of wonder that had fallen along the sides of her face when she read, that had cascaded over her shoulders when she threw her head back and laughed.

Once, when he was seven or eight, he'd come upon her at the bookstore, standing in the aisle with a customer. She was twirling strands of hair around her finger as she talked, each strand alive, electrical, luminous. He'd watched the end of it curl until it was a spiral, a DNA helix encoded with information specifically for him. Perhaps his love of women had begun then, as he'd sought to divine the mystery of Mother and, through her, the mystery of all women.

While Father had handled the business end of the bookstore, Mother had dealt with the public. She had organized events, ordered the stock, known the customers by name. Father was the brains and Mother was the driving force, the fuel, the wisdom of Kali.

Now here she lay, utterly still, as wrinkled as a peach pit.

Rick tugged her hospital gown over her knobby knees and covered her with the sheet. She stirred, made a soft, resigned sound, and her eyes opened. Nothing in them. No history, no past, no recognition. Out to lunch. Then she blinked and stifled a yawn and the ghost of her younger self flickered across her face, a shadow that promised nothing.

"Ricky."

"I didn't mean to wake you. Go back to sleep."

She pushed up on an elbow. "I'm so glad you're here, Ricky. They've been giving me the worst time. There was this disgusting moth on the TV screen tonight and that orderly wouldn't get it off. I couldn't very well reach it myself, now could I?"

"I spoke to him about it, Mom. It won't happen again." He stroked her hair, combing it over her shoulders with his fingers. It was okay to touch Mother's hair, to kiss it, to bury his face in it. It was sacred, magical,

58

germless. "We'll have breakfast together in the morning. I'll be right here, just go back to sleep."

"I don't want to sleep. I have terrible dreams. I think it's the drugs they give me. I don't want any more drugs, Ricky. Could you talk to the doctor about it? He doesn't listen to me. He just pats me on the shoulder and says, 'Yes, ma'am. You bet, ma'am. Don't worry about a thing, ma'am.' "

Rick laughed. She had the cardiologist's voice down perfectly. "I'll talk to him." He coaxed her back against the pillow, straightening tubes, the interstate of wires, careful not to let any of the liquids touch him. Then she reached suddenly for his hand, clutching it. Bacteria leaped from her skin to his. His intestines seized up. But he didn't jerk his hand away.

"What's wrong, Mom?"

She released his hand. He swayed, dizzy with relief. "Are you okay, Ricky?"

"I'm fine." Those caramel eyes, duplicates of his own, bored into him. "I'll be a lot better once you're out of here."

"I don't mean that." Cross, she turned her head away. "I . . . these dreams I have . . . violent, bloody . . ."

Dreams, hallucinations, like the moth on the TV screen. "The drugs," he said. "It's probably just the drugs."

She looked at him again, eyes narrowing. "You never could lie worth a damn, son." She snorted and rolled over, offering him her back. "Now leave me alone so I can get some sleep."

But he stood there, gazing down at her, and saw the ridges of Catherine McCleary's spine as he'd scrubbed her from head to toe with Clorox, her hair a dark, erratic border across her shoulders.

59

6

(1)

IN THE LIGHT of day, the farm depressed McCleary. Everything wrong with the place was no longer hidden: forty years of scuff marks on the pine floors, leaky faucets, drawers that sat crookedly when they fit at all, lopsided window frames, torn screens, dust, walls shrieking for fresh paint, toilets that clicked and burped and dripped. And those were just the things he could see without looking very hard.

When he showered in Cat's bathroom, the door slipped off the single hinge that held it upright and toppled onto the edge of the sink. It knocked down a piggy bank, which shattered, spewing a million pennies across the floor. The wall that separated the shower stall from the toilet was damp, indicating a leak somewhere in the plumbing. When he made a pot of coffee, the hot plate blew; he had to pour hot water through a paper towel with coffee in it that he held over his mug and Quin's. McCleary Drip Special. While hanging up his clothes in her closet, he uncovered a nest with twenty generations of ants in it.

Such details had never bothered his sister; her real life had been lived inside the skins of her characters. But they bothered him. He didn't mind clutter, but he liked order. He liked things to work. He liked knowing from day to day what was in which cabinet. He liked opening a refrigerator that was free of suspicious containers stashed at the back, the sort of thing that would give you ptomaine if you smelled it.

He made a list of everything in the house that needed to be repaired or replaced, then started a second list for farm supplies. Hay, feed, dog food, grain for the chickens. Ellie was awake by then, crawling after Flats, patting the side of the pool table on the porch and trying to reach the Christmas objects, grabbing on to his legs as he fixed breakfast and whining to be held.

McCleary gave her a piece of banana and set her on the counter where she could watch what he was doing. Her bright blue eyes swept over the strips of bacon sizzling in the frying pan, paused briefly on the simmering oatmeal, fixed on the pieces of bread waiting to be toasted. She pointed at the bacon and said, ''Uh?''

''Bacon.''

Then it became a game, Ellie pointing and McCleary naming until they'd covered everything within her immediate range of sight. When she grew bored with the game, she cried to be let down and then crawled into the living room looking for trouble. Although she could walk, she was unsteady on her feet and preferred moving on all fours when she was serious about getting someplace. At the moment, her goal appeared to be the fireplace, which she was eyeing with considerable interest. McCleary hastily scooped the bacon from the pan and went after her. Denied her destination, she burst into tears.

He fixed her a bottle, put her in the stroller, and wheeled it over to the stove. ''Five minutes to finish breakfast, El, that's all I'm asking. Then you can have my undivided attention.''

She clutched greedily at her bottle and peered at him with accusatory eyes that seemed to whisper: *I want to play in the fireplace and dig my hands into all those ashes.*

''Hey, what's all the racket out here?'' Quin appeared in shorts and a T-shirt, sleep deprivation written all over her face. She pointed at Ellie, who giggled and pointed back. ''For such a little munchkin, you make an awful lot of noise.'' She made a beeline toward Ellie, scooped her up, bottle and all, then continued toward the coffeepot. She filled a mug, snatched a slice of bacon. ''You should have gotten me up to watch her while you fixed breakfast, Mac. We'll be out on the porch.''

She sailed out of the kitchen, Ellie riding her hip like

a bag of groceries, and McCleary stared after her, astonished. On a typical morning at home, they would have had at least one argument now about whose turn it was to watch Ellie or feed her or whatever. He didn't know what had precipitated the change. He was merely grateful for it.

They ate breakfast out on the porch, where Quin studied the Yellow Pages and jotted down phone numbers and addresses for day-care centers. She read him some of the advertising blurbs and they agreed the local Montessori school sounded like the best of the lot.

While she stuck around to make a few calls, he and Ellie and Flats piled into the Wagoneer with cans of feed and headed out to make the feeding rounds. Ellie pointed at everything, jabbering away in her private language, giggling when one of the cows mooed at her, making a face when she sampled some hay and found it wanting.

When they stopped at the pond to feed the ducks, Ellie crawled toward the water and Flats intercepted her, herding her away from it like a sheep. It frustrated her and she howled until Flats licked her face. Then she rolled onto her back, laughing and kicking her feet, the light pouring over her, the dappled shadows of the trees dancing circles around her. McCleary saw Cat in his daughter's face, in her eyes, in those timeless facets of blood and bones and family trees.

With the animals taken care of, and the pregnant sheep not in labor yet, he drove over to the orchards and walked around, Ellie riding on top of his shoulders. His sister's farm records had been surprisingly informative, but he didn't have the vaguest idea what he was supposed to do with the information. The fifteen hundred blueberry plants, for instance, consisted of four types that matured at different times throughout the summer. With a little planning, you could spread out the harvest time—and therefore the earnings—over the entire three months. A beer carton filled with blueberries could bring as little as five bucks at the farmers' market or as much as seventy-five, depending on whether the berries were harvested before June 1. But he didn't know if blueberries required daily upkeep or which types were supposed to be harvested first. He couldn't even distinguish one type from another. To him, they all looked like gnarled tangles of thin branches locked in some hopeless struggle.

Cat's garden was supposed to be watered three times a week. But he couldn't find a hose long enough to stretch from the nearest faucet. He knew the farm's water came from a well, but he couldn't find an outside faucet that worked. He knew she grew asparagus in her garden, but what the hell was the rest of it? True to form, she'd entered only as much information as she'd thought she'd need. It had never occurred to her that someone else might have to wade through it all. But then, why should it? At thirty, death had not been on her agenda. Perhaps that was the real tragedy of murder, he thought, its suddenness, its gross indifference, its random finger pointing at you and you and you.

(2)

Twenty years had brought more of everything to Gainesville: more Pizza Hut and McDonald's franchises, more students and shops, bicycles and traffic. But basically, Quin decided, the city hadn't changed.

It was laid out neatly, in quadrants, with University Avenue as the east-west boundary and Main Street as the north-south boundary. But because the campus was the sun around which the rest of the city revolved, the center of things fell between University and Thirteenth Street. In practical terms, this meant it was nearly impossible for her to get lost. And for someone with her lousy sense of direction, this was no small detail.

She took a quick detour through the neighborhood where she'd lived off campus her first year. Two decades had left cracks in the curbs, sags in the porches, empty spaces where there had once been trees. Otherwise, it was essentially as she remembered it. She spotted her old place on a corner, a wooden building with jutting windows on the first floor and a porch on the second.

"Hey, Ellie. Look over there." She slowed down and pointed. "That's where Mommy lived when she was in college."

63

"Mama," Ellie said, and giggled.

"Yeah, I know. It's a hoot, isn't it?"

Sometimes when she thought about those years, they seemed to have been lived by another woman, perhaps an acquaintance. She could barely remember what she had looked like then, much less what she had thought or felt about anything. For her, the Sixties had died long before John Lennon crumpled in front of the Dakota.

It suddenly depressed her to be here, in this neighborhood, in this small block of her past, and she quickly wound her way back to University Avenue. She stopped at Office Depot to pick up the forms Ellie's pediatrician had faxed, then headed over to the Hippodrome.

The theatre was located in the oldest section of town, on the far side of the courthouse square and down the street from the courthouse and jail. The area was being refurbished with cobblestone roads, old-fashioned streetlights that resembled giant bubble-gum machines, and shopfronts that were eerily uniform.

The building was as grand as an opera house from the outside, with ornate pillars and a sweep of wide steps. Quin wheeled Ellie's stroller up the ramp into the lavish, deserted lobby. The floors reflected everything like mirrors.

A sign on the stairwell had a black arrow on it pointing up, with the word THEATRE under it. She didn't see an elevator; it was probably tucked away at the back of the building, just like it was in most department stores. She'd come to believe that the placement of elevators was actually a carefully construed conspiracy to discourage the presence of parents with young children, who seemed to be the only people who used them.

But in fairness to all concerned, she had to admit she'd developed a number of similar paranoid ideas since Ellie's birth: that she was the oldest new mother in South Florida; that Ellie was the only nine-month-old baby who rarely slept through the night; that when people looked at her now, they saw a woman and a baby and she was instantly categorized, marked, and labeled *Mama*. As though that was the only thing she was.

Screw the elevator. She carried Ellie up the stairs, with the stroller folded like an umbrella in her left hand.

On the second floor, she unfolded the stroller and put Ellie in it. A woman's laughter echoed from behind a closed door with a plaque on it that read MELODY BURNS: DIRECTOR.

When she knocked, a woman called out, "It's open, and since when does anyone knock around here?"

"I guess that means we're welcome, Ellie."

The woman was on the phone, sitting in the lotus position on a llama rug in the middle of a wood-paneled room furnished in dark leather, glass, and chrome. She wore black leg warmers and black high-tops, with a long red and black satin shirt. She had a cascade of blonde hair, flawless skin, eyes that were neither blue nor gray but some exquisite combination of the two. She was in her midthirties, Quin guessed, and regarded Ellie as though she were a rather curious bug that had wandered into a bug-free sanctuary.

"Got to run, sweets," she said to whomever she was talking. "We'll have lunch as soon as I've read the script. . . ." She hung up, gave a dramatic little sigh, and stabbed out the cigarette burning in the ashtray to her left. "God spare me the whining scriptwriters of the world. Well, don't just stand there." She tossed a script onto the couch and motioned for Quin to sit down. "Let's see what you can do. Try act one, scene three. Take a couple minutes to read it over, then we'll get started."

"You must have me confused with someone else." Quin set Ellie on the llama rug, where she immediately fell to her hands and knees and pressed her face into the soft fur, giggling. To her, it was a big, fluffy kitty. "I'm, uh, looking for Tess Schulman."

"Aren't you the talent I spoke to a while ago?"

"No."

"Oh." She laughed. "Then who are you?"

"Quin McCleary."

Her smile faded. "Catherine's sister?"

"In-law."

"Christ, I'm really sorry." She rolled onto her knees and extended her hand. "I'm Melody Burns. The director. She was incredibly talented and I don't know how the hell we're going to replace her. When I was in the business in New York, it was rare to find talent who had the spark she did. I thought she was wasting her time in theatre, you know. She belonged in a TV series, something classy and sophisticated. She had tremendous presence. Don't get me wrong," she went on, lighting a cigarette, "she was a marvelous stage actress, but all that talent . . ." She shook her head. "She could've made a fortune on the tube."

"I don't think she was particularly interested in amassing a fortune."

"So she said." She leaned toward Ellie, smoke drifting from her nostrils. "Don't drool on this rug, cutie. I'll have to get it dry-cleaned."

Ellie looked at her and began to cry. Great, just great, Quin thought, burning with embarrassment. She dug into the diaper bag for a vacuum-sealed container of milk, filled Ellie's bottle, handed it to her. She rolled onto her back, quiet and contented again.

"How old is she?"

"Almost nine months."

"I've got a niece who's eighteen months. She's such a good kid, she almost makes me want to have one."

Quin heard the makings of a perfect-baby story in the air, the baby who slept all night, talked in complete sentences before she was a year old, and never fussed. She steered the subject back to Cat. "Was Catherine involved with anyone?"

Melody sat back against a leather armchair and crossed her long legs at the ankles. Smoke curled from her cigarette into the pool of sunlight that streamed through the window behind her. "Probably. But I can't say for sure. Catherine was pretty private when it came to her personal life. The police asked me the same thing. They're being damn tight-lipped about everything, that's what really irritates me. I mean, my God, Catherine was a part of this company. Tess found her. We have a right to know if they've got any suspects. She was well liked here and this whole thing has upset everyone terribly. But you think that Detective Bristol gives a shit about us? Ha. The only concession he made was to assign a cop to the theatre in the evenings.''

''I understand she missed a rehearsal and that's what prompted Tess to go out to her place.''

''Yeah. And Cat *never* missed rehearsals. She was a real professional in every sense of the word.''

Quin gestured toward the computer on the desk. ''The theatre's linked up to Kazaam, isn't it?''

Melody nodded, crushed out her cigarette, brushed at the front of her blouse. ''Mainly because the Florida Actors Guild has a slot on it and a lot of people in the company have computers. It's a quick way to get a message out.''

''Is that the only computer in the theatre?''

''Yes, why?''

''Who has access to it?''

''Everyone does.''

Swell. ''How many people have keys to this office?''

Melody gave an exaggerated sigh, shoulders slumping. ''I have a key, so does my secretary, and that's it. Would you mind telling me what's going on? I'm sick to death of getting the runaround.''

''Someone left Catherine a message in her E-mail the night she was killed. It was unsigned but was posted from the Hippodrome at one minute after midnight. On November fourth.''

''Midnight? No way. This office is never unlocked past six, even when we're rehearsing. And my secretary leaves by five-thirty.''

''Is there a spare key?''

''Nope.''

''Not anywhere?''

''Well, I suppose the city manager's office has one somewhere, since the city owns the building.''

''Any chance your key could've been swiped and then returned?''

She laughed, fingering a gold chain around her neck that she slipped out from inside her shirt. A key hung on it next to a heart-shaped ruby. ''Bloody unlikely. What was the message?''

Quin told her and Melody's exquisite eyes slid close together as she frowned. How would it be to look like that? Quin wondered. "Weird. It sounds almost, I don't know, Gothic. Like something Heathcliff might have written. It could even be sort of romantic, you know. The fog's rolling in and lover boy's on his way."

Maybe, Quin thought. "Is it possible to trick a computer—or an electronic network—into posting a message from someplace it didn't originate?"

"You're asking the wrong person about computers. I've got absolutely no idea how any of this works. I just know how to use what I need to use." Then she frowned again, apparently realizing that her answer could possibly incriminate her since only she and her secretary had keys to the office. "And that detective has already checked out my alibi. I was staying with my sister on Cedar Key."

"I wasn't suggesting that—"

"Look, it's okay." A quick smile. "I'd do the same in your shoes." Her phone rang and she rose gracefully from the floor, flicking her hair over a shoulder. "Tess can really tell you more about Catherine's personal life than I can, Mrs. McCleary. She's probably backstage somewhere." Then she strode over to the phone and picked up the receiver, her back to Quin. "Sunshine Repertory . . . Jeremy, darling . . ."

The abrupt dismissal irritated Quin. She picked up Ellie, who had fallen asleep, put her into the stroller, and pushed it out into the hall. She shut the door behind her, then stood there, ear close to the wood, listening.

The conversation with Jeremy ended in about five seconds. Melody muttered something that Quin didn't catch, then punched out another number. "It's me. I thought you might like to know that Catherine's sister-in-law was here asking questions . . . Of course I didn't say anything . . . I just thought you might like to know, that's all . . . Oh, forget I even called, Christ. Goodbye."

She slammed down the receiver, and Quin quickly pushed the stroller down the hall toward the theatre.

7

(1)

"THIS MS. TULL?" asked a male voice.

"Yes, this is Andrea Tull."

"Name's King."

"What can I do for you, Mr. King?"

"No mister. Just King."

"Right." Two minutes to spare before her senior writing class started, she thought, and she'd stopped to answer a call from a Neanderthal. "So?"

"Picadillo gives me a toot yesterday. Tells me some things, says I should give you a toot when I got something. I think I got something. You interested or not?"

Picadillo was a high roller in Tampa with fingers in a dozen pies, a second-generation Cuban who had grown up in Miami next door to Carmen Mendez, star of *Home Before Dark*. Thanks to his recollections, Andy had devoted an entire chapter to Carmen's early background. Picadillo, who got a kick out of seeing his name in print, had offered his services on future projects, and was usually able to put her in touch with someone who had the answers she needed. He was the first person she'd called when she had a name for the Rasper's second victim.

"Yes, I'm interested." Even though this dullard didn't sound as though he could give her the time of day. "But I'd like some idea of what you've got before I pay you anything."

King laughed. "You don't pay me squat, lady. This is a favor. And I don't want my name in your book."

"No problem. When can we meet?"

"Now."

"I've got a class. I'll be free in an hour."

"Meet me at Link's."

He gave her directions, and an hour later Andy was seated at a small, round table inside Link's. It was no student hangout. This was strictly a neighborhood bar, and not a very good neighborhood at that. The floor was covered in crushed peanut shells, blinds on the windows kept the place very dark, and the AC must have been set at fifty. Three old-timers were at the bar, two bikers in leather were playing pool, and one of their floozy babes was perched on a nearby stool chewing noisily on peanuts and sucking down draft beers. None of them looked like a King.

Fifteen minutes into her wait, she ordered her second Coke and one of the hard-boiled eggs that floated in a fishbowl of vinegar like a fetus in some illegal experiment. She asked the bartender if King was around. He was a skinny geezer of about fifty who needed a shave and was sipping at a glass of what smelled like straight rum. "You Tull?" he asked in a southern Georgia drawl, without drawing his eyes away from the TV.

"Yes."

"He's in the alley out back, messing around with Virginia."

She wasn't going to ask for his definition of *messing around*. She started to get up, but Geezer dropped a Styrofoam cup on the bar and told her to pour her Coke into it. "No glasses outside. Too many get broke. Then people get cut and decide to sue me, right?"

Right. She left by the rear door. The heat in the alley felt good after the gelid air in the bar. The only person in sight was a guy in jeans and a sleeveless T-shirt, tinkering with a Harley-Davidson. His dark hair was very short except for a piggytail at the back. He wore two gold posts in his left ear, a rose tattoo shouted from his left shoulder, and on his right was another tattoo that said Nam '71.

Andy slipped on her sunglasses and walked over to him, Coke in one hand, the hard-boiled egg in the other.

"King?"

"You're late."

"Hardly. I've been waiting inside."

He slammed his wrench against something in the Harley's engine, then rocked back on the heels of his boots and raised his head. A pair of Andys stared back at her from the lenses of his reflective shades. "Virginia's pulling an attitude."

Uh-huh. And it was time for her to boogie back inside. Picadillo was wrong about this one. "Yeah, well, while you finish up there, I'll be inside."

He laughed and dropped his elbows to his knees, hands dangling between his legs, a motorcycle cowboy. "Virginia's the bike."

"Oh." She supposed that made him less of a fruitcake, but she wouldn't bet the farm on it. "So what do you have to tell me, Mr. King?"

He twirled the wrench between his fingers like a baton. "Word on the streets says Catherine McCleary was a witch."

"A witch," she repeated, mentally estimating the distance to the rear door.

"A white witch."

"She was white, all right."

He laughed again. "A good lady, okay? She was a good lady who maybe"—he rocked his hand from side to side—"even had a little power."

"What kind of power?"

"We're talking about magic, okay? I'm saying that maybe she knew how to do a little magic. That kind of power."

"Look, Mr. King—"

"King, no mister."

"Right. King. Could you be more specific?"

The wrench slipped from his fingers and clattered against the asphalt. He removed his shades and cleaned them with a soiled kerchief that he pulled from a back pocket. His eyes were much too small for his face, a pair of dark little raisins that seemed to float in his cheeks as if unanchored to muscles and tendons.

"She went to a tea-leaf reader named Ramona about a problem in money and love, okay? But Ramona's not too excited about talking with the cops. I think she'll talk to you."

71

"And how did you happen to hear about Ramona's acquaintance with Catherine McCleary?"

"She reads tea leaves for a friend of a friend."

"How much is this going to cost me?"

"Fifty."

This smelled bad, but she played it out, anyway. "And what assurance do I have that Ramona is on the level?"

"Hey, lady, I'm just passing on a lead, okay?"

Okay, okay, okay. One more okay and she'd scream. "Make it thirty and we have a deal."

A corner of his mouth twitched into a smile. "Thirty it is."

They headed out of the city, King's motorcycle a dark bullet racing into the sun. Just her luck to get a goddamn showoff. She patted the BMW's steering wheel. "Okay, babe, let's show him what you're made of."

The Beamer was fifty grand worth of car, a 320 SLI with an engine that had been modified by a mechanic in Key West who had once built race cars for a living. It accelerated to fifty in under eight seconds, topped out at a speed of one fifty, and could turn on a dime. She tailed King until they hit the interstate, then he opened Virginia as wide as she could go. Andy grinned, the autobahn in her blood, and swerved into the left lane. They raced, neck to neck, her speedometer climbing to one ten, the landscape blurring past. He hopscotched lanes; so did she. When he exited the interstate eight miles north of the city, he slowed to just under a hundred; so did she. He sailed through a yellow light at the first intersection; so did she.

This wasn't about speed at all, she thought. It was about nerves and breaking rules, about testing her parameters against his, as though she had to prove she wasn't just a woman in an expensive car. A man with an evolved attitude about women. Terrific.

Andy followed him into a neighborhood that tottered at the brink of negligence, where the small homes were outnumbered by trees. The oaks were huge and thriving, but everything else appeared to be dying of thirst. He pulled up in front of a little bungalow and hopped off the bike, helmet nestled in the crook of his arm.

"You don't drive like a woman."

"Now that's what I call a nonsexist remark."

He laughed. "You drive like an Andy, not an Andrea."

"Yeah, well, you drive like a maniac."

"No tickets, though."

They started up the walk. It was cracked, crumbling at the sides like an old cookie. Leaves crunched underfoot. Birds sang from the dense shade. Shadows flitted across the dirty front windows of the house.

"For fifty dollars, I think Ramona would talk more."

Yeah, and for twice that she'd probably run at the mouth. "Thirty for her to convince me she's on the level. If she can do that, then we'll negotiate."

"However it's good for you, okay? I'm just the tour guide."

"What do you get out of this?"

"I'm paying off a debt."

"For what?"

"You ask a lot of questions."

"Yeah, I do."

He punched the doorbell. "Ten years ago I got busted with fifty pounds of coke in a marina in Coconut Grove. Picadillo was dating my sister then. He talked to some friends, who talked to some other friends, and pretty soon my felony was a misdemeanor. I did five months and six days in the county jail, paid a fine, and I was out. No parole, no more dealing."

"The good citizen."

"Something like that." He grinned and rang the bell again. "King is now legit."

"What do you do?"

"I build Harley clones. The clones are better than the Harleys."

She glanced back at his bike, a dark loner at the curb. "That a clone?"

"Yeah."

An Oriental woman with graying hair answered the door. She and King spoke briefly in an Oriental language, then she pointed them down a hall, smiled at Andy, and left.

"Vietnamese?" Andy asked.

"Yeah. I did two stints in Nam. That was Ramona's mother. They own a Vietnamese restaurant here in town."

The faint odor of cat urine permeated the air; eight felines were on the patio where Ramona was sitting. Her black hair was swept up off her neck, fixed in a complicated knot at the back of her head. She possessed a strangely serene presence that Andy associated with Oriental women. But she was dressed like an American: Cavaricci jeans, a Liz Claiborne cotton shirt. Her nails were long, carefully tended, bright red except at the cuticles, where the half-moons were white and glistened with sparkles. Her makeup was minimal; she wore no jewelry. She might have been thirty or fifty. It was impossible to tell.

King spoke to her in Vietnamese; she replied. It sounded to Andy as though they were arguing. They both kept looking at her, then King introduced them and Ramona gestured for her to sit down.

"Tea? You like?" she asked in accented English.

"Yes, thanks."

"King, you get?"

"Sure." He left.

"My English not so good."

"King said you knew Catherine McCleary."

Ramona nodded. "She come alone. I read for her. I see she love a man. The man not so good for her. He taken."

"Taken?"

"A wife."

"Do you know his name?"

"No name. I see someone owe her money. Much money. I see friend who not a friend. Betrayal. I see violence."

"Did she tell you anything about this man?"

"No. I feel pain in man's leg, pain in man's heart. Pain and violence."

King returned with their tea and joined them at the table. "I'm a little unclear on who owed Catherine money," Andy said.

Ramona spoke to King in Vietnamese and he translated. "She says that Catherine had lent someone money and wanted to know if she would be repaid. Ramona didn't think she would be. She loved this man, but Ramona told her he would betray her."

Ramona pushed an appointment book toward King, said something, then he opened it and turned it so Andy could see the entries. "July second of last year was the first time Catherine came here, but there were a lot of visits after that. At least once a week until shortly before she was killed."

"She had her tea leaves read once a week?"

"No, no, no." Ramona waved her hand impatiently. "She my student."

"I don't understand."

Ramona sat forward, stirring her tea, the spoon clinking against the sides of the delicate cup as she spoke in her native language again. King nodded when she finished, then said: "Catherine was psychic, okay? She just didn't know how to, you know, focus it. That's what Ramona was teaching her."

"Psychic how?"

He repeated her question to Ramona. She sighed, rattled off something. King rubbed his jaw. "She, uh, says everyone is psychic, okay? But some people close it off. Catherine didn't. Toward the end she was doing readings for some of Ramona's clients. She joked about it, called Catherine the White Witch."

A chapter entitled "White Witch." Nice. "Was she involved in this stuff with anyone else?"

Ramona nodded. "Masks on side wrong." She realized Andy didn't understand and spoke to King, who nodded.

"Something called Masquerade," he said. "The only thing Ramona knows about it is that Catherine felt they were on the wrong side."

"The wrong side of what?"

"That they practiced the black arts. There isn't much more she can tell you."

There was something definite about the way King said this, so Andy didn't push for more information. She thanked Ramona and handed her two twenties and a ten. Ramona looked at the money and shook her head. "No reading, no money. I read leaves for you, yes?" She pushed her cup across the table. Andy glanced down at the leaves that had settled into patterns against the sides and the bottom.

"No, thanks. I'd just stay awake worrying about it. You keep the money. You've been very helpful."

King walked outside with her. "What will you tell Picadillo?" he asked.

"That the debt should be canceled."

He smiled and twisted one of the gold posts in his ear. "Be careful, Andy."

"You're the maniac."

He grinned. "If you ever want a bike, you call me and I'll give you a good price."

"Righto," she said with a laugh, and headed to her car.

(2)

Andy drove over to the police station. She figured it would probably be futile to try to convince Bristol that they should cooperate with each other. But before she wrote him off completely, she wanted to give it one more chance.

The woman at the front desk said Detective Bristol wasn't in, but his partner, Detective Wilkin, was in the staff room and could probably help her. Andy thanked her and hurried away before the woman realized she hadn't requested her name.

The only person in the room was a woman sitting at a long table, sipping coffee and paging through the newspaper. She didn't look like a cop. She was too well dressed, too precisely put together, and well, yes, too pretty, Andy thought, disgusted by her own preconceived notions.

"Hi," the woman said, glancing up with a smile. "Help you with something?"

"Is Detective Wilkin around?"

Bemused: "You're looking at her."

"I'm—"

"I know who you are, Ms. Tull."

Despite her smile, her voice held a hard, discomfiting edge. *The lady eats nails for breakfast.* "Mind if I sit down?"

"Not at all. As long as you don't want to discuss the homicides."

"The Homicides," as in a chapter heading. "So the policy has become official?"

Wilkin's laugh was quick, light, a fluted sound. It seemed to make the freckles across her cheeks quiver and dance in the fluorescent lights. "Where you're concerned, it's an unofficial policy. With the rest of the press, it's official. Personally, I don't see any harm in cooperating with you to a certain extent. But I'm not in charge."

"Then I'd appreciate it if you'd give Bristol a message for me."

"Sure."

"Tell him I think we'd find answers a lot quicker if we combined what we know. If he changes his mind, he's got my number."

"He won't change his mind. But I'll tell him."

Such certainty. "Thanks." Andy gestured toward the newspaper. "Did you people release disinformation on the murders?"

Wilkin rolled her painted nails against the table, a little drumbeat. "We withheld information."

"Same difference."

"Not at all."

"Semantics."

She held up her pretty hands. "Never argue with a writer."

"Does that mean I won?"

"You won." She drew a vertical line in the air. "One point for Ms. Tull, zero for the opposing team."

"You ought to be in charge."

"I'll pass that along to Detective Bristol, too."

"Good. Thanks again."

Farrah's on the Avenue was the sort of place you expected to find in a college town, Quin thought. It had been here for as long as she remembered and its big draw was the front patio. Shaded by a trellis of ivy, it was private without being isolated. From where Quin was sitting, she could see the rush of cars and bikes on University Avenue.

Tess Schulman sat across from her, trying to tell her about finding Cat's body. When she choked up, she reached for a French fry, dipped it in the honey and mustard sauce, and licked it off without ever nibbling at the fry. She wasn't pretty, but she had the sort of classic bone structure that took well to makeup, stage lights, cameras. Her hair was dark and ruler-straight, with a dozen tiny braids that grew out of her crown and fell to her shoulders. Her bangs followed a perfect line just above her brows, then the hair tapered back to the silver and turquoise earrings she wore. She also wore five silver bracelets on her right arm and a turquoise ring on her index finger. The silver enhanced the gray of her eyes so that when the light struck them right, they were the color of mercury.

The jewelry, excessive on another woman, was Tess's trademark, another eccentricity like the weird braids, the heavy makeup, the tight jeans, the glitter in her painted nails. She was theatre, after all, where eccentricities were expected, and she played it to the hilt. ". . . that Detective Bristol was pretty damn offensive," she was saying. "Here I'd found Cat, and he was interrogating me and asking me where I was the night before. I mean, c'mon, pal, she was my closest friend. You met him?"

"Not yet." Quin glanced at Ellie as she began to stir in her stroller. She pushed it gently, hoping she'd sleep a while longer. "He's been cooperative with Mac."

"Hey, why shouldn't he be? The quicker he cracks this, the better he looks."

"Was Cat dating anyone?"

"She said no, but I think she was. She liked her life real private, Quin, even with me." She sniffled, pulled a piece of Kleenex from her purse, blew her nose. "Damn sauce is making my sinuses act up." She wadded the tissue, stuck it inside her purse. "We didn't see each other much outside of work. I guess for the last eight or nine months we sort of grew apart. We sent messages back and forth on Kazaam, though. That's what tipped me off that something had happened."

"Yeah, I saw the notes. You think it was someone in the repertory company?"

"I doubt it. She didn't mix business with pleasure. She was going to this psychic a lot, though. That's how she got whenever things in her personal life weren't going well."

"You know the psychic's name?"

She frowned, shook her head, then went through her purse. "I think I've got her card in here somewhere. Cat said the woman was really good, but frankly I was never too interested in knowing what the future was going to be. I've got enough problems with the present." She slipped out a tattered business card. "Ramona. Yeah, this is it. Ramona, tea-leaf reader. You can keep this."

Quin put it into her purse. "What about Melody? How'd she and Cat get along?"

"She got along with everyone, Quin. You know how she was. But there was some bad blood between them because Melody thinks she's a director and isn't. She should've stayed in New York as a talent agent. Melody kept bugging Cat about representing her, too. She's kept a few clients."

She sniffled again and pushed the basket of fries toward Quin. "Eat some of these. I already need to lose five pounds."

"Five pounds and you'll be invisible, Tess."

She laughed, but the remark obviously pleased her. Quin picked at the fries as they talked about the play the company was doing, a comedy neither Tess nor Cat had liked but which Melody had insisted on. The shadows on the patio shortened to noon. Ellie finally woke up and began to cry. Quin fixed her a bottle of juice, but she held up her arms, wanting out. When Quin didn't comply immediately, she cried loudly enough to draw looks from the other customers.

"Jerk my strings and I'll dance," Quin mumbled, lifting her from the stroller.

"I was really surprised when I heard you were pregnant, Quin."

"Not half as surprised as I was."

"Has it been a big adjustment?"

It's been a breeze, Tess, can't you tell? "Somewhat." Quin started to elaborate, wanting to balance the remark with the hundreds of small wonders that Ellie had brought into their lives, but Tess wasn't interested. She sniffled again and fluttered off to get some Kleenex from the restroom.

She headed into the restaurant and Ellie, standing unsteadily at the stroller, pointed after her. "Mama?"

"No, I'm your mother." Quin held out a fork with a bite of scrambled egg on the end. "Here, cutie, it's cold, but I ordered it for you."

Ellie took it from the end of the fork, popped it into her mouth, moved with uncertain steps toward the other side of the table. Before Quin realized what she was doing, she dug her hands inside Tess's unzipped purse, which was hanging over the back of her chair, and proceeded to pull things out. Quin rescued the purse and reprimanded her. Ellie started to cry and now customers were glancing over, clearly irritated with the ruckus.

At this rate, Quin thought, she wasn't going to make it sane to Ellie's first birthday.

She quickly handed her daughter a spoon, which quieted her down, and stooped to gather up the things from Tess's purse. As she stuffed them back inside, she noticed a glass vial sticking out of an inside compartment. She slipped it out, uncapped it, sniffed it.

No wonder Tess had sinus problems.

"Hey, Ellie, good going. You can ravage as many purses as you want, kiddo."

Ellie giggled and clapped her hands.

When Tess returned, she seemed antsy, so Quin picked up the bill and said she had to get going and why didn't Tess come out to the house for dinner some night soon?

It sounded good to Tess, who said she'd call, which Quin doubted. She thanked Quin for lunch and looked embarrassed when she admitted that her budget had been severely strained lately.

"Daddy's been ill and I've been trying to help out with some of the bills."

Uh-huh, Quin thought, and wondered how expensive her coke habit was.

8

(1)

I'M THE MAN THEY'RE LOOKING FOR.

The thought struck him as he was hurrying across campus, struck him suddenly, and Rick stopped right where he was and slowly looked around. Throngs of students flew past him on bikes. Lovers and loners occupied the low brick walls in the warm sunlight. Several women stood near a vendor's cart paging through the campus newspapers. Two cops strolled by on the sidewalk. And here he was, standing in their midst beneath a startling blue sky, a man in khaki pants and a cotton print shirt who could still smell death on his hands. The death of a woman in Ocala whom nobody would miss. A death he had engineered alone. It thrilled him.

Rick started to walk again, past the low brick walls and the information booth and the bookstore, past landmarks that were as personal to him as the texture of his own skin. Details leaped out at him—how green the air smelled, how blue the sky tasted, his senses all mixed up and yet never more lucid.

The tendons in his legs stretched like rubber bands as he moved. His arms swung freely at his sides. His eyes connected with those of people he passed. *Hello, my name is Rick. I killed a woman last night in Ocala. Killed her alone, without my teacher.* He was the real McCoy in a row of imposters on *What's My Line?* He carried strands of his victims' hair in his pocket. Murder had made him privy to certain secrets in the hidden universe tucked away in every man, every woman, every child. He knew that if he squinted his eyes and peered at someone, at anyone, he would see them like X-rays. Hearts

82

beating, blood rushing, lungs pumping, souls churning toward whatever destinies awaited them.

Yes, that clearly.

Rick thought of weapons, both sacred and profane, knives and guns and daggers, nails and scissors, things made of the brightest, hardest metal. And he thought of women enfolded in their myriad mysteries, their private worlds, the worlds that he would sunder. Last night was a beginning. But of what? A new adventure? Some psychic journey through an unimagined darkness? He didn't know. For the moment, it was enough that last night had happened, that he had triumphed.

He walked on, smiling to himself, wondering if he no longer needed his teacher.

(2)

McCleary had spent the morning at the county courthouse. He'd talked with the coroner who'd done the autopsy on Davenport and his sister, had gotten copies of the photos taken in Cat's den as well as the rest of the crime-scene photos, had talked to the rookie who'd answered Tess's call the day she'd found Cat. He'd sifted through statements from Davenport's friends and fellow faculty, had used Bristol's computer to run an MO check through the FBI, and had attended to dozens of other details that brought back his decade in Homicide at Metro-Dade. By one, his head was pounding.

He gathered up his things, stacked them in the empty briefcase he'd brought with him this morning, and walked down the block to the police station. Bristol wasn't in his office, but Wilkin was, their individual spaces equally tidy, their desks equally neat, two peas in a little pod. She wore a short-sleeved shirtwaist with tiny red flowers against a navy-blue background. A wide leather belt accentuated her tiny waist. Her shoes, the same blue and red as her dress, were sensible enough to run in if she had to. Her hair was pulled into a loose ponytail with a red and blue scarf.

She smiled when she saw him, pointed at the phone, and rolled her pretty hazel eyes. "Yes, I understand, Mrs.

Samonsky. Thanks again.'' She hung up with a shake of her head. ''Our payroll supervisor just informed me I should be buying Disney stock with my savings deductions, that it'd be a better investment than the department credit union.''

''She's probably right. Steve around?''

She nodded, sat in her chair, unwrapped the cellophane from a sandwich. ''Yeah, I was going to call you. He just got back from talking to one of Davenport's neighbors and thinks there's a lead that should be checked out. He wants to know if you'd like to go with him.''

''Sure.''

''He's in the lunchroom.''

''You coming?''

''The captain's on the warpath.'' She pulled several files from a drawer. ''I need to clean up some paperwork.''

''Good luck.''

Her smile seemed both mocking and enigmatic. ''You really think luck has anything to do with any of it?''

''Probably not.''

''My sentiments exactly. Oh, I met Andrea Tull this morning. She stopped by looking for information.''

McCleary started to tell her about the .38 Tull had left behind but decided to keep it to himself for now. ''She as much of a pain as Steve says?''

''She's persistent, I'll give her that much. But basically I think she's pretty harmless. Steve had a fit when I told him.''

''Yeah, I bet.''

''Well, see you later.''

Her nose was already buried in files when he left.

Bristol was alone in the lunchroom, wolfing down an apple and studying a city map. ''What's the lead?'' McCleary asked.

''Davenport's neighbor on the right is a nosy old lady who's got insomnia. According to her, the professor had a lover for six or seven months before she died. She claims she's a bit paranoid about strangers in the neighborhood, so the first time she saw his car in the driveway she took down his license plate number. I ran a make on it. The guy's name is Jim Kliner.'' Bristol folded the map and looked up, smiling. "And he may be our first link between Davenport and your sister. He owns Phaedra Books out on West University.''

The message in Cat's E-mail, McCleary thought. "That was from someone named Emilio.''

"Fine. Then we have two boys to talk to. I called the store to make sure Kliner's there. How about if we talk to him, then I'll take you by Davenport's for a look around.''

"I'll drive.''

The air was still and lazily warm outside. There was no trace of yesterday's rain; the ground, denied too long, had sucked up every puddle. Bristol, like McCleary, didn't mind the heat, so they drove with the windows down. Bristol commented that it was a real treat to drive like this; his wife always insisted on air-conditioning when they were in the car together. McCleary laughed. His wife, he said, lived in AC for nine months out of the year. She claimed Florida was uninhabitable without it.

"It was worse when my wife was pregnant with our son,'' Bristol said. "Our electric bill went out of sight.''

"Ours was as high as our grocery bill.''

"Weird times, when they're pregnant, hormones going berserk, mood shifts like day and night.''

McCleary agreed. "How old's your son?''

"Almost nine.''

"So they really do grow up and sleep through the night like normal people?''

Bristol laughed. "Yeah, they do. I know it doesn't seem possible now, but take my word for it, they're big before you know it.'' He rubbed at his knee and shifted in his seat, trying to straighten his leg out all the way.

"Your seat isn't back all the way,'' McCleary said.

Bristol fiddled with the knob and suddenly had nearly another foot of room. "Great. That's better. Goddamn leg freezes up on me sometimes.''

"What happened?''

"A pair of slugs from a thirty-eight, one just above the ankle, the other just above the knee. I was flying for cover during a stakeout that went bad and forgot to pull my legs in. Two bones were shattered and were replaced with steel rods. I had about four months of physical therapy, was out of work for twice that."

He didn't say anything more and McCleary didn't pursue it. He steered the conversation to his morning search. "The coroner says both women were probably alive when their hands were amputated and that the tissues just above Davenport's wrists showed a trace of novocaine."

"She was found much earlier than your sister. Within a couple of hours of the murder. As far as I'm concerned, the novocaine and bleach points to someone with some medical or forensics knowledge."

"What about connections between Lucy and Catherine? Has anything besides the bookstore turned up?"

Bristol shook his head. "Lucy had a certain fondness for erotic art; your sister had an interest in the occult; Davenport was faculty, your sister was an actress. They didn't frequent the same restaurants, they had different social circles. . . ." He shrugged. "The bookstore seems to be it. For now."

"Optimist."

"There's got to be something more, Mike. Every student and faculty member in Gainesville has probably been into Phaedra's. Unless the shrink's right and we've got a serial sicko instead of a spree sicko."

Bristol seemed to need labels and felt comfortable with them. Labels were convenient, they defined parameters, and often made homicide investigations easier, McCleary thought, but they weren't always accurate. They didn't always apply. Nothing in this business was *always* or *never*.

"She have any family besides her ex?"

"A brother in Seattle who'll be here when the will's settled and a ninety-two-year-old grandmother in a nursing home who doesn't even know if the sun is shining. Angie and I talked to her, explained that Lucy had been killed, but nothing registered. It was like talking to an object."

"Can you arrange for Quin or me to see her?"

"Sure, but I doubt it'll do any good." He pointed

ahead. "The bookstore's just past this intersection on your right."

The lot was crowded. "Brisk business for the middle of the week," McCleary remarked as they got out.

"Yeah, the place is a gold mine. They have a coffee bar, poetry readings, discussion groups—all those things you associate with college. I've only been in here a couple of times. Their stock is too narrow for my plebeian tastes."

The building was white and squat, like an adobe hut. The narrow walk at the back angled through pines and clusters of bright pink flowers to a deck. Live oaks shaded tables and benches along the railing and most of them were occupied by students sipping coffee and reading.

Inside, it was crowded with browsers. Bristol went in search of Jim Kliner and Emilio and McCleary wandered around. The store was larger than it had looked from the road, yet maintained the feel of a secret place. The walls were decorated with book covers that had been blown up to eleven-by-fourteen posters, wooden plaques with quotes from famous philosophers, and an assortment of original art, some of it quite good, some of it awful. The giant bulletin board held announcements for the store's events as well as business cards that advertised everything from past-life regressions to health foods.

He went into a room at the back of the store that was furnished like a private library at the turn of the century. On an end table was a crystal bowl filled with individually wrapped dry fruit. On another end table was a vase with a bouquet of baby's breath in it. A beige Persian cat snoozed in one of the easy chairs. Everything about the room invited you to kick off your shoes, browse through the books on the shelves, and curl up with a book for as long as you wanted.

McCleary paused in front of a beautifully rendered oil painting that depicted a man standing under a vast blue sky and knocking at a door marked ASYLUM. Behind him rose a cloud of dust with a dark shape inside it that could have been anything—a car, a dervish, Satan on horseback.

"May I help you with something?"

The lanky man who'd come up behind him on feet

made of silk had curly brown hair, chocolate eyes, and a bushy mustache that he twisted at one end. He blinked a lot, as though he'd recently gotten contact lenses, and wore several gold chains that had tangled at his throat. The name tag on his pocket identified him as Emilio Turbeta, Manager.

"Yes, I think you can. I'm Mike McCleary."

The shock on Turbeta's face was brief but blatant. He took McCleary's outstretched hand in both of his, squeezing hard. "I can't tell you how sorry I am." The sincerity in his voice was edged with a trace of an accent. "Catherine was very special to me. Very special. So talented." His hands moved through the air now, punctuating his words. "This is such a tragedy, *señor*. I still expect her to walk in for a *cafecito*, you know? These habits . . ." He shook his head. "They linger. They haunt. They . . . ay, *dios mío*, I talk too much." He rubbed a hand over his face and his arm dropped to his side, motionless, as though he'd momentarily run out of steam. Then his hands began to move again. "Did you know we work closely with the theatre?"

McCleary shook his head, but Turbeta didn't even notice. He was a machine jammed on automatic. "We sell tickets for performances, do advertising, find things they need . . . and sometimes in the morning Catherine would stop by to pick up something and we would have coffee out on the porch and talk about theatre. Such fine times, good memories. She could talk about anything." He tapped his temple. "Very bright lady, very bright . . ."

"I'm sure he already knows how bright she was, Emilio. He was her brother."

The man in the doorway looked like an ex-hippie who would be stopped and searched in customs just on principle. He stood at least six foot four and was as skinny as a broomstick. He dwarfed Bristol, who stood next to him. His long hair was the color of honey and pulled into a loose ponytail that trailed over one shoulder. His jeans were faded, worn at the knees. "Nice to meet you, Mr. McCleary. I'm Jim Kliner." His pale eyes flicked back to Turbeta. "Em, why don't you get the gentleman some espresso?"

"Yes. Good idea. Excellent idea. Our coffee is the best." His relief trailed after him like an odor as he hurried from the room. Kliner, as slow-moving as Turbeta was quick, strode over to the chair where the Persian had lifted its head. He picked the cat up, sat down, and arranged the animal on his lap like a blanket, his long fingers sliding through its fur.

"I didn't know Catherine that well. Emilio is our theatre liaison. But I do know you aren't going to find anyone who has a bad thing to say about her." His pale eyes slipped to Bristol. There was a mesmerizing quality to the fixed intensity of his gaze, to the slow, languid way he stroked the cat, even to his voice.

"Actually, we're here about Lucy," Bristol said. "Her neighbor took down your license plate number during one of your visits, Mr. Kliner."

He didn't seem surprised. His fingers combed the Persian's fur; its purrs filled the room. "There isn't much to tell about my relationship with Lucy. The English department put on a book fair last year and we had a booth. That's how we met. She hadn't been divorced very long and she was lonely. We shared a love of books. I filled a gap for a while. End of story."

"No story's that short," McCleary said.

The remark clearly irritated Kliner. "This one was, Mr. McCleary."

"How long did you see each other?" Bristol asked.

"It wasn't like that, Detective. We slept together from time to time, sometimes at her place, sometimes at mine, but I never met any of her friends and she never met mine." His smile was small and sad. "I obviously don't fit the academic mold and that was a problem for her. Basically, she was looking for a guy who wears tweed jackets and smokes a pipe and teaches something obscure like medieval lit. I was a novelty for her, that's all.

"For about five months, we got together a couple times a week, spent part of every weekend together. Then it was just once a week. Then once every few weeks and finally the whole thing just died of inertia." He shrugged. "The last time I saw her was in early August sometime."

"Where were you on October twenty-fourth, Mr. Kliner, between midnight and five?" Bristol asked.

"Probably asleep. That's what I usually do between midnight and five."

Asshole, McCleary thought. "Alone?"

A flash of annoyance brought color to Kliner's cheeks. "Yeah, alone, Mr. McCleary, and no, there's no one who can verify it, so I guess that leaves me without an alibi, doesn't it."

McCleary felt his blood pressure rising. There was nothing worse than an asshole who thought he was bright and clever. "Good goddamn deduction, Kliner."

Bristol threw McCleary a warning look, but it was too late. Kliner was already pushing to his feet. "Look, I'm sorry about your sister, man. And I'm even sorrier about Lucy, but that doesn't give you the right to barge the fuck in here and—"

"Calm down, Mr. Kliner," said Bristol, patting the air with his hands. "We're just asking questions."

Kliner didn't sit down, but he didn't leave, either. Turbeta strolled in with four cups of espresso, apparently intending to join them. But he evidently sensed the tension in the room and beat a hasty retreat, shutting the door behind him as he left.

"What do you know about her interest in erotic art?" Bristol asked.

Kliner's smile this time was almost furtive, as though he were remembering something he had no intention of sharing with them. "It extended beyond art, Detective." He sipped from his cup.

"In what way?" Bristol prodded.

"Erotic literature, movies, everything. She was a very sensual woman."

"Kinky or sensual?" McCleary asked.

Anger tightened Kliner's mouth. "Sensual."

"What about paraphernalia? Videocameras? Drugs?"

"I don't like your—"

"I don't give a shit what you like or don't like," McCleary snapped, wanting to push him to the edge to see what he would do, how he would react. "Just answer the goddamn question."

90

"I don't have to answer you." He looked at Bristol. "Or you, unless you've got a warrant. So if you'll excuse me, guys, I've got other things to do." He crossed the room in three long strides and was gone.

"Touchy bastard," McCleary said with a low laugh, gazing through the empty doorway.

"You shouldn't have pushed him, Mike." Then Bristol grinned and raised his cup of espresso. "But if you hadn't, I would have. *Salud, amigo.*" And he knocked it back in a single gulp like a shot of whiskey.

(3)

"Hey, Cubanito, what gives?"

"Andy, *mí amor!*"

Emilio Turbeta hugged her hello as though they hadn't seen each other in months when, in fact, they'd had lunch only last week. He pulled a chair up to his table on the deck behind the bookstore, where light and shade seemed to float in equal quantities, painting the air the color of tea.

It was nearly three, the store's lull until around eight that evening, and the quiet was punctuated by the trill of a blackbird hopping along the railing. A warm breeze blew a few leaves from the branches overhead and they drifted through the light, tiny magic carpets. At the next table a woman was trying to calm down a fussy baby.

Andy had met Turbeta a year ago last summer when she'd given a three-day workshop on campus that he'd attended. He had no interest in writing; he'd signed up for the workshop only to meet her and get her autograph. Or so he'd said. They had lunch or dinner together occasionally, sharing their passion for Hispanic food and music and dancing, but he would never be anything more than a friend. He wasn't her type. She wasn't his type. There was a certain liberation in that.

When they were settled in with fresh espressos and a platter of piping-hot *arepitas*, she got right down to business. "You know of any groups on campus who're into the occult in a big way?"

He laughed. "Ask me something easy. There're forty thousand students on this campus."

"I guess that's what I get for going to a liberal arts college with eight hundred women in it."

"Everyone here belongs to something—ecology groups, language clubs, speech clubs, fraternities, sororities . . ."

"Cubanito, I'm talking about the occult, not about ecology, and I'm talking about the bad shit—"

He waved a hand impatiently. "The bulletin board inside is filled with occult stuff. Groups, healers, you name it. How should I know which ones are into bad shit, Andy?" His irritation seemed extreme, but he had a point. Ramona hadn't said anything about an *organized* occult group. For all she knew, Catherine and a few acquaintances had gotten together in someone's living room once a month and played with a Ouija board.

"Yeah, you're right. Never mind." She smiled. "Stupid question."

"Does this have something to do with the book?" His voice was hushed, like the book was some big secret.

"Probably not."

"But you think it might?" The fan digging for answers on how the writer worked: It made her uncomfortable when he did this.

"Yeah, with Catherine McCleary." She told him about Ramona without providing too many details. Emotions flickered across the surface of his face that she couldn't decipher. But she knew that he knew she saw them because he suddenly looked away, down at his cup. She felt a weird little stitch in her side, a stab of disappointment that he knew something and was hiding it from her.

"What is it, Cubanito? What's wrong?"

"I don't think you should get anywhere near this book, that's what's wrong, Andy. It's too dangerous. I don't like how it makes me feel inside."

His concern was flattering, but that wasn't what she'd seen on his face. "Don't worry about it." She gave his hand an affectionate pat, older sister reassuring little brother, and changed the subject.

But for a long time afterward, his face kept scrolling

in the upper corner of her right eye, Cubanito surprised, then scared, Cubanito with something to hide.

(4)

There were certain points in most investigations when you were in the right place at the right time, Quin thought, and this was one of them.

She'd stopped by Phaedra Books to poke around and had bought several books, including *Home Before Dark*, which she'd never read. Now here she was on the rear deck, staring at the photograph of Andrea Tull on the back of the book, certain that she was the woman seated at the next table. She was older, plumper, but it was Tull, all right.

Quin had overheard some of her conversation with the Cuban and was tempted to stroll over and tell her she could pick up her .38 any old time. And oh, by the way, just what the hell was she doing at the farm last night? But she didn't want to blow her anonymity just yet, so she waited until the Cuban had left, then pushed the stroller over and said, "Excuse me."

Andrea glanced up, her eyes a soft, winter blue, and smiled with the polite distraction of someone who has perfected a public persona. "Yes?"

"Could I bother you for an autograph?"

"Sure." She took the book, brought out a pen. "What's your name?"

"Quin."

"With a *Q*?"

"And one *n*. This is the only book of yours I've missed. I got the last copy and told them to reorder. I thoroughly enjoyed the others."

"Thanks."

"The *Herald* really covered this case. I can still remember reading about it."

"You live in Miami?"

"Used to. West Palm now. We moved before our daughter was born. Miami was getting to be like the Wild West."

"Isn't that the truth," Andy said with a laugh, and

93

scribbled something in the front of the book. "There you go."

"Thanks. Thanks very much." Quin slipped it in her purse. "You working on something new?"

"Trying to."

Ellie started to clap then for no apparent reason, and Andy laughed. "Yeah, no kidding." She brought her palms together softly, mimicking Ellie's clapping. "Yay, Andrea, right?"

Ellie giggled and covered her face with her hands, then peered out between her fingers, playing peek a boo. Andy mimicked her again, then opened her hands and whispered, "Boo."

Ellie burst out laughing. "You've made a friend for life," Quin said. "Thanks again."

"Hope you enjoy the book."

"I'm sure I will." You've got no idea how much, she thought, and smiled as she turned away.

9

(1)

RICHARD FARMER, PH.D., expert in criminal behavior, consultant to the sheriff's department, was the sort of man who made Quin uncomfortable. He exuded a kind of animal sexuality that made her acutely aware of her every movement, her every gesture, of the fall of her hair, the wrinkles in her clothes. And more, he was conscious of it, conscious of the effect he undoubtedly had on most women. She would bet this guy had every freshman woman in his classes swooning over Jung and Freud and vowing to major in psychology.

She had arrived at the psychology department ten minutes ago. McCleary, who was supposed to meet her here, was late, naturally, and Ellie was wired. Farmer's secretary was watching her at the moment, and Quin could hear her daughter's delighted gurgles through the closed door. She wondered why Ellie always seemed to laugh more when she was with other people. It bothered her nearly as much as Farmer's open scrutiny. She didn't have the faintest notion what he was talking about; it was the richness of his voice that captivated her, not the words. She could see this guy on TV, smiling as he asked you to send your Social Security check and your pension in care of his ministry, and you'd do it just because he'd asked. She could see him in Guyana, telling you to drink your Kool-Aid, and you'd do that, too, because you wanted him desperately to like you.

Quin watched his mouth, forcing herself to hear what he was saying. ". . . I made a copy of the profile for you and your husband, Mrs. McCleary. It's nothing that's set in stone by any means. These things never are. Profiling is a rather inexact science and I think it's primarily useful when combined with other similar tools.''

He passed her a folder. She opened it and was glancing through it when she heard McCleary in the front office. She was relieved that she wouldn't have to sit in here alone any longer with Farmer. She introduced them, McCleary pulled up a chair, and a few moments later Farmer continued as if there had been no interruption.

''The problem with solving any sort of serial killing is that these people seem to be racking up larger and larger body counts. Look at Jeffrey Dahmer or, at Randy Kraft, who zipped around L.A. freeways picking up young men. He may have killed as many as sixty-five people. When police are faced with that much carnage or, as with Dahmer such brutality, it becomes nearly impossible to put it all together.''

''Then you've definitely concluded he's a serial killer?'' McCleary asked.

Farmer sat back in his leather chair, hands locked behind his head. No half-moons of sweat under *his* arms, Quin thought. ''Like I said, nothing's absolute and regardless of what kind of label you want to give him, there are some inescapable facts. He thinks women are dirty, thus the cleanser, the bleach. He most likely has some medical knowledge, maybe something as basic as a first-aid or CPR course, or he's read a few medical textbooks. He's brighter than average, he plans carefully, he takes trophies.''

''But why hands?'' Quin asked.

''Perhaps a fetish of some sort.''

''Isn't it possible that the bleach is tied up with an aversion to germs and the hands represent a source of germs?''

''Anything's possible, but it's unlikely.'' He smiled at her like she was an amateur and it pissed her off.

''Why?''

''If a germ phobia's behind this, he would wash them down before he killed them.''

McCleary jumped on that one. ''How do we know he doesn't?''

''We don't *know* it.'' His hands dropped to the desk as he sat forward and reached for a pen. He tapped it

96

slowly and rhythmically against the edge of the desk, an irritating noise rather like a metronome. "But we can assume he doesn't. It would entail too much time, too much risk that something could go wrong. Think of the logistics, Mr. McCleary."

"There were rope burns on their wrists and arms. He took the time to tie them up, to inject them with novocaine so they wouldn't feel it too much when he chopped off their hands, and then he even hung around to arrange some clothing when he was finished. Don't talk to me about logistics, Dr. Farmer."

McCleary's agitation radiated from him in waves. She could feel them, almost taste them. It was one thing to discuss these things about people you'd never met; it was something else again when one of the victims was your sister. Farmer heard the dangerous edge in McCleary's voice and patted the air with his beautiful hands, as though McCleary was an irate patient he hoped to calm.

"I'm not the enemy, Mr. McCleary. I'm just giving you a picture of this guy."

It was uttered in that same dispassionate tone of voice. Draw up enough profiles on sick pups, she thought, and you became inured to the horror of the details. "Is he a necrophiliac, like Bundy?" she asked.

"Forensics didn't come up with anything to suggest it, and no, in my opinion, he isn't."

"But he could be a necrophiliac," McCleary prodded.

"Well, yes, of course. Like I keep saying, despite our need for hard-and-fast rules, there aren't any. There are only guidelines."

"Most of these kinds of killings have a sexual motivation," Quin said.

"That's a rather sweeping statement, Mrs. McCleary." He seemed to take umbrage at the mere suggestion.

"I don't think it's sweeping at all. Name one serial or spree killer who was a happily married man or who had a successful long-term relationship with a woman."

"Sex isn't even the issue here."

A slick evasion, she thought.

"Both of these murders " he went on, "are crimes of

97

violence and power and domination rather than sexually motivated acts.''

These days it was in vogue to say that a crime was just an act of violence and to ignore the possibility that the violence was based on sexual maladjustment. She started to say as much, but McCleary had already turned the conversation in another direction.

"What kind of profession would he be in?"

"Probably something in which methodical, fastidious thinking is required. Accounting, computers, mathematics, medicine.''

Oh, please, Quin thought. This was beginning to sound like the popular image of Ted Bundy, one-time law student, shrewd, clever enough to blend into a normal society. In reality, Bundy had been a failure at almost everything he'd done, except killing, and he had been the most cowardly kind of murderer, luring his victims by wearing a false cast on his arm. Once their backs were turned, he had struck them with a tire iron, driven them to a safe location, killed them, had sex with them. On occasion, the necrophilia had continued for a few days, with Bundy washing the women's hair and putting fresh makeup on their decaying faces.

Of course, the fact that she knew these things, that she sometimes lay awake at night thinking about them, probably indicated some aberration in her own personality, she thought. "I think he knew at least one of the victims.''

When Farmer shook his head, it seemed graceful, effortless. "Out of the question. Statistics say that more and more homicides are stranger homicides, the way they were in the late Seventies and early Eighties.''

"I'm not saying he knew one of them well, just that he had talked to her somewhere, maybe run into her at the grocery store, then he started watching her, learning her routine, and planned how he would kill her. When it got right down to the killing, he got off on it. The torture, her fear, her murder—it all aroused him. He's the worst kind of coward, just like Bundy was.''

Farmer's smile thinned like a piece of elastic when it's pulled too tightly. His dark eyes wouldn't let go of her.

They stared at her as if she were an apparition that had appeared suddenly in his midst and might, at any second, rattle her chains and emit some terrible noise.

"Bundy wasn't a coward, Mrs. McCleary. He was a sick man. A genius, but sick. Beyond help."

"Look, anyone who ties up someone else to torture and kill that person is a coward and I don't care what kind of psychobabble you want to attach to it."

She had offended some professional sensibility in him. It was apparent in his eyes, in the tight way he smiled, in the subtle shift of his attention to McCleary. She no longer existed for him, she thought. It was that simple. She listened to their conversation, two men analyzing a criminal mind, but in the abstract, as though it had nothing to do with either of them. She understood that it was easier, emotionally, for McCleary to discuss his sister's murder in the abstract, but what was Farmer's excuse? He obviously had strong convictions, but it was so *controlled*, as if he was afraid that his passion might show.

A knock at the door interrupted Farmer's discourse and his secretary poked her head into the room. "What is it, Opal?" he asked irritably.

"I was supposed to pick up my son at basketball practice twenty minutes ago, Dr. Farmer."

Ellie crawled past her saying, "Dadda, Dadda," her arms held out to McCleary.

He scooped her up and Farmer told his secretary to go on. McCleary said, "We've got to get going, too." He thanked Farmer for his time, stood, shook hands with him. Farmer said something to Ellie and she burrowed her face into McCleary's chest and started to cry.

She feels it, too.

Felt what? Just what the hell was she feeling besides pins and needles in her legs as she got to her feet and a light-headedness because she hadn't eaten anything since the hamburger this morning with Tess?

Uneasiness, discomfort, but something deeper than either of those things, especially when Farmer murmured it had been nice meeting her and the look in his eyes said otherwise. When he touched her shoulder on their way out the door, she flinched. She couldn't help it. It was as instinctive as scratching at a mosquito bite. The feeling drifted through her and away again, a seed that couldn't find proper soil to root in. Then the three of them were outside in the late afternoon light, a wash of soft, cool gold that transformed trees and buildings. McCleary took Quin's hand and Ellie laughed and waved at her, beads of the gold light rolling down her nose and spilling onto her mouth. Quin's eyes filled with tears and she didn't know why.

McCleary chuckled. "I don't think he liked you, Quin."

"The feeling's mutual."

"Why did you say the killer knew only one of the women?"

"I don't know. Just a hunch, I guess." They had reached the curb and stopped. A flurry of bikes passed on the other side of the street. The gold had leaked out of the air. She didn't want to talk about Farmer anymore. "You going to follow me over to Tot Stop? I've got to drop off these HRS forms."

"Sure. Where're you parked?"

"Over there somewhere." She gestured vaguely to the left.

"I'll walk you to the car."

"Like a date?"

"Like a date." He took her elbow as they crossed the street, his thumb making lazy circles on the inside of her arm.

(2)

The director of Tot Stop was a pleasant, sanguine woman named Helen Charles, one of those rare creatures who loved what she did. McCleary liked her instantly and realized that whatever misgivings he'd had about day care had vanished.

She clucked over Ellie's big blue eyes and talked to her as though she understood every word she said. Then she gave the three of them the grand tour, chattering incessantly as she ushered them into and out of rooms that were built and furnished with kids in mind.

The school was shaped like a T, with separate, sunny rooms for the ones, the twos, the threes, and the fours, and a central room with a TV, VCR, and several computers. Windows were wide and low, so kids could look out, the walls were decorated with colorful cutouts of *Sesame Street* characters, and the shelves were filled with an array of toys. The toddler playground was a Lilliputian world of tunnels and slides, swings and jungle gyms and sandboxes.

"They spend about an hour out here every morning," Helen explained. "Before lunch they always have some sort of project—art, music, story hour. Like I told you over the phone, Mrs. McCleary, we serve hot lunches prepared by a nutritionist, and you'd be amazed how well most of the kids eat. Around noon they go down for a two-hour nap."

A nap on demand? Not *his* daughter. Not in a room filled with kids. "They really sleep?" he asked.

"Oh, sure. We dim the lights, put on music, and most of them take a bottle. They grow accustomed to the routine. When they get up, they have juice and a snack, go out onto the playground again, then there's another project after that. We're open from six-thirty in the morning to six-thirty at night, six days a week. What hours are you all thinking about?"

McCleary demurred to Quin on the details. "I guess eight to four, nine to five, something like that," she said.

"That should work just fine. Let me introduce you to the ones teacher."

Miss Lianne, as she was known to the kids, was a short brunette with a face as round as a coin. She was sitting in the central room with the day's stragglers watching *The Jungle Book*. Helen took Ellie by the hand, walked her over to where they were sitting, and introduced them.

Ellie hung back, shy and uncertain, until Miss Lianne held out Big Bird and said, "Hi, Michelle, will you play with me?" Then Ellie grinned, reached for the bird, and settled on the rug with the others.

"I need to get some information from you both, so

101

why don't I show you where her cubbyhole will be? Then we'll go to my office for a few minutes.''

Quin and Helen walked off, but McCleary lingered, waiting for Ellie to notice their absence, hoping she would. She didn't. She continued to play with Big Bird and to watch the other kids, and after a few minutes he left, feeling older but no wiser.

(3)

Richard ''Rick'' Farmer biked home through the twilight, 2.2 miles of flat, smooth surfaces. The light on the front of his ten-speed pierced the ever-darkening air, but he barely saw it. His vision was focused inward on the bitch's face, those odd blue eyes, the pretty mouth that wouldn't stop talking, that kept spewing lies about what kind of man the killer was. Sexually maladjusted, a pervert. And he resented those unpleasant parallels she'd drawn to Bundy. Necrophilia, Christ. The germs. The contamination.

Quin McCleary, he thought, had things figured all wrong. He wasn't cowardly. He was careful. And he didn't screw corpses and he was certainly capable of sustaining an intimate relationship with a woman. He wasn't a psychopath. He was a student of life and death and transformation, an explorer of the hidden ocean of possibilities, a seeker who was slowly breaking free of the decades of conditioning laid down by the society in which he lived. She was wrong. What could possibly be cowardly about the Ocala kill, for instance? Wrong, he thought, but it didn't make him feel any better.

His home was at the end of a street shaded by hickories and live oaks. It was built of brick and stone and set back on two acres of land that abutted a field of pines. When the wind blew, Rick could hear the pines whispering, laughing, telling tall tales of the days before man. He often collected fallen pine cones and used them for tinder in the fireplace on chilly nights. He liked the way their smoke smelled, the sound of their crackling when they burned. Most of all, he liked the memories they evoked, of the days before his father had died, before Mother had gotten sick, when he was married and life was good.

He was quite the academic suburbanite then. He cut his lawn on Saturdays and went to neighborhood barbecues where he and other academics talked shop over ribs and cold beer. Every summer when classes were out he and his wife traveled for six or eight weeks. Mexico, the Caribbean, Europe, the Orient. He had belonged to a community that was a reflection of the one he'd grown up in, a world where things were black and white, either/or, good or bad, a simpler world, like in the Fifties. Then his wife had spoiled it and on a Saturday night in December the Good Life had ended.

He and Barb had just gotten home from one of the neighborhood barbecues. He'd had too much to drink, and she, ten weeks pregnant, had been in one of her dark hormonal moods, on his back about every goddamn thing.

As they were climbing the stairs, she started in about how many beers he'd had, how much time he'd spent talking to so and so's wife, how they hadn't had sex in two weeks because he couldn't stand the changes in her body, that was it, wasn't it, admit it, Ricky. He could no longer recall the exact context of these accusations. But he clearly remembered the whine of her voice, clawing at the inside of his head like a trapped animal, and how desperately he'd wanted to silence it.

He clearly recalled spinning around there at the top of the stairs and sinking his fist into her stomach. She toppled back, arms pinwheeling for balance, her mouth opening in shock and pain, her pale hair flying away from her head like a string of Christmas lights. Then she was falling, bouncing down the steps, the dull thud echoing hollowly in the stairwell.

When he reached her, she was sprawled in a pool of blood. She wasn't moving. She'd stopped screaming. Instantly sober, he knew what he had done and a blind, white panic seized him. He stumbled away from her and raced for the phone. Before he reached it, a part of him detached from the panic, planning, thinking, rehearsing what he would say. That he had been in the bedroom. That he'd heard her scream. That when he'd reached the stairs, she was already at the bottom.

Then he realized that if she lived, she would have her version of the truth, an ugly version that would make him look like a monster.

So he ran back to her, knelt beside her, felt for a pulse at her neck. It was faint and erratic and she'd lost a lot of blood, but he just couldn't take the chance. So he gently squeezed her nostrils shut and clamped his hand over her mouth and watched her face as she died.

The inquest had been merely a formality; no one had ever really doubted his story. He was from a respected Gainesville family, after all, that had been here since the turn of the century, a family that had helped make this community what it was.

In the aftermath of Barb's death, people had been sympathetic, kind, compassionate, but something essential had changed. He was single, a widower, the odd number at barbecues and parties. Neighbors and business associates had remained pleasant, but eventually the social invitations had ceased altogether.

Over the years, homes in the neighborhood were sold, families moved on, new families and couples moved in and Rick kept his distance. Now he knew no one on this street. His memories of the Good Life, of the man who had gone to barbecues and cut his lawn on Saturdays, of the man Barb had always called Ricky, seemed to belong to someone else. He could barely remember what she looked like.

And yet sometimes he sensed some small echo of her in these rooms, in the objects she'd touched, the books she'd read, as though a part of her still lived on in these things. In the beginning, it had spooked him badly enough so that he'd slept with the lights on at night, a kid afraid of the bogeyman. Now it was all simply part of the process of Becoming, the shedding of guilt as he penetrated the deeper mysteries.

On the enclosed patio at the back of the house, Rick settled on the wicker couch, on pastel cushions Barb had bought ten years ago when they'd moved into this place. The twilight green of the yard was broken up by colorful clusters of impatiens and marigolds and dwarf bushes with variegated leaves. Barb had started the garden and now he maintained it because he'd grown accustomed to it. It was as much a part of the house as its bricks and stones and eaves.

The property was bordered by tall ficus hedges that provided ample privacy from nosy neighbors. Ficus was a pesky plant, with a root system like an underground city. Some of the roots had exploded through the ground in his neighbors' yards like busted water mains. They were hazards for careless feet, killed the grass, guzzled rain as soon as it fell. His neighbors hated his ficus and because he wouldn't remove the hedges they hated him.

Despite all that, there was peace in this view. His view. His space. He momentarily forgot about the McClearys and the dead women. He forgot about Barb. He even forgot about Mother.

Then his thoughts circled back, they always did, and he picked up the receiver of the phone on the end table and punched out a number. The voice that answered held little power over him here and now. But in the darkness when they plundered, when they reaped, this voice had often terrified him.

"It's Rick."

"I was just about to call you. Are you free to-night?"

"No. I've got a mountain of papers to correct." It wasn't quite true, but tonight was for himself. "I'll call you tomorrow when I have some idea of how things look at work."

"Where do you want to meet?"

"The Island Hotel."

"On Cedar Key? That's nearly fifty miles. You're not having second thoughts, are you?"

He saw Lucy's hand, then Catherine's, and the rooms that were suffused with what they had done. Second thoughts? He nearly laughed out loud.

"It's a little late for second thoughts. I'll give you a ring tomorrow."

As he hung up, his own hands trembled. He held them level with his chest, fingers splayed, and willed the trembling to stop. When it did, he reached into the pocket of his slacks and slipped out the white handkerchief. He unfolded it and stared at the dark locks of hair, three of them. They were each taped at the top, holding the strands together. He could distinguish them quite easily. The cluster to the left, with the reddish highlights, belonged to Lucy. Catherine's lock on the right was absolutely black. And in the middle were Suzy's brittle strands.

Rick pressed the handkerchief to his face and stroked his cheek with the hairs. He thought of Mother that day so long ago in the aisle of the bookstore, Mother and that luminous cascade of hair.

10

(1)

ANDY OPERATED ON the premise that three battles had to be won before any book made the journey from the shelf to the cash register. A startling or intriguing cover prompted a browser unfamiliar with the author to pick the book off the shelf. Riveting back copy convinced the person to open the cover. Then the writer's job began.

The opening line, the first paragraph, could make or break a sale. It had to seize the browser, jerk him or her into the story, touch some sympathetic nerve. *In Cold Blood* did it. Her opening paragraph did not do it.

The five pages she'd written were shit, no two ways about it. But she saved them. She saved everything she wrote. There was always a chance that some poorly written sentence might contain a bit of information or the dark underpinning of a particular mood that would trigger the right brain to yield an original thought. It wouldn't be tonight, though. She was brain dead.

Andy pushed away from the kitchen table, rubbing her eyes. The hands of the clock over the sink stood at 3:10. And that was A.M., thanks. She'd sat down nine hours ago, had munched her way through a bag of M&M's, and an acceptable beginning was still as distant from her as Pluto.

The phone rang, a sharp sound that bounced through the quiet like a Ping-Pong ball. Two rings, four, five, and she sat there clenching and unclenching her hands. Six rings, eight, twelve, each louder and more shrill than the last, each lifting her to a new level of dread. Then silence, abrupt and unexpected.

The Rasper had never done that before.

Maybe it wasn't him. Plenty of people had this number. But how many of them would call at three in the morning?

She waited, her nails digging into her palms. The muscles between her shoulders began to ache. Wrong number.

She finally stood and the tension rushed out of her shoulders. Bath, she thought. A long, hot bath.

Andy got as far as the fridge when the phone rang again, and this time it didn't stop.

She hurried through the loft, through all the lights she'd left on, and braced herself for the rasp of his voice.

Bedroom. Recorder on. Notebook and pen. Okay. Get it together. Hoarse voice, as if she'd been sleeping.

On the tenth ring she answered.

"Andy." That rasp: dry leaves scraping against concrete. "You must've fallen asleep with all your lights on, huh?"

All the lights. He could definitely see the windows of the apartment. She started to scribble this in her notebook, but the pen slipped from her damp hand to the floor. And yet when she spoke there was a new courage in her voice. "Yeah, I guess I did. Look, if you want to chat, call during business hours."

"What's black and white and read all over, Andy?"

"What?"

"Just answer the riddle. C'mon, it's really simple."

"A newspaper. So what?"

"Very good, Andy. Her name is Barbara."

Dial tone. Andy hung up, rewound the tape, played it back again. A newspaper. Barbara. Had he killed someone named Barbara who worked for a newspaper? If so, why had he divulged the woman's name? He'd never done that before. Did it signal some new twist in the killings? Some new perversion?

Andy replayed the tape, listening for background noises. She might as well have been listening for the heartbeat of an alien on a clear summer night. She thought of her silhouette against the drawn Levolors, of the man outside tracking her from room to room, and suddenly craved darkness. She rushed through the apartment, turning off lights, then went into the front room where she could see the road. She parted the blinds at the side, peered out.

The bedroom faced the road. The only street lamp six doors down barely emitted a candle's flicker of illumination. Under the trees grew layers of shadows, cars stood fender to fender at the curb, nothing moved. He made a lucky guess about the lights, she thought, and wasn't within ten miles of her place.

She let the blinds fall back into place and returned to the kitchen to make a mug of chamomile tea. She waited for the microwave bell to ring and ran her fingers over the butcher-block counter. Her eyes wandered to the island in the middle of the room with its black stove. The white pine cabinets. White pine floor. The black refrigerator. *Black and white and read all over.*

A deviation from the other calls: why? He'd given her no details about the murder this time, had told her the woman's name, had implied she was connected somehow to a newspaper. Was he intentionally misleading her? Testing her? For what, her IQ? Was he losing it? Was she? Was he hoping to drive her crazy?

The microwave bell rang. She carried her mug of tea back into the bedroom, ran water for a bath, and listened to the tape again. The rasp of his voice curled up beside her on the bed. Licked at her skin. Mocked her.

In the bathroom she locked the door. No windows in here. Good. She eased into the hot water and raised the mug to her mouth. The tea was tasteless. She was hungry and too wired to sleep.

Thank you, Rasper, for tonight's insomnia.

She rubbed her eyes. Watched the swirl of tiny black dots against the insides of her eyelids, a pattern of black dots. She began to draw mental lines between the dots, connecting them, creating patterns.

Patterns, something about patterns. The change in the pattern of his calls reflected a deeper change, a shift in the tectonic plates of his complex emotions, the equivalent of an earthquake. So?

He hasn't killed Barbara yet.

Barbara, who had something to do with a newspaper. The only newspaper in town was the *Gainesville Star.*

She had one source there, Jules Scofeld, the man who was supposed to be digging up dirt on Bristol.

Good ole Jules would know if there was a Barbara who worked for the *Star*. In fact, if she was single and available and as attractive as Catherine and Lucy, Jules had probably hit on her.

In the bedroom, she found his number in her address book, where she'd scribbled it three years ago when he'd interviewed her for a profile in the *Miami Herald*. Although they'd seen each other for lunch shortly after Bristol had made it clear what he thought of her, she hadn't heard from him since.

The phone at the other end rang only twice before he answered. He sounded like he'd fallen into bed half-loaded only thirty minutes ago.

"Hey, Clark Kent, it's Andy. Got a minute?''

"Christ, Tull. You have any idea what time it is?

She heard a woman's voice in the background, then Jules asked her to hold on a second and covered the mouthpiece. She was pleased that he was so predictable. She liked predictable men. They were easy to deal with, to manipulate, to control. Her ex hadn't been the least bit predictable. It seemed she'd spent the entire three years of her marriage in a state of near panic because she couldn't anticipate anything about the man she brushed her teeth next to in the morning.

"Uh, sorry, doll.'

Doll: He'd apparently gotten on another phone.

"So what's going on?'' he asked.

"Jules, is there anyone named Barbara who works at the paper?''

"Not in Editorial.''

"In any department.''

"What's her last name?''

"I don't know. She's a slender brunet, lives alone.''

"I think there's a woman named Babs in Sales.''

"No, it's Barbara.'' That was what he'd said, so that was what he meant. Barbara, Not Babs or Barbie or Barb.

"Well, it wouldn't be Babs. She's a grandmother with white hair. So why the questions, doll? You on to something I should know about?''

"Probably not, but check it out for me, Jules, will you?"

"Brunets seem to be popular these days."

She ignored the remark, changed the subject. "You found anything on Bristol yet?"

"I was going to call you tonight, but I, uh, had to work late."

"Yeah, she sounded like good company for late hours, Clark Kent."

He let out a soft, drunken chuckle. "Meet me at Farrah's at ten tomorrow."

Andy hung up. She realized he hadn't said he would check out anything—not before breakfast, not after. But she knew he would. And then he would come to breakfast armed with some tidbit for which he would want to bargain. They'd bargained about the Bristol business and they would bargain about this and maybe someday down the road they would bargain about something else. Fine fine fine. Jules had connections, access to information at the police department, and, quite frankly, it would be a relief to have someone to work with, to confide in. The solo scene, especially at night, was starting to make her very uneasy.

(2)

Rick entered the townhouse at the back, by lifting the sliding-glass door up and off the track. He removed his shoes once he was inside and switched on a penlight. The narrow beam skipped over the dark tile floors as he moved toward the stairs.

The scents here were distinctly feminine, of perfume and lotions and shampoos. In the closets he knew he would find silks and porous cottons and textures, belts and scarves and purses that matched skirts and dresses and slacks.

The steps were carpeted and didn't squeak as he climbed them. So careless. If he were a woman, he would have special locks on the doors and the windows and heat sensors in every room that would set off an alarm loud enough to be heard in hell. And he would have a Doberman or a Rottweiler. Nothing discouraged a potential prowler more than a ferocious dog.

Halfway up the stairs he unsnapped the leather holder hanging at his belt and removed the knife inside. It felt correct in his hand, neither too light nor too heavy. He'd bought it in the sporting-goods department at K Mart along with a sleeping bag and a tent. A man who bought just a knife might be remembered; a man who bought camping gear would not be. Echoes of Ocala, he thought.

The blade wasn't particularly long, but it was serrated at the edge, those little teeth as sharp as a piranha's. It was also very clean. He'd washed it with soap and water, sterilized it with Clorox, then washed it again to get rid of the bleach stink.

At the top of the stairs, he paused and undressed. He folded his clothes and left them in a neat pile next to the banister, his wallet and car keys on top. He felt like Pan, like Zeus, like Nostradamus peeking through the window of the future.

The woman's bedroom door was ajar. A night light burned somewhere near the floor and cast the room in a pale blue glow. It was like swimming underwater with his eyes open, dark shapes eddying across the ceiling and spilling onto the walls and the bed, where the woman slept like an enchanted princess. He would wake her with a kiss. Her delicate foot would fit into the glass slipper.

He moved as soundlessly as water. The blue light liked his skin, stained it the color of ink, softened it until he felt like an alien up to no good.

Hello, sweet pea.

He smelled the soap on her skin before he'd reached the side of her bed. She had just bathed. Her hair was still a little damp. She slept on her side, facing him, the covers to her neck, her head dipped toward her chest, a fetus. That made it easy. He sat beside her, straining the sheet so that she was trapped like a pupa in a cocoon, clamped one hand over her mouth, touched the tip of the knife to her throat.

"Don't make me hurt you." His heart hammered in his chest, a wave of sweat crested across his palms. Sweet Christ, just the smell of her made him hard. He wanted to lick her skin, taste those lotions and perfumes, swallow up that blue light, absorb the sound she made against his hand.

"I take it that means you'll be a good girl?" He leaned forward until his face was within two inches of hers. Such pretty eyes. So wide. So terrified. Her head made a small, uncertain movement. "I can kill you faster than you can scream. Just remember that."

Another small nod.

"Okay, you're going to turn onto your back now." He lifted his hand slowly from her mouth and helped her roll. She didn't scream, didn't cry, didn't make any sound at all. He drew the tip of the knife lightly down her throat, then nudged back the covers, exposing her in layers. The swell of a breast, a nipple that hardened as soon as the cool air touched it, a belly as flat and pale as a sheet of paper. He touched his tongue to the tip of his index finger and drew wet designs against that belly, playful loops, little commas, highways that intersected one another.

And still she didn't speak or move.

But the muscles in her belly quivered as his hand crept under the covers, fingers trailing across the inside of her thighs. He said things to her, that she was a good girl and her skin felt so cool and soft, and didn't she like him just a wee bit? He coaxed her legs open a little wider and drew his hand between them, and didn't that feel nice?

She made an unintelligible sound. He threw off the covers and let his hand cruise over a hip, around her navel, then up across a breast, where it lingered. Beads of perspiration slicked her skin. He told her to bend her knees. He kissed them, those knobby hills, and his hands slipped down a shin and around her calf, defining it. He enclosed her delicate ankle with his thumb and index finger.

Rick touched her and smiled at how ready she was. He whispered that she was such a good girl, he was proud of her, and she wasn't going to make any noise, was she? She wouldn't tell Aunt Bess, would she? This would be their very own secret, his and hers.

He teased her but didn't satisfy her and she made a

noise and he assured her it was okay to feel good, really it was, there was nothing to worry about. Her hips moved ever so slightly against the pressure of his hand and he said he wanted to taste her, would she let him do that? It would feel very, very good and would make him happy and she wanted him to be happy, didn't she?

She made a deeper sound, almost a moan. He reassured her they weren't doing anything wrong, she trusted him, didn't she? Had he ever misled her? And while he talked, he kissed her knees and spread her legs with his hands, opening her like a curtain, and then found her soft, liquid center with his tongue. She tasted of pears and pastels, musks and sea, dark skies, a world that was hidden. She shuddered and moaned as she came and Rick drew her into his arms, holding her, feeling as though they were both sinking through the sea of blue light, drowning in it, dying in it. After what seemed a long time, but probably wasn't, he said, "Is that how it happened with your uncle?"

She sat up, away from him, and ran her hand under her nose. "More or less. Minus the knife." She fluffed the pillow, went through her nightstand drawer for cigarettes. She lit two, passed him one, set the ashtray on her tummy as she settled back. Their private ritual.

It had begun in the early stage of their affair, one night in this very bed, in this wash of light, when he'd asked her to tell him something she had never divulged to another human being. He'd intended it as a joke, a kid's game of Do You Trust Me? But instead of saying something silly, she'd lit two cigarettes and told him about a man she'd killed in Arizona just to see if she could do it. A hitchhiker she'd picked up.

When she'd reciprocated by asking him the same question, he'd told her about his wife, that night on the stairs. Two weeks later, during a four-day skiing trip in Aspen, they'd smothered a woman she had met in a gay bar. They'd taken the three hundred bucks in her wallet, wiped the motel room clean of prints, and fled back to their own cozy villa. The sex had never been better.

The second time was many weeks later, summer again, a drifter in Amarillo, a guy no one would miss. And

114

afterward, the sex, the endless hushed talk over cigarettes, and gradually a slow but undeniable addiction to killing. Twenty-three men and women so far, he thought, spread across seventeen states and four years, twenty-three without counting Lucy and Catherine and the ditzy bimbo in Ocala.

Rick inhaled the smoke, blew it out, watched it drift through the blue light, thinning, curling, vanishing.

"He wasn't really my uncle," she said. "He was just married to my aunt Bess. I used to visit on weekends. Doug was built like an ox."

"How old were you the first time it happened?"

"Thirteen."

"How long did it go on?"

"Until I was nearly sixteen and Bess followed him up to the attic one night. I used to sleep up there when I visited."

"How old was he?"

"Fifty, thereabouts."

"An honest-to-God pervert."

She laughed. "I must've liked it okay. I kept visiting them."

"What'd Bess do the night she found you?"

"Walked in with a rifle and told him to get out of bed. She didn't shout or anything. She was real calm. That scared me more than anything. She was nearly as big as he was. Not fat, just big, muscular."

"What'd he do?"

Her laugh was sharp. "He was scared shitless. He got up nice and slow, patting the air with his hands, saying, 'C'mon now, Bess honey, be careful with that thing.' I remember just lying there, shaking so bad my teeth were literally chattering. She never even looked at me. It was like I no longer existed. Then they left and I could hear the stairs creaking as they went downstairs.

"The next morning she handed me a bus ticket and said she thought it'd be a good idea if I left. I never saw either of them again. We were living in El Paso then."

The army brat.

"So what do you think, Doc?" She crushed out her cigarette, glanced at him. The blue light hugged her cheeks and left dark hollows under her eyes. "Have I broken down one more barrier?" She laughed as she said it, and for a second, he wondered if it was all an elaborate lie, one of her colorful little fictions.

"I think we should keep working on it."

She poked him in the ribs, passed him the ashtray. "You just like the sex part." She sat up and swung her legs over the side of the bed. "Let's go take a shower."

Rick watched her glide through the blue light. "It happened, didn't it?"

"Of course it happened." She turned, fixed her hands to her slender hips. "I never ask you if something's really happened, Rick. I take you at your word. Why can't you do the same for me?"

Because it was different if she lied to him. He knew how to compartmentalize things, how to tuck away the white lies, the black sins, the terrible secrets. She didn't. Sooner or later the lie would surface and he would call her on it and she would be compelled to lie again, further eroding the trust they had so carefully built up in their four years together.

"I take you at your word," he replied.

She returned to the bed, sat down, frowning. "You *are* having second thoughts. I knew it."

"We were just going to plan one murder here in Gainesville, remember? Then it was two. Now we're talking about pulling another one. Then it'll be four."

She touched his hand. "We'll stop now. At two. If that's what you want."

But that wasn't the real issue and they both knew it. The problem was them. For the past year, the kills just weren't affecting them as they once had. The time between kills had shortened, the thrill was waning. As a result, the sex wasn't as good, the communication was lacking, the intimacy was forced. Killing, he thought, was no longer a fuel that kept the relationship alive.

It had been her idea to try something new, to inject greater risk into a kill by planning it and pulling it off in Gainesville, where they lived and worked. "I don't like the choosing, the planning, the torture. And I especially don't like doing them here."

116

Her face hardened. "But we agreed . . ."

Rick jerked his hand away. "*We* didn't agree to anything. You suggested it and I went along with it."

"You chose them," she said.

As if they were divvying up the blame. He had a sudden vision of the two of them in a court of law, their attorneys standing by mutely as they argued over who had done what to whom and when. "I chose one. You chose the other. Get the facts right, princess."

She shrugged on her robe; she apparently didn't like arguing in the nude. Four years and he'd just discovered something about her that he hadn't known before. "You're afraid of being caught, right? Admit it, Rick, that's what this is about."

"It's crossed my mind, but that isn't what started this."

She threw up her hands. "Okay, fine, we'll stop at two, if that's what you want. And so what if I've already chosen the next one."

He felt he had to concede on at least one point. "Okay, one more, but that's it."

"We'll change the pattern."

"Change it to what?"

"So there isn't any pattern at all."

He thought of what Quin McCleary had said about the killer being cowardly. "We'll make it more fair."

"More fair? We're already making it relatively painless."

"It goes on too long."

"What about the rituals?"

"What rituals? Circles of laundry detergent? A bloodletting? Clothes?" He laughed. "Those aren't rituals. They're pretend."

"No more bleach, then, Rick."

Bartering now. "Fine." His voice tightened as he said it. No more bleach meant germs. Germs meant possible contamination. Contamination meant sickness. An endless cycle. If they eliminated the bleach, he wouldn't touch the women.

"No more bloodletting," she said.

"I never liked that part to begin with."

"Hell, it was your idea."

He didn't really remember whose idea it had been. But it was the kind of suggestion she was more likely to make if only to challenge his compulsion about cleanliness.

"Then we'll go back to the way it was before." She strode across the room. "We didn't argue about it then."

Only because there had been no time to argue, he thought. It had happened too quickly, too suddenly, like an act of God, and afterward there was the sex, the talk, that strange bond neither of them wanted to threaten.

She stood in front of the mirror, lighting another cigarette, and blew a pair of perfect rings into the air. They were linked at the side like Siamese twins. One couldn't rise or fall without the other, dissipate without the other.

Like us.

It wasn't a new thought, but was nonetheless disturbing, particularly when he labeled it in shrink terms. Psychopathic. Sociopathic. Anima and animus. They were each other's mirrors, connected in their common disregard for the ordinary lives in which they functioned somewhat normally.

"I thought part of the reason we were doing this was to build trust, not tear it down."

"That was my understanding."

She eyed him in the mirror. "Stop doing that."

"What?"

"Talking like a goddamn shrink."

"How do you want me to talk?"

"Oh, forget it. Just forget it."

Sound leaked out of the room, the blue of the air deepened. Some delicate balance between them had been disturbed and he felt, suddenly, as frail as a tree poised at the lip of some steep precipice, buffeted by high winds. A misplaced word and it was all going to slide into hell.

"Why don't you come to Masquerade with me sometime? You always said you—"

"Okay." He didn't want to talk about the parts of her life he hadn't shared. It wasn't jealousy, nothing as petty as that. It had to do with superstition, he thought, with some fixed idea in his mind that if they changed the rules too much now, the whole thing would collapse. He would lose her. And he didn't want to lose her, did he? He still loved her, didn't he?

She smiled and came over to the bed, folding her legs under her as she sat beside him on the mattress. "When this is all over, you know what I'd like to do?"

As though the murders and the investigation were a storm they had to weather. "What?"

"Get married, move someplace else, have a couple of kids."

Echoes of the Good Life, of the man he'd been eight years ago. No, thanks. "Let's get through this first."

"Okay."

He rubbed his hands over his arms as he got up. The germs were rallying on his skin now and he was anxious to shower, to get moving. He had a busy day ahead of him.

"So do we agree then?" she asked.

"On what?"

She cocked her head, a half smile on her face. "On what we were talking about. The details. No pattern and so on."

Oh, that. "Yeah, I thought we'd already decided."

"Just making sure," she said gaily, and followed him into the shower.

11

(1)

THE BIRTH OF the lamb at six-thirty that morning was no less miraculous to McCleary than the birth of his daughter nearly nine months ago. He wished that Cat had seen him midwifing, with Quin assisting and Ellie cheering them on from her perch on a mound of hay. And he wished she could see the little lamb now, struggling to its feet in the pale light and nuzzling its mother's belly in search of breakfast.

When he'd arrived yesterday, Cat's absence had still existed in the abstract for him, as though she were out of town and might return at any minute. But as his shock had worn off, her absence in his life had become a hard, palpable thing that grew like a tumor in the center of him. And around it gathered his anger, his grief, his need to know who had killed her and why.

These emotions were a tide that washed through him at unexpected moments, with no particular pattern. One minute he might be brushing his teeth and the next he would think of something he wanted to share with his sister and the reality would hit him. No more phone calls, no more visits, no more late-night chats, no more Thanksgivings.

Thanksgiving was a McCleary family tradition. Every year without fail the entire clan got together at his parents' farm in upstate New York. He didn't know what would happen this year. Less than three weeks from now.

"A penny," Quin said, glancing over at him as they stood knee-deep in hay.

"Thanksgiving," he replied.

"I know." She touched his shoulder, rubbing it lightly, a touch that communicated everything, then reached for his hand. "C'mon, let's get Mom and the baby into that separate pen."

Once the sheep and her lamb were comfortable in their own pen, they made the feeding round in the Wagoneer, Flats in tow. They returned to the house an hour later with four fresh eggs from the chicken coop and a batch of asparagus from Cat's garden, the makings for omelets.

McCleary had been the cook in the family since he and Quin had gotten married. It wasn't that Quin *couldn't* cook, only that she didn't do it well. She didn't use spices or herbs, didn't make sauces, knew virtually nothing about the nuances of cooking, and yet she ate all the time. In the early days of their relationship, breakfast at her place had consisted of fried eggs with hard yolks, burned muffins, charred bacon, grits that were as bland as Wonder bread.

He remembered dropping by her place unannounced one evening and was appalled to see that her dinner consisted of a charred hamburger with a couple of slices of Cheddar cheese on the side. No roll, no salad, no garnish or mustard or ketchup, just this disgusting dark blob in the middle of her plate. And back then he was afraid to open her refrigerator because some new life form was inevitably growing in a Tupperware container shoved to the back. When they'd gotten married, he'd made it clear that his realm was the kitchen. Damned if he was going to his grave from malnutrition or ptomaine poisoning.

Just as McCleary was setting breakfast out on the table, Flats started barking. A moment later a car pulled into the driveway. "Company," he called to Quin, who was in the bathroom bathing Ellie, then walked out onto the porch to see who it was.

Angie Wilkin stood at the screen door trying to convince a snarling Flats that she came in peace, but Flats wasn't listening. McCleary restrained her and pushed open the screen door; Wilkin remained where she was, eyeing the dog warily.

"It's safe," he said.

"I just love welcoming committees." She sidled

through the door, her back to the jamb. "I'm really a very nice person, Flats."

The sheepdog kept growling, so McCleary put her out and latched the door. "I don't suppose she knows how to get back in, does she?"

"Not yet."

"The way you say that bothers me, Mike."

Yesterday he'd been Mr. McCleary; today he was Mike. He wondered what had changed.

"I apologize for coming by so early." She relaxed her grip on her shoulder bag and hooked her hair behind her ears. Today's ensemble was a pair of brown Cavaricci slacks with a pink cotton shirt that had tiny brown designs in it. Her sandals and purse were also brown. She looked Florida casual with flair, but she wasn't going to any drug busts in these clothes. "I've been getting a busy signal with this number since last night. The operator said the phone was off the hook."

"Par for the course. Ellie probably hit the hold button on the phone in the bedroom."

"I just wanted to let you know that Steve got the okay from the nursing home about Grandma Davenport. He thought it'd be a good idea if your wife talked to her, since she seems more responsive to women, and suggested I tag along to run interference with the director. She's sort of difficult."

"We were just about to have breakfast. Can I interest you in an omelet?"

"I've eaten, but I'd love some coffee." She waved an arm at the clutter on the porch as they passed through it. "What're you going to do with all this stuff?"

"It depends on what I decide to do about the farm."

"You may have some valuable things buried in all this. That Wurlitzer alone is worth something."

"It's busted."

"Hell, a collector would love to fix it up. When my folks died, there was so much junk in their attic I hired someone to haul the stuff down and then got an appraiser to give me an estimate on what it was all worth. It saved me a lot of heartache."

"I'll keep that in mind."

"She had a will, right?"

"Yes." Despite his sister's love of clutter, her financial affairs had been in order.

"Was there anything unusual in it?"

He shook his head. He'd been named executor and had inherited the farm and everything that went with it. There was a trust fund for Ellie of about twenty-five thousand, and the rest of her estate—a hundred and fifty grand in cash, stocks, and money markets—had been divided equally among her sisters and parents. "Nothing unexpected. No bequeathments to people I've never heard of, no double-indemnity clauses in her life insurance. She wasn't murdered for money."

Wilkin shrugged. "It never hurts to ask."

True. But McCleary had the distinct impression that she was fishing for something other than a motive.

She made herself comfortable at the dining room table, her body positioned so she could peruse the books on the shelf behind her. She didn't chatter, didn't speak at all until he set her coffee and the plates on the table.

"Was your sister involved with anyone, Mike?"

"Not that I know of."

"Tess Schulman said she thought there was someone but didn't know who he was. I was just wondering if Catherine had ever mentioned anything to you."

"No, but she tended to be pretty private about certain things. It wouldn't surprise me if there was someone. There were always men in her—"

A squeal two octaves above middle C sundered the air and Ellie waddled into the room wearing just diapers, her hair dripping wet. She was waving her arms like a symphony conductor and stopped short when she saw Wilkin. Ellie stared at her, measuring her against whatever criteria kids used to assess strangers. Then she latched on to McCleary's leg like an overgrown flea and buried her face against his jeans.

"She's in the fear-of-strangers stage." Quin strolled in with a towel over her shoulder.

"Can't blame her. I'm in that stage myself and I'm thirty-eight."

Quin laughed and introduced herself. For the next forty minutes, she and Wilkin exchanged information in that way women always did, as if their gender alone were the basis for immediate camaraderie. During Quin's pregnancy, he'd realized just how prevalent this phenomenon was, when women she'd never seen before would strike up conversations about *their* pregnancies, *their* labors, *their* deliveries.

According to Quin, these conversations often led to intimate revelations about other areas of a particular woman's life. Any topic was apparently fair game: husbands, lovers, kids, sex, fantasies. It often occurred to him that Quin's dentist and her hairdresser, both women, probably knew a side of her he'd never seen.

Later, after Wilkin had left, Quin remarked that Wilkin was odd. Forty minutes of chitchat and that was all she could say about the woman? She was *odd*? "Why?"

"I'm not sure." She plucked the diaper bag off the bedroom bureau and slung it over her shoulder. "It's like she's got problems she tries to compensate for by being a cop."

"Bristol says she's good." To be exact, Bristol had commented that she'd risen through the ranks faster than a saint ascended into heaven.

"How long's she been in Homicide?"

"Five years, four here, one in Orlando, and three years of Vice before that."

"Well, whatever. She's got her own agenda, Mac, that's all I'm saying. And it may not mesh with *our* agenda. You want to meet at the theatre around three?"

"Depends on how much I get done here. Why don't you call when you finish at the nursing home?"

He walked out to the car with them, kissed Ellie goodbye, and told her to enjoy her first day at school. She waved as they drove off and he stood in the dusty driveway, watching the Wagoneer until it turned. He felt strange, dislocated, like a crab that has just discovered it's in the middle of the interstate instead of on a beach.

(2)

Quin set Ellie down in the toddler playground at Tot Stop, took her hand, and they walked over to where Lianne was pushing a little girl in one of the swings.

"Morning, Michelle. Would you like to try one of the swings?"

Ellie clung to Quin's leg and just stood there watching. Big mistake, Quin thought. This wasn't going to work. What had ever made her believe that it would? Ellie was too young, her exposure to other children had been minimal, and suppose she got onto the swing and fell out?

"Should we try the swing, El?" Quin asked, looking down at her.

Ellie giggled, then suddenly released Quin's leg and waddled over to the swings by herself. Lianne laughed, picked her up, and fitted her into the little leather seat with the leg holes. Ellie squealed as Lianne gave her a small push, then dropped her head back and peered up, up at the sky.

"I think she's going to do just fine, Mrs. McCleary."

"I'll stick around a few minutes to make sure."

Quin stood in the warm shade of a live oak watching Ellie swing through sunlight and shadow. Her only memory of her own first day at nursery school a hundred years ago was of standing at a wire-mesh fence, sobbing as her mother drove away. She had been four at the time and had been there just for the morning. But her stint had lasted less than a week; her mother said she couldn't stand the silence in the house. Quin knew what she meant. She could already feel that silence closing in on her.

She knew it would follow her. She knew she would glance in the backseat of the car to say something to Ellie or would reach for the diaper bag for a bottle and her daughter's absence would haunt her. She would fret about Ellie on the swing, on the slide, Ellie in the company of strangers. It was irrelevant that she'd fretted and worried when they'd first hired a sitter. This was different.

And it was also temporary, she reminded herself. Just until they found Cat's killer.

The most difficult thing Andy had learned in her life was patience. She'd come barreling into the world nearly forty-one years ago, an eight-pound baby in such a rush to be born that her mother had delivered her in just under four hours. She'd never mastered crawling because she was too busy learning how to walk and by fourteen months was speaking in simple sentences Lights off, oh-oh, Andy fall.

She finished high school in three years and sailed through college with a double major in just under four. And that was when her real life had begun, the life she'd been racing toward, her writing life. In one form or another, she'd been writing ever since. She'd been a reporter, a speechwriter, a ghostwriter. She'd written PR brochures, grant applications, and nearly starved one year as a free-lance writer. During research for a magazine piece eleven years ago on women who commit crimes, she'd met Carmen Mendez, who was then just another Looney Tune awaiting trial.

Mendez had taught her a great deal about patience. Andy had spent six months with her both during and after her trial, listening to her often-mad rantings about what had happened that night she'd murdered her husband and two kids. It had taken Andy another year and hundreds of interviews with family and friends to piece together who Carmen Mendez was and a year beyond that to write the book. But it had paid off, just as this would, even though Jules was already twenty minutes late.

There wasn't much business at Farrah's at this hour of the morning. Four studious types were sitting around a table near the door sipping espressos and arguing about the future of the Middle East. In her day, the hot topic had been the future of Southeast Asia. A generation from now it would probably be the future of man in space or man on a ruined planet. Assuming the planet was still here.

As she started on her third cup of coffee, she felt a sudden, acute homesickness for Key West. She missed her conch house, her cat, steamed clams at Paco's in the evenings, the smell of the sea. She missed the routine of her life, such as it was, with her small circle of friends, her work, her tidy passions. She felt displaced here among men and women born when she was marching for peace and equality and liberation. It seemed to her that the tragedy of the academic life if you were a professor was that you aged and your students did not.

A few other people arrived and among them was Melody Burns. Even in jeans and a denim jacket she looked sleek and untouchable, the kind of woman who never perspired, whose lipstick never wore off, whose blonde shiny hair always bounced. She was with Jim Kliner, Cubanito's boss, a towering scarecrow of a man. There was something absurd about the two of them together, an Abbott and Costello duo, mismatched from head to toe.

Andy had spoken with Melody briefly at the theatre the morning she'd found out about Catherine, but her timing had been all wrong. They'd been interrupted a million times by calls and visitors and Melody had asked her to come back another day. What day? Andy inquired. I'll call you, Melody replied, and hadn't and probably wouldn't.

But to her surprise Melody strolled over to the table with Kliner and said, "I owe you an apology for the other day, Andrea."

"You do?"

"She thinks she owes everyone an apology," Kliner remarked with a good-natured grin. "You have some persistent fans in Gainesville, Ms. Tull. Just had a woman in the other day who bought the last copy of *Home* and informed me I'd better reorder."

The woman with the baby and the weird name, Andy thought. Quin Somebody. "Just the sort of fans I like to hear about. How's the book selling generally?"

"Real good. It's required reading in a couple of psych courses, which helps."

"Why don't you grab us a table, Jim?" said Melody.

He gathered his long hair in his hand and pulled it to one side. "Right. So you can apologize. I know. Nice seeing you, Ms. Tull."

"Anyway, that morning you stopped by the theatre,

everything was in an uproar because of Catherine. You walked into a zoo and I apologize for being so brusque.''

"Don't worry about it. I understand, really. I'd still like to get together. At your convenience.''

She slipped a pack of Marlboros from her jacket pocket and dug out a cigarette with her bright red nails. She lit it with a monogrammed gold lighter, then dropped her head back slightly and blew smoke into the air. Never had smoking a cigarette seemed so elegant to Andy, so utterly correct. "There isn't much to tell, really. Catherine was terrific to work with and was one of those talents that dwarfs everyone else onstage. I guess you know that Tess Schulman found her.''

Andy nodded. "She's refused to speak to me.''

"I'm not surprised. Detective Bristol made it pretty clear that we're not supposed to discuss the murder with anyone.''

Yeah, I bet he did, Andy thought. "It's probably been tough on her, too, since she and Catherine were so close.''

"They used to work together in Coconut Grove.'' Her eyes had started to roam, checking out the new arrivals, glancing back to see if Kliner had found a table. "You should probably talk to her brother and sister-in-law.'' Those eyes returned to her, smiling. "They're staying out at her farm. Mike and Quin.''

Quin?

She leaned across Andy and stabbed her cigarette out in the ashtray. "I've really got to run. Nice seeing you again.''

Andy wanted to ask her what this Quin looked like, but Melody fluttered off, gold and exotic in the light.

Quin. How many women in Gainesville could there possibly be with a name like that?

She glanced out toward the street and saw Jules trotting up the walk, hands lost in his pockets. His gaze was fixed on a pair of coeds across the street who were checking out the display in the window of a sporting-goods shop. Both were thin and probably didn't have to work at it. Wait until they hit their late thirties, she thought, when their metabolisms slipped into first gear and refused to burn off the calories from a bag of M&M's. She looked down at the packet of sugar she'd just opened and dropped it quickly in the ashtray.

Thirty calories saved.

Jules waved when he saw her, Jules with his open, boyish face, his curly copper hair, his leanness like Pan. Although he was only five eight or nine, he didn't seem to suffer from the short-man syndrome; a lack of self-confidence had never been his problem.

"Clark Kent, late again. You're never going to save the universe at this rate, Jules."

He kissed her on the cheek. "It's hell trying to find a parking spot in this town. You order yet?"

"Three coffees so far."

"Christ, but I'm famished." He signaled the waitress, who hurried over, all smiles. Jules greeted her by name—Evelyn—and couldn't resist a little harmless flirting. Evelyn ate it up, chatting about her theatre courses, her professors, the weather.

Jules finally interrupted her. "Tell Andy about Catherine McCleary, Evelyn."

"What about her?"

"You know, that story you told me."

"Oh, yeah, about her being here the night she was killed."

Andy nearly choked on a mouthful of coffee. "You knew her?"

"Just to say hi. She came in here a lot with people from the Sunshine Repertory. First time I saw her, I liked to have died. *Magenta Nights* is only my favorite horror movie. I got her autograph. After that, she usually sat at one of my tables."

"Who was she with that night?"

"She was here alone for a long time. She was real quiet, seemed kind of depressed. Then she made a phone call and a little while later this guy showed up and they left together."

"What'd he look like?" Andy asked.

"Well, like I told Jules, I didn't pay all that much attention to his face. We were pretty busy that night. But I do remember that he walked with a cane."

Bristol. *I feel pain in man's leg*, Ramona had said about Catherine's lover. And he was married. Granted, there were probably other men in Gainesville besides Detective Bristol who used canes for their bum legs. But this would explain his antagonism toward her. He was in charge of the investigation of his murdered lover and was also a married man with a kid. Hardly the kind of thing he would want in a book.

It also raised the unpleasant possibility that Bristol had killed Catherine.

"You're sure?"

"Of that I am."

"Had you ever seen them together before?"

"No."

"You remember what time they left?"

"It must've been around ten, because I remember thinking I still had another four hours to work." She wagged their orders. "I better get these in or you two'll be ordering lunch."

"So, doll," said Jules when Evelyn had left. He was leaning forward, arms parallel to the edge of the table, his blue eyes a dazzle of light. "Is that the kind of dirt you're looking for?"

Andy laughed. "That'll do just fine, Jules, thanks."

"You think he killed her?"

"Do you?"

He rubbed his jaw, shrugged. "Hard to say. I've only met the guy a couple of times."

"Your editor know about this?"

"Not yet. I need proof before I can use it. Like a photograph." He grinned. "And I wanted to talk it over with you first, doll."

"Just hold on to it for a while."

Convince me, said his body language as he slipped a toothpick from his shirt pocket and proceeded to clean his nails with it. "I'd be passing up the scoop of the year."

"I'll guarantee you a bigger scoop."

"No offense, doll, but you said that before, and so far I haven't heard squat from you. Nothing's hotter than these homicides."

"You interested in a smear campaign, Jules, or in an exclusive?"

The end of the toothpick slid under his thumbnail. "Like I said, Andy, so far you're all talk."

"Mutilations have been involved."

"That isn't hard to figure, given how tight the cops have been with information." He didn't bother glancing up at her. "Give me something else."

"Hands, his thing is hands."

Jules raised his head, eyes bright with interest, curiosity, a bit of greed. "Hands? You're sure?"

"Yeah, I'm sure."

"I thought you said Bristol refused to cooperate with you."

She nodded.

"Then how can you be sure?"

"Trust me, Jules. I'm sure. Your turn."

"I hear a psych prof on campus is working with the cops."

"Which prof?"

"Richard Farmer. He teaches weird shit, aberrant criminal behavior. Okay, your turn."

"The killer also takes locks of their hair and uses bleach on them. Scrubs them down with it."

He paled. "Bleach?"

"Stop repeating everything I say and tell me about Barbara at the newspaper."

"No Barbara at the *Star*. But there's a Barbara L. Stillman who works for the campus newspaper. Thing is, she's blonde, plump, and her byline is B. L. Stillman, so I don't know if she counts."

"Are there any other presses in Gainesville?"

"A handful of college literary magazines, but no other newspapers. You have a snitch at the coroner's office?"

"I wish."

"Then how can you be so sure about your facts?"

"He's called me, that's how."

"Called you?" he hissed, leaning toward her again. "He's *called* you and you haven't gone to the cops? Good God, Andy."

"Just who the hell am I going to go to, Jules? Detective Bristol, who hates the ground I walk on and who may have been screwing Catherine? Or who maybe killed her? Or his sidekick, Wilkin? Or maybe that horse's ass of a captain? I don't know who to trust.''

"Me, doll, that's who."

"I have tapes of the calls, Jules."

"Tapes, Jesus, the lady has tapes."

"Three calls so far. In two of them he describes what he's done to the women, but he doesn't give me names. He eliminates a few details—to keep me guessing, he says—then gives me stuff the cops haven't released. Last night's call was different,'' she said, and told him how.

"Can I hear the tapes?'' he asked when she was finished.

"Depends.''

He squeezed his thumb and forefinger together and drew them across his mouth. "My lips are sealed, doll.''

12

NURSING HOMES, LIKE trailer parks, always seemed to have words in their names that suggested grandeur, Quin thought. But in all fairness to the Manor Nursing Home, there *was* something a little grand about the place.

It was a sprawling complex of brick buildings set in the midst of hardwood trees on the outskirts of Gainesville. Sidewalks curved past fountains shooting sleek arcs of water and ponds as round as tops. Everywhere she looked there were flowers and old people.

They sat in wheelchairs, on benches, on the emerald grass; they hobbled on crutches, in walkers, and leaned on canes. Some stood motionless in patches of sunlight, like basking flamingos. Others were talking to themselves. Quin wondered which was worse, to die like this, by degrees, trapped in a body of shrunken bones, your mind no longer connected to the planet, or to die suddenly, unexpectedly, a heart attack in the shower at forty or fifty-five. Given the choice, what would hers be?

Neither, she decided, and hurried into the building.

Angie Wilkin was waiting in the lobby for her, talking with a woman shaped like a pear. They looked ridiculous together, these two, Wilkin so well dressed and slender, the other woman so plump and stiff in her frilly blouse with the starched tie at the throat.

The woman's name was Mrs. LeForge, and that was exactly how Wilkin introduced her, as though her first name was Missus. Quin extended her hand, but LeForge's plump, dimpled fingers didn't move from where they were laced against the balloon of her belly. When she smiled, her flash of white teeth seemed almost predatory.

"I've assured Detective Wilkin we'll cooperate in whatever we can with the police, hmm? But I really don't see the point of this." LeForge was obviously a graduate of the don't-mince-words school. "Christine Davenport is ninety-two years old and has maybe thirty minutes of clarity a week. The body goes, the mind follows, hmm? But maybe you ladies will get lucky. Come along and we'll go see where the wheel of fortune leaves us off today."

As she turned away, Wilkin rolled her hazel eyes and Quin stifled a laugh.

At the door of the dayroom, LeForge keyed a code into the security system. It hummed, the door whispered open, then shut again as soon as they'd stepped through. It was like a big romper room, sunny and pleasant, with walls the color of seashells, heavy-duty plastic tables with rounded corners, two large-screen TVs, and comfortable old couches for sprawling and climbing. French doors on the left were thrown open to a shaded garden with a fence around it. Ceiling fans whirred, circulating the cool, fragrant air. Quin felt as if she'd walked into a dream where the characters were waiting for directions.

Some people shuffled in idle circles. Others seemed to have grown into the couches and chairs where they sat. Two women were arguing loudly, but not with each other, not with anyone. Two couples were playing cards.

"It's a pretty room, hmm?" LeForge didn't seem to see the patients. "But even this room hasn't done much for Christine's spirits lately, what with her friend in the hospital and all. She's right over there." She gestured vaguely to the other side of the room and moved forward with the lethargy of a sated mosquito.

Christine Davenport was sitting back against a nest of pillows on a dark couch in front of one of the oversized TV screens. Old wasn't an adjective that described her; she looked as though she'd been around since the Civil War ended. Bones and wrinkles and wisps of gray, a terry-cloth robe that engulfed her. Behind her thick glasses, her eyes were large blue saucers fixed on the screen, where *Play Misty for Me* was on.

"She's an avid Clint Eastwood fan." LeForge said this

as though Christine weren't present. "So that might be a way of encouraging her to talk." Then she touched the old woman's arm. "Christine honey, you've got some visitors and I've got some good news for you. Vicki's coming back in a few days." Then, to Quin, again as though Christine was absent: "Vicki's her closest friend."

Christine Davenport turned her head, looked blankly at LeForge, then crooked a finger at her, motioning her closer. LeForge leaned toward her and the old woman whispered something.

"I see." LeForge straightened up. "She, uh, said it's all right for Mrs. McCleary to stay, but she'd like you and me to leave them alone, Detective Wilkin."

"So she's lucid enough to know who we are?"

LeForge smiled. "Hardly. She said the lady with the strange blue eyes was okay and that you and I weren't and she would like us to leave her alone, hmm?"

Wilkin didn't look any too pleased about it, which confirmed Quin's suspicions that she and probably Bristol hadn't been entirely honest with her and McCleary about some things. "Hey, not to worry," Quin said. "Christine and I are going to watch *Play Misty for Me*."

"I'll be out in the garden," Wilkin said, still hovering.

"She's perfectly safe here, Detective." LeForge sounded a bit indignant at the implication that Quin might be in jeopardy. "No one here is violent."

"I'm not suggesting they are, Mrs. LeForge. Come get me when you're finished, Quin, okay?"

"Sure."

Christine raised her arm and pointed a spidery finger at the screen. "Oh-oh. Clint's in trouble."

It was the famous lovemaking scene between Eastwood and his girlfriend on Pebble Beach, the soft lighting and close-ups enhanced by Roberta Flack's singing of "The First Time Ever I Saw Your Face."

"I think it's the kind of trouble he can handle," Quin remarked.

"Goodness," LeForge breathed, staring at the screen.

Wilkin looked disgusted with all of it and walked off,

her shoes clicking against the wooden floors. LeForge said she'd "be around," like a friendly ghost, and made herself scarce as well.

"Will Clint marry her?" asked Christine, apparently oblivious to everything except what was happening on the screen. "Will she marry Clint? These are the questions inquiring minds want answers to."

A twisted version of the *National Enquirer* advertising jingle, Quin thought, and laughed. "With a circulation of three million or whatever it is these days, the *Enquirer* must be doing something right."

Christine smiled; it threw her mouth into a rete of wrinkles and deep folds. "My grandson, Jeremy, was a photographer for the *Enquirer* until he moved out of state. Made a lot of money. Lucy didn't make much money, but she was smart as a whip and married well, and when that ended, her settlement was quite good. Quite good, indeed." Her voice had begun as the squeak of a rusted spring but grew gradually clearer with use. "Mark, that was my Lucy's husband, wasn't ungenerous, you know. He just couldn't keep his pants on. He had that side to him. Then after the divorce she got interested in dirty pictures, started buying them up, hanging them in the house. She had a lot of problems, my Lucy did."

Quin noticed that she talked about Lucy in the past tense and decided she wasn't quite as addled as LeForge believed. "What kinds of problems, Christine?"

She shifted against the pillows. "Problems. Your kids have problems. Your grandkids have problems. Clint's got problems." She gestured toward the screen again, where Eastwood was about to find the bloodied corpse of his maid, stabbed by crazy Jessica Walter. "You have kids?"

"A daughter. She'll be nine months on the seventeenth."

"Nine months." She sighed. "God, they should never grow up. Ten's a fine age, I think. No problem at ten that you can't handle, 'cept for drugs, maybe, but in my time we didn't have problems with drugs. Where's she now?"

"At home," Quin lied.

"Not by herself, I hope."

"With my husband."

"Goodness. So many things have changed, haven't they? Husbands watching babies, husbands cooking, wives working . . . Now, my friend Vicki can sure tell you about problems with kids, dear. Her boy's a mess, you know. He shrinks heads and he's the one who oughta have his noggin looked at. I only saw him once, but you can tell. It's in the eyes. You have nice eyes, dear. That Mrs. LeForge has insect eyes. And I don't like that detective's eyes. She always looks at me like I'm crazy. I'm just old. There's a difference, you know."

"Vicki stays here, too?" Quin asked, hoping to keep her talking long enough to extract more information about her dead granddaughter.

"Sure does. She and I watch the soap operas. Sometimes when I'm feeling up to it, we play bridge. She's in the hospital right now. Heart's acting up. I think her heart's maybe broke, what with her daughter, Josie, drowning, then her daughter-in-law falling down them stairs and her being pregnant and all, then her husband dropping dead, bang bang bang, just like that."

"All at once?"

"No, no, no. There was years in between all these, but the heart remembers. I truly believe that. So then one more thing happens, bang, and it's too much. The heart starts acting funny. Like it's broke. I think it's got something to do with that Ricky of hers." Another sigh. "Kids. Did she suffer?"

She was gazing at the screen when she said it and it took Quin a moment to realize she wasn't referring to the movie. "You know about Lucy?"

"Course I know. The lady detective and another detective with a limp told me. Talked to me like I was still in diapers. Did she suffer?"

Quin started to lie but changed her mind. "Yes. And whoever killed Lucy also murdered my sister-in-law, Mrs. Davenport."

Her head moved, but it was so slight, Quin couldn't tell if it was a nod of acknowledgment or just a twitch. Her eyes were riveted on the screen again, where Eastwood was now playing disc jockey, his voice low and smooth. "Did you ever see *The Good, the Bad, and the Ugly*?" Quin asked.

"Eight times. One of my favorites."

"Mine, too."

"I like the one where the boys in Vegas lay odds on him getting some convict back across the country and he hooks up with that pretty blonde."

"The Gauntlet."

She snapped her fingers; it sounded like fire eating up dry paper. "That's it. He used to live with her. In real life. Then he dumped her and she got herself one of them fancy lawyers and sued the pants off him."

Quin wasn't up on her Hollywood gossip. "Really?"

"Sure thing. Read it right here." She lifted up with considerable effort; her thin hand dug into the pillows and came out with a wrinkled copy of the *National Enquirer*. "My Lucy used to bring me these every week." She smoothed it against her lap, her fingers gnarled like roots. "She had this young man with her once. His hair was so long, I thought at first that he was a girl. Didn't like him none until he sat right where you are and started reading to me from *Robinson Crusoe*."

"What was his name?"

"Don't recall."

"Was it Jim Kliner?"

"Jim. Yes. That was it. Jim with the long hair." She was staring down at the *Enquirer*, her hand still smoothing the wrinkled pages. "He was okay, but sometimes he and Lucy talked to each other like I couldn't understand them." Her mouth flattened out and seemed to cave in at the corners. "It's what people do when you get to be as old as me. The nurses and orderlies are the worst. They talk about sex and drugs and you name it like I'm not even here."

"What'd Jim and Lucy talk about?"

"Masquerades."

"That's a weird thing to talk about."

Christine's laughter was soft and phlegmy. Her eyes, as she raised them, were a watery blue now. "It's a . . . well, I don't know, like a group, I guess."

"What kind of group?"

"A dirty-pictures group."

"I don't understand."

"Me, neither. Jim wanted her to go with him. She said she wasn't interested." Christine shrugged. "She needed a man like Clint." Her hand fluttered toward the screen, a pale, translucent moth. "Is Clint married? Does Clint have children? Do his kids have problems? These are the questions inquiring minds want answers to."

The reference to the *Enquirer* was apparently some sort of signal that began and ended her period of lucidity. She didn't speak again after that, didn't even seem to know that Quin was sitting next to her. Quin jotted the farm's phone number on a business card and slipped it inside a pocket of Christine's robe.

"There's my card, Mrs. Davenport. If you remember anything that might be helpful, give me a call. Day or night, it doesn't matter."

"Bye-bye," Christine said softly, without looking away from the screen. "Bye-bye. Be always kind and good. Bye-bye."

Quin walked out to the garden to look for Wilkin, didn't see her, and returned to the lobby. She spotted Wilkin at the far end of the room on the pay phone, probably commiserating with Bristol. Quin guessed it wouldn't be long before she and McCleary suddenly found official channels choked, doors slamming shut in their faces, people refusing to cooperate. Sometimes greed or fear or both were at fault. In this case it would be ambition, that sweet taste of brief fame for cracking a case like this one, the reward of a promotion, a little more power within the infrastructure of small-city politics.

Mrs. LeForge strolled out of an office, saw Quin, and ambled over, one end of her frilly bow resting against the curve of her jaw like a hand. "Was Christine helpful, Mrs. McCleary?"

Quin didn't bother correcting her on the name. "Not really." The less LeForge knew, the better. "She really misses Vicki."

"They do get attached to people, hmm? But I think

Dr. Farmer will be bringing her back real soon, then things will improve for Christine.''

''Farmer?''

''Yes, you know him? He teaches at the university. Wonderful man, hmm? Very devoted to his mother. For years, Vicki and her husband owned the largest bookstore in town. Farmer Books. It isn't nearly what it used to be with the new owners.''

Ricky, whose sister drowned, whose wife fell down the stairs, whose father was dead and whose mother was in a nursing home. The Farmer Tragedies, like something from Shakespeare. No wonder the guy had personality problems.

''How'd it go?'' Wilkin asked, joining them.

Quin shrugged. ''Did you know Clint dumped his girlfriend and then she hired one of those fancy attorneys and sued the pants off him?''

Wilkin was pretty when she laughed. It crowded out the rigidness in her features. ''Fascinating. Clint got sued. Did the girlfriend win?''

''I don't know,'' Quin replied, and they both laughed as LeForge stood there wondering if the joke was on her.

(2)

McCleary spent most of the morning navigating through the many directories on Cat's computer. He wasn't looking for anything specific; he simply hoped to find an irregularity of some kind that would lead him to something else.

He eventually found two items that piqued his interest. The accounting program had a feature that kept track of your checkbook—withdrawals, deposits, balances. Cat had set it up for her various accounts: money markets, savings, checking, stocks. On May 14 of this year, she had withdrawn twenty grand from a money-market account in California and deposited it in her checking account here in Gainesville. On May 20, after the deposit had cleared, she wrote a check to cash for twenty grand.

It was the single largest withdrawal she'd made since she'd bought the farm eighteen months ago. There was no explanatory notation about what it was for. He knew she hadn't bought a new vehicle since the Wagoneer four years ago and that she wouldn't have blown twenty grand on clothes or jewelry. If she'd loaned money to someone in the family, she would have written the check to the individual and not to cash because everyone else in the McCleary clan lived out of state. It was possible that she'd stashed the money somewhere in the house, a hedge against the S&L failures. But if Cat had been paranoid enough to hide twenty grand, she would have hidden three times that. Sixty was what she had once claimed she needed to live here for a year, what with the mortgage, the salary to the caretaker, feed for the animals, taxes, and the vagaries of her profession.

The second item was in the electronic network. Kazaam made it possible for a user to flag the various categories on a particular bulletin board that were frequently accessed. Under Leisure Interests there were fifteen categories that ranged from photography to scuba diving. The two that were flagged were both private: the Florida Actors Guild, which he'd originally found under Professional Interests, and something called Adult Topics. When he accessed it, a brief explanation appeared on the screen:

Adult Topics provides a forum for sensitive issues. Membership costs an additional $30 a month and the usual prime-time and non-prime rates. For information on how to join, contact *Sugar/Adult* through the BB or by E-mail.

At the prompt, he tapped the ENTER key and the computer requested a handle. Easy enough. He entered:

Cat
Handle?

Not so easy, after all. He sat there thinking about it, plundering his memory for nicknames she'd had through the years, roles she'd played, characters in books she'd

141

loved. It was Claire, the woman she'd played in *Magenta Nights*, that got him in:

1. Categories
2. Topics
3. Set category
4. Reply
5. Exit bulletin board
6. Change handle
7. Feedback to Sugar
8. Ignore category

McCleary hit number one. The eighteen categories encompassed everything from erotic literature and films to a group discussion for survivors of rape, incest, and abuse. All had *private* next to them and one, Married Lovers, was flagged. He keyed it in and started reading the posts on the bulletin board.

Sugar, the topic contact, had started the topic over a year ago when her relationship with a married man had started to unravel. It wasn't clear to McCleary whether she'd been asking for advice or using the bulletin board as a confessional, and it didn't seem to make much difference. The topic had engendered more than fifty responses from other men and women in similar situations.

As he read through them, he realized there was a certain intimacy involved in this sort of exchange among strangers. You could turn yourself inside out without fearing ridicule or judgment. Since no one used his or her real name, anonymity was protected. Although notes were posted by individuals, it became obvious that the group was larger than its components, that the whole was greater than the sum of its parts. The group was your support system.

Cat's postings began eight months ago and at first, they were simply responses to other people's pain. *I think you should . . . I know how you feel . . .* Then, slowly, other elements had begun to creep in, a certain sadness, a trace of resignation, and, finally, a few facts.

The man Cat had been seeing had been separated when she'd met him but had apparently still been sleeping with his wife, a fact he'd neglected to mention. She found out by accident (she didn't say how), and when she confronted him, he swore the marriage was dead, that he was just going through the motions because his wife needed him right now. The group unanimously agreed that she should terminate the affair; she didn't.

I can't. My addiction to him is too deep. She'd written that on February 12, five days before Ellie was born, before he and Cat had shared a soda outside the room where Quin was in labor. She'd never given the slightest indication that she was in any sort of distress.

In early March, when she'd returned to Gainesville after helping out with Ellie, she'd noted that things had improved in her absence. But by summer she was despairing again: The man and his wife had reconciled and Cat continued to see him.

In early September she'd made a cryptic entry about how she hoped to even out the balance in the affair by her involvement in something called Masquerade. One of the respondents, a distinctly male voice who called himself Star Thrower, seemed to know what she was talking about. It was evident they'd discussed it at length in the private electronic mail.

I don't believe you're going to find any answers in anonymous sex, Claire, and I don't give a damn how avant-garde these people think they are.

Cat had taken offense and hadn't posted anything else until four days before she'd been killed.

Hey, Star Thrower, you'll be delighted to know I'm out of Masquerade. It got too weird, even for me. I'm not entirely free of my addiction, but I think I'm better.

McCleary exited the bulletin board and navigated to the E-mail menu. He made a search for Star Thrower, hoping his real name and address were in the mail directory. The only thing he found out was that Star Thrower lived in Honolulu.

Which eliminated Thrower as the author of the anonymous note posted the night Cat had been killed but didn't eliminate him as a possible source. McCleary sent him a brief and straight forward message: who he was, that Cat had been murdered, that he needed information about Masquerade, to please call. McCleary gave the number at the farm and promised him continued anonymity. When the message was sent, a note appeared, advising him that Star Thrower's E-mail was presently inactive and the letter couldn't be posted. In other words, McCleary thought, Thrower either hadn't paid his bill or was probably out of town.

He logged off and a great sorrow moved through him like a wall of water through a house. He began to weep, his fists pressed hard against his eyes. His favorite sister, his baby sister, the sister who was most like him in the ways that counted, had turned to the comfort of strangers.

When he opened his eyes, the light fell in dirty gold squares across his hands and the air had changed. It was noticeably cooler, as if the struggling AC window unit in the living room had suddenly found new life and was pumping twice its weight in air-conditioning in a valiant attempt to cool down the rest of the house. Flats, curled beside his chair, lifted her head and whimpered. He realized the room was suffused with the scent of his sister's perfume.

It seemed to float around him, an invisible ship that carried innumerable memories, all of them pleasant. He didn't question its source. It enveloped him, the scent, the uncanny silence, the light that seemed to come from everywhere and nowhere, a tidy package of fine and tenuous connections.

It left the room gradually, as though with reluctance, and in the end there was only the heat of the light against his knuckles.

13

(1)

ANDY HAD NEVER been to Cubanito's place but imagined that it would be several notches above student housing. She guessed the neighborhood would consist of small, old houses, the kind where the plumbing was ancient and sometimes failed, where hedges sometimes went untrimmed, where lawns sometimes were overtaken by weeds. There would be a certain carelessness about the way people lived, a feel of impermanence to the air, as though most everyone had only paused here en route to somewhere else. Somewhere better.

But it wasn't like that at all.

The homes were large and old, the fashionable kind of old that yuppies bought for a song, gutted, and refurbished. Yards weren't merely trimmed, they were landscaped, sculpted with an artist's eye for color, nuances, attention to detail. The trees were uniformly beautiful, thick and grand, trees that shaded and protected and had stories to tell. Cubanito's home looked as if it belonged to a professor who had reached the highest rung in his particular specialty, a man pulling in three times what Kliner paid him to manage the bookstore.

She swung into the half-moon driveway and stopped behind Cubanito's restored VW van. A calico cat was crouched on the front porch eyeing several birds that swooped, singing, through the water twirling from the sprinklers. A hammock, strung between a pair of willow trees, stirred in a faint, warm breeze.

Cubanito looked as if he'd just rolled out of bed in the clothes he'd worn last night: baggy white cotton slacks, a stained blue T-shirt, sweat socks, no shoes. The ends of his bushy mustache drooped. He held the fuel that he claimed got him started every morning: a mug of Bustelo coffee and a cigarette. But his voice reflected none of the disarray. It was pure staccato.

"Andy, *mí amor*. What a surprise. Come in, please, come in. Would you like coffee? Tea? Something cold to drink? Breakfast? I was just going to fix breakfast. Pancakes. Waffles. Something wicked, eh?"

She laughed and patted her hips. "No pancakes for me, Cubanito. Just coffee. I wasn't sure whether you'd already left for work, but I decided to take my chances."

"Today I go in at one. I like that, my mornings free to sleep and drink coffee and read the paper. Small pleasures. Necessary pleasures."

He led her through a Spanish-style living room where the expensive furniture was dust free and the white carpet had never known feet, bare or otherwise. The walls were decorated in African masks and vibrant weaves from Guatemala called *huipiles*. Pottery lined the top of a bookcase under the picture window. There was nothing random in this room.

"This place is great," she said.

He made a swift, impatient gesture with his hand. "I bought the house in a foreclosure, eh? Very good price, but *dios mío*, it still needs much work. So I do things a little at a time, a rug in one room, a piece of furniture for another. My forever project."

He chattered as he moved around the spacious kitchen, a man who might be consumed by his own energy if he stayed in one spot too long. He poured her a mug of coffee and prepared a platter of croissants. Everything laid out was of Waterford crystal: sugar bowl, creamer, bowl of jelly, a pitcher of honey. The delicate spoons and knives were sterling silver. She'd eaten out with him often enough to know that the trappings of a restaurant were often more important than the food that was served, but this was ridiculous. Crystal and silver with breakfast? What was next, an extensive wine list? Caviar as an hors d'oeuvre?

In time, his monologue about the house ran its course and he remarked that he hoped she'd changed her mind about the book. "But knowing you, you probably haven't, right?"

"Not yet."

He shook his head. "You're very stubborn, Andy."

"So my ex was fond of telling me. You know anything about a psych prof named Richard Farmer?"

"Farmer. Sure." His frown threw his bushy brows into odd angles over his eyes. "His parents used to own Farmer Books, his courses are popular on campus, and when he orders something from us, he does it mostly by phone. At the beginning of the semester he ordered three hundred copies of *Home Before Dark*."

"What's he like?"

"Seems okay, doesn't say much, likes his expresso hot and strong. Why?"

"He's acting as a consultant for the sheriff's department on these homicides."

"Yeah? I heard he's considered an expert in the kinky-crime shit. I also hear he's got a way with women."

"Who told you that?"

"These cute little freshmen come into the store for books he's recommended in class, giggling about how good-looking he is, how smart he is, how wonderful he is. He could tell them to read the Dick and Jane books and they'd do it, you know?"

"Any rumors about him?"

Cubanito grinned. "You looking to discredit him, *mí amor*?"

"Just curious."

"I've never heard that he screws his students or anything, if that's what you mean. He was married a long time ago, but his wife was killed, some sort of accident at home. As far as I know, he hasn't remarried."

"You think he'd be receptive to my asking him questions about these homicides?"

"Probably not."

"Thanks for the encouragement."

"You asked, *mí amor*. But you've got two things in your favor: he likes your books and you're female. It's worth a try, no?"

"Do you have a class schedule booklet handy?"

"Yeah, somewhere. Be back in a minute."

When he left the kitchen, Andy got up for a coffee refill. The adding machine in her head tallied the cost of the extras just in this room alone. Mexican tile floor: a grand, easy. Over-the-stove microwave: six bills, maybe more. The varnished-pine baseboards, the wallpaper, the track lighting: another grand. She glanced into the living room. The Southwest motif echoed mesas, deserts, dramatic landscapes, magic: Navajo throw rugs, pastel furniture, Indian wall hangings, cactuses in Southwest pots, photos of Monument Valley taken by Ansel Adams.

Either Cubanito was in debt to his eyeballs or he was making a lot more at Phaedra than she thought.

She walked over to the fridge for more cream. The front of it was covered with notes, postcards, to-do lists, snapshots of nieces and nephews. A real estate listing stuck out from the edge of the mess, with an exterior shot of a split-level home on several acres of land. Six bedrooms, full basement, five thousand square feet of space at a price that was ridiculously low by Key West standards. Hell, in Key West, she thought, a one-bedroom would cost this much.

Across the top Cubanito had scribbled: *Three for, one against, make an offer*. At the bottom he'd printed SOLD ON 07/11. She noted the address of the house and the name of the seller. She would look it up at the courthouse when she had time, look it up even though she felt a little guilty about sneaking around like this. But business was business, and she still had the feeling Cubanito was hiding something. You never knew when a serendipitous detail like this might lead to something else. Something bigger.

The doorbell rang. She called out that she would get it, and was surprised to find Tess Schulman on the front porch. Tess in her funny braids, her excessive silver and turquoise jewelry, Tess in jeans, a cotton shirt, and moccasins, looking as uncomfortable in the sunlight as a vampire.

"Hi, Tess. Come on in. Emilio's in here somewhere."

She tipped her sunglasses back onto her head, her bracelets clacking together like castanets. Her dove-gray eyes, although expertly made-up, failed to hide fatigue, anxiety, stress. Her expression was utterly blank; it was abundantly clear that she didn't recall that they'd met briefly the morning after she'd discovered Catherine's body. The morning, Andy thought, when Tess refused to speak to her.

"Have we, uh, met?" she asked as she stepped inside.

"Melody's office. I'm Andrea Tull."

Her thick brows knitted together. "Oh, right." She laughed nervously, sniffed, hooked strands of hair behind an ear. "The writer. Sure." Another small laugh, another sniffle. "Sorry. I don't seem to be doing too well these days on names and faces."

"Happens to me all the time. Emilio should be out in a sec. Would you like some coffee?"

She was twisting one of her little braids around the tip of her finger like a kid. "No, thanks. Uh, listen. I don't want to barge in or anything. I can come back later."

"You're not barging in." *I'm not one of his chiquitas, honey.* "Hey, Cubanito," she called. "Company!"

Minutes ticked by. Tess flitted around the kitchen with the same ennui that afflicted Cubanito, but hers was worse, accompanied by constantly sniffling, as though she were coming down with a cold. A nervous disorder, Andy mused, or some chemical imbalance deep within the brain. Or maybe just the result of too much coke?

When Cubanito appeared, he greeted her with about as much effusiveness as the fizz in a day-old Pepsi.

"Could I, uh, talk to you for a second, Em?" Her eyes flitted to Andy, then away again. Privately? she mouthed, as though Andy were blind.

"Yeah, sure." He offered Andy a stiff, uncomfortable smile, gave her the schedule of classes, then he and Tess stepped into the hallway. A moment later a door whispered shut.

Andy put the schedule in her purse. Lit a cigarette. Glanced into the hall. A little drama, she thought. The world is filled with little dramas. She slipped off her shoes and padded into the hall. Sometimes her gall appalled even her. But snooping and eavesdropping were talents she'd perfected during the last year of her marriage, when she was sure her husband was seeing someone else. He'd denied it, naturally, and she'd discovered that she wasn't above reading his mail, going through his glove compartment, his trunk, his wallet while he slept. And in the end she'd probably known more about the divorcée he was screwing than he had.

The divorcée he had eventually married.

She stopped outside the closed door and heard hoarse, angry whispers that she couldn't distinguish. She pressed her ear to the wood, listening, catching bits of conversation.

". . . kind of short on money," she was saying.

". . . nothing new . . ."

". . . always paid you," she said.

". . . besides the point . . ."

". . . just this once . . ."

". . . bad timing . . ."

". . . please . . ."

". . . Christ . . ."

". . . asked you for a goddamn thing . . ."

A drawer was jerked open, slammed again a few seconds later. ". . . all I've got . . ."

". . . lifesaver . . ."

His voice now cracked like ice: "No, I don't want a fucking line. I want you gone, Tess, and if you ever see that BMW in my driveway again, don't stop."

"You don't have to be so rude about it, Emilio."

"You got any idea who that woman is out there?" he hissed. "She could blow things open so wide, we'd all sink, and you'd be among the first to go, Tess. You got it?"

"Ex-*cuse* me, but let's get something straight. I don't give a shit if you're screwing her or half the women on campus. I don't give a shit who you screw. You seem to have this *very* mistaken idea that just because we went to bed a couple of times I'm puke green with jealousy whenever I see you with someone else, and hon, I got news for you, you just weren't that good. Thanks for the blow."

Andy slipped quickly down the hall, ducked into the bathroom. She shut the door, went over to the toilet,

150

flushed it, turned on the water in the sink, turned it off. She counted to twenty. Slowly. Then she opened the door and walked back into the kitchen. Cubanito was making a fresh pot of coffee.

"Tess left already?" she asked.

"Yeah, sorry about this interruption, *mí amor*. Tess is one of these women who's always . . ." His hand fluttered through the air, as if seeking something to grasp. "Oh, you know, involved in high drama. First her father is seriously ill, then she finds Catherine's body . . ." He shrugged. "She exhausts me."

"Oh, c'mon, Cubanito, I think she's got the hots for you. She seemed to think I was one of your ladies."

"Hey, twice I slept with her, right?" His hand lifted again, faltered, dropped to his side again as if from inertia. "And she's ready to get married. *Es una loca*."

A crazy. As though it were a generic term that applied to any woman who mistook casual sex for something else. Everything about Cubanito suddenly annoyed her: his constant motion, his caginess, his apparent belief that she was stupid. Yes, most of all that.

"Based on the number of times she sniffles per second, I'd say her main problem is going to be plastic sinuses before she hits forty."

"Yeah. Really."

He filled two new mugs. The silence between them was neither truce nor agreement but a tense expectancy, as if they were both sitting in a surgeon's office awaiting the bad news on their respective biopsies.

Andy finally broke it. "So, Cubanito. You dealing?"

The tenseness eased; he seemed relieved that she'd finally asked. "A little here, a little there. Strictly small-time."

Sure. Small-time bought him this house. This tile floor. The designer furniture. The gold jewelry he usually wore. "Was Catherine one of your clients?"

"No way." He shook his head and busied himself with cream, sugar, stirring. "Theatre was her addiction."

"So you knew her pretty well then."

"No one knew her well, except maybe Tess, and they weren't as close as they used to be."

"Why not?"

"Who knows? Shit happens."

For sure. "That's it?"

"That's all I know, Andy."

Cubanito, she thought, would never master the art of lying well.

(2)

Andy's ninety minutes in the university library were well spent. She uncovered a wealth of information on Richard Farmer and the picture that emerged was fascinating.

He was a Gainesville native, and for more than forty years his parents had owned Gainesville's largest independent bookstore, which still stood on the corner of University and Buckman Drive. One marriage, wife deceased, killed in a fall down a flight of stairs, no kids, although his wife was pregnant when she was killed. The death was ruled accidental.

Since Farmer had joined the UF faculty seventeen years ago, at the age of twenty-six, he'd become one of the top authorities in the country on aberrant criminal behavior. He had authored dozens of articles for scholastic journals and had acted as a consultant for state and federal law-enforcement agencies on cases that were yesterday's headlines: Adam Walsh, Christopher Wilder, Ted Bundy, the Green River killer. He was a member of the governor's commission on violent crime and had spent several summers counseling death row inmates at Raiford, which was where he'd met Ted Bundy.

And it was through Bundy that Farmer had achieved his fifteen minutes of fame: inclusion in an article in *People* about serial killers. His photo and Bundy's had appeared side by side, Mr. Sunshine and Rasputin, with a caption that said Farmer was one of the last people to speak to Bundy before his electrocution.

She didn't doubt that Farmer was ambitious. You didn't take on media cases and consent to your photo in *People* unless you were. And perhaps that ambition would squelch any misgivings he might have about discussing the murders with her. As Cubanito had said, it was worth a try.

Farmer's aberrant criminal behavior class met in the auditorium in the psych building at noon. It was an elective open to anyone who'd taken a basic intro course and had a hundred and eighteen students in it, more than half of them women. Andy did a head count twice just to be sure she'd gotten the number right.

He breezed in ten minutes late, six feet of leanness with a face that had undoubtedly stopped a few hearts in its time. Charisma radiated from him like an odor. It hushed the murmur of voices until it was so quiet in the auditorium that a sigh would sound like an explosion. Farmer's eyes swept across the crowd as he stood at the podium, mike in hand, a god about to perform a miracle no less astonishing than the parting of the Red Sea.

Andy sat forward, the recorder whirring in her purse, and strained to catch his first words. It was an involuntary physical response, an anticipation heightened by his silence. Then he cleared his throat and, very softly, started whistling "Dixie." The quick staccato notes flew from the speakers and struck the stillness, hail against glass, conjuring images of some poor barefoot Confederate shuffling down a dusty road with his rifle resting on his shoulder, a Southern mansion looming like a mirage behind him.

An explosion of laughter erupted from the crowd.

Before it had quieted, Farmer had left the podium and strode up the far aisle like a talk-show host, Geraldo on the warpath. "The purpose of that demonstration was to illustrate how our expectations about behavior are molded by our conditioning, by the ways in which society expects us to respond to a given situation. When someone doesn't act the way we expect him or her to, it shocks us, temporarily disorients us.

"So let's apply that to Ted Bundy. We don't remember him because he killed coeds or because he bit one of them in the buttocks or because he was executed. We remember him because he acted in a way that defied our expectations of how someone who looked like Bundy should act. . . ."

For the next hour, he talked and paced and held a hundred and eighteen people—and Andy—utterly spellbound. No question that he was a showman, with a manic comedian's wit and energy. If the university ever yanked Farmer from the faculty, Andy thought, the psychology program would collapse faster than a trailer park in a hurricane.

He opened the floor to questions and fifty hands shot into the air. The class was supposed to be ninety minutes long; it went on for two hours. No one left. When he finally called it quits, she walked to the front of the auditorium, where Farmer was gathering up his belongings. He was fielding questions from a handful of students, still charming them blind, but the strain was starting to show. He was not as quick to smile, not as patient.

The group dwindled to four students and Andy. Farmer said he was sorry, he really had to get going, would they hold their questions until the next class? Then he snapped his briefcase shut and headed for the aisle. She caught up with him just outside the door, fell into step beside him.

"Could I speak to you for a minute. Dr. Farmer?"

He didn't stop, but he glanced at her, frowned slightly. Up close, his face was as exquisite as his voice, chiseled from something immortal like granite or maybe diamonds. There was nothing personal in his gaze, but she felt it all the way to her toes, a strange, discomfiting warmth, as if she'd been sunbathing in the nude.

"It'll have to wait until next week. I'm . . ." He paused. "You're Andrea Tull."

She smiled, pleased that he'd recognized her. "I sat in on your class. It was . . ." What? Brilliant? Hypnotic? Definitely. But she wasn't about to fawn over him. ". . . unusual."

"That sounds so guarded," he said with a laugh.

"It wasn't meant to. I was impressed."

"We have fun in there." He began moving again. "You know as well as I do that there's a morbid fascination with serial killers, with Bundy as the most romanticized. He received literally thousands of love letters when he was on death row. After his death, I got letters

154

from women who claimed to be in love with him and wanted to talk to me just because I was one of the last people to talk to him. Go figure.''

"Nothing to figure." They stepped outside. The light hurt her eyes and she slipped on her sunglasses. "It's easier for people to think of him as an extraordinary man who was diabolically clever and driven by forces the rest of us don't understand. It removes him from us.''

"Bundy *was* clever.''

"So was W. C. Fields.''

He laughed again, looked at her again, but this time she knew he actually saw her and liked what he saw. "You have time for some coffee?''

"I thought you were in a hurry.''

"If I don't tell my students that, they follow me to the cafeteria.''

It was uttered without self-consciousness, a fact. "The Pied Piper of Gainesville.''

"Only of the psych department.''

Their discussion about Bundy continued throughout their stroll to the Market Street Pub. People on bikes sped past them. They were jostled by students on foot, shoppers, businessmen in coats and ties. The streets suddenly seemed as crowded as Tokyo's.

They took a booth at the back of the bar, away from the noise of the jukebox. Sitting across from him, she realized he was a fastidious man, as bad as her cats. The lay of his collar was perfect. His hair was trimmed just so. His navy-blue slacks retained their pleats. He didn't seem to sweat. When he stirred his coffee, it didn't splash over the sides of the cup and pool in the saucer. He took a cigarette when she offered it, lit hers, then his, and none of the ashes dropped to the table.

She discovered that the intensity of his gaze was as fixed as the rotation of a planet around the sun. It bothered her. It made her aware of her own appearance—the hastiness with which she'd braided her hair this morning, the wrinkles in her shirt, her extra pounds. She felt like apologizing for the way she looked.

But then he started to talk again, and, like his students, she was sucked into his story, his magnetism. The way he'd met Bundy was pretty much what she'd read, but far more personal. He had actually counseled Bundy during his summer at Raiford, prepared him for the denial of his final appeal, prepared him for death.

"Ironically, Ted had a real fear of dying."

Ted, the psychopath next door.

"I guess we met half a dozen times before he was electrocuted."

"Did he confess to any murders that he wasn't tried for?"

Farmer's smile was brilliant, secretive, a flash of sunlight on water. "Is it going in your book?"

"The book isn't about Bundy."

"That doesn't really answer my question." Shadow and light flickered across his face, changing it. His smile didn't touch his eyes.

"It won't be included if you don't want it to be."

"For now let's keep it off the record."

"Okay."

He grinned. "That's it? Just okay?"

"You want me to put it in writing?"

"That was a joke, Andrea."

Her name had never sounded so lovely, so different, so goddamn exotic. "Oh." She laughed, feeling young and foolish. On the jukebox Roy Orbison crooned about the lonely; she'd never been less lonely in her life. "So go on."

"In the beginning, Ted talked about murder the way we are. Like he was an interested observer. Then gradually his talk became more personal, but he still referred to himself in the third person. And yes, to answer your question, he did admit to committing several murders for which he wasn't tried."

Andy waited for him to elaborate, and when he didn't, she turned the conversation away from Bundy. "What about the Gainesville killer?"

"I'm working on these homicides with the sheriff's department and I'm not permitted to discuss them with the press."

"I'm not the press. And we're still off the record. Do you think he's a serial killer?"

"I really can't—"

"This is for me, all right? I won't use your name. I won't quote you directly. I'll put that in writing, too, if you want."

He sat forward, fingers laced together, his smile bright and patient. Roy Orbison's voice drifted away like smoke. There was only Farmer's voice, hushed, intimate, throaty. "I think we're looking at the classic serial killer, but there are a number of people who'll disagree with me on that point."

"Like Detective Bristol?"

"Yes. They think he's a spree killer, that he has some connection to his victims."

"I don't know about the label, but I agree that he has some connection to his victims. And he's got some weird hang-up with hands and hair."

Despite the constancy of Farmer's expression, she recognized astonishment when she saw it, and it blazed briefly in his eyes. "Where did you hear that?"

"From the horse's mouth."

"Bristol?"

"Hardly. He can't stand me."

"Then who?"

"Off the record?"

"Of course."

"The killer."

His silence coincided with that of the jukebox. He blinked, sat forward, hands gripping his cup. "Have you gone to the police?"

"No. Bristol's made it clear he doesn't want me within ten miles of his office, and if I went to him, he'd claim credit for everything."

Farmer smiled. "I think I hear the echoes of competition and ambition."

The remark made her bristle. "It's a little more complicated than that."

"I'm sure it is. It was just an observation, not a judgment. Tell me about the calls."

So she did, but she didn't mention her tapes of their conversations. She implied that Catherine had been seeing someone but didn't divulge that she believed it was

Bristol. She told him about the blatant change in the pattern of last night's call, about the Barbara connected to a newspaper, but didn't disclose the riddle that had led her to the conclusion.

"But there've only been two homicides," he said.

"It's a false lead. There isn't any slender brunet who works for a Gainesville newspaper."

"You checked all of them?"

"What all? They're only two, the *Star* and the *Sun*."

"There're literary magazines, corporate newspapers . . ."

"No, I'm pretty sure he meant a regular newspaper."

"You can't be sure of anything when you're dealing with a nut."

"Well, I'm sure of this."

"But why?"

"Richard, what's black and white and read all over?"

"A newspaper. But what's that got to do with anything?"

"It's what he asked me. When we were kids, that was the most popular riddle on the block and it referred to the newspaper that landed on your front porch every morning."

"I think I missed something."

"Look, it's a game to him, okay? He calls me. He scares me. But I listen. I don't go to the cops and he knows it. In this game there are certain ways to cheat that're fair. Planting false leads is fair. Not telling me everything is fair. But it wouldn't be fair for him to use the riddle and mean anything other than a newspaper that's delivered to your house every morning. He would see that as unfair as amputating these women's hands without using novocaine."

He seemed bemused by her conclusions. "Okay, let's see. In your framework, then, the personal objects he arranges at each scene are false leads."

"Yes."

"Totally irrelevant to the murders."

"I think so, yes."

"And the bleach? How does that figure? Is it another false lead?"

"Absolutely not. I think he's terrified of contamination, of disease, of death by disease."

"He told you that?"

The jukebox stopped and the quiet drone of voices grew around them, cool and damp like fungus. "No."

"Then how can you be sure? He could just be trying to mislead the police about what kind of person he is."

"Maybe, but I don't think so."

"And the circle of laundry detergent?"

"Cleanliness again."

He looked disappointed. "That's it?"

"Well, it could be part of the ritual of the killings."

"More specific than that."

She thought of Catherine's interest in the occult, of rituals, of incantations. "A magical circle?"

He nodded. "Yes, I think so. A circle of protection."

"The victim inside the circle as she was killed? Or as her hand was amputated?"

"Maybe, yes."

And the circle as a symbol of protection against germs, she thought. A circle for the killer's protection, a kind of amulet like a rabbit's foot. Yes, this had the right feel. Their waitress brought the check and she glanced at the time. "I'd love to sit here the rest of the afternoon, but I've got a class in twenty minutes."

"I need to get going, too." He picked up the check. "C'mon, I'll walk you back to campus."

Outside, the light seemed brighter, the heat more intense. He touched her elbow as they crossed the street and chose that particular moment to compliment her on *Home Before Dark*. "It's the best in-depth look at the female criminal mind that I've ever come across. I've made it required reading in all my courses."

"Music to an author's ears."

He laughed. "When will this book be coming out?"

"I've got to write it first."

"Without an ending?"

"Oh, it'll have an ending." If it didn't, she wouldn't have a book.

"You're always so certain about everything." It sounded wistful, the way he said it.

"Only about some things."

"So it'll be . . . what? Two years before the book is published?"

"More or less." They were on the other side of the street now and he hadn't let go of her elbow. She liked the feel of his hand, his palm warm and dry against her skin. "Far enough in the future so these murders will be ancient history to the sheriff's department."

"Then I guess we'll have to have lunch sometime soon and talk on the record."

The warmth of his presence rushed around her heart, squeezing it. She didn't like the way it made her feel and was relieved when he left her at the steps of the English department. Relieved, but just the same Andy watched him walk off through the crowd. She could still feel the shape of his hand against her elbow and imagined she would still be able to feel it tonight and maybe tomorrow, too.

14

(1)

THE AFTERNOON WAS hot and still and noisy with the cries of crickets. Light poked through holes in the curtains of Spanish moss and glistened against the tinsel hanging from the branches of last year's Christmas tree.

In South Florida, even in the midst of summer, the heat was mitigated by an ocean breeze, McCleary thought. But here it seemed to be landlocked, trapped under the blue dome of the sky, the sun burning through it, baking everything it touched. It made him wish for a hammock, a cold beer, a book he could get lost in.

He hesitated on the ramp outside the porch, Flats panting beside him, and wondered if a trip to town was worth the hassle. He wouldn't be hooking up with Quin, who'd called to say she didn't know for sure where she'd be, and he wouldn't be meeting with Ramona the psychic, who was out of town until tomorrow or the day after. But none of this, he knew, had much to do with his reluctance to leave. He blamed it on the scent of his sister's perfume surrounding him so quickly for those few moments in her den. A part of him wanted to believe that if he went back inside and sat at her desk long enough, it would happen again.

Flats butted his leg with her head, as if to say, *Hey, guy, pay attention to me*. She whimpered as he scratched her behind the ears. "You know, girl, I hate that goddamn Christmas tree. What do you say we get rid of it?"

She barked in agreement. McCleary marched down the ramp to the tree, jerked it out of the ground, and carted it over to the trash cans bound for the dump. Tinsel fluttered from the branches. The tired birdfeeder that had stood beside it toppled to the ground and rolled. An unseen bird hit a high note that could shatter crystal.

Mental fingers moved thoughts around in his head like pieces on a chessboard. On one side of the board were Star Thrower and the Married Lovers category on Kazaam. On the other side were the facts Quin had related when she'd called: Lucy Davenport and Jim Kliner sitting with her addled grandmother; Kliner reading *Robinson Crusoe* to the old woman; the grandmother pining in the absence of her good buddy, Vicki Farmer, mother of the shrink who'd profiled the killer.

Then there were other pieces: Masquerade, the withdrawal of twenty grand, Bristol warning him away from Tull, Tull's .38 found here in the yard. These fragments of his sister's life and death were linked somehow, but he couldn't see the connection yet.

A mail truck chugged up the driveway and Flats bounded off to greet it, barking but not fiercely. As the driver hopped out, she leaped at him, her front paws landing squarely against his chest, and slathered his youthful face in kisses. Laughing, he indulged her, then went over to McCleary with a stack of mail in his arms.

"Hi. I didn't know if anyone was here or not, but I figured I'd give it a shot. You family?"

"Catherine's brother. Mike."

He stuck out his hand. "I'm Kevin Davidson. Nice to meet you, Mr. McCleary. I was on vacation and came back and . . . and heard about what happened. I can't tell you how sorry I am. She was a really neat woman."

"Yes, she was." Past tense. He could use it now without experiencing that terrible dry clutch in his throat. "I didn't realize there was mail delivery out here."

"There isn't. It stops at the highway." He held out the bundle of mail. "This stuff was in her post office box in town. She only checked her box once a week or so, and whenever it got too full, I'd bring everything out here. I live just a couple of miles away."

"Thanks, I appreciate it. I'd forgotten all about her mailbox."

He glanced toward the house. "I'd bring the mail and then we'd sit up there on the porch with cold lemonades when it was hot and espressos when it was cold, talking about movies and plays. That's how she was.''

''When did you last see her?''

''Right before I left for vacation, must've been three weeks ago, I guess. I brought out some mail. She seemed, I don't know, sort of down. She wasn't crazy about the play they were doing and I think she was having problems with some of the people she worked with.''

''Did she say who?''

Davidson shook his head. ''Our conversations never got that specific. Is there going to be a funeral?''

''A memorial service in a couple of weeks. I'll give you a call at the post office when I know where and when, Kevin.''

''That'd be great. I'd better get going.''

''Thanks again.''

He patted Flats on the head, strolled back to his truck, and departed with a toot of the horn. McCleary set the mail on the Miata's roof and went through it. Catalogues, bills, flyers. There was only one personal item, a letter postmarked Gainesville on November 3, the day before Cat was killed. It didn't have a return address.

Inside the envelope were a note and a photograph. The picture was of Cat and Bristol, sitting close together on a pier, the sun setting behind them. Her arm was linked through his; he was laughing and shredding bread that presumably he was going to toss to one of the gulls swooping across the top of the picture. They looked as happy as honeymooners.

What surprised McCleary most was his own myopia. The possibility that Bristol was Cat's married man simply hadn't occurred to him. And yet the clues had been there all along—in Flats's attitude toward him, in the ease with which Bristol had moved around the farm that first day, in his references to the turmoil in his marriage.

He unfolded the note.

> You aren't fooling anyone except yourself. I know what's going on and I'm warning you to stay away from him.

163

It was signed by Janet Bristol.

Wronged wife hires detective to follow hubby. Detective takes pictures of hubby with other woman. Proof positive. A real old story, one with infinite variations, none of them pretty.

He started to crumple the note and photo, then realized they were evidence, and slipped them back into the envelope.

We need all the help we can get, Bristol had said.

Righto. Wrap it up fast and tuck it away before anyone discovers the truth.

McCleary returned to the house and called the station. The receptionist said Bristol wasn't in, was there a message? No message, he replied, and hung up. He found Bristol's home address in the phone book, located it on the city map.

Then he was gone, the Miata's tires eating up the road that led from the farm to the rest of the world.

(2)

Despite her years as a private investigator, Quin was still dismayed by the amount of information that was public. Lawsuits and liens, marriages and divorces, what you paid for your house, who owed you money, local arrests, convictions—it was all there at your local county courthouse.

The records at the Alachua County Courthouse weren't as voluminous as Dade's or as organized as Palm Beach's. But she found what she was looking for easily enough. She already knew that when Tess Schulman had left Coconut Grove and moved to Gainesville, she'd bought a two-bedroom house with a small inheritance from an aunt. What Quin hadn't known was that in the nearly four years since, three liens had been slapped against the house. Two of them—a plumbing company and a screening company—were still in effect. They totaled just under $12,000. The third lien, by Tile Roofs, Inc., for nineteen grand and change, had been cleared on May 28.

McCleary had said the $20,000 withdrawal from Cat's

164

account had been made on May 20. It didn't take a genius to figure this one.

On New Year's Eve of this year, Tess had been arrested for DWI. The charge was dropped the following day. Strings pulled in the right places, Quin thought, but by whom?

She continued her search with Melody Burns. No arrests or convictions, no marriages or divorces. She'd never been sued. There were no liens on her home, which had cost her $105,000 two years ago. But shortly before she'd purchased the place, she'd co-owned a house with Jim Kliner, who had bought her out to the tune of fifty grand two years after they'd closed on the property.

This bit of information elevated Kliner from the *coincidence* category to *significant*. She ran a check on him. He turned up clean in the arrest and conviction department. He'd never been married or sued. There were no liens on his house or his business. He owned quite a bit of property in Alachua County, most of it commercial real estate, and the bulk of it had been purchased in the last three years. A strip shopping center here, an office building there. Not megabucks, not a Trump in his heyday by any means, but bucks big enough to make her wonder if she ought to be in the bookstore business.

The last person she checked was Rick Farmer. There was absolutely nothing that raised even a glimmer of suspicion that he was anything other than what he appeared to be: an arrogant and opinionated psychology professor who had made a name for himself in criminology.

She called Tim Benson from a pay phone in the lobby. The wonderful thing about him was that he never questioned why she or McCleary needed the information they requested. He simply got it. So while they were on line, he ran her list of names through TRW, one of the three largest credit bureaus in the country, and through the Motor Vehicle Bureau.

In the credit department, Tess Schulman had maxed out six credit cards to the tune of $42,618.22. She'd missed so many payments on her Visa and MasterCard that her accounts had been turned over to a collection agency. Her DWI arrest had never made it as far as the MVB computer.

Melody Burns had made a few late payments in the last few years, but nothing outrageous. Her credit was considered good. Other than a speeding ticket three years ago, her driving record was clean.

Kliner's credit was gold star all the way, so outstanding, Quin thought, he was probably on every mailing list in the country for new credit cards. His driving record left something to be desired: two moving violations in the last three years, a ticket for not wearing a seat belt, a ticket for an expired registration and license.

By comparison, Farmer was the saint of the group. He had no credit cards, not even a gas card. His only credit was a mortgage and he'd never missed or been late on a payment since he'd purchased his home ten years ago. He'd never gotten so much as a parking ticket. He was so clean, in fact, Benson asked if the guy was for real and Quin laughed and said he was real, all right, and irritating as hell.

From the courthouse, she went to the university library and looked up Farmer in the *Who's Who* for the University of Florida faculty. His entry was impressive and mentioned in passing that he had been widowed in 1983. Vicki Farmer's daughter-in-law who had fallen down the stairs: Wasn't that what Christine Davenport had said?

Quin searched the 1983 index for the *Gainesville Star* until she found a listing for Barbara Farmer. She'd died two years after she and Farmer had married. She'd been thirty-one and pregnant at the time. They'd had no children, her own family was dead, and four hundred people had attended her funeral. The photograph that accompanied the article on page two of the *Star* was of an exceptionally pretty woman with tragic eyes.

Christine Davenport had also mentioned a sister who had died, but Quin didn't know what year it had happened and there was no cumulative index for the newspaper. It was the sort of fact Mrs. LeForge probably had at the tips of her dimpled fingers, she thought, and decided another visit to the Manor Nursing Home was in the cards.

(3)

Rick rubbed his palm against his slacks, rubbed hard and fast as he walked rapidly through the deep shade. But the impression of Andrea's elbow lingered against his skin. That sharpness. That perfect, jointed angle of cool, soft flesh and hard bone.

He didn't allow himself to think too closely about what he'd discovered, about its possible ramifications. But his anger didn't require thought. It moiled, gathering steam, power, the force of a thing that wouldn't be contained for long.

Dirtycocksuckingbitch. Pulling shit like this behind his back, violating the rules they'd agreed upon, bragging to the likes of Andrea Tull. And for what? To prove something? To show him that she called the shots?

To top it off, she'd chosen a woman named Barbara as their next victim, the name of his dead wife. Her private little joke.

His many and varied selves were suddenly clamoring for attention. He quickened his pace as if to outdistance them. But the voices pursued him. Richard the professor said he wasn't about to take the fall for anyone. Ricky, bearer of the Good Life memories, faithful son, trusted friend, muttered that she was just playing with Tull, matching wits with her, don't sweat the small shit, man. Richie the lover laughed it all off and asked who was at the helm here, anyway? Rick the killer whispered, *Cover your ass.*

He walked faster, the sun hot against his back, his soiled hand crawling with Tull's germs, so many germs, he shouldn't have touched her. At this very moment, the germs were marching across the surface of his skin, burrowing into creases, attaching themselves to hairs, sliding up under his nails, seeking a scrape, a tiny cut, an orifice through which they could enter his bloodstream. He knew how they behaved. He'd watched them under microscopes in medical school, had seen them swimming in drops of blood no larger than a pinhead, had studied them as they multiplied.

As soon as he stepped into the cool safety of his house, he raced upstairs, tore off his clothes, leaped into the shower. He scrubbed himself down with a strong soap, then with pHisoHex, then used a Betadine solution on his hands. When he finally got out, his skin literally squeaked and he felt much calmer. Calm enough to call her, his princess, his little whore, his betrayer.

How sweet she sounded over the phone, how guileless, her hello soft and breathless.

"It's Rick."

"I was just thinking of you."

Thinking what? "How about if we meet at the Island Hotel for dinner tomorrow night around six?"

"Great. I should be able to get away. You want to stay overnight?"

"Can't. Got an early class the next day."

"We could drive back in the morning."

Usually, the overnight stays had suited him. But not this time. "I'd rather not."

Her irritation radiated like heat through the electrical impulses that connected them. "Then what's the point of driving all the way out to Cedar Key if we're not going to stay overnight?"

"A surprise."

"Oh?" Her voice softened again. "What sort of surprise?"

He knew she was thinking in terms of a ring, a proposal, a formalization of their affair. It pleased him that in some ways she was still quite predictable. "If I told you, it wouldn't be a surprise."

She laughed. "See you tomorrow at six, then."

Rick hung up the receiver and walked over to the closet. He moved his shoe rack to the side and peeled back a square of carpeting, exposing a floor safe. He keyed in the combination, opened the lid. The stacks of bills inside were mostly in hundreds and five-hundreds and were bound in packets of $2,500. There was fifty grand here and another fifty grand socked away in safe investments, money he'd been stashing away for seventeen years. Some of it he'd inherited when his father had died, the rest of it had come from his paychecks, fifteen percent of his monthly income, his hedge against disaster.

Rick removed the stacks carefully, reverently, and lined them up to his right, straightening them, fussing with them, flipping through them. When he was a kid, Mother was always harping about how filthy money was, passing through so many hands that had been God only knew where. But the germs on money had never bothered him. Like the germs on dishes and utensils in restaurants, on handholds in buses and trains, like germs in public bathrooms, the germs that flourished on money were impersonal, prosaic, and therefore couldn't harm him. These germs were meant for ordinary people.

He emptied the safe of money, revealing a stash of weapons. Which one for tomorrow night? The Swiss Army knife? The dagger with the gold-plated handle? His grandmother's scissors? The Smith & Wesson .38? The Magnum? He picked out the scissors, which were small, compact, and fit into a leather case. They were ideal for snipping a lock of hair and not much else.

Rick finally settled on the dagger. He liked the way it felt when he held it and the gleam of its handle, unspoiled by smudges, fingerprints, the ravages of age. He liked the sleek curve of its blade, its sharpness. The end of it boasted a fine point like a needle. He'd bought it in a pawn shop in Miami years ago, not long after he was married. He remembered his wife wrinkling her nose at the musty smell in the shop, the dim light, the hairy fellow who'd taken the dagger out of the display case.

Why do you want an ugly thing like that, Ricky? He could still hear her voice, the disapproval, the bafflement, the pitch that was nearly a whine. *It's so useless.*

Useless, Christ. What the hell did she know?

He set the dagger down beside the pair of scissors, then removed the old aluminum box it had been resting on. It was perfectly square, the violet of a morning sea, decorated with dozens of tiny silver cats. It had belonged to Mother's mother, and it was where she'd tucked away money, amulets, jewelry, her cigarettes. The latch was brass and the lid squeaked when he opened it.

Among the valuable items inside were: his original diplomas; his first driver's license; a family snapshot taken the summer his sister, Josie, had died; a copy of his first paycheck as a full-blown professor; his correspondence with Ted Bundy; an autumn leaf his sister had pressed and waxed onto a piece of paper for him; and locks of hair. Mother's hair and Josie's, hair from both of his grandmothers, one dark lock salted with gray, the other bone white. If he ever had a daughter, some of her hair would be added to the collection.

Here, too, were the strands of hair he'd taken from Catherine and Lucy, and from other women, other victims, all long dead. The beauty of hair, he thought, was that it remained the same as the day you'd cut it. The color and texture of hair were unchanged by death. Hair endured like initials carved in stone.

Rick picked up the cluster of white hair. It had come from his father's mother, the woman he favored physically. When he touched it, pressing it against his cheek, and inhaled the faintest scent of lavender, he connected with his memories of her. Sweet memories, a child's memories, all of them vividly detailed, as though they'd happened yesterday. That's how it was with him and hair. A touch, a whiff, and everything about a particular woman returned to him, his history with women preserved in their hair.

He removed a single strand from the cluster and tucked it under a flap in his wallet. For luck. For whatever. Then he returned everything to the aluminum box, put the box in the safe. A few minutes later, whistling softly, he stood and studied his clothes, trying to decide what tomorrow night called for.

(4)

The Bristol home was a split-level ranch on a shaded street of nearly identical homes. Jungle gyms and swings grew from the emerald lawns, trikes and bikes stood waiting in the hot sun, Volvos and station wagons slumbered at curbs and in driveways.

This was a neighborhood, McCleary thought, where the families knew each other well enough for barbecues and picnics, and everyone probably attended the same church. Middle-class America hunkered down under the weight of mortgage payments and car payments and kids. Life lived on credit.

A school bus stopped at the end of the street, belching black smoke and kids who scattered into loose groups as soon as they hit the sidewalk. McCleary remembered walking to the end of the long road where his folks lived to meet Cat's bus after school when she was ten. He could still smell the stink of the bus's exhaust, hear the hiss of its brakes and the whisper of its front door as it opened. Cat had bopped down the street to greet him, her ponytail bouncing, her grin as wide as the outdoors.

He wondered if this memory, so bright and vivid now, would diminish or change as he grew older or perhaps fade altogether. His bout with amnesia several years ago had made him particularly appreciative of the complexity of memory, its labyrinths, the tricks it could play. He wanted, suddenly, to preserve his recollections of Cat on tape, on paper, it wouldn't matter. Then, in fifteen or twenty years, she would be more to his daughter than just photographs in a family album.

He started up the walk to the house. Bristol's Pontiac wasn't in the driveway, but a Volvo station wagon was. Leaves from a nearby hickory tree tracked across its pale hood like muddy footprints. As he rang the bell, a sandy-haired kid with freckles strode up the sidewalk, a knapsack on his back. He was a miniature Bristol, right down to the flat blue eyes.

"Hi," he said, all smiles. "You selling something?"

McCleary laughed. "Nope. I'm looking for your dad."

"He's at work, but Mom's home. She's probably out back in the garden. C'mon, I'll take you. You seen the new Ninja movie?"

"Not yet."

"Boy, it's awesome. Dad and I went last weekend."

Comic-book heroes. In his day, it was the guy from Krypton. Now it was streetwise turtles.

They went around the side of the house and into the backyard. Everywhere he looked there were roses, red and pink and white, large and small. Roses bloomed on thick, lustrous bushes and blanketed a trellis that covered the concrete patio. The air was redolent with their perfume.

A short, slender woman in tight denim cutoffs, a pink tank top, and a floppy straw hat was perched at the top of a ladder at the trellis, clipping dead leaves.

"Hi, Mom," the boy called.

"Hi yourself, big guy." She glanced around, most of her face hidden in the hat's shadow. "Who's your friend?"

"I'm Mike McCleary, Mrs. Bristol."

Even from where he stood he saw her jaw tighten. She descended the ladder and strode over, using the end of the clipper to tip her hat back farther onto her head. The fine lines of middle age added depth to an attractive face and deepened when she smiled at her son.

"Your snack's on the kitchen table, sweetie. And don't forget to put your dishes in the washer when you're done."

He bounded off with a wave. She gazed after him for a moment with an expression McCleary couldn't decipher, the light holding her profile like the lens of a camera. Then she looked at McCleary. "My husband's not home right now, Mr. McCleary. You can reach him at the station downtown."

McCleary brought out the note and the photograph. "I think these belong to you."

"Sent in haste, I'm sorry to say." She extended her hand. "I'd prefer that Steve not see those."

He slipped them back into his pocket. "I'd like some answers, Mrs. Bristol."

"I'm sure you would. But I'm not the person to give them to you. If you'll excuse me."

She brushed past him and he stared at her back, at the blonde ends of her curly hair poking out from under the hat, at the perfect curve of her buttocks. "How do you think Steve will react when I tell him you hired someone to follow him?''

A dirty blow, but it got her attention. She spun around. "Don't threaten me, Mr. McCleary. I hate to be the one to tell you, but your sister was a slut.''

Slut. Jesus. He hadn't heard that word in at least twenty years. He laughed, which only infuriated her.

"I'm glad you find it so amusing.'' She tossed the clippers into a patio chair and scooped a pack of Winstons off the steps. "What she failed to realize was that she just filled a gap for Steve while he and I were separated. She was filler, Mr. McCleary, like the goo in an Oreo cookie.''

It wouldn't take much to dislike this woman. "Then why didn't he stop seeing her when you two reconciled?''

"He was afraid she might go off the deep end.''

"If you really believed that, you wouldn't have sent Catherine the note and the photograph.''

She didn't answer. A tiny cloud of smoke floated around her face. The scent of roses thickened in the heat, nauseating him.

"He was still seeing her when she was killed, wasn't he?''

Her face started coming undone, a slackening here, a loosening there, and her tan shoulders stooped beneath the burden of her secrets. "Yes.'' The word seemed to get lost in the folds of heat.

"And he knew that you knew it.''

"Yes.'' She stared at a point over McCleary's left shoulder. Her eyes were glazed but not watery. She was the kind of woman who grieved in private. "The night she was killed, he got a call around nine-thirty or ten, I think it was. He said he had to run over to the station, but I knew it didn't have anything to do with work. So I followed him. He met her at Farrah's. I saw them leave together. I knew they were going to her place, so I turned around and went home.''

"And you're still living here?'' he blurted out.

Fury seized her face and shook it. "Steve didn't kill her, Mr. McCleary. He isn't capable of it.'' She spat the words, as though vehemence would convince him—and herself—that she wasn't living with a murderer. "And it's time for you to leave. Get off my property."

He ignored her warning. "What time did he get home that night?"

"Get. Off. My. Property."

"You don't remember or you don't know, Mrs. Bristol? Which is it?"

She dropped the cigarette she'd been smoking, crushed it under the heel of her shoe. "I'm calling the police." She started for the door and McCleary went after her, grabbed her none too gently by the arm, spun her around. She was so astonished, she just stood there, blinking, staring at him as though she expected him to pull a gun on her.

"You weren't even here, were you," he rushed on, and saw her flinch. "You were too angry to be here when he got back, right, Mrs. Bristol? So you took your son and went somewhere. Which means Steve doesn't have an alibi for that night and you don't exactly know what to do about it, do you? And the more time that passes, the more the details of that night blur for you. In ten years, you'll have convinced yourself that he was never involved with my sister."

He didn't see it coming. She slapped him with her open hand, slapped him so hard across the face that it rang out against the stillness in the yard with the clarity of a shriek. Then she ran for the door, ran for it as if to outdistance the truth of what he'd said.

McCleary's cheek stung. Stars floated through his eyes. The heat wrapped around him like a wet towel. A faint breeze stirred the roses on the trellis just above his head and their sweetness reached him again, smothering him. He walked to the front of the house, across the emerald lawn where the air smelled of mown grass, and waited to feel a sense of completion, of triumph. But it wouldn't come.

If Bristol had killed Catherine, then he had also killed Lucy Davenport. Or he'd made sure the MOs matched so that it would look as if the murders were committed by the same person. Bristol was probably the last person to see her alive and he had no alibi. It was enough to charge him with homicide. But when McCleary tried to visualize him cutting off her hand, washing her down with bleach, the image just wouldn't form.

He pulled away from the curb with the cloying stink of Janet Bristol's roses thick in his clothes and the imprint of her hand bright red against his face.

15

(1)

QUIN STOOD IN the shadows at the back of the theatre watching the rehearsal. It wasn't going well. Tess stumbled through her lines, got flustered, tried to recoup, and failed. Melody kept interrupting, waving her arms like a conductor, barking commands about how the scene was supposed to be played. The more Melody criticized, the more rattled Tess became, and the tension between them crackled like static. Tess finally burst into tears and flew off the stage. Melody told everyone to take a break and went after her.

When they didn't return, Quin strolled down the aisle as though she had every right to be here and slipped backstage. People milled in the hall, smoking and laughing and sipping endless cups of coffee. A guy experimenting with the lights said Melody had gone "back that-a-way" and stabbed a thumb toward the racks of clothes at the end of the hall. "Probably in Costumes," he said.

The door to Costumes was shut. Quin pulled one of the clothing racks closer to her, a shield that would block her from view from the rest of the hall, and pressed her ear to the door.

Not a sound from inside.

She opened the door, stepped in. A wall of mirrors on her left, more racks to her right, soft lights. She hunkered down between two racks and made her way to the far end of the room, the bright, colorful fabrics rustling with her movements. Voices now: Melody and Tess were arguing.

"If you weren't on my back every five seconds, Melody, I'd do just fine."

"Oh, Tessie, Tessie." Melody let out an exaggerated sigh, as though she was dealing with a precocious but stubborn child. "It's the coke, not me. And if you come to rehearsal high again, that's it, do you understand? You're out and I'll find someone to replace you."

"Replace me?" She burst out laughing. "You haven't even replaced Catherine yet."

Quin straightened up enough to see them in the mirror, facing each other on the other side of the room like adversaries about to engage in physical combat. And yet Melody's voice remained cool, unruffled. "Let me give you some advice, Tess. Catherine's tough to replace. But actresses like you are a dime a dozen on this campus. I could hire some drama student who'd do better at this part than you have. So straighten out if you want to remain with this company."

"You can't fire me. I've got a goddamn contract, Melody."

"And the fine print says you can be fired. Be back onstage in fifteen minutes."

Quin ducked down between the racks again. Melody's shoes clicked against the concrete floor, a steady clicking that didn't miss a beat even when Tess spat, "Fuck you."

The door opened and shut. Air hissed from a vent as the AC clicked on.

"Fuck you and your brother and your mother and your grandparents, too." Suddenly, wheels clattered and hangers knocked together as one of the racks crashed into another and sent it flying halfway across the room. Quin, exposed like a ghost on sensitive film, stood there mute, Tess staring at her.

She lifted her hand and smiled meekly. "Uh, hi, Tess."

"Oh, hey, this is really great." She threw up her hands. "People telling me I'm fucked, people spying on me . . . Yeah, fine, this is just great." She fell back into the nearest chair, unzipped her purse, pulled out a joint, and lit it. Then she crossed her slender legs at the knees and blew smoke in Quin's direction. "Isn't Melody a nice person? Isn't she a *wonderful* director? Welcome to the *real* Sunshine Repertory, Quin. Want a hit?"

"No, thanks."

"I bet Catherine didn't tell you about this part of things, did she? How we're all slaves to Ms. Asshole's whims. I don't know why *she* stayed, she didn't have to. But me, well, hell, with me it's a different story. I was never lucky enough to stumble into a gold mine like *Magenta Nights*, Quin. I didn't have the advantages Cat had right from the beginning, a family like hers, a brother like Mike, supportive people, people you could turn to . . to . . ."

Her voice broke then and tears coursed down her cheeks, smearing her makeup. Quin pulled a chair over next to her, sat down, touched her arm. "Tess, do you know anything about Cat's murder that you haven't told the cops?"

She swiped at her eyes. "Jesus, Quin. Why would I hide something like that? Cat was my closest friend. Do you have any idea what it was like to . . . to find her? To see what he'd done to her? To . . ." She sniffled, rubbed her nose with the back of her hand. "To know how she suffered? She was like my *sister*, for God's sakes."

"And good enough to lend you twenty grand so you could have one of the liens removed from your house."

"How . . . what . . . what're you talking about?"

"Let's not play games, Tess. I know about the liens, the loan, the coke that put you in this mess, and I know Cat was involved in something called Masquerade. One person I talked to called it a dirty pictures group, but I still don't know what it is and I still don't know who killed her and I think you may have the answer to at least one of those."

Her watery eyes widened and she pushed up from the chair with a brief, sharp laugh. "God, I can't believe it. You've been investigating me."

Why was it that people with secrets, people with something to hide, were always so deeply offended when they realized you were poking around in their private affairs? "Well, Tess, considering the loan, I don't know why it should come as any great surprise. People have killed for less."

"Killed?" Tess looked like she'd swallowed a fist. "Is that what you think? That I *killed* her?"

"I don't know." But it was an intriguing thought, that the killer might be a woman. "Did you?"

"That's sick."

Sick rather than *no*.

"I *found* her, for God's sakes."

As though discovery exonerated her.

"Christ, how can you—"

"Did you kill her, Tess? A simple yes or no will do."

"No, Jesus, no, of course I didn't kill her, I loved her, she was . . ."

"Yes, I know. You've already said all that. Tell me about Masquerade. What it is. How often it meets. About Cat's involvement?"

Tess's arms dropped to her sides, a gesture of defeat. She twisted the end of the joint against the wall, putting it out, and dropped it into her purse. "I've got to get back onstage or I'm going to be pounding the pavement for another job." She turned away; Quin caught her arm.

"Tess, please. It won't go any further than us. I swear. Just tell me whatever you know."

"Go home, Quin." Her voice was quiet and tired. "Just bury Cat and go home and enjoy your daughter."

She wrenched her arm free and hurried out. The sweet headiness of the marijuana smoke drifted around her. Quin thought about women who killed. Equality definitely existed where crime was concerned. In fact, except for rape, as it was presently defined, a woman was capable of committing any crime that a man could commit. But the data on which psychological profiles were based, and from which criminal behavioral theories were formed, came from the study of men who killed.

The killer as a woman.

Tess? Melody? Maybe even Andy Tull, who had dropped her gun in the driveway? Who was the expert on female killers? A woman. Yeah, it was something to think about.

(2)

Andy had put herself together for this meeting. She had done away with her braid and fixed tortoiseshell combs in her hair, pulling it away from her face. She had traded her jeans for khaki slacks and a short-sleeved red cotton sweater. Gone were her running shoes; sandals graced her feet. Not exactly Aphrodite, she thought, primping in the Beamer's rearview mirror. Too plump for a goddess. But, hell, she at least looked respectable.

She parked in the trees behind the farmhouse, where the Beamer wouldn't be seen as soon as someone drove in. While she waited, the sky turned from blue to purple. Venus popped out, winking brightly, and a breeze kicked up, redolent with pine and soil and water. It even got a little cooler—not much, but enough to make her long for the eternal balm of Key West.

When she got out of her car, the dog started barking again, its snout smashed against the porch screen, its front paws heavy against it. She walked down the dusty path to see the cows. One of them mooed as she approached the barbed-wire fence and another gazed at her with deep, mournful eyes and allowed her to stroke its ear. She strolled behind the house, where long curtains of Spanish moss stirred in the breeze. The grass, dry despite the rain, popped like corn under her shoes. She lingered at the chicken coop and paid a visit to the sheep and watched a very young lamb suckle from its mother. The simplicity of the act brought a lump to her throat.

She moved on until she reached the barn. Andy threw open the doors. The aroma of hay rushed at her, sweet and thick, inviting her in. She sat on one of the bales, watching the light outside grow dimmer, and thought about what she knew and what she didn't know and decided the latter still outweighed the former.

After a while the dog started barking again, and a few moments later she heard a car.

She pressed her palms to her thighs and stood. She hoped the McClearys were nice people. Reasonable people. Normal people. She hoped, but wasn't placing any bets. After all, she'd already met the wife, and how normal could someone be with a name like Quin?

As Andy came around the far side of the house, she saw a man—Mike McCleary—lifting a baby out of the red Miata. The same baby the woman named Quin had had with her the day she'd asked Andy to autograph her book.

He set her on the ground and laughed when she squealed and pointed at a bird that fluttered from a nearby tree. "That's a bird, Ellie. Can you say bird?"

"Dadda."

"No, bird. I'm Dadda, you're Ellie, and that's a bird."

She giggled, waddled away from him like a drunken sailor, her thumbs hooked in the waistband of her shorts, then tripped and sprawled in the grass. When she lifted her head, she spotted Andy, spotted her while McCleary was hoisting a bag of groceries from the trunk, and shrieked, "Dadda!"

McCleary's head snapped up. He shut the lid, his eyes on Andy. "Hello," he said, moving over to his daughter and grasping her hand. Ellie fell silent, looked up at Andy, then at her father, then at Andy again. "Something I can do for you?"

"I hope so, Mr. McCleary. I'm Andrea Tull."

He smiled. "I've been meaning to return your thirty-eight."

"How—"

"Tim Benson. He and I worked together at Metro-Dade for ten years."

"Small world."

"Very small. There're really only a thousand people in it, but don't tell anyone."

She laughed and he smiled, waiting for her to say something, to explain what she'd been doing here the night she'd lost her gun. When she didn't speak, he scratched at his beard. "If Benson didn't think as highly of you as he does, we wouldn't be standing here. I would have turned your gun over to Bristol as soon as I found it."

A suspect, she thought. That was what he was saying. That if it weren't for Benson, she would be up there on his list of suspects and so what if she wasn't the right gender. "Look, I, uh, well, I was going to break in that night. Detective Bristol hadn't given me any information and I needed to know what had happened. I didn't realize anyone was here."

"Bristol doesn't like you."

"Probably because he's afraid I'd find out he was having an affair with your sister."

She didn't expect him to know about it, but he nodded and moved away from the car. "I'm sure that has something to do with it. C'mon inside. My wife should be home in a few minutes." He scooped up his daughter. "I think the three of us have a lot of notes to compare."

As they walked up the ramp to the porch where the dog was barking, the evening light settled around them, soft and promising.

(3)

"If you'd called ahead, Mrs. McCleary, I could have arranged something, hmm?" said Mrs. LeForge. "But now they're having supper and after supper . . ."

"It won't take long."

LeForge, her hands laced together against her ample stomach, sighed heavily. "They dislike having their routine interrupted, hmm? Like children that way. On top of it, Christine isn't feeling up to par. She apparently remembered that her Lucy is dead and she's quite depressed, depressed even though Vicki is back with us, hmm?" Her arms dropped to her sides and swung there, simianlike. "So you'll have to make it very brief, Mrs. McCleary."

"No problem."

They moved along the hall toward the nursing-home dining room. Quin hadn't eaten anything since the greasy McDonald's burger she'd picked up for lunch; the smell of food turned her hunger inside out. Her stomach growled, a rude sound that was loud enough to be heard in the next county, but LeForge was apparently as deaf as some of her charges. She pushed through the double doors and into the dining room.

The room was large and pleasant. Vaulted ceilings, tall windows, murals on two of the four walls. The dozen teak tables seated a group of about fifty patients, some in wheelchairs, some in heavy teak chairs, each table with a floor lamp burning nearby. Music played softly in the background.

"We try to bring a little dignity to the evening meal," LeForge said.

The home's stab at gracious dining.

But most of the patients seated in the room looked as though they would have trouble remembering their days of gracious dining. Some of them couldn't seem to even remember what utensils were for and fed themselves with their fingers. Others were helped by solicitous attendants, private nurses in crisp white uniforms, a few family members. Some patients drooled and others had fallen fast asleep in their chairs, chins resting against their chests.

The place depressed Quin. She suddenly imagined herself at ninety or a hundred, in a place like this, wearing glasses so thick her eyes looked to be the size of billiard balls, her hearing failing, her taste buds gone. Ellie would visit once a week, a dutiful daughter who brought her newspapers and books she could no longer read and smuggled in home-cooked food that she couldn't taste. She imagined someone like LeForge moving through the corridors of her dimly lit life, murmuring *Hmm? Hmm?* like the refrain of an old song. She imagined sitting in a wheelchair, as ancient as Christine Davenport, but still possessing the capacity to wish that she were dead.

LeForge leaned close to the side of Christine's head and said, too loudly, "Hon, you've got a visitor. You remember Mrs. McCleary, don't you?"

The nurse seated next to her relinquished her chair to Quin, who sat down heavily, gratefully. Christine slowly turned her head. Behind her thick glasses those weary eyes were as empty as a summer sky. Then a light seemed to come on somewhere inside them and Christine's wrinkled mouth wrinkled even more as she attempted to smile.

"Clint's friend," she said.

"Yes, that's right. How are you, Christine?"

"Bad, so bad. Food's terrible, you know." She speared a green bean with her fork and held it up for Quin's inspection. "Would Clint eat this? Would Clint's children eat this? Does Clint have children?"

"Please," groaned a dignified little man on the other side of the table. "No more Clint. You sound like a couple of teenagers."

"Oh, shut up, Hans," said the woman sitting next to Christine. She had white hair that was wild, thick, and long. She looked younger than Christine. "Sometimes the home is for the best."

"The best for whom, Vicki?" asked Hans. "For you? For me? Or for our beloved children?" He exploded with laughter, his head thrown back, his pale, tiny eyes beseeching the ceiling.

"I don't have any children, so I wouldn't know." Vicki pushed away from the table and walked off toward one of the large-screen televisions.

"Now look what you've done, Hans," scolded Christine.

"Well, she *does* have children," said Hans.

Christine ignored him—or didn't hear him—and glanced at Quin. "Could you push me over there, dear? Vicki's not having a good day."

"Sure." Quin was delighted for the opportunity to pick Vicki Farmer's brain.

She was curled up in a corner of the couch, white hair falling around the sides of her face, hiding it, her legs drawn up to the side, folded together in a neat V. Quin parked the wheelchair alongside the couch and sat on Vicki's other side.

"Don't let that old fart bother you none," Christine told her, and gave her arm a maternal pat. "This is my friend . . . Oh, I forgot your name, dear."

"Quin. Quin McCleary."

"Quin, that's right. Her name's Quin, Vicki. She likes Clint, too."

Vicki cupped her chin in her hand and kept staring at the screen.

"Her sister was killed just like my Lucy, isn't that right, Quill?"

"Quin."

"Told her about the long-haired fellow, I did. And the dirty pictures group. Didn't like him much. You didn't either, remember, Vicki?"

"Of course I remember," Vicki replied. "My brain's not ailing, just my heart. I didn't like him any more than you liked Ricky, Christine."

"I liked your boy just fine."

"Did not."

"Did."

"Did not. But it doesn't matter. Sometimes I don't like him much, either." She pointed at the screen. "Would you shoo that moth off the screen, Quin?"

"Moth?"

"Oh, for heaven's sakes," Vicki snapped, and pushed up from the couch, her wild white hair flowing in waves across her shoulders. She hissed, "Shoo, shoo, you awful bug," and fluttered her hands at the empty TV screen. Then she dropped her head back as though she were watching the moth flutter off. She eased back against the cushions again and drew herself up into the same position as before.

"I've met your son, Mrs. Farmer," said Quin. "He's the consulting psychologist to the police department and drew up a profile of the man who killed Lucy and my sister-in-law."

"Killed Lucy." Vicki looked directly at Quin now and her eyes were just like Farmer's, the same odd brown flecked with gold, the same strange intensity. "You say that so easily."

"I didn't mean to."

She drew her gaze to Christine, who smiled and patted her arm again. "I'm okay. I'm fine. It's all right to hear the truth, Vicki. I don't mind the truth. It's the lies I hate."

"Sometimes I think I prefer the lies. So what's the profile say? Ricky's a smart boy, but he's not always right, especially when he's Richard."

"Richard?" Quin asked.

185

"The professor."

"Oh." As though Farmer were several men.

Quin tried to explain the difference between a serial killer and a spree killer, then gave Farmer's opinion. Vicki made an impatient gesture with her hand. "Hell, that serial stuff came straight from Ted Bundy. Ricky corresponded with him for a while, even talked to him right before he was executed. I mean, it wouldn't have surprised me if he'd brought the man home for dinner one night. That's how much he talked about him."

"That's a nice name," said Christine, nodding. "Ted. Yes, I like that. Did you ever wonder why Roosevelt didn't call himself Ted instead of Teddy? It would've been more dignified or something. Look at Kennedy. He's Ted, not Teddy."

"Doesn't help him much," said Vicki. "Ted or Teddy, he still isn't very dignified."

Christine covered her mouth with her hand and giggled. "No, I guess he's not." Then, as if remembering that Quin wasn't here to talk about Teds or Teddys, she said, "Did you have more questions. Quill? About my Lucy?"

"Actually, I was wondering if you could remember anything else about Masquerade."

"I don't believe I've read that book," said Vicki.

Christ, Quin thought. At this rate, she'd be here all night. "The Masquerade I'm referring to is—"

"A dirty pictures group," Christine said. "That longhair wanted my Lucy to join it. She said no."

Vicki Farmer was busy gathering her white, white hair at the back of her head with a rubber band. "Least she had sense enough to do that. There're plenty of things Ricky should have said no to in his life and didn't. But do you think he ever listens to me? Ha. I'm just his mother. But he's always been like that. So has Josie. She's better now about it than he is, though."

Josie, the dead sister.

"She would've picked me up from the hospital except that she . . . she . . ." Confusion flooded her eyes. She rubbed her palms hard and fast against the cushions as her eyes watered, as the tears spilled.

Christine patted Vicki's knee, comforting her. Quin felt like an intruder and turned to leave, but Vicki said, "He's always attracted bad women."

"Who?" Christine asked. "Clint?"

Her question made Vicki irritable. "No, not Clint. My son. Ricky. His wife, Barbara, was bad enough, but then, a year or two ago, there was another woman who had the worst of Barbara in her. Awful woman."

"Did I meet her?" Christine asked.

"No."

"You sure? What'd she look like?"

"Don't recall. I just remember that I didn't like her much."

Nowhere, Quin thought. This was going nowhere. "I'd love to stick around for a while, ladies, but I've got to get home."

"Lucky you," Vicki said.

"Bye-bye now. Be always kind and good," Christine called after her.

LeForge met her in the front lobby. "Was she lucid?"

"More or less. Thanks for letting me see her. I was wondering about something, Mrs. LeForge. Vicki's daughter is dead, isn't she?"

"Oh, my, yes, for many years now, hmm? She drowned in a lake in New Hampshire when they were vacationing one summer. I think she was nineteen or twenty at the time. She was actually quite a good swimmer, but she was alone that day and they think she swam out too far and got tired and couldn't make it back to shore. Sometimes Vicki gets a little confused and thinks Josie is still alive. Such tragedies, hmm?"

They were moving toward the front door. "Was she younger or older than Dr. Farmer?"

"Older, I believe, by several years." Her smile dimpled the corners of her mouth. "Why do you ask?"

"It's sometimes hard to follow what Vicki and Christine are talking about. I was just trying to keep things straight."

"Ah, well, I know just what you mean." She pushed open the door for Quin. "Just give me a little warning next time you want to see Christine."

"I will, thanks."

"Best of luck to you, Mrs. McCleary."

Like it was all a giant craps game, Quin thought, and hurried outside to the Wagoneer.

(4)

The porch, the dark, the breeze rustling branches, the sounds of the night: McCleary waited for these things to obliterate the voice that kept playing in his head, the voice on Andrea's tapes. That rasp, that whispery laughter. *"It was on a farm and there was a lot of fog . . . Washed her afterward with bleach . . . She didn't suffer when I took her hand. . . ."*

Details. The details shouted at him. A woman? Was it possible? Which woman? Tess? Was that Tess's voice on the tape? Was Quin right that the killer was female? Hard to tell from the tapes. They weren't that clear, the person was speaking too softly. A computer analysis might be able to determine the gender of the voice, but he couldn't give the tapes to Bristol. Not now. And if he gave them to Wilkin, she might turn them over to Bristol. No, it would have to be someone else. But who? Who did he know besides them? Who could he trust?

Benson, he thought. He trusted Benson in Miami. He would send him the copies he'd made. If he mailed them FedEx tomorrow, Benson would have them the morning after. It would take a day or two beyond that to have them analyzed. But suppose, in the meantime, this bastard killed a Barbara who worked at a newspaper? Unlikely. Andrea had checked the newspapers and hadn't turned up a slender brunet named Barbara at either newspaper. It was a false lead, the caller playing mind-fuck games.

McCleary went into the bedroom for his sneakers. The night light cast pale, buttery circles against the floor. There was enough illumination for him to see Ellie as she slept, one arm thrown over her head, the other curled up under her chin. *You shouldn't be here.* He would send her and Quin home. Home was six hundred miles south. Home was safe. Home was . . . Hell, who was he kidding? Quin would never leave.

Barking erupted in the yard. Flats had been off hunting for hours, but this wasn't the sound of a huntress returning home with a kill. This was loud, frenzied. Flats enraged, Flats threatened.

McCleary rushed into the kitchen, grabbed a flashlight from the drawer, and ran outside. As he hit the ramp, he heard Ellie crying. The bedroom light came on. He loped past the cars, following Flats's bark toward the front gate. It was shut, but the sheepdog had leaped it, he could hear her somewhere beyond it, hear her and the rumble of a car tearing down the road.

He threw open the gate and charged out, shouting for Flats. The rumble grew more distant and the barks tapered off as the sheepdog limped into the beam of light. She whimpered and plopped at his feet, panting and licking at her right rear leg. When he touched her leg, she growled, a soft, warning growl.

"It's okay, girl. I won't hurt you. Let me just take a look." She whimpered but let him look. She was bleeding from a nasty gash. "Did you miscalculate the height of the fence and catch a nail or something? Who was in the car? Jesus, I wish you could talk. C'mon, let's go back to the house and clean this up." McCleary, veterinarian, he thought.

She tried to get up, but her leg gave out. McCleary lifted her carefully, 140 pounds of dog. She whimpered again and licked his face. The gate swung and creaked in the breeze, and as he caught it with the toe of his shoe, the beam of light hit a piece of paper stuck into the wood with a long nail. Three little bears had been drawn in black crayon and labeled Papa Bear, Mama Bear, and Little Baby Bear. A red X covered the baby bear. Beneath this was:

GO HOME MCCLEARYS.

(5)

The veterinarian had come and gone and Flats was now curled up near the fireplace, on a bed of old blankets Quin had fixed for her. The gash had required eight stitches and the vet, a young guy who had been treating

Cat's menagerie since she'd moved here, had advised them that Flats should stay off the leg for a day or so.

That had about as much of a chance of happening, Quin thought, as her and Ellie returning home. McCleary hadn't said as much yet, but she knew he was thinking it as he sat at the dining room table, folding and unfolding the grotesque drawing.

"We'll keep her with one of us all the time," Quin said, sinking into a chair across the table from him.

"It's not that simple, Quin."

"We'll make it that simple."

He rubbed a hand over his face. "I want you two on the next plane out."

She leaned forward. "Then I think we'd better start thinking about doing something else for a living. Even if just one of us stays in this business, the threat to Ellie is always going to be a possibility."

McCleary looked over at Flats, then at the snapshots that covered the wall to his right, then at Quin. "It all comes down to what Benson said. The only people who should be in this line of work are loners. No spouse, no family, no personal life."

Then he got up and walked out of the room. Quin remained at the table, staring at the drawing as though a part of her believed it would eventually surrender a name. The shower came on; pipes clattered. The wind rose. If they left, if they didn't leave, if they went to the police, if they didn't go to the police, if if if.

She would give it another day. But whatever she decided would reach well beyond this place, this tragedy.

16

1

THE LOCAL JOKE about Cedar Key was that you went back two years in time for every mile driven on State Road 24. That would be about forty years, Rick thought, the early Fifties. Norman Rockwell and the Cold War and the pre–rock 'n' roll days of bebop and Elvis. Simpler times.

The island was a punctuation point at the dead end of SR24, a dot off Florida's scalloped Gulf coast. It started where the salt marsh did, a vast expanse of tall grasses already darkening in the evening light. The grasses seemed to rush away from him toward the horizon, the breeze bending them until they kissed the surrounding acrid mud flats. Next to the flats were exposed beds of oyster shells, fragmented, glinting like bits of glass.

A few homes were scattered along the shores of the marsh, rambling, private places. Only the tongues of their docks or the tips of their chimneys were visible from the road. This didn't look like a place that had problems. But it did.

The number of oyster fishermen had dropped from a peak of a hundred and fifty in its heyday to a bare eighteen. It was the result of beds that had been overharvested and of unchecked septic-tank leakage that had damaged others. Since oysters were particularly susceptible to waterborne bacteria, the state had closed down nearly all the beds around the island. A Cedar Key oyster was now about as rare as snow in Miami.

Fishing, which had once been a driving force on the island, Rick thought, now represented less than ten percent of its local revenue. There was a moratorium on sewage hookups until the new sewage plant was built, which had stalled growth at just eleven hundred residents, most of them seasonal retirees and affluent part-timers. Tourism was on the rise, but at best that was a mixed blessing. Although it bolstered the island's economy, it had also produced tacky embarrassments like the horse-and-buggy tour and the Mullet Train, a clone of Key West's Conch Train. The feuds among the town's politicians were like family squabbles, endless and futile, with nothing agreed upon or resolved. There had been more than twenty police chiefs in the last ten years.

But despite its problems, Cedar Key had one thing in abundance: ambience. This was laid-back island living at its best. The taste of the sea was in everything, gulls wheeled through the purple sky, and the light had a peculiar quality to it that didn't seem quite real. The Main Street was wide, lined with quaint shops that Rick thought of as ad-hoc architecture. In the center of the block was the Island Hotel, steeped in lengthening shadows.

It was a rustic two-story inn built in the nineteenth century, and when Rick walked through the front door, he walked back in time. He was thirteen again, a midget in a giant's world where the ceiling was as unreachable as the sky. By squinting his eyes and gazing obliquely to the left or right, he could see the past juxtaposed over the present like a pair of translucent photographs: Mother checking in at the front desk, Dad hauling in bags from the car, and Josie, his sister, off to his left, gesturing for him to come and look at the tropical fish aquarium.

Moray eels, Ricky. Aren't they pretty?

She tapped the glass with her nail and the morays slid out from between the rocks where they'd been hiding. The smaller one slipped across the top of the other, the two pressed so closely together he couldn't tell where one ended and the other began. Their brilliant colors melted together like oils. The upper parts of their bodies entwined.

"They're making love, Ricky."

Her hair brushed his cheek as she leaned closer to the glass, the scent of her skin swirling around him, and she laughed when he grew suddenly hard.

"Mom'll see."

But Mother had seen only the things that she wanted to see. If she'd known about the nights when Josie tiptoed down the hall to his room, she'd given no indication. If she'd thought it odd that they'd spent so much time together that long, hot summer when he was fourteen, she'd never remarked on it. And yet she'd been forever chastising Josie for the provocative clothes that she wore tight and braless, for her foul mouth, for the company she kept. Only Dad had seemed to have any control over her at all, but he'd been at home even less than Mother, so Josie had pretty much done what she wanted, when she wanted, and with whom she wanted.

Until that trip to New Hampshire.

Rick hurried past the aquarium and through the funky bar, the restaurant, onto the patio. It was enclosed on two sides by trellises that were thick with ivy. At the back, it sloped down to a garden, a fountain, trees, a few tables.

It was too early for the dinner crowd, so he was alone out here. He ordered a beer and a dozen raw oysters. The beer was Mexican and the oysters probably came from the Caribbean somewhere, but what the hell. He always had oysters on Cedar Key. It was a tradition, like eggnog at Christmas.

Josie had started the tradition the afternoon she'd shucked an oyster, held the half shell between her fingers, and worked her tongue into the glistening glob of muscle, loosening it. He could still remember how her tongue had looked, pointed and pink, like a finger without a nail. The glob had made a wet, sucking sound as it popped free of the shell and she'd tilted her head back and it had glided down her throat. She'd licked her lips afterward and smiled at him.

The light was nearly gone now, the last of it bleeding from the sky, and she was late, his princess, his little whore.

Calling Andrea, bragging to her . . .

He wouldn't think about that now.

A woman strode out onto the patio with a drink in her hand and a bag over her shoulder. She took the table in the corner, where ivy hung over the sides of the trellis, a green veil. She lit the lamp on the table, opened her purse, removed a paperback, a pack of cigarettes, a lighter. She got comfortable in the chair, her right leg thrown over its arm, her sandal dangling from the ends of her toes, then dropping off. Her foot was tan, small, and perfectly shaped, like Cinderella's. Her flowered skirt hiked above her knees, revealing the V of darkness between her thighs, the shifting shadows

A drop of liquid lingered against her lower lip when she sipped at her drink. Her tongue darted out, as pointed and pink as Josie's, chasing it. Then she opened her book, lit a cigarette, and started reading, her naked foot swinging like a pendulum in the darkening heat.

She glanced up once from her book, not smiling, not acknowledging him in any way, looking around as though she were expecting someone. But she knew he was watching her, that he saw her pale hand slipping over the knob of her knee and up along her inner thigh, a slow, intimate journey of soft curves and silken skin.

Then her eyes fixed on him, points of cold heat like the stars, the moon. Her foot kept swinging, sweat glistened on her upper lip, and he saw the small, almost imperceptible movements as her finger found the secret place. His heart slammed up against his ribs. He couldn't wrench his eyes away. A flush spread across her cheeks. She made a soft hissing noise; a slow smile burned across her face.

He was suddenly on his feet, his head pounding, his legs eating up the distance between them. Then he was in front of her and she was looking up at him, that maddening smile mocking him. "That's how it happened, isn't it, Rick?"

"Not here." He grabbed her by the wrist and jerked her to her feet, smelling her now, the same soap and perfume Josie had worn, and that other, deeper, exciting odor, musky and thick, that was only hers.

Laughing, she yanked her arm free of his grasp and ran for the garden, barefoot and fleet, a wood nymph, his whore. She darted between rows of hibiscus, ducked under low-hanging branches, melted into the shadows, here one minute, gone the next.

He caught her at the far end of the garden, near the fence where the live oaks grew, and took her just as he'd once taken Josie, on a bed of dry leaves, her skirt bunched at her waist, her legs locked around him.

(2)

"Was that how it happened?" she asked.

"More or less."

"Which?"

"It doesn't matter." They were on the pier now, strolling past fishermen and tourists. A few people had gathered around one of the many pelicans that hung around for handouts, birds so tame they allowed you to come within a foot of them. "It was a long time ago."

"That's what makes it important, Rick."

He didn't feel like talking about it. A part of him, though, would always be swimming in the waters of Lake Winnipesaukee the summer that he was sixteen. He had only to close his eyes to feel the warm sun against his back and the chill of the water from the waist down, numbing his legs. Josie had swum up behind him, encircling his waist with her arms, and pressed against him, taunting him. *"Bet you can't get it up in water this cold, Ricky, bet you can't . . ."*

It was late in the day and the lake was deserted. They had taken a raft out and were pretty far off shore when she came up behind him and tugged at his swimming trunks. Her mouth had been close to his ear and she'd been whispering things to him, dirty things, things she did with guys at college. And suddenly he'd whipped around and dunked her. She'd come up sputtering, incensed, calling him names, and he'd dunked her again and this time he hadn't let go.

The more she struggled, the harder he held her, air bubbles hissing around his arms, the sun bright and hot in his eyes. When she stopped struggling, Rick thought it was a trick and held her under the cold Winnipesaukee waters a little longer. Then he let go of her head and she floated to the surface, facedown, arms out at her sides, her hair floating like black seaweed around her. He knew she was dead, was sorry that she was dead, but she shouldn't have talked to him like that.

Rick pushed her away from him and swam back to shore. Shivering, his teeth chattering, he hauled himself out of the water and fell back on the sand. For a while, he didn't move. He watched the sun glide across the sky, a blazing white ship, and wished he were on it. He finally picked up his towel and wrapped it around his shoulders and gazed out across the water. His sister was drifting toward the island in the distance. She looked like a log.

He left her towel and clothes on the beach, retrieved his shorts, T-shirt, and sneakers, and walked over to the men's room to dress. His story was already neatly laid out in his mind, a map he would follow. Since his parents didn't know he had bicycled to the lake, he would tell them he hadn't seen Josie. They would believe him. They always did.

When he emerged from the restroom, the blazing white ship had sailed out of the sky. He could hardly detect the lump that was Josie. He mounted his bike and rode back to the cabin his parents were renting. Josie didn't come home for dinner. Mother was frantic. Dad called the sheriff's department. Her body was found the next morning by someone in the search party. The coroner said she'd drowned. No one ever suspected.

"Are you pissed off at something, Rick?"

They had stopped and she was holding out a crust of bread to a pelican. The bird snatched it from her hand. He watched it vanish in the pelican's fleshy throat. "I'm not pissed off. I'm just curious about something."

"What?"

"What's black and white and read all over?"

A muscle ticked under her eye; she was still watching the pelican. "A newspaper. Everyone knows the answer to that one."

"Yeah, and her name's Barbara."

She drew her eyes to him. "I didn't mention you, Ricky."

"That makes it all fucking right?" He fought to control his voice. "Christ, what's wrong with you?"

Anger leaped into her face. "Nothing's *wrong* with me. I just want to know if she's as good as she thinks she is."

"You told her the next woman would be *Barbara*, for Christ's sakes."

"Oh, stop it, will you?" She laughed. "No one would ever draw a connection to your wife, that's ludicrous. You're making this into something it isn't, Rick."

His fury was so extreme, he wanted to hit her, to sink his fist into those beautiful white teeth and watch her choke on them. He took her roughly by the arm and led her quickly away from the pier, where there weren't so many people. She wrenched her arm free when they reached the street and hissed, "That hurt, you fuck."

She stood there at the curb, rubbing her arm, her face cast in stone, and glared at him accusingly. As though everything were his fault. Everything. He slapped her hard and she stumbled back, her mouth frozen in an O of astonishment, her hand fluttering to her cheek. The heel of her shoe caught on something and she fell, arms pinwheeling, and landed on her ass in the dirt.

Rick looked at her, hating her. He spun around and walked back toward Main Street and the hotel and his car. His rage knocked around inside him. He began to shake. He clutched his arms against him, trying to contain and control it, and moved faster, faster, his entire being focused on diffusing the rage.

By the time it had passed through him, he was beyond the hotel and the parking lot and stood at the top of a shallow rise at the end of Main Street. Neat little bungalows were set back from the road, their shades and curtains pulled against the darkness. Lights glowed behind them, illuminating the ordinary lives of the people who inhabited them. He envied these people, whoever they were. He envied their routines, their predictability, their goodness. Even that.

Genes, he thought. The genes made you what you were, not environment, not upbringing, but the complex weaves of the generations before you, the tight spirals of DNA encoded with everything from the color of your eyes to your propensity for violence.

His princess, his little whore, disagreed. She said it was all in the soul, that etheric ball of energy that was born and reborn through the millennia, accumulating knowledge like interest on an unpaid debt. By making the unconscious conscious, she said, it was possible to dip into the memories of other lives, to find such specifics as the names of who you were before, where you had lived, what you had done. She claimed that their connection in this life, for instance, went back to when she was a witch in Salem, burned at the stake by the man he had been, a man who had actually been her apprentice in the black arts. He had called it fanciful; she swore it was truth.

He sat on a bench at the end of the street and gazed down at the streetlights on the other side of the rise. Beyond the lights was a beach, then the Gulf, its waters dark and shiny. He thought about killing her. He thought about binding her to a pole, piling dry wood at her feet, setting a torch to it, watching her burn.

"Rick?"

He didn't look at her. She sat beside him on the bench, struck a match, lit a cigarette. He felt the shape of the scissors in the left pocket of his windbreaker and the weight of the dagger in the other. He would kill her right here, just slide the blade into her ribs and twist it up into her heart, then pull it out and walk away.

"I'm sorry," she said. "I should have told you about those calls."

Her soft, compliant voice didn't fool him for a second. He didn't say anything. He thought he could see the flicker of firelight across the dark Gulf waters, but it was just the reflection of the streetlights.

"I was going to set her up. I thought she'd be worthy. For us, I mean. For the two of us. Like Catherine and Lucy."

"And Barbara."

"I wasn't thinking. The name didn't even occur to me, I swear. It was my turn to choose, but I just wasn't thinking." Then, her voice softer, her hand touching his: "I'm sorry, Ricky. It won't happen again. I don't know what else I can say."

"There won't be any Barbara."

"Okay." She dropped her cigarette to the street, crushed it out with the heel of her shoe.

"No more calls to Tull."

"Okay."

"We'll do it my way."

"Okay, baby." She stroked the back of his hair. "Whatever you say."

He looked at her finally, at her pretty eyes shiny with tears. "We're going to do it like before."

"The island's not big enough."

Excuses, excuses. "Are you with me or not?" he snapped.

"Of course I am, Rick. You know I am. It's just . . ."

"What? Just what?"

"We don't have any weapons, we—"

"I have a knife. C'mon." He clasped her hand and they got up and walked down the hill toward the beach, the water, and the jetty in the distance. She didn't protest, didn't ask questions, didn't say anything at all.

They kicked off their shoes when they hit the sand and claimed a bench under a palm tree. She sat very close to him, smoking again, and they talked about the stars. She didn't ask him why they were sitting there. She didn't say anything about his hand dangling over her shoulder, stroking her breast through the fabric of her blouse.

Cars passed on the road behind them, headlights grazing them. From the back, he imagined they looked quite innocent, a couple enjoying the night air and the slivered moon that pushed up from the water in the distance.

"You want to toss for the knife?" she asked.

"We'll see."

"Okay." No argument, no impatience, no urgency. She lit another cigarette from the embers of the last, passed it to him. He puffed, drew the smoke deeply into his lungs, passed it back. He pushed her skirt up high on her thigh, enjoying the sight of her legs crossed demurely at the knees. "Make me come, Ricky." That dark, husky voice, the voice that killing had created. It excited him. Even now. Especially now. He touched her chin, turning her head toward him, and kissed her. Her tongue tasted of salt and beer and something else, something indescribably good. The pulse at her neck leaped against his fingers as his other hand slipped up under her skirt.

She uncrossed her legs and slid down lower on the bench until her head rested against it, one leg coming up, bending into a perfect V, her heel hooked at the edge of the bench, her eyes fixed on his, inviting him. He did what she wanted him to do, in the way he knew she liked, did it as they sat there on the public bench. The pleasure of anticipation, he thought, and afterward it would be even better, the long talking, their cigarettes glowing in the blackness of an unfamiliar room, the scent of their passion scattered like seeds in the dark. He couldn't relinquish that yet, couldn't despite everything. So when her hands came to his head, urging him down, he slipped off the bench and knelt before her in the sand and ate her like a fig.

(3)

"Someone's coming," she whispered.

He was instantly on his feet, brushing off his jeans, shaking his head as though he'd been looking for something in the sand that he hadn't been able to find. "We'll come back in the morning when it's light. It's probably buried in the sand." He spoke loudly enough for the approaching couple to hear.

But the couple passed without so much as a glance in their direction. Tourists, he thought, watching them until they moved under a streetlight. He slipped a hand into his pocket and brought out a quarter. "Call it, babe."

She looked at him, excitement glimmering in her eyes as she gazed after the couple. Then she smiled at him. "Heads."

"Tails."

He flipped the quarter, caught it. "Heads it is." He reached out and she grabbed on to his hand and he pulled her to her feet.

"Where?" she asked, brushing her hands over her skirt, slipping her sandals back on.

"We'll play it by ear."

"Maybe they'll go as far as the jetty. The jetty would be ideal."

"Yeah, it would."

She clasped his hand, humming softly to herself, and together they started down the walk, following the man and the woman just ahead of them.

(4)

After saying good evening to the couple, Rick and the woman took them there on the jetty. While they were doing it, Madonna sang about American girls from the couple's transistor radio. The warm breeze whispered through the pines around them. Water purled over the rocks below. Twenty, maybe thirty seconds, and it was over.

Death is just a breath that isn't taken, he thought.

They removed the money from the man's wallet to make it look like robbery and he even got some of the woman's hair before they rolled the bodies over the side of the jetty. The bodies tumbled, knocking loose stones and clumps of dirt. Rick realized that he was light-headed, breathing hard, that his shirt was drenched in sweat, but the metallic taste in his mouth was absent. His hands weren't crawling with germs and bacteria, either. A clean kill, a snap of the woman's neck as his princess took care of the man, and the woman slumping in his arms, so light she was practically weightless. Euphoria filled him.

They moved quickly through quiet side streets, under long arcades of leaves, through the scent of night-blooming jasmine. "I like the ritual better, Rick."

"This was clean."

"There wasn't any time for them to be afraid. I don't know why, but that fear, *their* fear, makes a difference."

How quickly she'd forgotten the way it was before. The rush of adrenaline, the headiness. "But *we* were afraid. Like we used to be."

She thought about this, then nodded slowly and held out her arms. "No blood."

"Exactly. How do you feel?"

"Like I could run a marathon." She laughed then, tugged on his arm. "Let's do it again."

"We'll go back and get our cars."

"Good idea."

They hurried through the darkness, wedded in their corruption, isolated by it, just as they had been for four years. Their time together had always been spent alone. They had no friends in common, didn't frequent restaurants or nightclubs together unless they were out of town. They sneaked around, stealing time like a man and a woman married to other people. He didn't understand it, but he didn't need to. He loved her as much as he often hated her and that was enough.

For now.

On their way out of town, they bought a six-pack of malt liquor. They chugged down one each, their cars pulled side by side at the salt flats. Then they took down a lone fisherman under a bridge, a guy who was half in the bag, and rolled him into the still, dark waters. Exhilarated, laughing, slapping the blade clean on the sand, his princess flopped into the old man's chair. She pulled two beers from his open cooler and tossed Rick one. They drank them in the shadow of the bridge, smoking and laughing and talking. An occasional car trundled by overhead. The noise of crickets and frogs surrounded them as completely as the darkness.

When they made their way up the shallow slope toward their cars, her arm was tight around his waist, the skin soft, the bones hard and firm beneath it. "Again," she said with a breathless laugh. "You follow me."

He felt something then—heartburn or prescience, he couldn't tell which, maybe neither, maybe nothing more than a sense that they should not push their luck. But he nodded at everything she said, astonished at the clarity of her mind despite all they'd drunk. Then he was back inside his Firebird, following her up the highway and out onto the mainland again.

State Road 24 was deserted, fifty miles of asphalt that

unfurled into a blackness broken only by two stoplights. He could see the first one in the distance, a rhythmic red flashing that spilled into the road like radioactive waste, illuminating the roof of her car as they neared it. She drove the speed limit, his princess did. But he felt her alertness, the tautness of her body, the anticipation, and from time to time the scent of her on his hands seemed as fresh as it had on the beach, and it aroused him.

A couple of miles past the flashing red light, where the road was darkest and the trees were tall and thick and unforgiving, she suddenly slowed down. He thought at first that she had car trouble, but as she continued to slow, tapping her brakes so he wouldn't run into her, someone on a bike pedaled into the glare of her headlights. A woman, hunched over the handlebars of a ten-speed.

Princess lowered the passenger window and leaned toward it, saying something to the woman. She kept pedaling, faster, faster, and didn't even glance toward the car. Princess stuck her arm out the driver's window and motioned him around her. He stepped on the accelerator and the Firebird leaped forward, a black jungle cat. He swerved to the right, around her car, and the woman on the bike hunched lower over the handlebars, aware now that she was in danger.

The Firebird shrieked past her. Rick glanced in the rearview mirror. She'd swung off the road, headed for the trees, Princess following her, bearing down on her, closing the gap between them. All he could think of was that she was going to ram the bike and crush the woman. That meant there would be paint from her car embedded in the metal of the bike that might be identified and traced. It meant, quite simply, that if she went down, he would also.

So he swerved the wheel savagely and spun in the road. The Firebird's rear end fishtailed, straightened, then he raced for the woman, intending to cut her off before she reached the trees. His headlights caught her, held her, suspended her in the liquid darkness. And then, from the right, blazed the other headlights, and he saw the fear burning in the woman's face and knew he would remember it forever.

Rick slammed on the Firebird's brakes seconds before he would have struck the bike. The suddenness of it startled the woman. She lost her balance, fell, and in the seconds before she scrambled to her feet, the other car had screeched to a halt. Now the woman was running, her arms pumping at her sides, the trees a dark wall just beyond her. He leaped from the car, stumbled and struck the ground hard, sprawling like some graceless thug.

When he lifted his head, Princess was racing after the woman, into and out of the spill of lights from the cars. He scrambled to his feet, his vision hazy, then blurred, then offering up doubles of each of them, doubles of the trees, the darkness, even of the ground.

She reached the woman first. He saw it clearly, as if in slow motion: the way her body seemed to lift from the ground like a gymnast's, the way her legs swung out from the rest of her body, the impact of her shoes against the small of the woman's back. Then they were both falling, falling back into the darkness. He raced on, but it was as if he were in a dream, moving through air like syrup, going nowhere fast.

He heard a scream, brief and sharp, and for seconds he saw his princess, her arm rising and falling, rising and falling, again and again. Her hair was a wild nimbus around her head, her back was hunched like an animal's. Then he reached her and grabbed her wrist, stopping her arm before it descended again, and pulled her off the woman, away from her, into the grass.

She panted and sobbed and suddenly wrenched around, the dagger still in her hand, *his* dagger, the dagger she'd won when they'd tossed the quarter. It whistled past his ear, then the blade tore through his windbreaker, his shirt, and into the skin on his right shoulder, burning like acid as it continued its downward descent. It would have plunged into his thigh if he hadn't moved, if he hadn't grabbed her wrist and twisted it, forcing the dagger from her hand. She screamed, struggled, tried to bite him. He shoved her back and her head struck the ground hard, knocking her out.

He rocked back on his heels, one hand gripping his shoulder, the other clenching and unclenching against his thigh. Blood seeped through his fingers. Pain radiated up and down his arm. His eyes swept from her to the dead woman to the cars. Two cars, one driver. Two bodies, one of them dead, the other unconscious. He pushed to his feet, wincing at the pain, and stumbled back to the Firebird.

He drove it over to Princess's car, backed up to the front of it. From the trunk, he pulled out a thick, heavy chain. He connected one end to his rear fender and the other to her front fender. It was illegal to tow a vehicle without a tow bar, but better to risk this than to leave one of the cars here. By morning, this place would be crawling with cops.

He somehow got her into the Firebird's passenger seat, then tore a strip of terry cloth from a beach towel and wrapped it around his injured shoulder. He tried not to dwell on the germs that had swarmed into the open wound like mosquitoes, germs he could feel even now, germs from the people they'd killed, from the ground, from the grass where animals had defecated. No time to think about germs, infection, disease.

He cranked up the Firebird, gave it a little gas, and swung in a slow, wide circle onto the road. The wheels rolled over the bike, crushing it like a Coke can. Then he was back on the pavement, his shoulder still bleeding, his princess slumped against the door, her car a dead weight behind him. And he drove with both hands gripping the steering wheel, his eyes fixed on the empty dark and his mind frozen around a single image: her arm, pale in the moonlight, rising and falling again and again.

17

(1)

THEY WERE SPEEDING through the rain on a dark road. Cat was driving much too fast and straining forward in her seat, wiping at the foggy windshield with the palm of her hand. Quin kept asking her to slow down, but Cat said there wasn't time, she had to show her something.

Quin didn't know what she was talking about. They were on their way to pick up a pizza, weren't they? King size, all the trimmings, even anchovies. What was the big hurry? She couldn't see five feet in front of her, and on either side of the car, the world fell away into rain, darkness, emptiness. The headlights illumined a wall of water. Now and then lightning burst against the wall, burning a path through it, and the light pulsed inside the car, coloring it a cold, hard blue. In those moments, Quin could see the dashboard, the silent radio, Cat's pale hands knitted to the steering wheel. And she could see the speedometer needle, swinging toward eighty.

She pleaded with Cat to slow down, but she didn't seem to hear. They were picking up speed. The wind whistled against the windows and doors and shook the car as if it were made of tin. Then Cat's arm jerked up like a puppet's and she pointed at a figure on the shoulder of the road, someone on a bike who was hunkered over the handlebars, pedaling madly, frantically, wildly.

"Her," Cat said, *"remember her. She knows."*

As they sped past the woman, the car fishtailed and went into a skid. Quin screamed. Her car door flew open and she was thrown clear, out of the dream, and came to with a start in bed. Thunder rolled through the dark like bowling balls. The storm had followed her, leaked into her real life, and its fury paralyzed her. Lightning burned through the room, turning it that same hard, unforgiving blue. Its stroboscopic flash exposed McCleary's motionless shape on the other side of the bed, the silhouette of the playpen, the flapping porch screen beyond the open door.

Then the skies opened up and a gust of wind drove rain through the screen and into the bedroom. She leaped up to shut the door, realized that Flats had gone outside earlier and hadn't come in before they'd gone to bed.

She hurried out onto the porch. In the gloom of its dim light, she saw that the wind had knocked things off the pool table. A dozen ornaments rolled noisily around on the floor, a plastic reindeer lay on its side on a chair, a little Santa Claus was stuck upside down in a pocket of the pool table, mistletoe was plastered against the wet screen. She kicked aside a wreath and plastic containers of flowers and plants that had tumbled from the ledge and called for Flats.

The sheepdog limped up the ramp, barking, and slipped through the door as Quin opened it. She shook herself, spraying water everywhere. Quin grabbed an old towel from the back of the piano to dry her off, but Flats, spooked by the thunder, was already headed at a fast three-legged hobble toward the bedroom.

"No, Flats, no!" Quin hissed.

But she wasn't stopping for anyone or anything. She skidded as she took the turn into the bedroom and Quin hastened after her, envisioning muddy sheets, Ellie waking up to company in the playpen.

Flats was cowering in a corner just inside the door, alternately whimpering and growling as her tail thumped against the floor. The fragrance of perfume swelled in the air. It had no particular source, but seemed to come from everywhere, seeping from the very pores in the wall, through the floorboards, the glass, the light fixtures.

"Quin," McCleary whispered. "Do you—"

"Yes."

She pressed up against the jamb, the damp, cool wood biting into her spine. Her eyes darted around the room, seeking a shape, a shadow flickering across the wall, a mist solidifying and moving toward her. Special effects in a Spielberg movie. But she saw nothing unusual. There was just the scent, thickening and tightening and gathering strength like a tidal wave. It was so strong, so overpowering, it was as if her nose were jammed in a bottle of White Linen, as if the stuff coated her tongue. She could drown in it, choke on it. That strong.

First the dream, now this.

And she and McCleary were both awake and Flats was reacting to it.

Quin didn't know how long it lasted, fifteen seconds, maybe as long as thirty. There was no particular point where it was present one moment and gone the next; it seemed, rather, to leave the room gradually, like the smell of smoke or gas.

When it was completely gone, her feet were encased in ice. She felt as if the room had been turned inside out and shaken like a purse and she was one of the objects that had fallen out. The cool air was quickly displaced by the humidity, the dampness, the heaviness of the storm. She stumbled clumsily toward the bed, crawled across the mattress to McCleary, groped blindly for his hand. It was as cold as her feet.

"What did you smell?"

They asked the question at the same time, stopped at the same moment, laughed nervously in perfect sync.

"You first, Mac." She didn't need his confirmation; she knew what she'd smelled. But perhaps to him it was chocolate cake or coffee and he'd seen little green men. If so, she needed to know.

"Her perfume." His voice was very, very soft.

"Did you see anything?"

"No." Thunder, lightning again. Then: "Did you?"

She shook her head. "Were you awake when I went out onto the porch?"

"I heard you leave. I was still half-asleep. I started smelling perfume and at first I thought it was coming from your pillow." His fingers tightened across the back of her hand; she welcomed the connection. "Then I realized what it was and sat up and . . . and suddenly it was everywhere. It happened the other day, in Cat's den, but it didn't last as long and the scent wasn't as powerful.''

She drew back. Only his beard was utterly clear to her; shadow hid the rest of his face. ''Mac, it happened to me, too.''

''What? When?''

It sounded foolish in the telling, a spook story without the spook. But now that she knew they'd experienced the same thing, separately and simultaneously, it wasn't as easy to rationalize as imagination, wasn't as easy to dismiss.

They began to analyze it the way they would any event in an investigation, as a puzzle whose missing pieces not only had to be uncovered but fit into a reasonable whole. Reasonable. How could such a thing be reasonable?

They agreed on the basics: that the scent was White Linen, Cat's favorite, an aroma Quin didn't wear, and that the only bottle was on the other side of the house, in the bathroom adjoining Cat's bedroom. Beyond that, they agreed on nothing.

He believed it had lasted several minutes and that the signals were random, like those from an emergency beacon in a downed plane. She didn't think it had lasted more than thirty seconds and believed the incidents had been targeted specifically for them, that Cat wanted them to know she was still around.

''That explanation's too convenient, Quin.'' McCleary's voice was still soft but no longer startled.

''Then how do you explain it?''

They were out in the kitchen by then, Quin straddling a stool at the counter, McCleary fixing a pot of coffee. ''It's a scent we both associate with Cat. Maybe we conjured it to comfort ourselves or something.''

''For a flatliner graduate, you're pretty cynical.''

''Look, all I'm saying is that we should explore other possibilities.''

''Like what?''

He set out the mugs, a pitcher of cream, claimed the stool across from her. It was a relief to be able to see him clearly now, the smoky eyes, the dark hair laced with white, the salt-and-pepper beard that rounded his chin, completed his features. He seemed, just then, as solid as the wall behind him.

"Maybe each time it's happened, it's because we needed confirmation about something and that need stimulated our olfactory nerves in a certain way so that we'd smell it. You smelled it at home, before leaving to come up here. It's possible you subconsciously needed to know you'd made the right decision. For me, it happened right after I'd found that adult topic entry on Kazaam. I guess I needed to be sure that I wasn't wasting my time trying to find out about Masquerade and the married man she was involved with."

"Psychobabble, Mac. The odds are against both of us subconsciously choosing White Linen."

"The odds would be astronomical if Bristol and I both smelled it. Or if Andrea Tull did, since she never even knew Cat. But not with you and me, Quin. We both know that White Linen was like a tradition with her."

"But what about my dream? I think that's significant."

"In what way?"

"Cat's urgency. She *wanted* me to see the woman on the bike. She told me to remember her."

"That doesn't prove anything, Quin."

"Well, to me it does. These incidents aren't random and they aren't self-created. She's trying to tell us something. You're just too pigheaded to admit it. Besides, if I wanted to conjure a smell, Mac, it'd be something to do with food, not perfume."

His laugh signaled an impasse, an uneasy truce. This, like the issue about her and Ellie leaving, an issue shelved for the last twenty-four hours, was better left alone for now. "You tired?" she asked.

"Not really. Besides, Ellie will be up in a couple of hours."

"Let's arrange those things on the floor of the den, Mac."

"I already did that," he said.

"But I haven't. We haven't."

They carried their coffee into the den. McCleary had been able to find duplicates of only four of the six items. They were missing a garter belt and a sweatband, two rather common articles of clothing, Quin thought. If a woman had one of each, why not several? Especially Cat, who never bought one of anything.

"You sure there aren't another sweatband and a garter belt in her drawers?"

"Positive."

She looked at the list from the police file, at the photograph of the items, at the items themselves, and frowned. She glanced at McCleary, who was at Cat's desk, shifting through the contents of the file. She started to say something, changed her mind, and went into Cat's bedroom. She pulled out all of her bras and underwear, checked the tags, and smiled smugly to herself. Since their disagreement the night before last about her leaving with Ellie, they'd uncovered nothing new in their investigation, as though the two events were somehow linked. Now, suddenly, she'd made one of those marvelous leaps and Christ, it felt good. She returned to the den with her bundle, dropped it on Cat's desk.

McCleary sat back, hands hooked behind his head. "Okay, you've got my attention."

"On the list, it says the bra that was found was a thirty-six B."

"So?"

"Cat didn't wear a thirty-six B. She wore a thirty-four A." *Like me.* "Look." She showed him the tags on several bras. "And the underwear. Wrong again. The list says a size six, made of silk, red and pink." She showed him the tags on several pairs of underwear from Cat's drawers. "These are fours, cotton bikinis, one color. Cat would never buy red and pink, and she definitely wouldn't buy them in silk. Too impractical. They'd probably have to be dry-cleaned. And I bet if we made this same comparison with Lucy Davenport's things, we'd find the same discrepancies. The killer bought this stuff."

McCleary grinned. "He isn't very good at guessing sizes."

"Bristol would do better than this, Mac. He might not know her exact size, but he'd come a lot closer than this."

His eyes slipped from her head to her toes and back again, a frankly appraising look that, under other circumstances, would have been flattering. But she suspected it meant he didn't have the slightest idea what sizes she wore.

"Size six dress?" he asked.

"Eight. A six would be up to my thighs."

"Small in a blouse?"

"Safe guess. Blouses and shorts don't count. You've bought some for me. Bra?"

He leaned back in the chair, smiling slightly now. "Thirty-four C?"

Dreamer. "Only when I was pregnant. Underwear?"

"Four."

"One point for you. Shoes?"

He leaned forward, peering over the edge of the desk at her bare feet. "Eight and a half, medium width."

"Nine."

"But I'm close. Closer than the killer was."

"Exactly my point. Bristol's guesses would have been more accurate, too."

McCleary went through Lucy Davenport's file. "Lucy and Cat were similar in height and weight and body structure. If the killer knew one or the other, then he probably would have bought the same sizes for each of them, right?"

"That makes sense."

"But he didn't. The only common items on both lists are bras and belts. The bra found at Lucy's was a thirty-two C, the belt was size thirty. Cat's belt is a twenty-nine."

"Meaning what?"

"I'm not sure."

But she knew that look on his face. "What's your idea?"

"Two killers. They're partners. They each selected a victim. That would explain the discrepancy and the lack of any solid connection between Lucy and Cat. Then we make one of them a woman, like you theorized. The bra and belt sizes for the two women don't match because for the victim the woman chose, she used her own clothes. The man guessed for his victim and bought the clothes."

"You may have something, Mac."

Excited now, he dug a pencil and paper out of the desk drawer and went to work. Quin moved around behind him and looked over his shoulder as he jotted notes, made columns, lists, comparing the sheet to the information in the files.

When he was finished, the paper was divided into thirds that were labeled *Tess*, *Melody*, *Killer*, with physical descriptions for the first two, including probable heights and weights. Tess (five foot five, less than a hundred pounds) was the shorter and thinner of the two and would fit the thirty-two C bra. Melody (five eight, a hundred and twenty or twenty-five pounds) would fit nicely into the thirty-six B. The belt sizes were too close to guess which woman wore a twenty-nine and which one wore a thirty.

"It can go either way," McCleary said. "That's the problem."

"There's another problem, too. When I last saw Tess, she wasn't as thin as she is now. She was more Melody's size."

McCleary's memory of what Tess had looked like differed from Quin's. He remembered her as lean, rather than the anorexic skinny she was now, and said she'd never been buxom.

"Melody's not buxom," Quin said.

"Compared to Tess she is."

"Mac, Dolly Parton is buxom. Melody's just got a nice figure."

"Okay, okay. We've narrowed it to Tess and Melody. But who's the guy? Kliner? Bristol? Emilio?"

"Not Bristol. Everything else aside, I just don't think he'd be able to juggle a wife, Cat, and some other woman. Kliner, on the other hand, was screwing Lucy and used to live with Melody. I say that makes him a fairly good contender."

"Agreed."

"But how's Masquerade fit?"

"I don't know."

"Maybe it has more to do with her affair with Bristol than with her murder."

"No, I think it's involved somehow, and I think Tess is our best lead."

"Want a warm-up?"

"What?"

"The coffee, Mac."

"Oh. Yeah, thanks."

Bemused by his distraction, she picked up his mug and started out of the room. Before she reached the doorway, he said, "Quin?"

"I know, light on the cream."

But his expression said this wasn't about cream; this was about The Issue. "We seem to work best together, don't we."

Not an easy admission for a stubborn ex-cop who prided himself on being a loner. "Yeah, I think we do."

"If we take extra precautions with Ellie . . ." His voice trailed off.

"We already have. Helen Charles didn't let Ellie out of her sight today and she's with us when she's not there. Whoever these people are, they aren't going to go anywhere near that day-care center. It'd be too damn obvious. They don't work like that. They'd be more likely to follow Ellie and me if we left."

But even as she said this, she wondered if she really believed it. Wasn't it entirely possible that in some dark, dank cellar of her mind she equated leaving with failure, with an admission that she couldn't be both a mother and a gumshoe? Was that it? Was that really what her little speech was about? Was it? Was she that insecure? And if so, what kind of monster did that make her, willing to jeopardize her daughter's safety to prove her own worth? What worth?

She had an abrupt and terrible vision of herself draped over a tiny casket, prostrate with grief, and . . . A door slammed shut in her mind. She hurried out of the room, wishing the fragrance would reach out and touch her here, now, as she stood in the kitchen alone.

Tell me I'm right, Cat, please, please.

But there was only the scent and sound of the rain, soft and unobtrusive, a cushion against which her doubts and her questions clamored.

2

"Hey, doll, you awake?"

Jules's voice boomed from the answering machine, rousing Andy from a surprisingly pleasant dream about her ex. As she rolled over to grope for the receiver, the dream continued behind her closed eyes and her ex's face became Rick Farmer's.

"Yo, Clark Kent." She glanced at the clock. Not even seven yet. "This better be good. It's obscenely early."

"You free for a couple of hours?"

"No class until three."

"Great. We're going to Cedar Key. Our guy's struck again. I'll pick you up in ten minutes."

She literally threw herself together and eight minutes later stood on the curb beneath a gray sky sagging with clouds. It was no longer raining, but water dripped from nearby trees and rushed through gutters, out into the street, carrying away twigs and dead leaves.

She felt, as she often did, a stab of nostalgia for home, for the way it rained in the Keys, fast and furiously for ten minutes, the sky black as pitch. Then it was over and the sun would come out and the sky would turn a breathtaking blue. Half an hour later there wouldn't be a trace of the rain. But inclement weather in northern Florida seemed to stick around like the flu.

Jules's Scirocco screeched to a stop at the curb and the passenger door swung open. His copper hair was still damp from the shower and curled like commas across his forehead. "We've got the jump on this one, kiddo. Hop in."

As soon as she was sealed inside, the AC blasting her in the face, she wished she'd offered to drive. She'd forgotten how lousy he was behind the wheel. He drove either too slowly or too fast, like an old lady one minute and a maniac on the autobahn the next.

He was in his fast mode right now, whipping up and down slumbering neighborhood streets, an open thermos of coffee between his legs. He was trying to balance two cups on the dashboard and tell her the story at the same time.

"You're going to broil your cock and kill us, Jules." She moved the cups and thermos out of his reach. "Drive and talk. I'll do this."

Jules gave her a dirty look. "*You* drive. I'll do breakfast. There're some rolls in a bag somewhere in the back." He swerved off the road, bouncing through puddles and potholes, then jammed on the brakes. They traded places. She immediately turned off the AC and lowered her window. Jules grunted his discontent but was too keyed up to make a fuss about it.

His story was simple. He'd gotten a call from a buddy at the Cedar Key newspaper who said a man and a woman had been pulled out of the water near the jetty this morning. A third body, a local fisherman, had been found under a bridge. A credit card belonging to one of the first victims had been discovered in the sticks on State Road 24, where a young woman had been stabbed to death.

"This fuck took down four people in a single spree, Andy."

"Look, I don't want to sound ungrateful or anything, but I've got my hands full with this other story, Jules."

"They're connected."

"They are?"

"The couple killed near the jetty? She was a brunet. And I remembered what you'd said about this guy taking hair from his victims, right? Well, a huge chunk of this woman's hair is missing at the back, like someone or something took a bite out of it, that's how my buddy at the paper put it. They were tourists from Michigan and had just gotten to Cedar Key yesterday morning."

The tourist bit didn't fit and neither did the male victim. But the hair . . . That had never been in the news. Either it was something Bristol and his boys had withheld or they just didn't know about it. But *she* knew and that was enough.

She pumped Jules dry and by the time they reached the clinic on Cedar Key where the bodies had been taken, she knew everything he did about the murders. But none of it explained why the killer's pattern had changed, a change that appeared to have started with his last call to her. It was the kind of loose end that affected her like open spaces did; left unchecked, it could reduce her to a barely subdued panic.

18

(1)

LIGHT THE COLOR of pus: that was the first thing Rick saw. It oozed through the Levolors in her bedroom and spilled onto the chair near the window where his clothes were scattered.

He pushed up on his elbows. His joints and muscles creaked like rusted springs and a herd of elephants stampeded through his head, waking up the pain in his shoulder. It began to ache and throb. Heat flashed through the length of his arm. Then he felt the germs, thousands of them, crawling and slithering over his skin, digging into the wound at his shoulder, diving into his bloodstream, breeding in his body's cavities. He made a tight, choking sound, leaped out of bed, and stumbled into the bathroom.

Shower soap fast get them off

He tore the bandage from his shoulder and nearly puked when he saw it. The skin around the gash was inflamed, puffy and soft at the edges. Bright red ribbons of infection led away from it. Germs inside already. Eating at the flesh. Consuming it.

He turned the shower on so hard, so fast, the pipes clattered and clanked in the wall. A monsoon of chilled nails poured over him and the soap shot out of his hand and he nearly lost his balance as he stooped over to pick it up. The germs rallied and cackled like carnival geeks, mocking him, challenging him, biting into his tainted, burning flesh. He scrubbed and scrubbed, his mind a vast white tundra empty of everything except the need to purge, to cleanse, to purify.

But the soap didn't work. The germs clung to him, clung to the hairs on his arms and legs, moved en masse through the hairs on his head, balanced at the tips of his lashes like Olympic divers. He snatched a bottle of pHisoHex from the plastic holder that hung on the shower door, spun off the top, poured it into his hands, slapped it on his body. Hair and arms, groin and legs, chest, back, between his toes and behind his ears. Then he used a hand brush on himself, grinding the bristles into his skin, working the brush back and forth on this spot, that spot, wherever the germs were most stubborn.

He scrubbed too hard at a place on his arm and it began to bleed. Rick stared in horror as germs rushed toward the abrasion. They were visible now, several dozen of them, tiny black things that wiggled like worms and held on to his skin with what felt like suckers on their undersides. Rick mashed the brush into the midst of them, then picked off those that remained, squeezing them between his thumb and forefinger. They burst like bloated ticks and he laughed wildly and flicked them off his fingers.

But there were always more, climbing up his neck, circling the openings to his ears, burrowing under his nails to hide. So he turned the water as hot as he could stand it and stood under the spray, grimacing with pain, steam rising around him. They were impervious to heat; these were tropical germs. Desperate, terrified, he shut off the water, scrambled out of the shower, jerked open the doors of the cabinet under the sink.

A dizzying array of bottles and jars were lined up inside. Creams and lotions and perfumes, shampoos and soaps and disinfectants. Betadine, iodine, merthiolate, alcohol. He grabbed the bottle of alcohol, poured some into a washcloth, rubbed it over his arms and legs and chest, wherever he saw the wiggling fuckers.

The wound at his shoulder started to seep again, the blood a festive pink as it mixed with the alcohol and water on his skin. Rick tipped the bottle and poured alcohol directly into the deep gash and nearly went through the roof. Sweet Christ, how it burned, sinking down through the damaged tissues like acid. But he felt the germs shriveling, dying, scorching. He poured in more alcohol, emptying the bottle. He hurled it away from him, opened the Betadine, stuck the nozzle directly into the gash, squeezed.

Blood bubbled to the surface and the germs' corpses floated in it, no larger than specks of dust. He squeezed at the gash and watched the blood. With it came memories of last night, flashes of her arm rising and falling, of himself driving back to Gainesville, of her car hooked to his, of the blood on her clothes, her face, her hands, and of how he had bathed her as she lay there mute and compliant. By the time he had finally tended to his own injury, he had known it was too late.

Just as it was too late now. The alcohol and Betadine would prevent further infection, but the nasty red lines snaking out from the wound meant that he needed an antibiotic, preferably a shot of penicillin, followed by a ten-day regimen of pills. And stitches, he needed stitches to keep the germs out.

Needle, thread, clean bandages.

He found everything under the sink, in the traveling sewing kit she'd used frequently in their early days together. It was supplied with the essentials for repair and restoration: broken zippers, missing buttons, tears in conspicuous places.

He prepared a place on the counter, sterilizing it with Betadine. His hand trembled violently as he tried to thread the needle and he had to prop his elbow against the edge of the sink to steady it. *Easy now, take it slow, that's right* . . . He pulled the thread through the eye of the needle, doubling it, knotted it at the end. Then he saturated needle and thread in Betadine and went to work.

Stitches? shrieked Richie the lover. *What the fuck you need stitches for?*

To keep out the germs. The goddamn germs. Yes. Prevention. He knew all about prevention.

He barely felt the first poke of the needle through the skin. But as the second stitch became the third and the fourth and the fifth, the discomfort increased. By the tenth stitch, his teeth were gritted and sweat rolled down the sides of his face. By the twelfth, he thought he was going to puke.

His intent focus blocked out awareness of everything

220

except his shoulder, the pain, the slowly closing wound. He didn't hear the door squeak open, didn't know she was there until she spoke. "What're you doing, Rick?"

She startled him, but not enough to foul the knot he was tying. "What I should've done last night."

She couldn't see his shoulder from where she was standing and came around to his other side, stood next to him. A sour stink emanated from her skin, her nightshirt. She smelled used-up. "It looks bad."

"No thanks to you."

"What's that supposed to mean?"

He snipped the thread and prepared a bandage.

"Rick?"

He raised his eyes. In the unkind glare of the fluorescent light, she looked as used-up as she smelled. Her skin was pale and dry, her lips were cracked, her hair was tangled. Dirt and blood were caked under her chipped nails. He considered killing her here, now, getting it over with. He would snap her neck like a toothpick, then ransack the place so the cops would think robbery was the motive. But someone might have seen his car outside or seen him hauling her into the house last night.

"You lost it, babe, that's what it means." He pressed tape over the bandage. "You lost it real bad." He brushed past her; she padded along behind him like a faithful pet.

"Is that why I have a knot the size of a baseball on the back of my head?"

"Yeah." He opened the bottom drawer of her bureau, where he kept a change of clothes. The shirt was slightly wrinkled, but it was clean and felt like silk against his raw, tingling skin. His shoulder still ached, but now that he'd sealed off the wound, it was easier to block out the pain. "You fell, hit the ground, passed out cold."

"Where's my car?"

"Downstairs. I towed it back into town."

He drew his fingers through his hair, watched her in the mirror. She bit at a thumbnail, examined something on her palm, fretted and puzzled over the details. "The last thing I remember is . . . is the woman on the bike."

"Yeah."

221

"Did we—"

"You did. You had the knife."

A shadow curled through her eyes like something living; she was remembering—not all of it, but enough to know that he spoke the truth. "It wasn't like Aspen."

"No," he replied. "Definitely not like Aspen."

"Or Amarillo."

"No."

"Or Albuquerque."

"No, and it wasn't like Los Angeles or Seattle or Boston."

He walked past her, got a plastic grocery bag from the kitchen, then returned to the bedroom. She hadn't moved, didn't say anything, but her eyes followed him to the chair. He pulled the plastic bag over his hand and used it to protect himself from contamination as he picked up his clothes. Then he fitted the bag around them, tied it at the top. The clothes would be burned.

"Got to split," he said without looking at her. "Talk to you later."

"Split for where? You don't have a class until this afternoon."

He scooped his wallet and loose change off the bureau. "Mother's expecting me." He headed for the door, but she started after him, her footsteps quick, urgent.

"Rick, wait."

He stopped in the living room, snapped, "What is it? I'm already late."

Something tragic happened to her face. The muscles all seemed to atrophy at once and the skin suddenly sagged, as if pulled by excess gravity. The corners of her eyes and mouth drooped, her nostrils fell, her cheeks loosened from their bones. For a few brief seconds, he saw germs crawling from her nose, her ears, and wiggling against her lower lip. Then she rubbed her hands over her face and started to cry, and the germs were invisible again.

"I . . . I'm sorry if I cut you, Ricky, I don't remember doing it, you know I would never hurt you, I . . . everything's so mixed up . . ."

Tears. He hated it when she cried, it hurt him. But he

222

couldn't make himself move toward her, to touch her, to comfort her. She reached out and he wrenched back, certain that her touch would transfer the germs from her skin to his. Her arm dropped to her side, resigned, defeated. She looked as if he'd struck her.

"Ricky . . ."

"Not. Now." The words were weighted, stuck to his tongue.

"I'll shower." Obsequious, panicked. He'd never withdrawn from her before, not even in the beginning. "It'll be all right."

"No." He moved back a few more steps. "I'll call you later."

"But—"

"Your car keys are on the chair in the bedroom."

She stayed where she was, arms clenched tightly to her waist, that stricken expression in her liquid eyes. He turned and fled, the memory of the black things on her skin pursuing him into the warm, damp morning.

(2)

The Cedar Key clinic was a short, squat building two blocks off Main Street. It didn't look equipped to deal with anything more serious than sunburn.

"I figure we've got an hour before this place is hopping with reporters," Jules said as they got out of his car.

"Are the autopsies going to be done here?"

"I doubt it. The chief of police had the bodies brought here until they could be identified. He'll probably have them transferred to the morgue in Gainesville. Let's make the most of the time we have."

Jules's buddy, Ralph, met them inside. She guessed he wasn't a day over twenty-five. He had a deep tan and a nose like Pinocchio's after he'd lied. His expression, the electricity in his voice as he led them down a hall, indicated that he hadn't been a reporter long. This was easily the most exciting thing that had ever happened to him.

They ended up in a room with a physician in a white lab coat and the chief of police, a guy no older than

223

Ralph who seemed to think he was Doc Halliday. Ralph was on a first-name basis with both of them and slipped right into their conversation about the wording of the official statement that would be released to the press. In due course, he introduced her and Jules as *friends*—and asked if it would be okay if they took a look at the bodies.

"Wouldn't recommend it if you just finished chow," the chief of police said, hooking his thumbs in his belt. He tilted his head to the left. "Through that door."

Light glinted off the four metal gurneys lined up side by side in the chilly holding room. The bodies were lying in unzipped body bags, two women, two men. The couple pulled from the water near the jetty weren't bloated yet. But fish or crabs or both had been chewing at the woman's fingertips and her black hair had dried into stiff clumps from the salt water.

Andy turned the woman's head until she could see the gap of missing hair. It went from the nape of her neck to halfway up her skull, whacked off like a cluster of stubborn weeds. When she let go of the woman's head, it lolled, a piece of fruit rotting on a vine.

Broken neck.

She dug out her recorder, switched it on, and talked softly as she moved slowly around the body, dispassionately noting the details. The awful blue lips, the way the woman's clothes stuck to her pale skin. Her companion was just as pale but had died of knife wounds, not a broken neck. The marks were visible in his shirt, three stabs in the back, one of them at the upper part of his spine that would have probably paralyzed him if he had lived. No blood: The sea had taken care of that.

Their personal belongings were drying on a table between them, each item tagged with a name and the location of where it had been found. Next to the man's wallet were his driver's license, a soggy insurance card, four credit cards. No money: It suggested that robbery had been the motive. Nice try, but she wasn't buying it.

The fisherman's neck had also been broken and he'd been stabbed once.

The last victim was a young woman who'd been biking on State Road 24. From the neck up she looked to be sleeping, a pretty thing with wispy blonde hair. Below the neck she was Swiss cheese. Her clothes were stained with blood despite last night's downpour. Grass was stuck in her hair and to the corners of her mouth, as though she'd been screaming with her mouth open against the ground.

When Jules came up alongside her, he made an unpleasant sound, then muttered, "I'm gonna puke, man."

Ralph, standing on the other side of the gurney, pointed Jules in the direction of the restroom. He alternately looked at the woman, then at Andy, as though seeking some family resemblance. "The first two were found about three this morning, the other two around five," he said. "They think the guy did her last and really lost it, that's why there're so many stab wounds."

"Who thinks that?"

"Sheriff Partridge."

Ah, yes, Doc Halliday, the youthful expert. But she agreed that this woman had been the last victim, dessert at the end of the spree. And yes, the killer had probably lost it and had probably been six sheets to the wind, booze or drugs or both. She was suddenly certain that two people had done this, one armed with a knife, a small knife, and the other armed with nothing except bare hands and rage. And suppose, just suppose, Quin was right? That one of the killers was a woman? Another Carmen Mendez with loose screws, but brighter, educated, shrewd?

But it still didn't explain why the pattern had changed, and that, she knew, was the key.

"Who is she?"

"Off-islander." Ralph had lit a cigarette and blew smoke over the woman's body. "But I've seen her around. She works at a bar over the bridge. Always on her bike, don't think she even owns a car. What paper you work for?"

Like they were standing in the middle of a singles bar. "I don't."

"Oh, I got the impression from Jules that you did."

When she didn't reply, he walked away to check on Jules. She moved on and stopped at the remains of the woman's bike. The tires were flatter than pancakes, the handlebars were twisted, the gearbox was squashed like a bug. Run over, Ralph had said. Yeah, she thought, and the right handlebar must have been sticking up. Flecks of black paint were ground into the metal. Somewhere a black car was driving around with a scratch or a gouge in the paint job. It wasn't as telling as the calling card Bundy had left—a bite mark was hard to top—but hell, it was something.

(3)

A plumber was due at the farmhouse that morning to give an estimate on repairing the leaky shower. Quin had volunteered to wait for him, which gave her an excuse to keep Ellie at home a few hours longer. There was nothing like a good dose of guilt to kindle the domestic fires.

She called Helen Charles to tell her Ellie would be in later, then got her daughter situated in the living room with a wooden spoon and a couple of pots and pans, every kid's favorite version of a steel band. She pounded away as Quin stacked the breakfast dishes and was still pounding when she went into the utility room to start a load of laundry.

The pounding stopped and Ellie's jabbering floated through the rooms, noises strung together like the rudimentaries of some foreign language. Then something fell in the kitchen and Flats started barking. Trouble, Quin thought, and walked into the kitchen. Ellie was sitting on the floor, slapping her hands against little mounds of Purina Dog Chow that had spilled from the ten-pound bag that had been in the pantry. Flats was sucking up the stuff like a vacuum cleaner.

''Mama!'' Ellie squealed, and scooped up handfuls of chow, then let the pieces rain through her fingers.

''Nice, very nice.'' Quin jerked open the door of the broom closet and things sprang out at her. A broom, a mop, a bucket, a bag of cleaning rags, the vacuum cleaner, a box of books, a coffee tin. Flats hobbled out of the way as the broom slapped the floor.

Ellie murmured, "Oh-oh!" and watched the tin roll across the floor, its contents clattering.

"Great. Thanks a lot, you guys. Look at this mess."

Dog and child peered at her with perfunctory contriteness, then Flats grabbed the broom by the handle and pulled it free of the mess and Ellie caught the tin and held it up to Quin. "Mama." She shook it and the lid fell off. Loose keys poured out, a dozen of them in varying shapes and sizes.

Quin stooped to pick them up and realized they were labeled. Spare keys—to the front door, the Wagoneer, the storage room, the theatre, the caretaker's house.

She didn't recall anyone mentioning that the caretaker's place had been searched. There was no compelling reason to take a look at the house; the caretaker's alibi was solid, after all. But it was careless that they'd all overlooked it.

Quin cleaned up the mess, scribbled a note to the repairman in case he arrived, then loaded Flats and Ellie into the Wagoneer to drive over and check out the house. The only time she'd visited Cat here at the farm, she'd been five months pregnant, a regular hippo. Cat had given her the grand tour of the property, and Quin remembered the road to the caretaker's as dusty and riddled with potholes. But the drought had been at its pinnacle then; today much of the road was underwater from last night's deluge.

She had to detour through the orchard at one point. The sun peeked out briefly from the magma of clouds, showering the gnarled apple trees with light. They shimmered and glistened and a few leaves drifted to the soft jade grass around them. The light sculpted the trees into shapes; they were men or women or animals that had been frozen by a witch's spell for some obscure infraction.

Even the caretaker's place seemed enchanted somehow. It was small and wooden, much older than the main house. The roof was gabled, the windows were tall and dirty. Weeds in the tiny garden at the side had choked the tomato plants. Insects had consumed most of the lettuce. The stone path to the front door was strewn with leaves. In front of the garage, which was detached from the house, was an old Buick with a flat tire. Behind her, maybe thirty yards away, was a barbed-wire fence and a rickety wooden gate that separated the property from the access road.

Flats led the way up the stone path, hobbling and barking, and slipped inside as soon as the door was open. The front room was still and warm; the caretaker hadn't left the air conditioner on. A faintly disagreeable odor lingered in the air and seemed to emanate from the kitchen. Flats was already on her way in there, with Ellie waddling along right behind her, and Quin hurried after them.

She stepped into a tidy little country kitchen: gingham curtains, butcher-block counters and table, gas stove, cast-iron skillet on a back burner. Flats snapped at the flies hovering around the garbage can against the wall and Ellie swatted at them with her hand and wrinkled up her nose at the smell.

"Yeah, I know what you mean." Quin removed the garbage bag from the trash can, tied it shut, set it aside. As she leaned over the sink to open the window, a thick black cloud of flies lifted from it, swarming, buzzing. She realized the odor was worse here and guessed there was unground food in the garbage disposal. Quin turned on the water, hit the switch. The disposal motor shrieked as its blade struggled to grind up what sounded like loose stones.

She quickly turned the disposal off and stuck a barbecue fork down through the opening, seeking the offender. She speared something, pulled it out. Impaled on the prongs was a woman's hand, the fingertips and nails chewed up by the blades, the skin like shredded Kleenex. Quin dropped the fork and jerked back, emitting a small, choked sound. The fork clattered to the floor and landed with the ruined fingers facing her, hooked like claws against the wood.

Flats and Ellie moved toward it instantly to investigate. "No, stay away from that!" Quin scooped up Ellie with one arm, grabbed Flats's collar with the other hand, deposited them in the other room, shut the door. She stood there blinking, sweat dimpling her forehead, and stared at the hand. That gray flesh. The ruined fingertips. The fork sticking out of it. A part of her expected it to twitch, to inch toward her, to rise up and wave. Her breakfast began to come up her throat and she swallowed hard and lurched for the phone.

19

(1)

MCCLEARY'S FIRST STOP was Federal Express, where he mailed the tapes to Benson. Then he drove over to the courthouse to wade through the real estate records, a task he detested.

In Dade County, it was a lesson in bureaucratic inefficiency. In Palm Beach County, it seemed the clerks were always on a break or at lunch when you needed them. The story wasn't much different here, but since Alachua County was smaller, there were fewer transactions, which simplified the task.

Eight real estate transactions were recorded for July 11 of this year and one of them was the house whose address and picture Andy had seen on the door of Emilio Turbeta's refrigerator. It had been sold for $82,500 to Kali, Inc. No mortgage holder was listed.

In the courthouse listings of local businesses, the company was described as a wholesale office supply and printing warehouse with a Gainesville address near campus. The president and chairman were one and the same: Emilio Turbeta. No other officers were listed.

McCleary consulted the county map that was kept under glass like the Declaration of Independence. He located Kali's downtown address easily enough, but the road the house was supposedly on didn't exist. According to the map, the entire area, in fact, was pasture.

He asked the woman at the desk about it. He expected her to reply that she was about to take her break and could he come back later? But to his surprise, she actually had an answer. The map had been drawn up three years ago, she said, before the pasture had been sold to a developer for a housing project. Then the developer went bankrupt and she'd heard there were only a few completed homes. It probably explained why Turbeta had gotten a house with five thousand square feet for a song.

The Gainesville headquarters for Kali was in a strip shopping center two blocks off University Avenue. It was flanked by a pizza joint on the right and a tacky Florida souvenir shop on the left. The woman at the desk was reading a book as he stepped inside and quickly stashed it in a drawer. She was too young to be anything but a coed. She had that part-timer look about her, too, that said this was not her life's work.

"Hi," she said. "Help you with something?"

"I just need some information. How fast are you able to place orders for supplies?"

"We're a wholesaler, sir."

"And I'm a retailer. How fast?"

"Our minimum order is a thousand dollars and generally we can get you that from our warehouse by the next day. We don't deliver, though. You'll have to pick up here. Anything over twenty-five hundred usually takes three to four days. Would you like to open an account with us, sir?"

"That depends. Is your warehouse local?"

"Yes. Just outside of Gainesville."

"Oh, so you only take orders here."

"Yes, that's right."

"Would it be faster if I picked up my order at the warehouse?"

"Not really. Sorting is what takes the time, not delivering."

"How long have you been in business?"

"This is our third year."

"What's involved in opening an account?"

She plucked a form from a stack of forms in a wire basket. "Just fill this out, and be sure you include a credit-card number we can bill to. It takes three days to run a credit check." A big smile: He guessed she got a bonus for every new account she brought in. "And that's it."

He glanced at it. "Mind if I take this with me and drop it off later?"

"No, sir, whatever's easiest for you."

"Do you also sell printing equipment?"

"No, just supplies."

"Do you have a catalogue?"

"Sure." She opened a drawer, pulled out a flimsy catalogue, passed it to him.

He flipped through it, unimpressed. High prices, not much merchandise. "Is this your only office?"

The smile vanished; she was tiring of his questions. "As far as I know."

"I was looking for something a little closer to Archer."

"Oh."

"But thanks."

Frosty now: "Don't mention it."

The company was probably legit, he decided as he left. But neither it nor Turbeta's salary as manager of Phaedra Books would explain where he'd gotten eighty-two grand in cash for the house. But if you had expendable income from a tidy sideline in the local coke business, you could funnel some of the cash through your corporation, and on paper it would look convincing enough to the IRS.

In the end, who else mattered but the IRS?

(2)

The sky was clouding up and wind gusted off the Gulf, kicking leaves down Main Street as Andy walked from the clinic toward the jetty with Jules and Ralph.

This was her first time on Cedar Key and she couldn't help but compare it to Key West. It lacked the carnival tackiness of Duval Street, the raucous college crowd, the drunks, but not for long. There was already a Mullet Train crowded with tourists wearing flowered shirts and bermuda shorts, cameras slung over their shoulders. That was never a good sign. And she sensed a certain self-consciousness in the quaintness of the buildings, in the price tags that shouted from shop windows, even in the Island Hotel's sign: ENJOY HAPPY HOUR IN THE KEY'S FUNKIEST BAR, 4–6 DAILY.

"When you write this up, Jules," said Ralph, "it's got

to be straight facts, no speculation. That's how Sheriff Partridge wants it for now.''

''Yeah, well, I'm not working for the sheriff. It depends on my editor.''

Ralph wiped the back of his hand across his sweaty brow and glanced at Andy, looking for support. She reminded him that she didn't write for a paper.

''So who *do* you write for?''

''She writes books.'' Jules was still pale and the heat had made him irritable. ''True-crime books.''

''Yeah? So have I read anything you've written?''

''Probably not.''

''I like Wambaugh's stuff. You read him?''

''Yes.''

''I've got this manuscript I'm working on now that's as good as anything he's written.''

Right, pal.

''It's about . . .''

Andy tuned him out and kept on walking.

The jetty didn't have much to tell her. But seeing it helped her fix it in memory: the shallow slope of rocks and dirt, water foaming over stones and shells, the pale, almost translucent crabs scurrying about.

Killed them, rolled them into the water, walked off.

Walked or drove?

Had they stayed on the island? Probably not. Too risky. But perhaps they'd eaten here (and paid in cash) and left their car on Main Street somewhere and walked down here to the jetty. The trees blocked the view of the road and at night, under a starless sky, they probably weren't even noticed. They were just two people out for an evening walk.

Andy strolled the length of the jetty, talking softly into her recorder. As she started back, she saw two men approaching Ralph and Jules. One of them was Sheriff Partridge and the other was Detective Bristol. He was leaning heavily on his cane, staring past Jules at her. She waved; he didn't.

Shame, shame, she thought. Such hostility. The bigger they were, the harder they fell, and she was certainly going to enjoy watching Bristol's life turn to shit.

"Hi, Detective."

His jaw tightened. "I thought I made it clear that I didn't want you anywhere near my investigations, Ms. Tull."

"Tull?" Ralph looked at Jules. "You didn't tell me she's Andrea Tull, man."

"The musician?" asked the sheriff, scratching his cheek with his car key.

"That's Jethro Tull," said Ralph.

"Excuse us a minute." Bristol took her firmly by the elbow to lead her off to the side, but Andy pulled her arm free.

"The last time I checked, this was still a free country, Detective, and we *are* in a different county and you don't have any jurisdiction here."

"But I do," said Sheriff Partridge, hooking his thumbs in his belt. "And I think it'd be best if you and your friend left the island, Ms. Tull."

Jules puffed out his chest like a rooster. "My editor will be real pleased to know that these murders are connected to the Gainesville killings." He whipped out the notepad in his back pocket and flipped to a blank page. "You have a quote, Detective Bristol?"

"Sure." Bristol grabbed his notepad and flung it. "Fuck off."

Jules laughed. "Thanks for the quote, sport."

With that, he started back toward the road, arms swinging at his sides, his copper hair shining in the gloom like a pan that had just been polished. Ralph was already trotting after him; Bristol and the sheriff were looking at her, daring her not to join her friends in their departure. Nothing pissed her off more than a man who didn't take her seriously. So she tucked her fingers in the back pockets of her jeans, smiled, and said, "Well, guys. Your move. Let's find an ending for this story."

The sheriff's thumbs slipped out of his belt and he glanced at Bristol, a good citizen waiting for his orders.

"Arrest her," Bristol snapped.

"Yes, sir." Then: "For what?"

"Obstruction of justice." Andy's blood pressure inched upward. "Interfering with a homicide investigation." Her pressure crept up another notch. "Withholding information." She clenched her fist, swung, and struck Bristol on the jaw. "Assaulting a police officer," she added, and watched him stumble back, his cane slipping from his hand, astonishment bright in his face as he fell.

Then she looked down at her hand and wondered if she'd broken it.

(3)

Quin was sitting on the front steps with Flats and Ellie when a cruiser finally pulled through the rickety gate. Forty-two minutes to answer a 911 call, she thought. She could have been dead by now.

It had just started to sprinkle and she welcomed the warmth of the raindrops against her face, the fresh air, the absence of flies. The cruiser stopped behind the Wagoneer. A cop in uniform stepped from the passenger side and Angie Wilkin swung out from behind the wheel. Her sensible cotton print dress had short sleeves and a leather belt that accentuated her tiny waist and the flare of her hips. Her shoes were canvas, low-heeled, the same dark blue as the dress. From a distance, she looked as fresh and untouched as a newly plucked peach. But as she drew closer, the pinch of fatigue at her eyes became apparent. So did the hard set of her mouth. She was strictly business when she spoke.

"Quin, this is Sergeant Rollins."

He looked like the Pillsbury Doughboy, plump cheeks, a tire starting at his middle. "Nice to meet you, ma'am."

"We would have been here twenty minutes ago," Wilkin said, "but we had trouble finding the access road. What's the problem?"

Flats, growling softly as the two approached, now began to snarl, her lips curling back from her teeth. Quin caught Wilkin's nervous glance in the dog's direction, saw Rollins's hand move toward the gun in his holster, and took hold of Flats's collar. "It's okay, girl." She looked up at Wilkin. "I found a"—she couldn't spit out the word—"something inside the house."

Wilkin sensed her discomfort; she didn't ask what kind of something. "We'll have a look."

"It's in the kitchen."

Quin held on to Flats as the two cops stepped toward the door. The sheepdog snapped at Wilkin's ankle but missed. "Dogs love me, Flats. I wish you'd believe that." Then she slipped past, Rollins tight at her heels.

"She smell funny or something, Flats, or do you just have PMS?"

The sheepdog growled.

"Yeah, well, chill out, girl. You bite her and we'll get sued." Quin left Flats on the stoop, picked up Ellie, gave her a bottle of juice, and went inside just as it started to rain.

Rollins was on the phone and Wilkin was sealing a transparent bag that now contained the hand.

"It'd been in the disposal for a while. I don't know how much Forensics is going to be able to tell us."

"What's there to tell? It's Catherine's."

"Probably. But we'll get a blood type on it to make sure."

"It's definitely her hand."

Wilkin raised her eyes from the bag. "How do you know?"

Because that was part of what the perfume meant, Quin thought, but didn't say it. "It just makes sense."

"Forensics is on the way," Rollins said as he turned away from the phone. "I'll check upstairs."

"Okay, Gary, thanks." Wilkin waited until he left, then said, "Why didn't you call me or Detective Bristol, Quin?"

"I couldn't remember the number."

"What brought you over here?"

"I realized that none of us had checked it out."

"A bad oversight on my part."

Quin noticed that she didn't include Bristol in the statement.

"If anything else happens, I'd appreciate it if you'd call me directly, Quin."

"How come I get the impression there's something going on you're not mentioning?"

Wilkin slipped a pack of cigarettes from a pocket in her dress and leaned against the counter as she lit one. She smoked with the same graceful style with which she groomed herself. "I don't think this is the place to talk about it."

"I do. It's about Steve, isn't it?"

She wasn't very adept at masking her surprise. "Yes. He's been suspended from duty pending further investigation."

"For what?"

Wilkin flicked her ashes into the sink. Through the window behind her rain shimmered in the melancholy light. "He was having an affair with your sister-in-law and was seen leaving Farrah's restaurant with her the night she was killed. And unless he's got a solid alibi, my guess is that the captain will arrest him before the end of the day."

Quin guessed that Wilkin or some other cop had talked to the same waitress Andrea Tull had.

"He doesn't even know this yet, Quin. He was on his way to Cedar Key when the captain decided. So keep it to yourself."

"Cedar Key isn't in your jurisdiction, is it?"

"No. But there were four murders on or near Cedar Key last night that the captain thinks may be connected to these. Personally, I rather doubt it, but . . ." She shrugged and offered a wan smile. "I'm not the boss."

"All women?"

"No. A couple of tourists on the jetty, a fisherman, a woman on a bike on State Road 24 . . ."

Blood rushed out of Quin's head and with it went the sound of Wilkin's voice. She was suddenly back inside her dream where Cat was stabbing a finger at a woman pedaling a bike madly through the wet dark.

"Quin?"

She knuckled her eyes and the image vanished. She was still standing in the uncomfortably warm kitchen in the caretaker's house, the dream like a bad taste in her mouth. Smoke from Wilkin's cigarette drifted toward her and she waved it away with her hand.

"Oh, sorry." Wilkin twisted the end of the cigarette

against the inner wall of the sink, then used a paper towel to turn on the faucet. She splashed water against the ashes, washing them away, turned off the faucet, and dropped the spent cigarette into the paper towel. She wadded the towel and dropped it into the empty trash can. "You looked sort of funny there for a minute."

"Do you think Steve killed her?"

"I hope not, Quin."

"All clear up here," Rollins called, his footfalls heavy and loud on the stairs.

"Look, you don't have to hang around here. We're going to wait for Forensics to arrive," Wilkin said.

"I'm expecting a plumber, so I'll be up at the house for a while if you need anything."

"Fine." For the first time since she'd arrived, she winked at Ellie and wiggled her fingers. "Bye-bye, cutie."

Ellie promptly burst into tears and buried her face against Quin's chest. Wilkin stepped back with a shrug. "Oh, well. Today's not my day for kids and dogs, I guess."

It was a relief to get outside, away from the hand, the stifling air, the foul odor, and even from Wilkin.

(4)

The house Turbeta had bought was way the hell out in West Jesus, in an area that had been sectioned and partitioned into lots and blocks but had nothing except trees on them. There were signs on the dirt roads, but no cars, no bikes, no people. It was a neighborhood waiting to happen, McCleary thought, a probable neighborhood.

Then he turned down Forest Boulevard and saw four houses, all with driveways and curbs and landscaped yards. Model homes for the now bankrupt development, he thought, and three of them had FOR SALE signs in their overgrown front yards. An old story in the boom-and-bust economy of Florida's real estate market.

He stopped in front of the last house. It occupied a lush corner lot and was set back from the road, shrouded in hickories and willows. He started to park in the driveway, then changed his mind. He left the Miata in the trees on a lot in the next block and hoofed it back.

The lot was at least three acres, with the house sprawling in the center of it, a cedar split-level that was fenced at the back. It started to rain as McCleary scaled the fence, a light summer rain that was sweet if you weren't in it and irritating if you were. He dropped onto an elevated deck replete with a swimming pool, a Jacuzzi, lounging chairs, and a wet bar under the awning.

The bar was fully stocked with hard liquor and the small refrigerator under it was jammed with half a dozen kinds of beer and every conceivable kind of mixer. From the looks of things, Turbeta was expecting company.

The sliding-glass doors lacked the security extras—steel pins, a board in the track, a latch at the bottom—and didn't appear to be connected to an alarm. It took him about twenty seconds to lift the door off the track, which popped the flimsy lock. He stepped into the cool silence; the noise of the rain receded.

Black marble floors, coral-colored walls, coral and mint green in the fabric of the furniture. Even the accents didn't deviate from the color scheme: Navajo throw rugs, paintings of Indian women, tiles that depicted Indian life. Pottery graced the bookcases, the end tables, the windowsills. There were cactuses and flowering plants and a gravel atrium on one side of the house in which flourished trees and bushes and more cactuses.

All the electronic equipment was Japanese, state-of-the-art. McCleary wouldn't even venture a guess at what it had cost. The rooms were connected by intercoms. The bedrooms, two downstairs and four on the upper level, were lavishly decorated, each with a different motif. Next to each bedroom door was a ceramic tile that bore the name of the room. His least favorite was the China Suite, heavy on reds and satins; the one he liked best was the Country Suite.

There were clothes in the bedroom closets—men's and women's robes in an array of sizes, kimonos, slippers, bathing suits, a supply of linens and towels. In the bathrooms, the tubs were made to lounge in, the ceilings were mirrored, the cabinets were supplied with expensive soaps, shampoos with names he couldn't pronounce, and delicate bottles of exotic oils. There were hair dryers and electric razors and toothbrushes still in their containers. In the kitchen, the refrigerator was stocked with food. But the place didn't look lived in.

The odor of fresh paint and dust still lingered in the air. The washer and dryer in the utility room hadn't been connected yet. When he picked up the phone to call Quin, there wasn't any dial tone; no hookup yet. It was as if the house eagerly awaited inhabitants.

While he was in the kitchen, he heard a car chug into the driveway. He couldn't see it; it was hidden on the other side of the drooping willow branches. But after a moment a woman appeared, her umbrella tipped forward, obscuring her face. McCleary slipped inside the pantry, left the door open a crack, and pressed back as far as he could against the wall to wait.

Presently, the clicking of her shoes grew louder and she came into the kitchen. Her back was to McCleary and since she was wearing a raincoat and a hat, he couldn't tell anything about her. She set a box on the counter, felt under the kitchen cupboard, then picked up the receiver and punched out a number.

"Em? It's Tess. Where do you want me to put all this stuff? . . . Yeah, about five boxes' worth. I've still got to unload the car . . . Uh-huh . . .'' Then, in a soft, little-girl voice, she said: "Em, you sleeping with her? With Andrea?'' Whatever he said, it was the right answer, because she laughed. "Okay, later . . . No, I won't.'' She hung up, reached under the cupboard again, then whipped off her hat and shook her hair free of the rain.

As she turned, she was still smiling, a private, secretive smile. Then McCleary stepped out of the pantry and her smile shriveled like dry meat. "Mike. What—''

"I think it's time we had a little talk, you and me. For old times' sake, Tess.'' He took her by the arm and led her toward the living room. "Remember all those great conversations we had when you and Cat lived in the Grove? All those Saturday nights, Tess? Remember how many times you told me that Cat was like a sister to you?

I think she was better than a sister, though, since she even lent you twenty grand that she probably knew she would never get back. So I'm going to get it back for her, Tess. Twenty grand worth of information.''

He pushed her down into one of the thick Southwest chairs. She looked at him with wounded eyes that filled until the tears spilled, then she covered her face with her hands. McCleary waited with all the time in the world suddenly on his side.

20

(1)

THE SUN CAME out while it was still raining and screamed through the many windows in the living room. It brought out the auburn highlights in Tess's straight hair, making it shine, but it was far less kind to the rest of her. Stripped of makeup, flashy clothes, and most of her jewelry, the ravages of cocaine abuse were evident in the scarcity of flesh that covered her bones, in the circles like bruises under her eyes, in the trembling of her hand as she lit a cigarette, in the way her cotton shirt hung loosely on her shoulders.

She blew a cloud of smoke directly at McCleary. "I didn't do anything. You don't have any right to hold me here."

"I'm not holding you here, Tess. You're free to walk out the door whenever you want."

"Oh, sure. I'm free to leave. Sure, Mike. And then you'll go straight to the cops and lie about me."

"I won't have to lie."

"What's that supposed to mean? Never mind. I know what it means. You and Quin both think I killed her. But I didn't. I signed a note for the loan, you know. Cat didn't want me to, but I did. I insisted on it. *Insisted*. And I was going to pay her back. But it isn't like the loan broke her or anything. She had plenty of money. But I had to postpone payments when Dad got sick . . ."

"And when your coke habit got more expensive."

Her voice sharpened like glass. "I just do it socially. I . . ."

"Sure you do, Tess. And when you're strapped for cash, you pay Emilio in other ways."

She leaped up, her fingers hooked like claws, and

242

swiped at his face. "That's a filthy thing to say, you bastard!"

McCleary caught her by the wrists, was shocked at how thin they were, at how fragile they felt, and pushed her back into the chair. Then he leaned toward her, a hand on either armrest so that his body trapped her in the chair. "Did Emilio kill her?"

She pressed her palms against his chest and tried to shove him back. "Get out of my face, Mike."

"Answer my question."

"Why would Emilio kill her?" Hysteria quivered just beneath the surface of her voice; McCleary knew he'd touched a nerve. "He liked her."

"But you're not sure, are you, Tess."

Silence.

"What's he doing with this house?"

Silence.

"Coke money buy this house, Tess?"

"For your information, he's got an office-supply business."

McCleary laughed. "Kali Inc. doesn't make enough for him to be able to pay eighty-two grand in cash for this place. Or to furnish it like this."

Silence.

"Okay, let's move on to something else, Tess." He pulled up a chair and sat in front of her. "What's in the box in the kitchen? And in the boxes in your car?"

Silence.

"Have it your way."

He went into the kitchen, picked up the box, carried it back into the living room, set it on the floor at Tess's feet, jerked it open.

The array of sexual paraphernalia inside, all of it still in cellophane wrappings, included some objects he'd never seen before and whose purpose was anyone's guess. There were a dozen videotapes in black boxes with nothing written on them (no title, no plot capsule, no stars, no rating) and a stack of soft-porn magazines.

At the bottom of the carton were three round aluminum containers, the kind Christmas cookies came in. One was stuffed with M&M's, another with chocolate chip cookies, and a third with white powder. He dampened the end of his index finger, dipped it into the powder, touched it to the tip of his tongue. It went numb almost instantly.

"And the other boxes?"

"Mostly food." Her voice sounded dead.

"So you're Emilio's lackey."

"Lackey." Her laughter was a low, bitter sound. "Yeah, I guess that's as good a word as any. I run errands for him and he sometimes pays me in coke. And when there aren't any errands to run, I earn my keep by making sure the guests are happy." She threw out her arms. "Imagine this room, Mike, with, oh, anywhere from thirty to fifty people in costumes and masks. Important, sophisticated people, some of them very rich, all of them here for kinky kicks, and no one quite sure of the identity of anyone else. That's the key, really. Anonymity."

She crushed the smoldering filter of her cigarette, lit another, got up, and walked over to the sliding doors. Rain smeared like spit against the glass. The sun had vanished again, and outlined in the pale light Tess seemed terribly small and fragile.

"When it started four or five years ago, it was just Emilio and Jim Kliner and a few friends. They dabbled in the occult. Séances, spells, shit like that. Then they started experimenting sexually and that became the focus of things. It sort of grew from there. The friends brought friends who brought other friends. They wore masks and costumes, tried different drugs. Now it's kind of a club. Masquerade. You pay five hundred bucks at the door every time you attend."

"Expensive membership."

"It's worth it."

He laughed. "For what? You don't have golf, swimming, or tennis."

"Very funny." She turned around. "Masquerade provides a worry-free environment for experimentation."

She was starting to sound like an ad for an avant-garde version of Club Med. "In other words, a percentage of the take goes to paying off the cops."

"It goes to overhead. There're expenses, you know. Food and entertainment and the mortgage . . ."

"And the cops."

"I suppose so, but I don't know for sure."

"How often are these costume balls?"

"Once a month or so."

"And one night you brought Cat along."

Tess's eyes burned. "Don't you dare judge me, Mike. I didn't *make* Catherine come, you know. I thought she might enjoy it, thought it might help her through the rough time she was having with whomever she was seeing. She wasn't very happy toward the end. And people who attend aren't obligated to do anything they don't want to do."

"If it helped her so much, why'd she quit coming?"

Her eyes flicked away and slipped around the room, as though she were remembering it filled with people, music. "I don't know."

"You're a lousy liar, Tess."

"Look, your concern about her well-being is a little late, Mike. I didn't see her turning to you when she was so down in the dumps. I didn't see you coming up here to advise her."

She knew where to hit, he thought. "How long did she come to these things?"

Tess shrugged, paced across the room, stabbed out her cigarette. "I don't know. Four or five months, I guess."

"And the parties are always here?"

"For the last year or so, yeah."

"Emilio just bought the house in July, Tess."

Her smile was sly, mocking. "Okay, so I'm impressed that you've done your homework, Mike. But Emilio rented the place for a while until he bought it, then renovated it. Before that we sometimes met at the store, in the basement. It was fixed up nice."

As though she were referring to someone's restored car. "I get the impression that Emilio is just Jim Kliner's gofer."

She drew her shoulders up, defensive now. "That's not true. They're partners."

"Oh, so Jim has some money in this place."

She flopped down on the couch in the middle of the room and picked at her thumbnail, evasive again. "I wouldn't know."

"I suppose you don't know that Jim was having an affair with Lucy Davenport, either."

"News to me."

"Was Lucy ever here?"

She gave an exaggerated sigh. "How should I know? Everyone wears masks and costumes, remember?"

"I want a list of the members, Tess."

"Oh, for Christ's sakes," she said irritably, throwing her arms out to her sides, then letting them drop to the back of the couch. "There isn't any list, and even if there was, I wouldn't have access to it. Don't you get it, Mike? I'm like an employee, okay? Emilio says do this and I do it. That's all. I know about him and I know about Jim. I don't know about anyone else."

"Who takes the five hundred bucks at the door?"

"It varies."

McCleary thought about Quin's description of the scene she'd witnessed between Tess and Melody backstage at the Hippodrome. "Where does Melody fit?"

Something new crept into her face, something very much like fear. "Melody? Who said anything about her?"

"Afraid she'll fire you, Tess? Is that it?"

"Go away, Mike." She got up, began tossing the items back into the box.

"Help me, Tess."

She raised her head. "Why? Why should I help you with anything? You insult me, accuse me of killing her. . . . Give me one good reason why I should help you, Mike."

"Because she loved you like a sister."

Into her face came a terrible stillness that froze her eyes, paralyzed her mouth, even seemed to smother the breath in her lungs. Then it caved in, laying bare her private struggles, the layered conflicts of grief, conscience, drugs. Her eyes filled with tears, but the tears didn't fall, and she turned her head to the side, rolling her lower lip between her teeth.

"I can't get you a list of members. I don't even know for sure if there *is* a written list."

"Fine. I just want to attend tonight."

She looked at him then. "No cops."

"Okay."

"No trouble."

"You have my word."

"You need to know the protocol."

He didn't say anything, but he stepped aside so that he was no longer blocking her, and her body sagged as though lightened of some terrible burden. It crossed his mind that all of it had been an elaborate act, a duplicitous performance to bring them exactly to this point, where she could set him up. But when she put the box down, sank onto it, and began to talk, McCleary dismissed his misgivings and listened.

(2)

The women came to him while he slept: Lucy with her dark sorrowful eyes; Catherine with her thick black hair; his dead wife with her hands folded against her belly, protecting her unborn child; his wicked sister whispering about the moray eels; and then the others, the many others from cities he'd never been to again. And when Rick opened his eyes, they were in the room with him, as visible as the germs had been, angels of death that surrounded his bed, grinning, waving, giggling.

He bolted forward, a scream trundling down his tongue like a semi jammed in overdrive. He leaped out of bed, ran into the bathroom, slammed the door. He stood against it, shaking, breathing hard, a sob exploding from his mouth.

He heard them now, heard them giggling and whispering and conspiring against him. He flattened against the floor on his stomach, his cheek squashed against the tile, and tried to peer under the door. Shapes, that was all, dark shapes that shifted and oozed, bubbled and changed, shapes of the past, the present, the future, all of them crowding into this one place together.

They banged their fists against the door and called him

by his various names: Rick and Ricky, Richie and Richard, brother and husband and son, lover and teacher and killer. He got up and stumbled to the other side of the room, his blood running hot, then cold, then hot again, and the voices kept on and on, shouting and laughing. He slapped his hands over his ears, turned on the shower to drown out their voices. Then, just that fast, silence clamped down over the house, possessed it, turned it inside out.

His arms dropped to his sides and he listened, straining to catch some small noise. Silence licked at his skin like a dog. His knees gave out. He crumpled to the floor. His exhaustion was so profound, he couldn't move and lay there panting, spit oozing from a corner of his mouth.

After a while, he got up, his knees rubbery. He unlocked the door and opened it. His bedroom was empty. Of course it was.

Bright afternoon light streamed through the windows and across the unmade bed. His clean clothes, the clothes he would wear to the nursing home, were hanging on the inside of the closet door, washed, ironed, ready.

He walked over to the nightstand and picked up the vial of penicillin tablets. He'd already taken one when he got home and now he swallowed another. He kept certain antibiotics around the house the way other people did Tylenol. At the first sign of a scratchy throat or a stuffy nose, he increased his intake of vitamins and started in on some kind of drug. With a thousand milligrams of penicillin pumping through his blood, the red lines shooting away from his shoulder no longer seemed as pronounced. The skin wasn't as puffy, as swollen. And the stitches were holding nicely.

He showered. He didn't see any germs. What had happened earlier seemed distant from him now, not quite real, as though some other man had been hiding in here. Rick dressed and locked up the house and left for the nursing home. He started thinking about last night, but it disturbed him, so he stopped. Richard's calmness stayed with him, held him together like glue.

Mother was out on the lawn with her friend, Christine Davenport. Their wheelchairs were parked side by side in the shade near the fish pond. Mother liked the fish. She liked watching them, naming them, talking to them, feeding them. Right now, the fish were lined up in a neat little row like animals in a circus, waiting as she shredded a piece of bread she'd salvaged from lunch.

"Someone's coming," Christine said without looking around.

Christine reminded him of Lucy when he'd first met her here, Lucy with her long, delicate bones, wearing her beautiful hair pulled away from her face, Lucy with that hopeful expression all lonely, hungry women wore. He had chosen her because she lived alone, because she was recently divorced and in between men, because she had marvelous hair. He'd enjoyed killing her, but he didn't like the way Christine's eyes bore straight through him. He didn't like the way she just backed up her goddamn wheelchair and left without a greeting, an excuse, a word. *She knows,* he thought. *She knows.*

"What's wrong with Christine?" He settled in the grass next to Mother's wheelchair, wondering who would believe Christine if she told. Mrs. LeForge? Bristol? Mother? Would Mother believe her? "Is she having a bad day?"

"She's off to see Clint."

"Who's Clint?"

"Eastwood."

Uh-huh. Clint Eastwood. And he was worried that someone might believe her? He might as well fret about the sun not rising tomorrow. "How're you feeling?"

"Not so good, Ricky. Bad dreams again."

"I'm sorry to hear that, Mom."

"Ricky, can you do something for me?"

"Anything."

"Take me out of here."

Anything but that. "How about next weekend? We'll drive up to—"

"Not for a weekend," she said crossly. "For good. I want to go home."

"I'll talk to your doctor about it."

"He doesn't have anything to do with it. He works for me. I can fire him at any time, you know."

He patted her hand and her fingers closed over his, holding on, squeezing. His skin tingled, but the sensation didn't last long. The elderly were like newborns, nearly pure, practically germ free.

"I don't like it here anymore. Christine is so . . . oh, so damn ornery."

"It's her age, Mom."

"That's got nothing to do with it. It's all these people stopping by to ask questions about her Lucy. Detectives, that McCleary woman—she and I had a fine discussion about Ted Bundy and she asked Christine some questions about Masquerade, you know, that dirty-pictures group that the longhair tried to get Lucy to join."

No, he didn't know, he'd never heard this story, but he knew about Masquerade, straight from the mouth of his princess.

"And while she and I were talking, I got a little mixed up and thought Josie was still alive. Funny, how that happens sometimes . . ."

The glue of his calmness began to dry and crack. That metallic taste—of fear, apprehension—flooded his mouth. He leaned forward, hanging on to Mother's every word and to the spaces in between to divine what Quin McCleary suspected.

Everything, whispered Josie in her wicked, seductive voice.

You reap what you sow, laughed his ex-wife.

Never trust a woman, cooed Lucy.

His eyes began to burn. He could feel something growing inside him, a compact vegetable thing, hard as a squash ball but with long, fibrous fingers that pinched and squeezed at him, telegraphing some urgent message. A year ago, six months ago, even three weeks ago, he might have been able to decipher it. Now it was a code as arcane to him as signals from another planet.

It panicked him. He knew what was happening to him. He knew. He was becoming like Bundy had been toward the end of his life, the core of his personality unraveling, eroded by events he could no longer control, his genius splintered into a thousand ordinary pieces. He felt parts of himself scrambling for safety like ants in a fire that found only another wall of flames. And another. And another. And beyond that tidal waves, earthquakes, erupting volcanos.

Seize something, anything.

His fingers twitched closed on grass and he tore the blades out by the roots. Bits of dirt fell away. An earthworm squirmed through the hole in his fist, its disgusting head poking through the hole in his fist, and he smashed it, squashed it dry. His fingers dived into the grass again, plucking, tearing, ripping, shredding, destroying.

Pretty soon the ground at his side was denuded of green. He controlled this tiny mound of overturned soil and everything that lived in it, worms and spiders, ants and microbes. He was king of this little hill and his power was no less than life and death. That was the lesson, always and forever. Remember. Life, death, nothing less.

"Oh, Ricky."

Mother's voice, soft and pained, reached him as if from a vast distance. Her hand cooled the back of his neck. He looked up, up into those eyes that had always seen too deeply, and realized that he was clutching her knees, that his face had been buried against her breast, that he was weeping. She drew him closer, whispering that it was okay, everything would be okay, and her hair fell around the sides of his head, hair that in his mind was just as dark and lustrous as it had been in his youth. He shut his eyes and drifted away on the music of Mother's voice, the two of them rocking. Rocking gently.

(3)

Lunch arrived in midafternoon. Andy's stomach was twisted up with hunger and she had a wicked headache. She hadn't eaten anything since the rolls she and Jules had shared during their ride to Cedar Key. And after one look at what was on her plate, she knew she probably wouldn't be eating again until she got out of here. It was some sort of mush the color of bird crap, with a slice of Wonder bread and a plop of what might have been rice pudding for dessert.

She slipped the plate back into the metal slot in her

cell door and shouted, "Hey, Corporal. You forget about my phone call?"

Her voice echoed in the chilly, metallic air. She was the only person inhabiting any of the eight cells, and the dipshit sheriff had put her in the one at the very end of the row. Only by craning her neck could she see the metal door between her and the rest of the world.

After she shouted again, the corporal appeared, a man pushing sixty who looked to have a fondness for dark, heavy beer. He moved with the maddening slowness of honey from a jar, trying to light a pipe and talk to her at the same time.

"I heard you, I heard you, ma'am. Just hold your horses."

"I was entitled to a phone call as soon as I walked through that door, Corporal, and it's . . . what? Two P.M. now? That's six hours."

"That's true, ma'am. But I had to track down Sheriff Partridge to make sure you hadn't already made a call." He unfastened a remote-control device from his belt and aimed it at the door. Nothing happened. "Hell, these electric doors never work like they're supposed to." He shook the device, aimed it again. Still nothing. "Finally found him up in Gainesville. He drove the bodies to Gainesville and stuck around for the coroner's report. And in the meantime that detective you floored got himself arrested for one of them murders."

"Detective Bristol?"

"If he's the one you slugged, then that's who we're talking about, yes, ma'am. That'd be him, all right." He'd been fiddling with a button on the device and now, when he tried it again, her door whispered open.

They stood facing each other with nothing between them. He motioned her out, took hold of her arm, and they started up the hallway. "You have a quarter on you, ma'am?"

"No. My money's in my purse."

"It's locked up in the safe and only the sheriff's got the combination."

"Can you lend me one? It'll be a collect call, so you'll get it back."

252

"Can't, ma'am. Regulations." He fitted his pipe between his lips, lit it without letting go of her arm, puffed on it. "But I reckon your lawyer's got one."

"My lawyer's here?"

"Yes, ma'am."

She didn't have a lawyer, not in Gainesville.

He ushered her into a room with nothing in it but a table and four chairs. Sitting at the head of the table was King, minus his pigtail, wearing a suit, with a leather briefcase open in front of him.

"Have a seat, Ms. Tull, and let's figure out how to get you released. Could you excuse us, Corporal?"

The old coot looked as though he was going to mutter something about regulations, but even he knew she was entitled to time alone with her attorney. "I'll be outside if you need anything, counselor."

The door shut. "How the—"

King touched a finger to his mouth. "There isn't much time," he whispered. Then, in a louder voice, so the corporal could hear if he was listening: "The courthouse here on the island closes at four, Ms. Tull, so I won't be able to get you released today . . ."

Outside the door the floor creaked as the corporal went about his business. "You're breaking a dozen laws doing this, King," she said softly.

"Picadillo tells me to keep an eye on you. To make sure you don't get into trouble. I followed you and your friend here this morning. So when you got in trouble, I called Picadillo. He called his lawyer. The lawyer made a few calls, okay? He's trying to get you transferred to Gainesville sometime this evening, then he'll meet you there with a bondsman. But Picadillo wanted you to know this, face-to-face, no phones, he says, so here I am. You know about Detective Bristol?"

She nodded. "And I've got tapes that I think will prove they've got the wrong man. Catherine's brother has them. Call him for me and tell him to hold on to them until he hears from me. Not to give them to anyone."

"No problem. Anything else?"

"Yeah, thanks."

"Just canceling my debt to Picadillo." He pulled

something out of his pocket, crouched, slipped it inside her sneaker, stood again. "It's just a small knife, okay? You don't have to take it. But I figure you're always better off with something just in case. Picadillo says to trust no one." He grinned. "Except me."

He opened the door and the corporal was waiting for her on the other side of the door. "Still need that quarter, ma'am?"

"No, my attorney will make the call. Thanks again, Mr. King."

"No problem." He waved and walked out into the rain.

As the corporal led her back down the hall, she felt the knife snuggled up against the inner wall of her shoe.

Trust no one.

21

(1)

THE PLUMBER HAD finally shown up early that afternoon. Quin had been so irritated that he was late, she had nearly told him she'd changed her mind about the repairs. But he had given her such a low estimate on repairing the shower, she had hired him on the spot. He'd returned a while later with an assistant and his gear and had been in the bathroom ever since. Even from her spot next to the smashed Wurlitzer on the porch, the racket sounded as though they were rebuilding the entire east end of the house.

The rain had tapered off and water dripped steadily from the chains of Spanish moss. Now and then the sun struggled through banks of clouds, a fuzzy white disk no larger than a throat lozenge. The light made the puddles in the yard glisten like broken eggs. It was a strange, flat light, she thought, not conducive to photographs, for instance, something that added luster but not depth, like the illumination cast from a lamp without a shade. And more, it failed to alter in any way the geography of the case board in front of her.

Quin had combined their separate case boards into one, then arranged and rearranged it, hoping the marriage of the two would yield the secret she sensed but couldn't find. It was here, she knew it was, tucked somewhere in the folds of facts and suspicions that she, McCleary, and Andy Tull had compiled. But no matter how she arranged the information, she kept coming up with nothing.

The hammering inside the house didn't help. All this for a leaky shower pan? No telling what they might find once they were in: carpenter ants the size of bumblebees, rotting boards, rusted pipes, dead rats.

The incessant noise had constricted to a tight, hard knot in her right temple. But it wasn't just the hammering. It was the waiting—for the plumber to arrive, for McCleary's call, for Ellie to take a nap—waiting for that moment of illumination when the disparate pieces would fall into place.

Perhaps the missing piece, she thought, lay in Masquerade.

In their life before Ellie, she and McCleary would have pulled this job together, and until Cat's murder, it would have irritated her no end that she would miss it. But the course of her sorrow about Cat had taken unexpected turns, she thought, and mostly she was grateful for a night with Ellie, just the two of them and Flats. If it was chilly, she would build a fire and they would settle down in front of it with Ellie's books and blocks and toys.

"Mrs. McCleary?" Jake, the plumber, strode out onto the porch with dust on his cheeks and a spot of grease at the tip of his hawk nose. His partner passed them, carrying gear out to the car.

"Finished?" she asked.

He laughed. "Hardly. It's the shower pan, all right. It's got more holes in it than a brick of Swiss cheese. If you could come back here for a second, ma'am, I need to show you something."

"Sure." She glanced toward Ellie, who was sitting with Flats near the dusty piano stacking Tupperware containers. "Watch the munchkin, Flats, okay?"

The sheepdog barked and Jake laughed. "They make great baby-sitters. We've got a Lab and I swear she's the only one in the family our son listens to."

On their way to the back of the house, they exchanged information about their respective offspring. Such comparisons always included odd bits of information you couldn't find in books: a new method of potty training, for instance, or some home remedy for a child's bad dreams. And, invariably, Quin's anxieties about Ellie's development were always soothed. But even this exchange did nothing to mitigate her shock when she saw the bathroom.

It looked as though it had been bombed. Loose tiles

and chunks of plaster were everywhere, only one wall of the shower was left standing, the maze of pipes and plumbing were exposed, the wall between the stall and the toilet had a hole in it that a grown man could squeeze through. "Just take a look behind that wall, Mrs. Mc-Cleary."

She did, then wished she hadn't. The floor had rotted out; she could see straight down to a mound of earth under the house. "The whole floor has to be replaced?"

"That'd be the smart thing to do, but it'd cost a fortune. You could get by with just replacing everything about two feet out in every direction from the shower."

They negotiated a price. "We can come back tomorrow afternoon, if that's okay with you, ma'am, and finish it up then."

"Sure, that's fine."

"I used to try to finish a job I'd started, but I was working so late, my wife felt like a widow. There's hell to pay when a woman starts feeling like that."

They left shortly afterward and Quin stood on the porch, watching them as they drove out. That phrase, "hell to pay," turned slowly in her mind, a squeaky little pinwheel. Was that it? The elusive X in the equation? Had the change in the killer's pattern resulted from a change in the relationship between him and his partner, a woman who was also his lover?

A tenuous balance disturbed by some random event, she thought, and suddenly a trust was shattered and the pivot of power had spun out of whack, shifting the entire geography of their relationship. Was that what had happened? What had set it off? Which of them had wielded the knife last night? Which one had stabbed the woman on the bike, the woman in her dream? Which one had sought redemption in the utter madness of the kills? Him or her?

Quin picked up the case board and carried it inside. She fixed Ellie a bottle, a hard-boiled egg, and a bowl of applesauce, got her situated in an overstuffed chair and went into the den for the tapes and the recorder. She set it up on the dining room table, popped in a tape, switched it on.

There was a lot of static, then she heard Andrea's voice, thick with sleep; "Hello?"

The sound of the caller's breathing was now close enough to taste. Goose bumps rose on Quin's arms as that raspy voice said, "I woke you."

She fast-forwarded through Andrea's reply. Now the caller was laughing, quick expulsions of air that remained soft and slippery, the way moss sounded if rubbed against the palm of a hand. "It's morning, Andrea. Not light yet, but morning. That's important."

Male or female? She couldn't tell. The tape just wasn't that good and the voice was too soft.

Quin spun the tape ahead to the caller's description of Cat's murder. "It was on a farm and there was a lot of fog . . ."

They had listened to the tapes three times when Andrea was here. But it was different now, alone with Ellie and Flats, alone with the noise of the dripping trees and the weird light, alone with this voice. Different, too, because of what she knew now.

"What's black and white and read all over, Andy?"

"A newspaper . . ."

"Very good, Andy. Her name is Barbara."

Barbara, who worked at a newspaper.

Who had made the calls? Did the one who hadn't know about the calls?

Lovers who killed. Start there, she thought. Follow it. Okay, then. Before last night the killers had agreed on certain commonalities about the murders to create a particular MO: the chalk, the bleach, brunets, the locks of hair, the mutilations, novocaine, the arrangement of clothes and personal items. But beyond that each had chosen a victim, planned the respective details of the murder, and the other had gone along with it. The decision, then, about where and how to dispose of the women's hands was probably as individual as the victims they'd chosen.

The bleach, the absence of fingerprints, the conscious shaping of an MO, pointed to someone familiar with police work, forensics, with the criminal mind. Someone who was an expert in criminal behavior? Someone whose dead wife's name just happened to be Barbara?

"Jesus." Quin stabbed at the stop button, a chill whipping through her. She popped the tape from the recorder.

Barbara. A coincidence? Or did Farmer's partner intend to pin the murders on him? *Is that it?*

Quin got up and shut the French doors. Ellie had fallen asleep in the chair, the last of the hard-boiled egg clutched in her hand, the bowl of applesauce in the crook of her arm. Quin removed the bowl, picked the egg out of her hand, lifted her carefully.

She felt a sudden softening in her muscles, as though her body were a buttery wasteland held together by a few thin bones. She held her daughter tightly as she carried her into the bedroom, held her and felt like weeping for the countless times she had resented Ellie's demands on her time, her life, her very being, for the times she had allowed Ellie to come between her and McCleary. And for what? To prove something to herself?

In the end, the only things that mattered were these: the reality of Ellie's warmth, her softness, her trust and laughter, and all of the small, bright quirks and minutiae that made up who she was.

But she had also loved McCleary's sister and that love demanded its own completion—from her, from him.

She realized she had moved across the room and was now packing a diaper bag, her hands reaching automatically into the bureau for the articles Ellie would need. Now she was changing into jeans, a dark shirt, running shoes. Now she was rifling through McCleary's suitcase for the Browning. She snapped in a clip. Thirteen rounds. Not enough. She dropped two more rounds into her purse.

Quin turned to Ellie and pulled off her sunsuit; its collar was stained with breakfast, with lunch, with playtime in the rain. She fitted her head and arms into a T-shirt from Disney World that was too big for her. Quin changed her diaper.

I need to do this, El. I need to.

She would follow him. Follow Farmer. She would follow him all night if that was what it took. But first she

259

would make sure her daughter was safe. She would ask Helen Charles to keep her for the night. She trusted Helen.

Quin propped a couple of pillows at the edge of the bed so Ellie wouldn't roll off. Then she hastened into the living room to call Helen.

The phone rang before she reached it. When she picked it up, a man asked for McCleary. She said he wasn't home, this was his wife, could she help him? "My name is King and Andy Tull asked me to call you. . . ."

(2)

The last thing he remembered was the softness of Mother's hair surrounding him, enfolding him, protecting him. But here he was, standing in front of the refrigerator in his kitchen, wearing latex gloves, a doctor's gloves. The light in the windows indicated that it was much later in the day. He didn't know what he'd done in the intervening hours, but it didn't matter. The important thing was that he knew what he was doing now.

He opened the freezer and rummaged through the packages of wrapped food until he pulled out the Baggie that contained Lucy Davenport's hand. He could still visualize how it had looked in those last few minutes of her life. He could see the coral nails filed into perfect ovals, the long, graceful fingers hooked over the armrest of the chair, tendons straining against the skin on the back of her hand. It wasn't very pretty now. But stripped of artifice, it was closer to its true nature as a carrier of filth and germs.

He shut the freezer door, tossed the Baggie onto the table. It clunked like a rock. He lifted the receiver and punched out her number. She picked up on the second ring and the sound of her voice shocked him. It was harsh, ugly, cruel, as though it, like Lucy's hand, had somehow been reduced to its true essence.

"It's Rick."

"Hi. I was just about to call you."

How quickly her voice was transformed into something of beauty, changing like a chameleon's color. He looked at Lucy's hand and wondered what she had done with Catherine's. The hands had symbolized their pact with each other, their trust. But for her the trust had been only another lie, a means of gaining power over him, controlling him, and ultimately betraying him, if that suited her purpose. The amputated hand of a dead woman, after all, would be incontrovertible evidence of guilt.

"Rick? You still there?"

Where else would I be, babe? "Sure. You free tonight?"

She laughed gaily. "I was just going to ask you the same thing. I thought you might like to celebrate Bristol's arrest."

A small memory clicked into place as she said this, of himself listening to the local news on the radio as he'd driven home from his visit with Mother. "I can't think of a better reason to celebrate." He paused. "Did you know about him and Catherine?"

"I suspected. It was just a matter of dropping hints in the right places."

Such a clever woman. Even if Bristol could never be tied to the other murders, people would assumed he'd committed them, the investigation would wane, the heat would be off. But it didn't change his plan one goddamn iota.

"So, what time will you be free?" How smooth and effortless his voice sounded, how convincing.

"I'll be tied up until later."

Tied up: a perfect metaphor. "How much later?"

"I'm not sure."

Masquerade, he thought. Another perfect metaphor.

"How about if I call you?" she asked.

No, that wouldn't do at all. She was trying to seize control again. He knew her tricks. He told her where he'd meet her and when and why. He expected her to argue, to protest, to twist things so she would be in control again. But she laughed, a small, coy laugh. He had a sudden, disquieting sensation of the sky coming unhinged, of clouds falling, of the sun spinning like a roulette wheel in the kitchen window. He felt dizzy and grabbed onto the back of the chair to steady himself. The feeling had passed when they hung up a few minutes later, but the faint taste of metal lingered against his tongue, a warning.

(3)

Their meeting took place in a large room, with a plate of glass between them. It was observed by at least four cops, two on Bristol's side of the glass and two on McCleary's side.

Though the cops weren't close enough to eavesdrop on the conversation, their presence obviously made Bristol uneasy. He hunkered down in his chair and kept his mouth very close to the speaker as he whispered, "How the hell did you get in here, Mike?"

"Pulled a few strings." It was actually Tim Benson who'd done the pulling, but Bristol didn't need to know that. "And I've got fifteen minutes, so start talking, Steve."

Bristol's flat blue eyes spit at him; color exploded in his cheeks. "You had no fucking right to go to my wife."

"I had every right. Now tell me what my sister was involved in. Tell me about Masquerade. Convince me you're not the asshole you appear to be and that I shouldn't be cheering Andrea Tull for slugging you."

"Fuck off." He got up.

"The killer made calls, Steve, and they were taped. Talk to me and I'll release them."

He turned back, frowning. "Calls? When? To whom? You?"

"To Andrea Tull."

"Jesus." He sank into the chair. "What'd he say?"

"I'm not entirely convinced it was a man, but whoever it was gave Tull specific details on the murders." He explained what he knew and what he suspected and Bristol listened without interruption, growing paler by the moment. "So I need to know everything you do about Masquerade."

"I didn't know anything about it until that last night."

"When you and Cat left Farrah's?"

Bristol nodded, rubbed his hands over his face. "We

262

went back to the farm and started arguing about my wife. That's when she told me she'd gone to these parties. Civilized sex games, I think that's how she described them. She said that in the beginning she felt like they evened the score between us. If I was going to sleep with my wife, then she would sleep around, too.''

"Did she?''

Bristol hesitated, uncomfortable with the memory. "She got involved with a woman. I don't know who it was, I don't even know the extent of the involvement. But when she was talking about it, I got the impression that what happened between them took place only within the context of these parties, that maybe she never even knew the woman's identity.''

Of all the things Bristol might have told him, this possibility hadn't even occurred to McCleary. His sister with a woman, the comfort of gender: It made a terrible kind of sense, given the state of her relationship with Bristol at the time.

"It would fit in with your theory about two killers, Mike.''

"Did she say why she stopped going to the parties?''

"It complicated things for her emotionally and I think it also began to affect her work. Even in the worst of times, Catherine was able to keep her work and her life separate and then suddenly she couldn't. That was her bottom line. If anything got in her way where acting was concerned, she got rid of it.''

"Did she ever say anything about Tess that would make you think she might have been the woman?''

Bristol stared down at his hands, turned them over, seemed to contemplate the sweat that glistened in the lines. "She felt sorry for Tess, cared for her deeply, but no, I don't think there was ever anything sexual between them. But there was a lot of tension between her and Melody. Melody wanted to represent Catherine, Melody couldn't direct worth a damn, Melody was empty between the ears: comments like that. And put them together in the same room anywhere except onstage . . .'' He shook his head. "You could feel the tension then. But her alibi for that night checked out, Mike. She was on Cedar Key, staying with a friend at the Island Hotel.''

So what, McCleary thought. She could have left and come back, and given last night's murders on Cedar Key, it was another one of those so-called coincidences that bothered him. He said as much. ''Melody was also involved with Jim Kliner a few years ago, and Kliner's one of the people behind Masquerade.''

Bristol started to say something but clammed up when one of the cops came up behind him. ''Time's up.''

''Give me just another minute, okay?'' he asked.

''Then that's it.''

The man moved away. Bristol leaned toward the glass and in a voice so soft McCleary barely heard him said, ''One thing my wife probably didn't tell you, Mike, but I want you to know it. The morning after Catherine and I argued that last time, I told Janet I was filing for a divorce. Catherine was already dead then, but I didn't know it. So whatever happens to me won't be nearly bad as living with the knowledge that my inability to make a decision may have inadvertently killed her.'' He swallowed hard. ''She was the best thing that ever happened to me.''

Then he got up and walked off, favoring his bum leg, his shoulders hunched like a very old man's.

(4)

The tapes, put the tapes someplace safe, King had said with a disturbing urgency in his voice. Quin finally stashed them behind some books on the shelf in Cat's den.

She tried Helen again, but the phone at Tot Stop was still busy. She paced, called again, got another busy signal. More waiting, she thought, forget it. She decided to drive to Tot Stop and take her chances that Helen wasn't busy tonight.

She let Flats outside and propped the door open so that she could get back in if it started to rain. The sheepdog stood for a moment at the bottom of the steps, sniffing the air, then hobbled out into the waning light, her nose to the ground, following some critter scent. ''Don't jump any fences, girl,'' Quin called after her.

En route to town she thought of Andrea in jail, of McCleary somewhere in Gainesville, of Ellie, who would be with Helen, of herself tailing Farmer, everyone isolated, divided, separated. But the alternative, of more waiting as night fell like some dense curtain, was worse. She pressed the accelerator to the floor and drove.

22

(1)

". . . IN THE WEATHER news for this evening, we've got a tornado watch for northern Alachua County until midnight tonight. A twister touched down in a trailer park twelve miles north of the city, but there's no word yet on the exact location or the extent of the damage. Stay tuned for further bulletins."

Just what he needed, McCleary thought, switching off the radio. A goddamn tornado watch to cancel Masquerade's festivities tonight. But he supposed it was preferable to a hurricane watch, where people took cover behind boarded-up windows and settled in with food and supplies to ride out the storm, which could last for hours. A tornado lasted less than twenty minutes and rarely traveled more than fifteen miles. And there wasn't much you could do to prepare except hide in a cellar, if you had one.

But on the down side, a tornado often packed winds in excess of two hundred miles and struck with such violence and fury that it instantly demolished whatever it touched. The twister that roared through Xenia, Ohio, nearly twenty years ago had flattened three thousand buildings in just three minutes, he recalled. In high winds, the stilts that held up the farmhouse would snap like matchsticks in seconds.

He would call Quin once he was inside the theatre to make sure she had the radio or TV on. She would kid him about being an alarmist, which was usually her role, but two decades in South Florida had taught him to respect violent weather.

The Hippodrome's parking lot was almost empty. McCleary parked near the entrance, pulled the Magnum from the glove compartment, loaded it, and slipped it into the shoulder holster that his windbreaker covered. As he got out, leaves fluttered from the trees and swirled in little dervishes around his feet. The air smelled thickly of rain. Lightning flashed in the distance.

From the trunk, he removed a gym bag. He dumped the stuff that was inside it, slung it over his shoulder, and trotted up the steps to the side door. The only people in the lobby were a man and a woman sharing a cigarette who didn't even glance at him. He hoped they were refugees from the theatre's library and not members of the repertory company.

He called the house from the pay phone, reached the answering machine; Quin had probably gone into town for groceries. He left a message about the tornado watch, then climbed the rear stairs to the second floor and used one of the keys Tess had given him to unlock the backstage door. A few lights were on and he heard music coming from a radio somewhere. Otherwise, the hall was strangely quiet, a waiting quiet, as though the building were holding its breath.

On his right was a room marked PROPERTIES and to his left was COSTUMES. He listened before he tried the knob, heard nothing, walked in. Track lights illuminated the racks of costumes—blacks and golds and pinks and purples, satins and silks and cottons, sequins and beads, hats and shoes, socks and stockings, capes and coats and shawls. Stage magic.

He had a sudden, clear image of Cat playing dress-up when she was a kid, her little feet flopping around in high heels, her mouth painted a sloppy red, a hat with a feather in it sitting lopsided on her head. *Look at me, Mikey.* He rubbed his hands over his face, shocked at how deeply the memory hurt, at how deeply it angered him. Anger at whom? At himself for failing her? At Bristol for appreciating her too late to make a difference? At Tess who'd betrayed her? At Cat for dying? At the bastard who'd killed her, amputated her hand, and stuck it in a garbage disposal?

All of them, none of them, he didn't know, it didn't matter. The anger was a thing unto itself, like a force of nature. It sharpened the edges in him that grief had dulled, and he moved quickly and purposefully between the racks of costumes, jerking out this hanger, that one. He went through the plastic bins stacked against the wall like blocks. They contained bras and slips and stockings, shoes and socks, T-shirts, undershirts, costume jewelry. He picked out everything he needed, then shoved it all into the gym bag.

In the adjoining bathroom, he searched the cabinets for a razor but couldn't find one. A drugstore, he thought. He would have to go by a drugstore. But there was time, plenty of time. This was one event where it wouldn't matter if he arrived late.

He was halfway across the room when he heard voices in the hall. Voices coming this way. One more irritant. He turned quickly toward the wall, where several empty cardboard cartons had been fitted together like Chinese puzzle boxes. He pulled out the top one, dropped the gym bag inside, closed the flaps, picked it up.

The door swung open and Melody Burns breezed in, saying something about common sense to Jim Kliner, who was with her. She stopped in midsentence when she saw McCleary.

"Mike." There was something undeniably arresting about her face, a wryness, a cleverness. She was the type who supplied the punchline when the teller forgot it, answered the obscure question on geography in Trivial Pursuit, knew who had made the cover of *Variety* last week. That kind of woman. "What're you doing here?" Her lovely eyes narrowed, assessing, measuring. Her concentration etched faint lines against her pale, otherwise flawless complexion, lines that deepened at the mouth when she smiled. "Did we have an appointment I forgot or something?"

"No, nothing like that." He nodded at Kliner, who didn't nod back, who didn't acknowledge him in any way. He stood behind Melody, his long hair loose and flowing over his shoulders: Christ without the halo. Yeah, fuck you, too, pal, McCleary thought, and looked back at Melody and held up the box. "I'm packing the things in Catherine's dressing room and needed another box."

"Oh, take as many of those things as you want. They'll just fill with hangers."

"Thanks, I will." He chose another larger box and fitted the smaller one into it. "I'll have to come back tomorrow and finish. How early does the building open?"

"Sevenish. It'd be easier to load your car if you park on the ramp at the rear door."

"Great. I will."

"I guess you'll be heading south now that an arrest has been made." This came from Kliner.

"In a couple of days." He smiled at Melody. "Thanks again."

"Sure."

He shut the door on his way out. Melody, the planner, the diplomat, the brains behind Masquerade? Melody, his sister's lover?

He set the boxes on the floor of Cat's dressing room and slipped back across the hall. He listened at the door. Whispers, then nothing but the noise of a rack on wheels clattering across the room. He returned to Cat's dressing room, deciding what to pack to make his story look good. Books from the low shelves under the window (theatre, metaphysics), old magazines in the bottom desk drawer, the odds and ends stuffed in the cubbyholes of the rolltop desk.

He found a framed family photograph that had been taken at a Thanksgiving reunion several years ago, before Ellie was born, before Cat's life had slipped into darkness. She stood between him and Quin, her arms around their waists, her black hair tumbling over her shoulders in loose waves. She was laughing at something Quin had said, but he couldn't remember what it was. No White Linen that day, though. And no White Linen now.

McCleary wished suddenly, desperately, that the scent would come to him someplace other than the farmhouse, as it had for Quin. Then it would be easier for him to believe that its source was Cat. It was one thing to die, he thought, and to know that your consciousness continued in some form, but quite another to believe that communication was possible with the people who had survived you.

He pressed his thumb over the surface of the photograph and wondered what had happened to the glass. The cops, he thought. The cops had probably broken it accidentally when they'd searched the room. The photo slid around in the frame, came away from the right edge, and exposed a slip of paper inside, airmail paper, very thin. McCleary quickly removed it.

It had been folded once, and inside, the note was typed, undated, unsigned. It read:

I thought of silk that night, of unexplored canyons, of worlds I'd imagined but never seen, you stirring under my hands in air that smelled green. Your heart, beating like a sparrow's, your long arms stretching up, up over your head as if to seize the moon, your knee bending, disturbing the perfect length of your leg and ending in a perfect upside down V, the geometry of your bones: These are the things I remember.

Does it bother you to read this, Catherine? To remember the moment of unmasking? Can you feel my teeth against your skin? Does their imprint linger? Can you remember your pleasure? How you felt? Can you still feel any of that? Can you? Or was it just another part for you, another role, the incarnation of another character, an act for some hidden camera?

I sit here in the heat, naked in the heat, and my hands become your hands, touching in the ways you touched me, Catherine, your long fingers playing me like a violin, your touch quick and certain and never cruel. It's only afterward that your cruelty shows, after those long, fine bones have tightened and loosened and tightened again, after you've taken from me and claim you have nothing to give in return.

Those are the times I hate you, hate the sight of you, running your fingers through your hair, patting your clothes, rearranging your mask, your goddamn disguise. But I know what you are, Catherine. I know who you are and what you need and no one else can give you what I can.

No one.

Don't do this, Catherine. Come to me, come the

way you have in the past, in the softness of laughter,
under the black sky, in the invisible heat that we have
dreamed.

McCleary's head throbbed. His fingers left damp marks
against the sheet of paper as he folded it, slipped it into
an inner pocket in his windbreaker. *No date. No signa-*
ture. He picked up the carton he'd packed and left the
building the same way he'd entered it.

It was nearly dark outside now. It had begun to sprinkle. *I sit here in the heat, naked in the heat.* Bristol was
wrong about one thing. Whoever the woman was, Cat's
relationship with her had not been confined to Masquerade.

(2)

Supper wasn't much of an improvement over lunch,
Andy thought, but she was too hungry not to eat. So she
sat at the edge of the cot, forcing herself to eat slowly,
hoping she could kill twenty or thirty minutes. And that
was the point, really, food as a means of passing the
time, as an excuse not to dwell on the knife in her shoe
and on what she might or might not do with it when the
opportunity arrived.

If it arrived.

It would arrive, wouldn't it? She would be transferred
to Gainesville, wouldn't she?

She heard the phone ring in the main room, heard the
gruffness of the old corporal's voice, but couldn't make
out a word of what he was saying. She slipped her nearly
empty plate back into the tray slot in the door and strained
to catch a word, a phrase, anything.

Jules, she thought. It was Jules calling to check on how
she was doing. She rather liked the idea of Jules in the
throes of guilt for deserting her at the first sign of trouble. But given the choice, she would prefer a call from
King, letting her know he'd gotten in touch with the
McClearys.

The door at the end of the hall slid open and the corporal shuffled in. He was trying to light his pipe again,

271

like a character in some surreal story, whose lot in life was this corridor and that goddamn pipe.

"Call for me?" she asked hopefully as he aimed the remote control device at the door of her cell.

"Nope." He puffed on the pipe; the sweet aroma of the tobacco reminded her of gentle things, ordinary things, sunlight on water, a gull in flight. "Just the cop who's driving you to Gainesville. Calling from up the road a piece."

Andy had a sense of things sliding together, coalescing, congealing like blood. "So then I'm definitely being transferred."

"Ayup." the old man snorted. "Assuming that one cold beer up the road don't turn into a dozen."

Wonderful. An intoxicated cop was going to drive her the fifty miles to Gainesville.

The door whispered open. The corporal said he had to cuff her. *Regulations. You know how it is.* Andy held out her arms, wrists mashed together, the smoke from his pipe drifting into her eyes. "Oh, I almost forgot. Your lawyer done called a while ago. He'll meet you in Gainesville when you arrive."

In the front room, the corporal reached behind a counter with a hundred cigarette burns on it and pulled out a white plastic bag. It was tied neatly at the top, like a bag of garbage, with a tag that bore her name.

"Your things," he said, scribbling his name on a clipboard.

"Ah, right."

"You want some coffee?"

"Sure. Thanks."

He led her to one of the wooden chairs against the windows, unlocked the handcuffs, then snapped the left cuff around the arm of the chair.

"Is this really necessary?" she asked. "I'm not going anywhere."

"Regulations. I'm by myself tonight. How do you take your coffee?"

"Cream and three sugars." What were thirty calories when her entire intake of calories today probably hadn't amounted to enough to keep a bird flying?

While the corporal fussed with the coffeemaker, Andy shifted around and gazed out the window. The sodium vapor lamps cast a Halloween glow on Main Street, which was virtually empty. A fine mist was falling and tendrils of a light fog snaked across the wet road, dissolving when the wind blew, only to re-form again a moment later, like a line of conga dancers.

The knife in her shoe.

She squeezed the bridge of her nose and rubbed her eyes. The ticking of the clock on the wall, the hiss and sputter of the coffeemaker, seemed abnormally loud. Headlights flashed against the window as a car turned down Main Street. She watched it drive on past, a dark beast prowling the mist. She sensed a stirring of something out there in the wet dark, a culling of elemental forces that would breathe life into events that were still only probable. A ball of ice formed in her stomach. Her hands began to perspire. Her bladder suddenly ached. She asked the corporal if she could use the restroom.

"Reckon it'll be okay. Long drive to Gainesville, 'specially in weather like this." He unlocked her cuffs, led her to a restroom down the hall, and locked her in.

She quickly pulled off her shoe, liberating the small knife. A switchblade. An anachronistic weapon, she thought. *West Side Story*, gangs, hoodlums. It was very narrow, about four inches long, bright red, badly scratched, cool to the touch. She had to press the button several times before the blade snapped out. It wasn't long, but it was sharp enough to cut the hair on her legs.

So what? Who was she kidding? She wasn't going to use it.

Trust no one.

She pulled her sock and shoe back on and pressed the switchblade down deeply into her shoe. Then she relieved herself and a few moments later, called for the corporal.

(3)

Quin eyed the clock on the dashboard. Sixty-one minutes now, but who was counting?

273

She was parked in the trees at the dead end of Farmer's street. She knew he was home; she'd seen him dart out into the rain an hour ago to fetch a newspaper at the end of his driveway. But he hadn't appeared since and she was beginning to think he probably wasn't going anywhere tonight except to bed.

It was already eight.

Thirty more minutes. If he hadn't shown up by then, she would drive back to Helen's and pick up Ellie and that would be that.

She was fiddling with the radio dial when a dark car pulled out of Farmer's garage. A Firebird. Funny, she'd pegged him as the type who would drive a Corvette. Something phallic. Something that made a statement. A Firebird was a teenager's car, fast and noisy, a car that cruised South Florida streets in search of girls in string bikinis.

It hung a right at the end of the street. As soon as it had turned, Quin cranked up the Wagoneer, hit the headlights, pulled out of the trees. The wipers made their slow and infuriating noise—*squish*, *squish*—like feet in a pair of wet galoshes. She swung out onto the road, saw the Firebird at the light just ahead, its engine idling noisily, a distant thunder.

The light turned. The car didn't leap, didn't lunge, didn't peel rubber through the intersection. It just rolled on through the dark, in no apparent hurry, and Quin followed, pacing herself to him, sliding into the groove he cut through the air.

(4)

When the corporal led Andy into the front room again, Detective Angie Wilkin was standing there in a gray raincoat. She didn't look as carefully put together as she had the last time Andy had seen her. No glossy lipstick now. No makeup at all, in fact. Her hazel eyes seemed almost as pale as her cheeks, the freckles across the bridge of her nose were like imperfections, and her brows needed plucking. Her hair was damp from the mist and she'd hooked it behind her ears, which gave her face an odd severity, a cop look, Andy thought.

"Hello, Miss Tull."

"Hi."

"You're signed out and I've got the transfer paperwork, but I've got to search you first."

Panic. The knife in her shoe. "Search me? For what? No one's back there but me."

"Usually in transfers we have someone riding shotgun. But I'm solo tonight." She seemed apologetic, but it didn't change anything. "Hands against the wall."

Don't check my shoes, she thought.

The detective took her time patting her down. "Do you know about Steve's arrest?" she asked.

"Yes. And I've got tapes with the killer's voice on it, and I'll tell you right now, the voice isn't Steve's."

"Tapes?" Wilkin's fingers slipped into Andy's back pockets, touching, feeling, as though seeking federal secrets. "What tapes?"

"Phone calls."

Her hands were moving down Andy's left leg now. "How do you know the voice isn't his?"

"I can tell."

"Then whose voice is it?"

"I don't know. I just know it isn't Steve's."

Now her hands were slipping up Andy's right leg. "Tell me about them."

So Andy did, talking rapidly, hoping to distract her from moving her hands lower to her shoes. Besides, she needed an ally and what better ally than Bristol's partner?

"Turn around, Ms. Tull."

She turned. Wilkin's hands slipped across the breast pockets on her shirt, over her ribs. Then she stepped back. "Look, I know you and Steve don't get along, but we're talking about a homicide investigation." She spoke softly, glancing now and then toward the corporal, who stood behind the counter patting tobacco into his pipe. "You should have turned them over to *somebody*. You could have given them to me. If you had, Steve probably wouldn't be sitting in jail."

"Don't rub it in. I feel guilty enough about that already."

"They're transferring him out later tonight, up to a holding cell in Lake Butler."

"What for?"

"I'm not sure. I think it probably has something to do with the feds wanting to talk to him. I'd like to be able to turn over those tapes to the captain before that happens."

"Then you think he's innocent."

Wilkin's voice dropped to a whisper. "Of course he is. The only thing he's guilty of is bad judgment. Where're the tapes?"

"The McClearys have them."

"Do you have copies?"

"No."

"I'll call them on the way and we can pick them up." She opened the door. "Let's get going. The bad weather's moving this way."

A few minutes later, they stepped outside into the mist and the orange glow of the parking-lot lights. The air was at least twenty degrees cooler than when Andy had arrived on Cedar Key this morning. Midsixties, she guessed. "I'll still have to take you in," Wilkin said, stopping beside the Acura. "But let's get rid of the handcuffs. And call me Angie, okay?"

Andy grinned and rubbed her wrists as she unfastened the handcuffs. "You got it."

23

(1)

THE RAIN WAS light but steady when McCleary neared Turbeta's place. The humidity, the dampness, and the heat made him uncomfortable as hell in his costume.

None of the street lamps worked, but a soft glow rose from the trees that surrounded the house, as though a giant fist held a radioactive isotope inside it. Across the street from the house the lot was crowded with cars that were parked in four neat rows, eight or ten across. All of the vehicles had been backed into their respective spots so that they faced away from the house. It struck him as a deliberate arrangement, since natural inclination was to pull in facing the lot.

He cruised through, noting the absence of expensive models—no Porsches, no BMWs, not a Mercedes in sight. These models were straight out of middle-class America, as ordinary as cans of Coke and about as memorable.

He wondered if he would have to pass through a metal detector at the door. Tess hadn't mentioned it, but he suspected her omissions had outweighed the details she *had* divulged. So he slipped the Magnum out of its shoulder holster and locked it in the glove compartment.

As he slowed, looking for a parking space, Dracula appeared out of nowhere and flagged him down with a flashlight. McCleary stopped, lowered the window.

"Space at the end of the second row, sir." The mask muffled his voice, so even if he were someone McCleary knew, it would be impossible to identify him. "Just circle and back in."

So it *was* deliberate. "Thanks."

As he went around, he saw Dracula in the side mirror,

a handheld radio close to his mouth. What was there to report? The arrival of a red Miata? A description of his costume? His license plate number?

McCleary pulled into the designated spot. Before he killed the headlights, they illuminated the back of the car in the row in front of him. The numbers on its license had been covered with tape that blended with the plate. Nothing like a little paranoia to keep a party interesting.

He got out, opened his umbrella, locked the door. Dracula was waiting and handed him a plain white envelope. "Just give this to the person at the door, sir. And you can check your umbrella in the cloakroom. Enjoy your evening, sir." Then, chuckling softly: "No other tin men tonight. Nice choice."

"Thanks, don't bite too many necks."

Dracula laughed. "All the tasty necks are inside, sir."

Yeah, I bet they are.

He crossed the street, slipped the five hundred bucks into the white envelope. He'd gotten the money from the automatic teller machine outside the drugstore where he'd bought a battery-operated razor, which he'd used to shave off his beard on his way over here. Under his silver mask, his jaw itched something fierce. He felt ludicrous in costume, like a misfit who had never gotten enough of Halloween as a kid. The silver hat, shaped like a triangle, the silver mask, the shimmering silver pants, the silver jacket—and his muddy running shoes. He would probably rust before he made it to the front door.

Had the tin man made it to the wizard? Would he?

Up the walk now, under the dripping trees. Lights from the house twinkled through the branches like fallen stars. Shadows moved past the curtains. Margaret Thatcher opened the door, her face cast perfectly in a full mask, her body cloned in a conservative blue suit, sensible shoes, a blouse with a bow under the chin. Thatcher. He nearly laughed out loud.

She greeted him in a voice striving to be British, a voice that might have belonged to Melody Burns. McCleary nodded and stepped into a vestibule that was separated from the rest of the house by a heavy oak door. At one end was the cloakroom, where Groucho Marx was

278

smoking a cigar and arranging wet raincoats and umbrellas. Thatcher was to his right, behind a podium, as though she were about to give a speech. "I trust the rain hasn't troubled you too much, sir."

He shook his head, handed her the envelope. She counted the money inside, counted discreetly, then licked it shut and set it aside. She tapped keys on a keyboard hidden behind the podium, then passed the envelope through an electronic gizmo on top of the podium that coded the back of the envelope. Next, she slipped a blank plastic card through the gizmo, coding it as well, and handed it to him.

"Put the card in the slot in the door and wait until you hear it click before you open it. Groucho will give you a ticket for your umbrella. And hold on to the card, sir. It's your ticket for enjoyment."

He nodded again and went over to the cloakroom with his umbrella, his thumb slipping over the code's impression on the card. A hunch said it was tied to Dracula's radio transmission, and on Thatcher's computer it was probably linked up to his license plate number.

Groucho wasn't as chatty as Thatcher. In fact, he didn't say anything at all. He just chomped on the end of his cigar, blew a cloud of smoke into McCleary's face, and handed him a ticket in exchange for the umbrella. *Yeah, same to you, dipshit.*

He slipped his card into the slot in the door, heard the telling click, stepped inside. The house was transformed by light and shadow, by quiet music and voices and the rustle of costumes. The air was redolent with fresh flowers and some sort of potpourri. And behind these scents were others: cigarette smoke, the sharp sweetness of grass or hashish, and the aroma of food from the long banquet table against the wall to his left.

McCleary headed toward the bar at the end of the table, threading his way through the press of bodies, the clouds of perfume and aftershave. He passed two clowns, a witch, Humpty-Dumpty. An elf poured him a beer. Tinkerbell flitted past him, laughing and waving her wand. He moved along the length of the banquet table, perusing the cuisine.

There was American and Chinese food, Italian and Greek and Indian, something to satisfy every palate. There were red and white potatoes, steaming long-grained rice, vegetables that were yellow and green and red. There were desserts that ranged from breads to cakes and pies to exotic cheeses. Silver bowls were brimming with jelly beans and M&M's as colorful as butterflies.

McCleary helped himself to a handful of M&M's and ate them as he walked around the room, listening to the undercurrents in the air, the soft trills of laughter, the voices, the music at just the right volume so that it wasn't intrusive. He passed Franklin Roosevelt, John Kennedy, Marilyn Monroe, a confluence of the dead. He spotted Cleopatra hanging on Marc Antony's arm. Princess Stephanie passed him a joint on her way toward the banquet table. He dropped it on the black marble floor and crushed it with the heel of his shoe.

He stopped near the steps that led to the next level of the house, sipped his beer, waited for someone to approach him. For something to happen. After a few minutes, a cigarette girl strolled over. She was straight out of a lost era, wearing a little box hat, a short skirt, black net stockings, the display of goods lined up in a neat wooden tray that was hooked over her neck with a strap. A simple white mask covered her eyes and nose.

"How about it, Tin Man?" Her voice was a gravelly imitation of Tess doing Mae West. "Anything here that interests you?"

He shrugged, then pointed at what looked like a pack of Juicy Fruit gum.

"Good choice." She picked it up, popped off the top. Clever. It was a metal box painted to look like a pack of Juicy Fruit. She tapped out a purple pill no larger than the tip of a pencil. "Psilocybin. Starts fast, peaks slow, lasts about four hours, very visual, very mellow. It's a nice high to share with someone."

"Like whom, Tess? You?"

"Shit." She flicked the pill back into the container, started to move away.

He caught her arm. "Not so fast."

"You said no trouble, Mike."

I lied. "Give me a tour of the house, Tess."

"I can't. Let go of my arm."

"You're here to please the guests, Tess. You said it yourself." He urged her up the curve of steps, where they passed two Boy Scouts. They went through the French doors and into the thickly carpeted hallway. Empty. The lighting here was subdued, a soft blue; the noise downstairs was strangely muted, as though the hallway were insulated somehow.

"You forgot to tell me about the coded cards, Tess. Where's the main computer?"

She tried to jerk her arm free. "You're hurting me," she whined.

"The computer, Tess. Where's the main computer?"

"I don't know. I don't know anything about that. I swear."

"What else is the card used for, Tess?"

"I don't know."

"For these?" Still gripping her arm, McCleary reached past her for the knob of the nearest door. A red light glowed above it, presumably a signal that it was in use. He rattled it hard. "Does it open these doors?"

"Don't do that." She yanked her arm free, took several steps backward. Hysteria edged her voice. "I've told you everything I know. I can't help you anymore. Just leave me the hell alone."

She spun and hurried toward the French doors, her little hat now lopsided on her head, her uniform mussed in back, her net stockings crooked. She nearly collided with a very tall Goofy, a Goofy well over six feet who moved as though he were on a pogo stick. He swung his long arms back in a parody of lost balance, then looked at McCleary and stabbed a thumb in Tess's direction, as if asking what her problem was.

"I guess she doesn't like tin men."

McCleary instantly regretted breaking his silence, but Goofy apparently wasn't anyone who knew him. He just threw up his hands in a silent burst of laughter, then slapped his palms against his thighs. His shoulders rolled as he let out a low, gleeful chuckle. One more fruitcake, McCleary thought, and started down the hall as though he knew where he was going and had every right to be headed there.

He'd gone three or four steps when he felt a surge of air behind him. He whirled. The world seemed to fall into a slow-motion clarity: Goofy airborne in the soft blue light, long legs jacked up, hands poised for a lethal chop, body angled, aimed, a missile of flesh and bones.

Kliner, he thought. Kliner, who was well over six feet tall, had recognized his voice.

McCleary leaped back, but he wasn't quick enough. Kliner's shoes slammed into the edge of his shoulder, knocking him to the left. He fell to one knee, scrambled up, balled his fist, and swung as Kliner rushed him. He caught him hard on the chin, felt the skin on his knuckles tearing like a piece of Kleenex, splitting wide open. Kliner flew back, arms pinwheeling for real this time, his legs coming up from under him. His mask was askew: Goofy's left eye was somewhere in the vicinity of his temple, the mouth nearly touching his ear. Then he hit the floor and his head slammed into the wall. The vibration rippled through the soles of McCleary's shoes and dislodged the tile next to the China Suite. It dropped like a stone, bounced on the carpet. Where it had been was a slot that seemed to grow against the wall like a dark, humorless smile. A slot identical to the one on the front door. For the plastic card.

Then McCleary was up and running, charging through the French doors, down the steps, around the corner. He stopped cold on the last step, his knuckles throbbing.

Music, people, noise.

Go easy, he thought. Back to the wall. Fix the mask. Good, very good, you're doing fine. Back right out of this room.

But his legs refused to move. They felt rubbery, loose, unconnected to his hipbones, a puppet's legs severed from the strings that powered them. He looked down and his shoes were no longer solid. They were dissolving like aspirin in water, melting into the floor. A tide of panic swept through him, sweat sprang from his pores like some living substance, something other than water. He squeezed his eyes shut, forced himself to breathe deeply, evenly, slowly, and pressed back against the wall, seeking the reality of cold, hard wood. Something solid. But the wall was as soft as gelatin and his fingers were sinking into it, being sucked into it. He could feel it, the wall *swallowing* his fingers.

McCleary jerked his hands away. His arms dropped like lead weights at his sides. In front of him, the room pulsed, a giant heart straining to pump blood to distant organs, a heart lurching to find its proper rhythm, a heart in overdrive. Now the walls were breathing, those soft chests rising and falling, again and again, making the room tilt until people were falling into one small corner where their flesh and bones ran together like paint in water. And the noise, dear God, the noise. It throbbed, it beat, it pounded. A fork scraped across a plate and it was the shriek of metal against hot cement, the shriek of a thousand nails clawing at a blackboard, a shriek that shredded his insides like tissue paper.

He couldn't remember why he was standing here, what he was supposed to do, who these people were, what was required of him. His right hand grabbed his left and held on hard. *Think think think.* The words slammed back and forth against the walls of the squash court in his head. The words echoed. The words became faces, the faces turned into symbols, the symbols flashed like neon.

M&M's. He saw the old ad, a pair of M&M's dancing, M&M's coated in milk chocolate, M&M's that melted on your tongue. *How many? How many did I eat?* The thought raced through him, laughing. A hallucinogenic. Acid? Psilocybin? Dust? What? What had they been coated in?

He commanded his legs to move and they did, flopping like fish struggling at the end of hooks. His fingers sank into the gelatinous wall again, into that cool sucking, that seductive sucking, the house was alive, the house was going to devour him.

Then he was around the corner, away from the crowd. He pushed back into the shadows under the stairs, knees exploding like firecrackers as he slipped down the wall into a tight crouch. He ripped off his mask, wiped his face on his shirt, tried to focus his vision on what was in front of him. A door. The kitchen. Yes, he was sure it was the kitchen and . . .

And what?

Kitchen/food, food/M&M's, M&M's/acid. No, not acid. He had done acid, years ago in college he had done acid and mescaline and mushrooms. This was mushrooms with a twist of something else. Speed? Coke? Did it matter?

McCleary pressed the heels of his hands against his eyes and seized an image of Quin, Quin and Ellie. And then he held on to it like a dying man, wrapped his soul around it, and pushed back into the shadows until he became a shadow, thin and flat and as simple as a protozoan.

(2)

Quin bit into the apple she'd brought with her and checked the time. Moving up on twenty-two minutes now since Farmer had turned into the nursing home and pulled into a parking spot. He hadn't gotten out of his car. He was just sitting in there, engine off, headlights off. What the hell was he doing? Waiting for someone? Drinking? Jerking off? What?

The hands of the dashboard clock ticked off another minute. "C'mon, Farmer, do something."

And suddenly the Firebird roared to life, almost as though he'd heard her.

(3)

The wipers whipped across the glass, the radio was on, but Rick couldn't remember what he was doing here. Couldn't even recall the drive. Had he already gone inside? Had he spoken to Mother? Was she alone? He remembered . . . what? Weeping in her lap? Tearing out clumps of grass down near the lake? When did that happen? When?

He looked at the time. Late. He was late. He was supposed to be with *her*. They were going to, they had talked about, she was tied up . . . yes, he remembered that phrase, *tied up*, like Lucy, like Catherine, tied up up up up . . .

Rick slammed the Firebird into gear and screeched out of the lot, away from the Halloween-orange lights, away from Mother. *Away. Fast.*

(4)

The rain had started to fall in earnest once they were off the island. Now Andy hated its noise, its tedious rhythm against the Acura's roof, its blinding slant across the road, its relentless repetition. She hated it almost as much as she hated the way the Acura hugged the road like some small, clever spider, catching a curve at just the right moment, racing through a light in the second before it turned red, everything timed at sharp, painful edge.

Wilkin was a terrible driver, sitting forward in her seat, hunched over the wheel, gripping it tightly. Now and then one of her small, lovely hands would dart out, rub quickly at the fogged windshield, and drop to the steering wheel again. When she spoke, it was only to ask something about the tapes. Was there any background noise on them? How was Catherine's murder described? How was Lucy's murder described? Did anyone else besides the McClearys know about the tapes?

Emilio and Jules, she thought, but neither of them had heard the tapes, so she shook her head. "No."

"You're sure?"

"Of course I'm sure."

"What about your editor?"

"No way."

"Were you going to use them in the book?"

"I don't know. Look, it's better if you just listen to them yourself."

Wilkin looked over at her. In the glow of the headlights, Andy saw a corner of her mouth lifting in a half-smile. "I'm just trying to decide the best way of presenting them to the captain, that's all."

"Sure, I understand."

But she didn't understand. Her vague intuition that

285

something didn't fit persisted with the stubbornness of the flu. Walk through it, she thought. You slugged Bristol, he filed charges, you both end up in jail. And then what? Why would Bristol be transferred to Lake Butler, the reception and medical center for all inmates entering the Florida penal system? Why there? Why would the feds want to talk to him there?

"There's a convenience store just ahead. I'm going to pull in and call the captain, tell him the rain's delaying me. That way he won't send out the army when we're late," Wilkin said.

"Okay."

A few moments later they pulled up in front of a 7-Eleven and Wilkin got out and darted through the rain to the pay phone. Andy watched her through the rain-smeared window. The tapes, she thought. Something about the tapes. What?

It would come to her. Sooner or later it would come to her.

Rain and wind rushed into the car as Wilkin opened her door and swung behind the wheel again. "We're set," she said, slamming the door. "I've arranged it so that they won't transfer Steve until we've gotten there."

"Arranged it with whom?"

"The driver. He owes me a favor."

They were moving again, moving through the rain, the dark, and the riddle of the tapes clattered in Andy's head like loose tools. Not much farther to the farm, to the tapes. She wondered why she found no comfort in the thought.

(5)

The kitchen door in front of McCleary breathed as it swung open, and Aunt Jemima waddled out with a tray of food. McCleary moved more deeply into the cubbyhole formed in the right angle where the two walls met. She didn't see him. But sooner or later someone would.

He pressed his hands against the floor to push himself to his feet. The wood still felt soft, but like cotton now, not Jello-O. His body was adjusting and the effect of whatever he'd eaten was evening out, stretching into a plateau that would rise gradually until he peaked. Move now, he thought, now.

McCleary stood. His legs were weak sticks, trembling with his weight. He reached for the edge of the wall to steady himself but grabbed on to a doorknob instead. There, hidden under the stairs, was a short, squat door, a hobbit's door with an old-fashioned key protruding from an old-fashioned keyhole. Hallucination. He nearly laughed. But the key felt solid when he touched it. The key turned. The door opened.

He ducked and stepped inside. Stairs. A wooden railing. The dank odor of subterranean places floated from the darkness below. He shut the door and the darkness swallowed him.

24

(1)

A YELLOW LIGHT. Wonderful.

C'mon, Quin thought at the station wagon in front of her. Run it. Run the damn thing. But the wagon eased to a stop. Quin swung into the left lane, hoping to cut in front of the Pontiac swerving in from the turn lane, but she didn't make it. She sat there fuming. Farmer was well beyond the intersection now. By the time the light was green again, his Darth Vader car would be halfway to another planet.

Nearly two hours shot. She'd discovered nothing new about Farmer except that he was indecisive when it came to visiting his mother. She'd missed dinner, squandered gas, imposed on Helen Charles, and wasted two hours she could have spent with Ellie. And for what? To feel useful? To prove her love for Cat? To convince herself she could be mother and gumshoe and wife?

The only thing that seemed perfectly obvious now was that she needed to have her head examined.

Traffic began to move. She rummaged in her purse for the graham crackers she carried around for Ellie and felt like crying. Like ranting. Like raving. For herself, for Ellie who would grow up with a fruitcake for a mother, and for Cat, murdered by the bastard who had given her the slip.

Home, she thought, all she wanted to do was go home with Ellie and forget that she had even left the house.

(2)

The basement was twenty-eight steps deep. At the bottom, the air was cooler and the blackness not as dense, as pervasive. Vague shapes fluttered past him, phantoms the drug created and destroyed in the blink of an eye. He could feel the weight of the house above his head, feel the throb of the music and dancing feet through the floor.

He moved toward a beam to his right, then inched around it, feeling his way with the uncertainty of a blind man who has regained some of his sight but doesn't trust it yet. Now and then the wood turned soft and gooey under his fingers, like rice pudding. But he could distinguish the effects of the drug now. He concentrated on the faint humming around him, the noise of the house on automatic: AC, water heater, electrical impulses. That was real. And so was the thin crack of light that lay against the blackness like a pale ruler.

He crept toward it, his knees creaking. He felt as if he were swimming in an underwater cave, a man without an oxygen tank, a man holding his breath and moving toward a light at the surface that promised more than fresh air and warmth.

Ear to the wood, he listened. Then he cracked the door, saw a couple of old wooden crates jammed with gardening tools, lengths of rope, balls of string, a rusted can opener, a broom, things tossed there to be dealt with later. He pushed the door open wider.

At the opposite end of the room was a man seated at a computer terminal and surrounded by video monitors. McCleary had the sensation that he'd crossed some curious barrier, drawn aside a curtain between himself and his sister's death, but instead of answers and sunlight, he'd found only a spacious twilit room filled with more questions.

He moved closer to get a good look at the monitors. For a moment, his vision divided and he saw doubles of everything. He rubbed his eyes with hands that felt larger than they should be, thicker, the hands of some other man, and he wanted to examine them, poke at them, divine the mystery of these hands. He forced himself to ignore the sensation, to concentrate on the monitors, on the man at the computer.

The man was scanning the monitors, his head moving from side to side like someone in the stands at Wimbledon. He hit a key and zoomed in for a close-up of the couple in a bright red room. The China Suite, McCleary thought. The man and the woman were unmasked, unclothed, and feeding each other plump red strawberries. Sybarites in paradise.

Now a close-up of the Blue Suite. Two women and a man. Only the man was unmasked. His face was vaguely familiar, a politician's face, one of the powers in Tallahassee, but his name escaped McCleary.

In the Country Suite the woman was a member of the state parole board. She and her companion, a woman, were passing a pipe back and forth, giggling like teenagers.

In the Forest Suite it was a state lobbyist and a woman who didn't look a day over sixteen. In another suite it was a prominent real estate developer with a younger man. Somewhere in here, he knew, there were tapes of his sister with the woman she'd met here, tapes kept for the day they might be useful.

He was dimly aware that he was moving again, hunkered down, an urban commando. The room breathed and pulsed around him, but he barely noticed it. His anger had blotted out everything but the back of the man's head. His anger was a thing apart from him, an entity that had possessed him. He was its conduit, its expression. And suddenly it sprang away from him and grabbed the man around the neck, squeezing his throat, pulling him back, back, until McCleary saw the man's face.

Emilio Turbeta.

McCleary squeezed his neck, hoping it would break. Turbeta gasped, struggled, clawed blindly at the air. His legs jerked up as his chair toppled and they both fell back. The chair clattered, its wheels spinning impotently. For a second, the ceiling above McCleary whirled like a dervish, shadows rushed toward him, then he kicked the chair away and scrambled to his feet. Turbeta had staggered up, coughing and rubbing his throat. McCleary grabbed him by the shoulder, threw him against the wall, sank his bleeding knuckles into Turbeta's gut. Air exploded from his mouth, his eyes bulged in his cheeks, and when McCleary let go of him, he slid down the wall, a marionette with severed strings.

McCleary frisked him, pulled a Beretta from a shoulder holster inside his sweater. It felt like plastic in his hands.

"Get up, dipshit. You're going to access information for me."

"*Señor*, please . . ."

McCleary flicked off the safety on the gun, cocked it, aimed it at Turbeta's chest. "A list of the members. Now. The list with names and the license plate numbers, Emilio. Do it!"

Turbeta didn't argue, didn't say anything at all.

(3)

Flats was waiting on the porch when Quin drove up and started barking as soon as she climbed out of the Wagoneer. It woke Ellie, who laughed and kept trying to poke her head out from under the raincoat Quin had thrown over them for the run to the porch.

Quin let her down once they were on the porch, and she and Flats greeted each other like long-lost friends. It became abundantly clear to Quin that Flats belonged in the family, and she wondered how the sheepdog and three cats would take to one another.

"Okay, guys, into the house. We're going to make popcorn and pig out."

She herded them toward the doors. Flats was soaked; every time she shook herself or scratched, water flew off her back. Quin made her stay outside while she put Ellie down in the living room. She stripped off her mud-splattered Disney World T-shirt and went into the bathroom for a towel to use on the dog. Ellie waddled along behind her, yawning and fussing to go outside.

Quin wiped Ellie clean with the towel, then they both rubbed down Flats. The splint had come off her leg, allowing her to get at the bandage. It was sodden and dirty, so Quin cut it off, applied Betadine on the stitches, then wrapped it in fresh gauze. This procedure would send a cat into paroxysms of terror, she thought. But Flats ate up the attention and lay still for most of it. When Quin was finished, she put fresh PJs on Ellie, fed Flats, then finally attended to her own hunger. Fruit, a platter of cheese and crackers, a yogurt. She carried them over to the easy chair near the door.

Babies, dogs, and then adults, she thought, that was the order of things in the world. She sighed as she sank into the chair and Ellie snuggled in her lap, dozing off again. Flats curled up at her feet. The sound of the rain cushioned her fatigue but didn't allay her irritation with how the night had ended up.

It was then that she noticed the light glowing on the answering machine on the other side of the room. She got up slowly so that she wouldn't awaken Ellie and carried her over to the couch.

The message was from McCleary and was noisy with traffic and falling rain, but she heard enough of it to understand about the tornado watch. She turned on the TV, volume low, and tuned into the weather channel. Suddenly, Flats's head came up and she growled very softly.

"Shit, just what I don't need, girl. Don't spook me like that. It's just a critter out there, right?"

Flats went to the door. The growling grew louder. Quin looked around for her purse, which held the Browning, and realized she'd left it in the car. A tight, hard knot formed in her throat that she couldn't swallow. She crept over to the door and peered out.

Headlights washed through the rain. In the dim spill of the porch light she saw Wilkin's Acura. No bogeyman at all, she thought, annoyed by how quickly her mind seized on the worst.

Flats was snarling now, so Quin put her in Cat's bedroom and shut the door. Then she went out onto the porch and held open the screen door as Wilkin and Andy dashed up the ramp.

"I thought you were in jail," Quin exclaimed.

Andy grinned and ran her hands through the front of her hair. "It's a long story."

"C'mon in. How about some coffee or a bite to eat?"

"Coffee," she and Wilkin said.

Flats clawed at the door and barked as soon as they

stepped inside the house. "Oh-oh," Wilkin murmured. "I hear the dog who hates me."

"She's in the bedroom."

"I can't believe your daughter sleeps through that racket."

"Nothing short of a nuclear attack will wake her now." Quin was already at the coffeemaker. "Just toss your raincoats over the chairs. So what's going on?"

"They're transferring Steve tonight. We need those tapes, Quin. Angie's going to take them to the captain when she brings me in."

"Transfer him where?"

"Lake Butler," Wilkin said. "Something to do with the feds." She made an impatient gesture with her hand, then picked up a dishtowel and rubbed it through her wet hair. "The driver says he'll delay the trip as long as he can."

"Well, sure, let me finish this and I'll get them."

"God, what a relief," Wilkin said, and winced as Flats's barking reached new heights of frenzy. "It sounds like she may dig through that door, Quin. Where's Mike, anyway?"

"In town. He'll be home in a while."

She could see that Wilkin the cop wanted to ask where in town and what he was doing but yielded to a sense of propriety and didn't. Quin went into the den, puzzled by her own vagueness concerning McCleary's whereabouts. But what the hell. It was nice to have company and she hoped they would stick around awhile.

(4)

The germs were back. In the wash of the Firebird's headlights, he could see several of them, black as coffee grounds, wiggling across the backs of his hands as he steered the car. They slipped down into the valleys between his knuckles, curled around the hairs on his wrists, dug under his thumbnails. They were a sign that she had poisoned him, that the affair had gone sour.

In the end, he thought, she'd proven to be no better

than Josie or his wife. Only Mother had never betrayed him.

He swung his right arm out, smashing the back of his hand against the passenger seat, killing the fuckers. Then he rubbed the back of his left hand against the side of the door. He unlocked the glove compartment and removed the .38 and the Baggie with Lucy's hand in it. It was completely thawed now, a gray, ill-defined mass of dead flesh. But Forensics would be able to identify it and that was all that mattered.

He flicked off the safety on the gun and thought about how he would kill her. Then he would drive back into his life, life as it had been before *she* had entered it, and he would be free of her and the germs forever.

The wind blew, hurling rain against the windows. He thought of Bundy clasping him on the shoulder, Bundy laughing. *"We're a lot alike, you and me."*

And they were. *But I'm smarter, Ted. I won't get caught. I won't fry.*

(5)

"Señor McCleary, listen to me, you are making a big mistake. . . ."

Mistakemistake: The word hammered against the walls of McCleary's skull as his hearing faltered again. The hum of the monitors, the tap of the computer keys, the wheeze of his own breathing: All of it sounded hollowed-out, weird, as though he were trapped inside a small, invisible dome.

". . . Jim is looking for you. I am supposed to be watching the monitors for you. . . ."

Youyou

". . . for the tin man. In a few minutes he will call me on the intercom. Have I seen the tin man? No? I am positive? And then he will come down here to look for himself. He will be armed. He is *loco* when it comes to Masquerade, Mr. McCleary. It is like his child. . . ."

Childchildchild

"I also want the tapes you have of my sister."

"Bueno, señor. I will give you whatever you want. But no one here killed Catherine, no one—"

"Shut the fuck up." *Shuthfup.* That was how it sounded. Words running together, sounds running together, short circuits in the gray matter. Get what you want and split before this stuff peaks, he thought. "Hurry up." *Hurup.*

"I will tell you anything, Señor McCleary. I only ask that you remember how cooperative I am."

Turbeta turning state's evidence in exchange for immunity, Turbeta with diarrhea of the mouth on the witness stand, Turbeta blowing Masquerade wide open to save his lousy ass. "Who else besides you, Jim, and Tess?" *Whoesbesyou.*

"Melody Burns."

The name echoing. Turbeta's fingers tapping, tapping.

"She and Jim started it when they lived together. I came in when they split. But she was still a partner. She brought in many members."

Printer on now.

"And the monitors?" *Antimons.*

"We are information wholesalers, *señor.*"

Wholesalers. The word slammed around in his head, a marble in a glass cage.

"We sell to whomever can afford the price. Political opponents, attorneys, judges, husbands, wives . . . It depends on the situation. These are details that Jim and Melody handle. I am in charge of the computers. The equipment."

Sheets spat from the printer. Turbeta pointed at a drawer to his left. "In there you will find the tapes of your sister."

McCleary moved toward it but kept the gun trained on Turbeta. The Cuban's face was starting to melt like hot wax. "Why her?"

"Melody wanted it. A disagreement about representation, I think. I'm not sure. The tapes are numbered. I believe Catherine is on tapes nineteen through twenty-one."

"Be sure," McCleary barked.

"I . . . I am sure, *señor.*"

McCleary found the tapes, stuffed them into a plastic bag Turbeta handed him, tied it to the side of his belt. The printer had stopped. McCleary tore off the sheets, folded them, stuffed them inside his pocket, then put the gun to Turbeta's head. "Two things. The key to this room, then you get Melody and Jim down here. Make it convincing, *amigo*." *Maitconving*.

"No problem, *señor*." He reached into his pocket, brought out a set of keys. "The blue one fits this door. You see, I cooperate completely with you. No problem."

As he scanned the monitors to locate them, his face kept melting. A cheek sank in, his nose fell off, an eyebrow vanished. McCleary averted his eyes, hoped he was out of here before the stuff incapacitated him.

When Turbeta had finished speaking to Melody and Kliner on the intercom, McCleary removed the gun from his temple and congratulated him on a job well done. "Does the computer control the intercom down here?"

"Yes, all over the house."

"Disengage it."

He did, then looked up at McCleary with a wide smile. "Now what would you like me to do, *Señor* McCleary?"

"Go to sleep." McCleary struck him on the back of the head with the gun. He slumped, his head lolling against the keyboard. "Sorry, *amigo*."

McCleary propped him up again and pushed the chair closer to the computer. Then he hurried across the room, jerked the broom from the old crate, and stood against the wall, where the door would hide him when it opened.

It didn't take them long to get downstairs, and their arrival was noisy—heavy footfalls and loud, argumentative voices. Tinkerbell swept through the door first, one of her wire wings bent, her mask gone, her blonde hair bouncing against her shoulders. Goofy was right behind her. He slammed the door and McCleary swung the broom like a batter intent on a home run.

The handle slammed into Kliner's chest, knocking him off his feet. As Melody whirled around to see what was going on, the handle whistled toward her and caught her at the knees with a sharp, resounding crack. She stumbled back, her face skewed with acute agony, tripped over Kliner, and went down.

McCleary leveled the gun at her, then at Kliner when he moved. "Don't. Don't make me do to you what you did to Cat."

"Mike, you're making a mistake," Melody gasped, trying to sit up. "No one—"

A white, blinding rage filled him and he squeezed the trigger. Once. Twice. Three times. The slugs slammed into the floor between them. Splinters flew. Melody shrieked. McCleary backed out of the room, his hand trembling, his rage moiling, then slammed the door and locked it before he could change his mind.

As he reached the top of the stairs, he heard pounding, shouts. Then he was on the other side of the hobbit door, turning the old-fashioned key in that wonderful old-fashioned lock, and couldn't hear anything from the basement.

He pushed through the kitchen door. Aunt Jemima looked up from a wad of dough she was kneading and seemed surprised to see an unmasked guest. "Help you with something, sir?"

"The phone. Where's the phone?"

She lifted a plump, dimpled arm and pointed. The end of her finger melted. The dough in front of her suddenly grew little legs, got up, and walked away. "If I were you, I'd get my ass out of this house," he told her, then made two calls, one to Andy's buddy, the reporter, and the other to 911.

A murder, he said, and spat out the address. He didn't give his name. Damned if he was going to be within ten miles of this place when it was busted. All those sweet careers in here swirling down the drain to front-page news. Good fucking riddance. He had what he'd come for.

He left through the utility-room door, rain pouring over him, and raced across the yard. He scaled the fence, had a bad moment at the top when his legs refused to cooperate, and fell gracelessly to the sodden ground on the other side. He sprinted toward the front of the house, paused at the corner looking for Dracula, didn't see him, and raced across the road to the lot.

Once he was inside the Miata, his fingers turned to stone and he couldn't get the key in the ignition. Holes opened up in the dashboard. A knob on the radio turned into a mouth and began to cackle. Panic churned somewhere deep inside him and he pressed the heels of his hands into his eyes, pressed until black dots exploded like stars against the insides.

Drive. Get somewhere. Anywhere.

When had he eaten the candy? What time? He couldn't remember. But one thing was certain. The plateau was gone; he was rising again. He opened his eyes, steadied his right hand with his left, guided the key into the ignition. The Miata purred to life. He eased it into first gear, pulled slowly out of the lot, realized his headlights were off, and switched them on.

He lowered his window, letting the wind and rain blow over him as he drove. When he reached the main road, he didn't know which way to turn. His sense of direction had abandoned him. He finally hung a right and crawled at twenty down the road. The rain shimmered and danced, sometimes solid, sometimes as loose as a handful of pebbles, and sometimes not there at all. The road beneath him shifted, the windshield dissolved, warts grew and vanished on the backs of his hands.

Flashing red lights blazed in his side mirror and now he heard the shriek of sirens. His smile froze in a rictus that might have been pleasure or pain. "Bye-bye, fuckers," he muttered.

Just ahead was a pool of neon. Gas station. Call Quin. Take a leak. Get off the road. He pulled up to a pump and went inside to pay for the gas. The fluorescent lights assaulted him. The old coot behind the counter had a grin as huge as Texas.

McCleary dug into his pocket for his wallet and realized the papers from the basement, the list of Masquerade members, were still stuffed in his raincoat pocket. He pulled them out, damp and creased, found his wallet, slipped out a ten.

"Ten of unleaded," McCleary said. His eyes burned.

The wall behind the old coot's face changed colors, throbbed, dissolved.

"Righto. Road out there startin' to flood yet?"

For all he knew, his Miata was floating. "It's plenty bad. Where's your phone?"

"Around the side, near the restrooms. But it ain't workin'. You're welcome to use this one." He pushed a black phone across the counter. "Long as it's local."

"It is, thanks." McCleary dialed the number at the farm and smoothed the papers with his hands as he listened to the ringing. His eyes wandered down the list, pausing here and there when he recognized a name.

Two rings. Three.

A name leaped off the list just as the phone was picked up. But it wasn't Quin's voice he heard; it was another woman's, saying, "Hello?"

And there it was, her name right in front of him, the cop who was being paid off, the cop who had framed her partner, the cop whose voice he now heard, the woman who had been his sister's lover. His heart clutched.

"Hello? Is anyone there? Hello?"

He opened his mouth to speak, but a hot tightness squeezed at his vocal cords, pulled on them like rubber bands.

"Hello?"

McCleary's finger slammed down on the disconnect button. He stared at the name, panic clawing at his chest, the blood in his legs rushing hot, cold, hot again.

"You okay, son?"

His words fell out of his mouth like dead birds. "Tree Frog Farm off Ninety-fifth. Catherine McCleary's place. Call 911." Then he raced for the door, a man possessed.

25

(1)

"WHO WAS THAT?" Andy asked, glancing up from the mug of coffee she had just poured.

"Wrong number, I guess," Wilkin said. "Coffee done?"

"Yeah. How do you take yours?"

"Black."

"You find those tapes, Quin?" Wilkin called.

"Yup, right here." She came out of the den, wagging the tapes. "You want to listen to them before you leave?"

"Sure. Might as well let the rain taper off before we head into town."

"Okay, I'll get the recorder."

As Quin hurried back into the den, Andy carried the mugs of coffee out to the dining room. Flats had quieted down in the last few minutes, but now her barking renewed and, on the couch, Ellie stirred. A moment later a car pulled into the driveway.

"That's probably Mike," Andy said, and started to get up to look, but Wilkin motioned her to stay where she was.

"I'll look, Andy. Stay put."

Andy. Not Andrea, not Ms. Tull, but Andy.

Andy.

What's black and white and read all over, Andy?

That's not how we do things, Andy.

A hole ripped open inside her and she was falling through it, being sucked into it, unable to breathe, to pull air into her lungs. She saw Wilkin moving toward the French doors, heard Quin coming out of the den, felt her head turning with agonizing slowness, a rusted, squeaking ball bearing. Time crawled. It seemed to take

300

forever for her hand to get to her shoe, for her fingers to close around the switchblade. Half a lifetime passed before Quin stopped, frowning at the stricken expression on her face. Andy nodded slowly at Wilkin's back, nodded even as she was pushing up from the table. She saw the blood leak from Quin's face, saw her eyes dart toward the couch. At Ellie. Then everything clicked into fast forward.

Quin rushed past her, heading for Ellie, and Andy was on her feet, the switchblade at her side. She was aware of the noise of the rain, the wind filling the room, aware of her heart hammering. But these details seemed removed from her, distant, like details she had written about in a book that was finished and almost forgotten.

When she was within two feet of Wilkin, the detective looked around, a corner of her mouth creeping up in what promised to be a secretive smile. Their eyes locked in a brief, blinding instant, an instant in which Andy was suddenly back in the dark of the loft, the phone ringing, that raspy voice whispering: *I woke you.*

She saw Wilkin go for her gun, but her arm was faster. It flew up and the blade caught Wilkin at the chin and tore up the right side of her face. She made a sound that wasn't human, then she was stumbling back, one hand at her cheek, blood streaming through her fingers, the other hand gripping her gun. It fired. The slug slammed into the floor. The switchblade slipped from Andy's hand. She stooped to grab it and something charged past her, the dog, the goddamn dog, released from the room when Quin had run into it.

Flats leaped, her muscular body literally arching up, up, a perfect projectile, and then her front paws struck Wilkin in the chest, knocking her over like a bowling pin. Her gun struck the floor. She fell into the table, toppling it, screaming, shrieking, "Get it off, get it off, oh God, help me!"

Andy stumbled back, her stomach heaving, then spun and ran into the bedroom where Quin had vanished with Ellie. She slammed the door, locked it, backed away shaking, certain the door was going to explode inward at any second. She knew she was saying Quin's name over and over, like a mantra, a prayer, but didn't know if she was shouting or whispering.

The bathroom door suddenly jerked open, Quin hissed her name, and she lurched inside.

(2)

He saw the whole thing, saw it as he stood paralyzed in the screened doorway, Tull, Wilkin, the dog. He raised his arm and squeezed the trigger of the .38 again and again and again, not knowing if he hit the beast. He couldn't see well; his arm was shaking. Then the chamber was empty and the gun slipped from his hand and struck the porch and he heard the rain. That was all, just the rain.

He waited. For the dog, for redemption. Wilkin groaned. Rick picked up the gun, reloading it as he moved toward her on wooden legs, his fingers fumbling with bullets, dropping them, spinning the chamber. He looked down at her. Her eyes were small, bright holes in her bloody face, eyes that tried to command him even now, eyes that beseeched him.

She opened her mouth, whispered something. This, he thought, was where they parted company. He raised the gun, aimed it between her eyes, then reconsidered, lowered it, and smiled. ''Suffer, babe. Be back when I finish up.'' He stepped over her and didn't look back.

Closed door. He rattled the knob, stood to the side, fired until the door yawned open. He turned on the light. Catherine's bedroom and another closed door. A bathroom. Inside, the kid was crying. Smart kid. A dead kid. Goodbye, ladies, he thought, and started firing.

(3)

The plumber's hole in the floor. Andy dropped through it first, then reached up to grab Ellie as Quin slowly lowered her down, lowered her by the arms as she kicked and wailed. Gunshots hammered the old door and Quin threw herself to the floor, arms covering her head.

Hurry, Andy, get out of the way, Jesus, hurry.

Quin had one leg inside the hole when Farmer's fist crashed through the splintered wood. She shoved her other leg through the wood and pushed away from the lip of the hole and dropped. She landed hard on her right ankle, twisting it. Andy grabbed her elbow and jerked her up. She reached for Ellie, clutching her so hard that when the rain hit them, it felt as though their skins were seamed together.

She tore through the dark, her fear so acute she barely felt the shoots of pain in her ankle. She tried to shield Ellie from the rain with her arms, but there was too much rain. Her daughter bounced against her until it seemed as though she were tucked inside a pouch at the front of her, a little marsupial. She had stopped crying and her arms were wrapped around Quin's neck, clinging to it.

Behind her, another shot rang out. She ran faster, faster, weaving through the blackness.

(4)

McCleary remembered nothing of the drive to the farm. One moment he was swerving onto the limestone road, and the next he was speeding through the gate. The air around him pulsed and shifted and the Christmas trees on his left bent toward him, an army at attention, paying homage to an unknown god.

The driveway emptied into the yard and two facts registered immediately: the cars and the figure running down the ramp, straight into the glare of the Miata's headlights. Farmer. Farmer stopping. Farmer taking aim. McCleary floored the accelerator and jerked the steering wheel right, left, right. The Miata weaved toward him as he fired, missed, fired again, and blew off the car's side mirror. Then he turned and charged down the muddy path toward the pasture. McCleary slammed on the brakes, leaped out gripping the Magnum, steadied his hand against the upper edge of the door, squinted an eye shut, squeezed back on the trigger.

The explosion tore through the air, but Farmer was still moving and, a moment later, was beyond the reach of the headlights. McCleary ran up the ramp to the house, terrified of what awaited him inside. The screen door banged open in the wind. He burst onto the porch.

At the end, in a dim pool of light, he saw a broken, bloody thing that had once been human trying to grab on to the toppled table to lift itself.

Wilkin.

McCleary ran past her into the house, shouting for Quin. The house was empty. He ran back onto the porch, where Wilkin was sitting up against the table, her breath a slow, racking wheeze. "I . . . loved her, Mike." Blood oozed from a corner of her mouth. "More than he did. But she . . . she shouldn't have broken things off. She shouldn't. That was bad. That—"

He grabbed her by the arms. "Where are they? Where the fuck are they?"

"She left me for him, Mike—"

"Where are they?" he shouted.

She blinked and smiled. "Dead," she said. "They're dead." And then she began to laugh, a wild, erratic sound broken by coughs and flying spittle laced with blood. *Dead dead dead*: The word rose and fell inside him as he backed away from her, wiping her blood from his cheeks.

Her right arm moved, the arm farthest from him, and he suddenly realized why she'd been crawling toward the table. He saw the gun, the gun in her hand, her hand lifting slowly, with tremendous effort, and he didn't even think twice.

He blew her away.

(5)

McCleary was outside when he saw it coming, a black, swirling wall fissured with lightning, a beast from the primal soup, an awesome power possessed of intelligence, will, ambition. The tornado tore a swath through the darkness, shrieking like metal against metal as it approached, sundering the very texture of the air.

He raced across the yard, his ears pounding and pulsing from the sudden change in pressure, and dived under the trees. He hit the wet ground, rolled into a ditch filled with water. Seconds later, the ditch where he lay was sucked dry, grass was torn out by the roots, dirt and debris swirled around him. The trees closest to him vanished. Things poured over him. He rolled onto his side, covered his head with his arms, drew his legs up against him, and prayed, prayed for his wife, his daughter, himself.

(6)

The shrieking tunnel bore down on the farm with winds approaching two hundred miles an hour. The stilts that held up the farmhouse collapsed, the roof was wrenched away, the porch vanished. The chicken coop was flattened. The sheep's pen fell in on itself. The tip of the funnel snapped the barn and it dissolved. It snapped again and the entire second story of the caretaker's house was torn away. Half of the orchards disappeared in the blink of an eye.

Rick, who was trying to get back to the house and his car, saw it moving toward him, a whirling black wall, a living, ravenous thing that raced across the pasture swallowing everything in its path. Trees, fences, cows. He weaved left and it pursued him, tracked him, hunted him. His ears throbbed. A tremendous pressure was building in his head. His arms pumped frantically at his sides, but it didn't matter. It kept coming, closer, closer. Its winds sucked at his clothes, his limbs, the hair on his head. Dirt swirled into his eyes, blinding him. He stumbled, fell, curled into a tight ball on the ground.

Then it was on him, crushing him like garbage in a compactor.

(7)

Silence. That was all he heard, just the silence, smooth and creamy and thick. He shouted for Quin, for Ellie, but his words were muffled and he realized he was buried under something. He kicked his legs, moved his arms, and slowly dug himself out from under a heap of rubble.

He sat up, blinking, his body screaming in a hundred

places from bruises, cuts, abrasions. He rubbed his face, felt the warm ooze of blood on his right cheek, brushed mud and leaves from his hair. His head felt as though it had been torn off and then sewed on backward.

The stars were coming out. A slivered moon poked through a thin layer of clouds. There was enough light to see the ruin in front of him. The house gone. Everything beyond it gone. The lay of the land was completely transformed, as though the earth had belched when the twister hit, heaving upward as the funnel bore down.

He rocked forward onto his knees. Although he no longer felt the effects from whatever he'd ingested, he wobbled when he stood. He shouted for Quin again, his voice hoarse, echoing in the silence. He moved unsteadily toward the path that led to the pasture, but it was an obstacle course strewn with debris. The pool table that had been on the porch was on its top, its legs sticking straight up in the air like an animal that had keeled over. Next to it was the kitchen sink.

The pasture fence was gone. One of its boards had been driven into the trunk of a tree like a nail. He came across two cows standing motionless in the starlight, mooing softly. He found the backseat of the Firebird with three chickens in it, clucking wildly. He found a dead sheep, a carton of eggs with every egg inside unbroken, and the Wurlitzer, its old 45s still inside.

There was just a deep hole where the pond had been. On the other side of it was his car, headlights on, doors thrown open as though it had been abandoned when its occupants fled. McCleary peered inside. A box of Christmas ornaments was in the passenger seat. A tennis racket stuck up next to the gear shift. His keys were still in the ignition.

He sat on the edge of the seat but didn't pull his legs in or touch anything. He was afraid that some fragment of the storm had possessed the car and would seal him in. He pressed his hands against his eyes. Dead, he thought. They were dead.

Emotion filled him, water in an empty vessel, and threatened to drown him, suffocate him. Then he heard something, a sound he couldn't connect with anything, and he raised his head. He saw a shape thirty yards away and realized it was Flats. Flats, limping toward him, whimpering.

McCleary leaped up and ran toward her, certain that she wasn't real, that she was some vestige of the hallucinogenic, something his grief had conjured. But when he dropped to his knees beside her, she licked him and barked and wagged her tail. He hugged her, weeping, his face buried in her wet fur. She squirmed free, barked, grabbed on to the sleeve of his shirt, and tried to stand.

"What is it, girl? What're you trying to tell me?"

She struggled up, turned east, barked again. East, he thought. What the hell lay east? "The caretaker's house? Is that what you're saying?"

Another bark. His spirits soared. The caretaker's house. The cellar. McCleary lifted her carefully, hurried back to the Miata, placed her gently in the passenger seat. He sped across the pasture, slamming into holes, swerving around fallen trees. Hope swelled inside him as he neared the house.

His headlights struck two walls and the front steps. The rest of the house was gone. Inside the empty hull were Andy and Quin, who was clutching Ellie. As he stumbled toward them, his daughter's cries filled the night like music.

Thanksgiving
Gainesville, Florida

THE PEOPLE WHO had known his sister descended on the
Hippodrome in suits and ties, in jeans and T-shirts, in
spiffy leather shoes, and in sneakers without laces.
McCleary greeted them at the door: Ramona and King
and Andy Tull, the mailman and the waitress from Farrah's, actors and actresses from the repertory company.
Steve Bristol arrived alone, hobbling in on his polished
cane.

Bristol opened the memorial service with a moving
tribute that was also, McCleary knew, a kind of penance
for him, a public confession. There were other speakers:
Quin, Ramona, several people from the company, and
himself. At the end, slides that depicted scenes from Cat's
life were projected onto a screen onstage. McCleary, sitting with Quin, Ellie, his parents, and his three sisters,
watched Cat as a baby, a toddler, a teenager in jeans;
Cat with her family, her theatres, her animals; Cat with
Bristol.

In the last few seconds before the lights came on, when
the darkness separated each of them, he caught the scent
of her perfume. It drifted from no particular place but
seemed, rather, to come from everywhere in the theatre,
as if candles were being lit, bottles were being opened,
homages were being paid. It was pure and light, a fragrance whose source is dreams, memory, and the elusive
quality that is love.

And then it was gone.